"What C.A. Pack has produced is a genuinely thrilling adventure with vivid descriptions and a fully built world, with rules you can learn and immerse yourself in. The story was highly unpredictable due to its inventive concept and multi-genre style, making it an exciting yet sophisticated read for both young adults and their elders."

— *Readers' Favorite*

"Pack's aptitude for spinning plots major (time travel) and minor (Pru Tellerence's missing child) continues to make this a singularly engaging series. The stakes have never been higher in Pack's inventive epic.

—*Kirkus Reviews*

SECOND

CHRONICLES OF

ILLUMINATION

SECOND

CHRONICLES OF

ILLUMINATION

Library of Illumination:

Books Five, Six, and Seven

C. A. Pack

Artiqua Press

info@artiquapress.com

Artiqua Press

www.ArtiquaPress.com

ARTIQUA PRESS

info@artiquapress.com

Westbury, NY 11590

ARTIQUA PRESS TRADE PAPERBACK

August 25 2015

SECOND CHRONICLES OF ILLUMINATION

Library of Illumination—Books Five, Six, and Seven

Library of Congress Control Number: 2015900954

"A people without the knowledge of their past history, origin and culture is like a tree without roots."
— Marcus Garvey

TABLE OF CONTENTS

PREFACE

You may get a sense of déjà vu reading the *Second Chronicles of Illumination.*

The Library of Illumination (LOI) is an ongoing series of novelettes, novellas, and novels about a special library where books literally come to life. In 2014, I published *Chronicles: The Library of Illumination,* comprised of the first five stories in the series. It included an adventure entitled *Portals,* in which LOI curators Johanna Charette and Jackson Roth discovered gateways to libraries similar to their own—on other worlds.

I've chosen to include *Portals* in this book as well, because it kicks off a continuing story line. Think of it as a bonus. If you've already read it and wish to jump straight to *The Overseers,* start this book with chapter eleven. The *Second Chronicles of Illumination* also includes the novel *Myrddin's Memoir.* The three titles are all part of the same storyline but are not the entire adventure. This is an ongoing saga, and that means it will continue in future "Chronicles."

Call it episodic. Call it Dickensian. Call it *opus magnus interruptus.*

I hope you enjoy it.

PORTALS

1

JACKSON CARRIED AN armful of returned books to a dimly lit alcove in the Library of Illumination's cupola. It was a special area reserved for some of the library's quirkier offerings. The teen enjoyed reading the various titles, but after looking inside *The Pop-Up Book of Phobias,* he refrained from opening any of the others. Unleashing overpowering arachnophobia is not fun.

He hesitated as he shelved *Lamb: The Gospel According to Biff, Christ's Childhood Pal.* When he had some time, he would have to come back and take a closer look at that one. He wasn't sure what a few of the other books were about. *Prodigiorum Ac Ostentorums Chronicon* was Greek to him, and he had never heard of *The Codex Seraphinianus.* There was the *Egyptian Book of the Dead,* but there was no way he would ever open that one. And no library would be complete without *Ripley Scrowle* and *Prophecies* by M. Michel de Nostredame. *I wonder if Johanna has unenchanted versions of these.*

The recess appeared shadowy, which mystified Jackson because there was an octagonal window at the end of the alcove. It should have allowed light to flow into the library, but the aging etched glass looked frosted and did not permit a view of the outside.

Jackson shook his head. *Something's not right here.* After shelving the last book, he ran down the cupola stairs and shouted, "Illumination," as he took off out the front door. He looked up at the area where he thought the alcove should be located, but didn't see a window.

He tried circumnavigating the library, which wasn't an easy thing to do considering it had no side alleys, so he had to go around the entire block. Still, he couldn't find that particular octagonal window.

Johanna stood waiting by the door when he walked back in. "What's wrong?"

"Nothing, really."

"Where did you disappear to? I thought somebody died, the way you ran out of here."

"The thing is," Jackson mused, "there's a little window in the alcove where we keep the wacko books, which should be visible from outside, but there's no corresponding window out there."

"Repeat after me, there is no such thing as a wacko book. And there has to be a window. If there's one in here, you should be able to see it from out there."

He grabbed her arm and dragged her out the door. "Look up. If the cupola stairs are near the center of the building and the weirdo-book alcove is on the left, the window should be right there." He pointed. "But it's not."

"Wait. That doesn't make any sense. I've got to go back inside and get my bearings." Johanna went all the way up to the cupola, and then carefully traced her way back down and out the front entrance. "You're right. There should be a window there. I guess the one in the alcove is a fake."

"Why would anyone put a fake window in a library hundreds of years ago?"

"I don't know. It doesn't make sense."

"So I'm thinking, maybe it hides a safe and there are piles of gold in there."

Johanna covered her face with both her hands for a few seconds. When she finally looked up, she said, "That is so ... you."

"C'mon. Let's go look." Jackson grabbed her hand and dragged her back to the alcove window.

For several minutes, they stood and stared at the octagonal wooden frame filled with radiating triangles of leaded glass. "I never realized you couldn't see outside," she said. "I wonder what would happen if we cleaned it."

"Your wish is my command." Jackson practically flew down the cupola stairs to retrieve some rags and a spray bottle of glass cleaner from the utility room.

He returned before Johanna had a chance to miss him. He doused the fabric with cleanser and started rubbing the window. Grime came off on the rag, but the view remained obscured. "It's not a window, so no matter how much I clean it, we won't be able to see through it. I'm telling you, it's hiding something."

"Forget it. There's no way we're going to open it," Johanna said dismissively. "Besides, it looks like it's painted in place."

Jackson tried prying it with his fingers. "Wait ..."

He bolted down the stairs again, and returned a few minutes later with a box cutter. This time his breathing sounded a little more ragged. The cupola steps spiraled straight to the first floor—five stories below—with no exits along the way. Running up and down the staircase several times took a toll on the teen, but not enough to derail his overall enthusiasm. He used the box cutter to slice through the paint that sealed the window to the wall. Once he had cut through all eight sides, he tried to pry the window open again.

"I don't think it's going to open," Johanna said. "Let's quit before you hurt yourself."

"No. This is my mystery, and I want to solve it." He ran downstairs again, and returned with a crowbar.

"No." Johanna grabbed it away from him. "I can't allow you to destroy library property."

"I'll fix anything I destroy."

"Oh really?"

"Yeah. Ask my mother. I'm the one who fixes everything around the house. If I destroy this, I'll fix it and you can deduct the cost of materials from my salary."

"I don't know ..."

Before she had a chance to think it over, Jackson jammed the edge of the crowbar under the window frame and tried to pry it off.

"They must have screwed this thing in place, because it's not giving way. Nails would have pulled out by now." He inspected the wood, but it had been covered by so many centuries of paint and varnish, he couldn't determine where the screws would be. "I need to give this one more try." He grimaced as he shoved the crowbar against the window frame with all his strength. Little beads of sweat broke out on his brow, and a vein in his forehead became clearly visible. He stopped to rest for a moment.

"This is crazy," Johanna said. "It's not going to open. There is no safe behind it. Why are you wasting your energy?"

"It's my energy to waste. Besides, I think I can do it this time." Jackson took a deep breath before applying force against the crowbar. "Aarrgghh!" He grunted as he worked to remove the window frame. *Crack.* A one-inch chunk of wood broke away and dropped to the floor.

"At this rate, you should be done in less than a week."

"Not funny. The least you could do is help me. If we both pushed against the crowbar, I bet it would work."

Johanna sighed. "Okay. Whenever you're ready."

"On the count of three. One ... two ... three." They pushed as hard as they could, but nothing happened.

"Okay," he said reluctantly. "Forget it. I'm throwing in the towel."

"It's not like opening it is going to provide any illumination for this space."

As soon as Johanna uttered the word *illumination*, the octagonal window flew open, and the great outdoors did *not* appear on the other side.

Johanna and Jackson each held their breath for a few seconds.

"You said, 'illumination.'"

As soon as he repeated the word, the two of them were sucked through the portal to a place that was extremely strange, yet eerily familiar. It had the same proportions as the Library of Illumination, but instead of books, row upon row of crystal obelisks lined the narrow shelves. They walked out of the alcove and found the surrounding area laid out exactly like the cupola in their library.

"Where are we?" Johanna whispered.

"It looks like a mirror image of the library, but it has all these tall, pointy things where the books should be."

"Let's get out of here."

"Wait. I want to see where we are."

Johanna shook her head. "I don't think that's a good idea."

"Where's your spirit of adventure? Where's your plucky, can-do attitude? Where's your imagination?"

"It's my imagination that's telling me to go back where we belong."

"Okay, see you later." Jackson said it breezily as he walked to the cupola steps. "Look." He pointed to a strange symbol embedded in the stair post. "This must be *their* equivalent of the number one. I'll never understand why this floor is considered the *first* level, while the main floor is called level five. It doesn't make any sense."

Johanna walked closer to look at the symbol. "I read about it in Mal's diary," she explained, as Jackson grabbed her hand and pulled her down the stairs. "The cupola is the highest level, so it's number one. Think of it like winning a prize. If you win first place, that's the highest you can go. It's *first*, not *fifth*. With that in mind, it makes sense that the window level right below it is the second level. Those massive arched windows were designed to flood the library with light, although the light in this library is sort of unearthly."

"Yeah, like they're lighting the place for a horror film."

"The third level," she continued, "is the halo. It's just a single layer of shelves on a narrow balcony that overlook the floors below. The fourth level is known as the residence level."

"That's a no-brainer, considering that's where your apartment is."

"And the main floor is the fifth level."

They had reached the main reading room. The circulation desk was the same familiar shape, but the shelves still held crystal obelisks.

JOHANNA REACHED FOR Jackson's hand and relaxed when his warm fingers curled around her own.

He pulled her toward the curator's staircase. It was right by the residence, and it was the staircase they used most often. There were also stone steps built into the foundation near the front door that linked the main reading room to the residence level, but that staircase was rarely used because the books closest to it were about obscure musical tonalities with archaic chord-scale relationships—not a trendy topic. The more popular books on music could be found closer to the curator's apartment.

Johanna studied the main floor as they walked across it. The reading room looked downright uncom-fortable. The furniture, or what she supposed was furniture, included an assortment of oddly shaped surfaces dwarfed by the thousands of obelisks crowding the shelves. She looked up. The windows, opaque with grime, looked like they hadn't been cleaned in a millennium. It looked like their library, and yet it wasn't their library.

"Let's go up to the next floor," Jackson urged.

"I don't think that's such a good idea," she whispered.

"Why? I don't think there's anyone here."

"How can you be so sure?"

"Do you hear anybody?"

"Maybe they're in the antechamber, binding books."

"What books?"

"All right, they're polishing the crystal."

"One more level isn't going to hurt." He tried to pull her up the steps.

"No," Johanna said, wrenching her hand away from his. "That's the residence level, and I have no intention of finding out who lives there."

"I hadn't thought of that. Wouldn't it be cool to see how your other half lives?"

"My other half!"

"Shhh. They'll hear you," he whispered.

"Exactly." She turned to go back.

"I'm going without you." He quickly climbed to the next level.

Johanna couldn't help herself. Instead of returning to the cupola, she walked into the middle of the reading room, where she could keep an eye on him. The balconies on the residence level were fairly visible, and Johanna followed Jackson's progress until he stopped just outside the curator's apartment. She waved to get his attention, but either he didn't see her or he ignored her. *Why does he have to be so difficult? He's playing with fire.*

JACKSON BEGAN TO notice subtle differences in the obelisks, not just in their height and width but on their surfaces as well. At first he thought they were dusty, but on closer examination he saw that they had subtle etchings on them, like a design, or another language, or code. He looked down at Johanna and waved at her to come up.

She adamantly shook her head from side to side.

She's so stubborn. He felt sure they had discovered something monumental about this library, but he didn't know what it was. He wanted to discuss it with her, but knew if he walked back down the stairs, she would interpret that as a signal they could leave and would head back up to the cupola. *There has to be a way I can get her up here.*

JOHANNA'S IMPATIENCE GREW. *Why tempt fate? Why can't he wait until I ask Mal about this?* She needed to know what to expect. She motioned for Jackson to return. He held up one finger, as if to say, *wait a minute.* She didn't want to waste another moment. *I should just leave, and if he wants to follow, fine.* She raised her arm to wave goodbye, but could not stop herself from shouting "No" when Jackson reached for the crystal lever that opened the bookcase-door to the residence. He looked down at her and waved.

She watched in horror as a dark tentacle shot out of the residence, wrapped itself around Jackson's neck, and dragged him inside. Her heart nearly stopped. Jackson had been caught trespassing, but by what? And who knew what kind of trouble he had gotten himself into? Her fear was for him rather than herself. She practically flew up the stairs to the residence. When she got there, the shelf that disguised the entrance had swung back into position and the crystal lever was gone. She began hammering on the wall behind the obelisks, hoping for Jackson's sake that there would be strength in numbers—hopefully, two against one. After not receiving any response to her pounding, she decided the best way to get attention would be to make some *real* noise. She picked up the closest obelisk and hurled it across the aisle, sending it crashing into a shelf crammed with more of the literary crystals.

Instantly, the balcony filled with swirling fog. An odd being that looked like he had been formed out of molten gold rose from the depths of the mist. A blue diamond band surrounded the entity's head, and lightning bolts shot out of it at varying intervals. It began communicating in a language Johanna could not understand. Even the translation app on the iPad would not have been able to help her. The words sounded more like grunts—"iks" and "ogs," "nnhs" and "utzs."

She shrank back against the shelf that had held the obelisk. She suddenly realized she couldn't calmly close a book and make the apparition go away. There was no book to close, and the obelisk that she had sent sailing through a sea of air had broken into tiny pieces. She thought about how she would feel if someone had trashed one of her precious books. Her shoulders sagged. She had done something childish, something to gain attention, although not the kind of attention she wanted. In the process she had destroyed something precious, if not to her, to someone else. Not to mention she could be electrocuted at any moment.

Before she could give it any more thought, something wrapped around her neck and dragged her into the residence. The sudden loss of oxygen coupled with surprise caused Johanna to black out. When she came to, she saw Jackson standing in the middle of the room.

"I knew you'd come," he said.

She struggled to her feet, choking on the oily mist that enveloped her. She looked around, but couldn't see much in the hazy darkness. "Where's ..."

"He went out after dragging you in."

"Come on, then, let's get out of here."

"I'd love to, but I can't move."

"What do you mean, you can't move?" She took a step toward him, afraid that she, too, might be unable to move, but if that were true, she would have never been able to get up off the floor. She reached for his hand. *Zap.* She felt electrified, in a bad way.

"Force field ..." they said in unison.

"I have to get you out of here." She thought of how they had handled the force field surrounding the blue orb. "Illumination."

"Uurrgg." Jackson gurgled and squirmed. He suddenly looked like he would choke to death.

"Delumination," she cried out.

He loudly gasped, taking in great gulps of air.

"Can you move?"

"No."

"I was hoping 'delumination' would work."

His body relaxed. He took another deep breath,

then a step. "The second one worked, which is good, because for a moment I thought you might kill me."

"I guess it's like the little window. You have to say it twice for it to work. Anyway, we need to get out of here. But I did something stupid. I broke one of their obelisks ... on purpose, and it released an odd being with lightning coming out of its ... head. Since the obelisk is broken, I don't know what they're going to do to contain it. Whoever captured you may still be out there."

"Unless it took the obelisk to the antechamber to glue it back together," Jackson speculated.

"There must be something it can do to repair it. Anyway, just be prepared for anything when I open the door."

"Frit."

"Excuse me?"

"Just a family saying. My brother, Chris, once said 'friggan shit' in front of my mother, and she had a conniption. So he got into the habit of condensing it into 'frit,' and now we all say it, even my mother and my little sister."

"That's nice. Can we get back to the problem at hand?" She had no idea what kind of beings they were dealing with. "Do you think they're human?"

"My mother and my sister?"

"Don't joke. I'm talking about whatever captured you."

"I don't think so. I didn't get a chance to pay much attention to what captured me, but I can tell you, it had an iron grip."

"Just be prepared to run. But—and this is a big 'but'—if we can't outrun it, we shouldn't go back the way we came, because we don't want it following us back into *our library*."

"How are we supposed to stop it from doing that?"

"I don't know."

"I wonder if there are any more windows to nowhere, in any of the other alcoves."

"What good would that do us? We might just end up in a library that's scarier than this one."

"Yeah, but there's usually no one up in the cupola. We could just hide out until we think it's safe."

"Unless whatever is chasing us follows us there." She sighed. "Let's just make a run for it and try to get back home. Ready?"

They each took a deep breath. Jackson nodded to Johanna, and she hit the lever that opened the door to the residence. No one was there. They tiptoed down to the main level and across the floor, and then broke into a run—straight up the stairs to the cupola. They didn't slow down to see if anything was behind them. They couldn't afford to waste precious time.

"Illumination," Johanna cried as they ran into the alcove. They hit the wall hard but remained in the same unfamiliar library. She could hear someone, or something, stomping up the cupola stairs.

"What are we going to do now?" Jackson asked.

Johanna thought about him being trapped behind the force field in the residence, and how she had said the wrong thing at first. "Delumination."

Nothing happened.

"Why did you say, 'Delumination'?" As soon as Jackson repeated her command, they felt themselves swoosh away to another place.

"Oh my God," Jackson exclaimed.

"What?" she cried, looking around in a panic.

"It's the *Pop-Up Book of Phobias.*" He smiled at her, and in a singsong voice said, "Honey, we're ho-ome."

"Maybe not," Johanna whispered.

"What do you mean?"

She looked down.

Jackson immediately knew what she meant. The floors were as transparent as glass.

—LOI—

2

J OHANNA WHISPERED. "DO YOU SEE ANYONE?"
"No, but even if I did, how often does anybody look up at the cupola?"

A chime went off, followed by the whirring sound of the front wall sliding open four stories below. Johanna and Jackson stooped down to peer through the transparent floor. They saw a large man covered with curly, red hair stomp into the library. He wore a caftan of rich, blue silk emblazoned with a bright gold design. "FURST," he screamed.

He walked over to the circulation desk and relentlessly rang a bell until a small man, also covered with curly, red hair, came running from a back room. He, too, wore a caftan, but it only reached as far as his knobby knees and appeared to be made of plain sackcloth.

"At your service, I am." The smaller man pulled the bell out of the larger one's hand and placed it out of reach, behind the desk.

"The book I ordered, I want."

"Here, it is not."

"On Tuesday, you promised."

"Here, it is not," the little man said a tiny bit louder.

"It, where is?"

"Of our region, outside."

"Beyond us, it is?"

"By force, taken."

"Get it back, you will?"

"An army, I would need."

"Stop, this must."

"An army, I would need," the little man said a tiny bit louder.

"To the council, I will speak."

"With my regard, go forth."

"Furst," the larger man said, nodding his head.

"Dungen," the smaller man replied, nodding to the big man's back as he exited the library. When the wall slid back into place, the little man retreated.

Johanna and Jackson watched as he walked back in the direction of the antechamber.

"How odd," Johanna whispered.

"Did you understand any of that?"

"No. And I don't want to. I want to get back home."

"How are we going to do that?"

She gave it some thought. "I think we ran up the wrong alcove and through a different window."

"I'd be more than happy to look in the other alcoves to see if there are more windows. Too bad the walls aren't made out of glass."

"Don't do anything foolish," she warned.

"I won't." On impulse, he kissed the tip of her nose and then winked as he slipped away.

The cupola formed a triquetra, three intersecting ellipses intertwined with a circle. The winding aisles snaked like a puzzle, and the points of the ellipses formed the alcoves. Johanna saw Jackson only for a second, as he crossed the far side of the cupola. She sighed with relief when he finally returned to where she waited. "So?"

"There's an identical hazy window at the end of each alcove."

"You're kidding ..."

"Not only that. There are similar windows in some of the hallways. That opens up a lot of possibilities, and we can only guess at picking the right one."

"From what you could see, did it look like we're in the wrong alcove?"

He shook his head. "As far as I can tell, this is the alcove we started out from."

"Great." The word belied her feeling of frustration.

"Look, when we ran in what we thought was the right direction, we ended up here, not back at home. So I'm thinking, even if we go through this same window, we shouldn't end up back in scary town."

"I think I'd rather take my chances talking to the little red-haired man. Maybe he knows something about these windows."

"And if he starts chasing us?"

"We run."

"Okay, let's go."

"Quietly."

Jackson nodded.

They crept down the stairs, and Johanna pulled Jackson toward the circulation desk. "Let's ring, so it doesn't look like we're invading his space."

"Where's the bell?"

She made a face. "I'm pretty sure he put it on a shelf." She walked around the circulation desk and slipped inside the gate leading behind the counter. She saw the bell and grabbed it, but didn't get a chance to ring it.

"Behind my circulation desk, what business have you?" The curator practically roared at her, not at all like the meek little man who had just cowered before his much-larger kinsman.

Johanna placed the bell on the counter. "I'm Johanna Charette, curator of the Library of Illumination ... uh ... another Library of Illumination. We came in through a window in one of the alcoves, and we're wondering if some sort of map exists that can help us get back to our own library."

The man just stared at her.

She gave it another try. "We're not supposed to be here. Can you help us?"

"Operating, the portals are." He said it barely above a whisper, with a look of dread upon his face.

"We mean you no harm," Johanna continued. "We just want to go home."

"Use the portals, why did you?"

"Know what they are, we did not," Jackson broke in.

Johanna poked him. "Why are you talking like that?"

"Because that's how he speaks. It's almost like Yoda from *Star Wars*."

"Want to go, where do you?" the man asked.

"Where are we now?"

"The Realm of Dramatica, this Library of Illumination is in."

That piqued Jackson's interest. "You're a realm? That's so cool!"

"A realm, you must be from," the curator said decisively.

Jackson looked at Johanna. "What realm are we from?"

"I have no idea."

"Of your library, what are the properties?"

"Do you mean the different levels of the books? Mostly twos and threes, although we recently had a four, and Casanova caused all kinds of havoc."

"Come alive, do your books?"

"Yes."

"Here, wait."

He disappeared into the antechamber, and returned a moment later with a large, tattered book, which had a heavy, metal padlock. He held the palm of his left hand about an inch above the lock, and it popped open.

Furst slowly turned the pages. Jackson leaned over to see what he was reading, but could not see any words. He whispered in Johanna's ear, "The pages are blank."

She smiled. "That's because you're not the curator."

"Right."

"Found it, I have," Furst said, with a satisfied smile. "Of the Eleventh Realm, Johanna Charette, you are. Fantasia, it is called."

"Really?"

"Fantasia? Fantastic. At least, I think it's fantastic that you found us," Jackson said. "The Eleventh Realm, huh?"

"And you said we are now in ...?" Johanna asked.

"In the Sixth Realm, Dramatica is."

"Wow," Jackson said. "We traveled five realms."

Johanna shook her head. "Like that means anything to you."

"Well, at least this isn't like the scary library with the guy with the tentacles."

Furst paled. "Another library, you have been to?"

"Yeah. A scary place with obelisks instead of books, that's run by someone or something with tentacles."

Furst consulted the gold book.

Johanna watched his hand start to tremble. He looked at her with horror in his eyes. "Terroria, that is, the Twelfth Realm. Talk to the Library Council, I must. The Two Millennia War, Terroria started."

"Why did they start a war?" Johanna inquired.

"To take over all the libraries, they wanted. Very serious, this is."

"Can you tell us how to get back to our own library?" Jackson asked.

"Go, you cannot. Talk to the Library Council, you must."

JACKSON GNAWED ON his thumbnail. He leaned close to Johanna. "How long do you think they're going to keep us?"

"You actually look worried."

20

"It's just that I promised Logan I'd be there tomorrow for our community-service project. He's depending on me."

"You didn't tell me you're working on a project."

"Yeah, we have to do it to graduate. Logan and I got some of the local home-improvement stores to donate materials, and we're going to fix up the outside of Old Lady Caruthers's place, which is falling apart."

"It sounded wonderful until you ruined it all by calling her 'Old Lady' Caruthers."

"Point taken. Anyway, like I told you before, I'm handy around the house. So we're going to paint the exterior and replace the shutters, and Cassie's father is a contractor, so he volunteered to help us rebuild the porch. Chris is getting a few of his friends to chop up the broken front walkway, and Cassie's dad is going to show us how to pour concrete. Plus, Cassie and Brittany got the Mothers' Club to donate flowers and stuff that they're going to plant in front of the new porch and along the sidewalk. It's a lot of work, but we're hoping to finish it all in one day. I've got to be there. We made a commitment."

Johanna was impressed by the scope of work Jackson and Logan had taken on. Plus they managed to get promises and donations from others, to make the revitalization project a success. "You should shoot video of it and put it to music, so you can upload it to the Internet."

"I won't be able to shoot anything, because I'll be too busy working. But *you* can volunteer to shoot it." He put his arm around her. "It'll be fun."

"First, we have to get out of here," she said pragmatically.

"The next time I come up with a bright idea, like opening a library window, you have my permission to fire me."

"Thanks. I'll remember that."

It did not take long for the Dramatican Library Council to convene. Their library had a giant bell in an open tower over the entryway, and the peals immediately drew council members from all over the city. They dropped whatever they were doing to respond to the perceived emergency.

"For five hundred years, the bell has not rung," Furst told them. "Great danger, we are in."

The council members stared at Johanna and Jackson as they gathered around a table in Dramatica's version of the executive boardroom. The stone walls and leaded glass windows reminded Johanna of her own library, however, this one had a glass ceiling and a glass table.

Jackson knocked twice on the tabletop. "I like this. It's really cool."

Furst leaned over and whispered, "Secret deals made under the table, it is to prevent."

"Ahhh," Jackson answered.

"Explain," one of the council members demanded.

"Speak, you must," Furst told Johanna.

She stood up and looked at the assembly of people before her. They were all covered with curly red hair and wore caftans of varying degrees of richness. "I'm Johanna Charette, curator of the Library of Illumination on Fantasia." She looked at Furst for reassurance, and he nodded at her. "We found a small window that could not be seen from the outside of our library, and we tried to open it to see what was behind it. When we managed to do that, we were transported to another library, much like our own, except instead of books we found obelisks." This statement incited an increase in murmurings among the Library Council members. "When Jackson"—she pointed to her assistant—"went to find out where we were, someone or something with tentacles imprisoned him and placed him behind a force field." The sound level increased even more. "I saw him get pulled into the residence, but by the time I got there, I couldn't get inside. No one would come to the door, so to get their attention—and this pains me deeply to say—I threw one of their obelisks, breaking it." The murmuring grew quite loud.

"Here now, you are. Get away, how did you?"

She took a deep breath. "I was pulled into the residence after I broke the obelisk, but whatever dragged me inside must have rushed to inspect the damage, without bothering to secure me behind a force field. Jackson was immobilized, but because of something that happened recently in our own library, I managed to say the right thing to get the force field to release him.

"We left the residence and ran up to the cupola, where the window is located. We went back through it, but instead of returning to our own library, we ended up here."

"Through the window, did anyone see you leave?"

"We heard someone coming up the steps, but I don't know if he, or she, or it, saw us disappear through the window."

Torran, the largest of the Library Council

members, stood. Gold embroidery covered every inch of his caftan, and jewels encrusted the neckline and edges. He had a deep, resonant voice. "The portals, you have breached."

"So they're like the portals from *Stargate*?" Jackson asked.

"A system of portals that connect all the libraries, it is said there exists. But hidden by the College of Overseers many years ago they were, when the Two Millennia War Terroria started. Seek to take over all the libraries, they did."

"Can you tell us how to get back to our own library?" Johanna asked.

"Breach the portals, we cannot. Know their true directions, we do not. Summon the College of Overseers, we must. Now."

"How do you do that?" Jackson asked.

"The Curator Key, Furst must engage."

Furst turned his head upward and looked through the glass ceiling to the very top of the cupola.

"Easy, it will not be," he mumbled.

"Do it, you must," Torran demanded.

Furst left the room, and the other council members trailed behind him. They talked among themselves as they waited, while the curator descended to a sub-level.

"What's this Curator Key they're talking about?" Jackson asked Johanna.

"I don't know. I could probably ask Mal's diary, but I don't have it with me. I didn't realize we were going on an excursion or precipitating a war."

"Sorry."

They heard scraping and turned to see Furst

dragging a large ladder behind him. "Here, let me help you with that," Jackson said, picking up the back of the ladder. "Where are you taking it?"

Furst pointed straight up.

Jackson grimaced. He ended up on the lower end of the ladder as they lugged it up the cupola stairs, toward the highest point in the building.

"Place it across the railings, we must," Furst said, pointing to where he wanted Jackson to carry his end of the ladder. They extended it as far as it would go and laid it horizontally across the rails.

"Now what?"

"A rope, I must get." Furst disappeared down the stairs, pushing through the stream of council members who climbed up to watch. He returned several minutes later with a coil of rope. He tied one end into a lasso and the other around his waist. Then he climbed on top of the ladder.

"Whoa, whoa, whoa, what are you doing?" Jackson called out, grabbing the end of the ladder.

"Reach the hook with the rope, I must."

Furst started to crawl across the makeshift wooden bridge that now spanned the open space in the middle of the cupola. He moved very slowly. Jackson couldn't tell if Furst wobbled because of nerves, or because the ladder wasn't strong enough to hold his weight. None of Furst's countrymen moved to help him accomplish his task.

"Johanna," Jackson called out. "Can you grab the other end of the ladder and hold it still?"

"Will do," she responded, grabbing the opposite side.

The two teens watched as Furst shakily stood

up in the middle of the ladder. He took the section of rope that he had tied into a lasso and threw it toward the uppermost part of the ceiling. It missed whatever target the curator had hoped it would catch onto, and fell downward, pulling Furst off balance. Everyone gasped as the curator fell. Furst managed to grab on to the edge of the ladder and dangled several stories above the library's main reading room.

—LOI—

3

THE LIBRARY COUNCIL members discussed Furst's dilemma in detail, but not one of them moved to help him.

Jackson climbed onto the edge of the ladder.

"What are you doing?" Johanna screamed.

"Someone's got to save him," he told her. "Hey, I'd appreciate a little help here," he yelled at the council members at large.

One of them, a man in a brown silk caftan without much ornamentation, grabbed hold of Jackson's end of the ladder. The teen crawled out to where Furst clung, all the while praying that the ladder was strong enough to support them both. He straddled the ladder when he reached the curator and locked his ankles together. Grabbing Furst by his arms, Jackson pulled him up high enough so the Dramatican could get a better grip.

Jackson contemplated his next move. Normally,

he would reach over and grab Furst's waistband to haul him up, but the man wore a caftan. Instead, the teen grabbed the rope Furst had attached to his waist. It had been tied with a slipknot, and Jackson could only reach the part that pulled it loose. As a last resort, the young man grabbed a handful of fabric from Furst's caftan and hauled him up, hoping the man wore underwear, or else Johanna would get an eyeful.

Furst managed to scramble back on the ladder to the cheers of the council members. He trembled as he sat catching his breath—sweat oozing from every pore.

"What, exactly, are you trying to do?" Jackson asked.

Furst looked up and pointed. "A hook up at the top, there is. Try to lasso it to pull myself up, I did."

"Okay, first things first. Untie that rope from your waist and tie it to the ladder instead." Jackson took the lasso end in his hand. Taking a deep breath, he narrowed his eyes in concentration, and tossed it. Everyone released a collective sigh when the rope missed its mark. Jackson retrieved the line, which now dangled from the ladder, grabbed the lasso again, and thought about how Johanna never missed the trash bin when she free-tossed a wadded-up piece of paper across the length of the circulation desk. *I can do this,* he thought. He stared at the hook. He envisioned the lasso snagging it. He thought about how contacting the College of Overseers could pave the way for them to get back home. He raised his elbow so the noose hung open from his wrist and, without taking his eye off the hook, flung the rope upward. He watched as it climbed, willing it to snag the hook.

"That's what I'm talking about," he screamed,

when the rope caught hold.

Enthusiastic shouts and whistles erupted from the group.

Jackson looked at Furst, who had broken into a wide smile. "What do I need to do when I get up there?"

Furst's face fell. "You cannot. The curator, I am. Contact the college, only the curator can."

"Are you going to be okay doing this?"

"Know, I do not."

"Have you ever climbed a rope before?"

"No."

"We should have knotted the rope before we tossed it," he said, thinking out loud. He looked at Furst, who still looked scared. "Wait here."

Jackson untied the rope from the ladder and climbed to the top of it. He took a moment to study the Curator's Key. It wasn't a key at all, but an intricate dialing mechanism. The odd configuration of brass gears and ivory numbered buttons reminded him of Jules Verne's *Time Machine. I wonder if we have one of these.* Jackson shifted his gaze to the hook. It had been solidly integrated in the framework of the cupola. From up close, it was fairly large. He slowly slid back down to the ladder. "Do you have another rope?"

Furst nodded.

"Do you want to get it?"

Furst turned and tentatively stared at the end of the ladder.

"Better yet," Jackson continued, "tell me where it is, and I'll go and get it, that way you can save your energy for climbing it."

"Sub-level six, it is in. Next to the cellar stairs, it

is."

"I'll be right back."

Jackson crawled to the edge of the ladder and jumped down onto the floor of the cupola. He didn't waste any time answering questions. He just ignored them all and ran down the stairs. The buzz level increased, as council members stared at Furst and called out their questions to him.

"Another rope, we need," he answered, not exactly knowing why they needed it.

Jackson returned a couple of minutes later, with the second coil of rope hanging from his shoulder. He crawled back on the ladder and formed a noose on one end and proceeded to tie knots at one-foot intervals. Then he scrambled up the rope that he'd already attached to the ceiling and secured the knotted line to the same hook.

He returned to Furst. "Those knots will keep you from sliding back down as you climb up. Just grab the rope above the knot, pull up your knees, and then wrap the loose end of the rope around one foot and use your other foot to hold it in place. Every time you straighten your legs, you'll be able to reach higher, and you just need to keep doing that until you reach the top."

Furst nodded. He grabbed the rope and used it to pull himself up to a standing position. He reached as high as he could and pulled up his knees as Jackson had advised, but had difficulty wrapping the rope around his foot and using the other foot to hold it in place. After three tries, he returned to a sitting position on the ladder. "Do it, I cannot. Doomed, we are."

Jackson gave it some thought. "You can do it," he

said, with a smile. "Try it again."

Furst slowly stood up and grabbed the rope. Jackson stood up as well. When Furst pulled his feet up, Jackson looped the rope around one foot and pushed Furst's other foot into place. "Straighten your legs and move your hands higher," Jackson told him. Furst did, and Jackson climbed the second rope to help the man wrap his foot again. Together, the two men climbed the pair of ropes—student and teacher—until they reached the top.

"Okay, do your thing," Jackson said.

"Afraid to let go, I am," Furst replied, his voice filled with panic.

"You won't fall. I'll hold you in place. Are your feet tight against the rope?"

"Yes."

"Okay." Jackson pulled himself up and wrapped his legs around Furst's waist, holding him in place. "Do what you gotta do."

Furst tentatively let go with one hand and manipulated the dial. Jackson watched as the gears slowly turned, screeching with years of non-use.

"Descend, we must," Furst said nervously.

"Just loosen your grip a little at a time and slide."

Jackson released Furst and slid down the rope. The Dramatican curator slowly made his way down to the ladder, at the bottom of which Jackson waited to guide him in. Above them, the gears continued to turn as the opening in the cupola slowly grew larger. They headed in opposite directions, and when they each reached firm ground, Furst motioned Jackson to help him remove the ladder from the railing and place it out of the way. Then they stood and watched with the others as the cupola yawned wider.

METAL ON METAL clanged thunderously as the gears in Dramatica's cupola locked into place. The crowd gasped when a magnificent white light shot upward from the center medallion embedded in the library floor, straight through the opening in the roof. After a minute, the light stopped as suddenly as it had appeared.

"Now what?" Jackson asked.

"Look," Johanna said, pointing toward the various alcoves. A dozen men—nearly identical in appearance— emerged from the twelve portals. Each one had a long, white beard and even longer, white hair that touched the floor. They all wore purple robes and matching miter hats.

"A plethora of popes," Jackson whispered.

Johanna jammed her elbow in his side. "Stop," she said under her breath.

Torran addressed the overseers. "Torran, I am, Dean of the Library Council."

♄ *Who is the curator?* the twelve overseers asked in unison.

Furst pushed forward through the throng of men.

"Furst, I am. Curator." He bowed deeply.

♄ *There is another.*

Furst looked for Johanna in the crowd and signaled for her to join him.

She walked over to where he stood and addressed the twelve men. "I am Johanna Charette, curator of a library in a different realm."

Ω *Realm Eleven.* She heard the words, as did

everyone else, but did not know who spoke them.

𝄞 *She breached the portals on Realm Twelve. We must extract Nero 51."*

The light shot up through the portal, and two of the overseers disappeared. When the light suddenly turned off, they retuned, flanking the curator known as Nero 51.

The Dramaticans gasped. Nero 51 had the body of a man, but his feet were larger and flatter—like swollen platypus feet—and he had multiple tentacles for arms that could stretch out to untold lengths. His wide head dipped in the middle, rising on either side over large black eyes that commanded more than half his face. He had a flat nose and a very small mouth.

He made a series of unintelligible sounds. One of the overseers waved his hand, and Nero 51's words instantly became understandable. "Terroria has been invaded," he declared, "and our property maliciously destroyed."

The overseers addressed Johanna. 𝄞 *Why did you breach the portal and destroy library property?*

"We did not know about the portals or how they work. When we were unexpectedly transported to another world, my assistant Jackson wanted to explore it. But he was taken and locked in a force field."

"TAKEN? I did no such thing. I found him trying to break into my residence."

"I wasn't really trying to break into the residence," Jackson volunteered. "I only wanted to get Johanna's attention."

𝄞 *You are Jackson?* the overseers asked in unison.
"Yes."

33

They all nodded.

"Who is Jackson?" Nero 51 demanded. "A curator?"

🎵 *A curator-in-training.*

"A curator-in-training who has broken the laws of the Library of Illumination, just like his master." Nero 51 glared at Johanna. "I demand justice, with a trial on Terroria before a jury of Terrorians."

🎵 *Library law is regulated only by a jury populated by overseers. There will be no jury of Terrorians. But we will acquiesce to your request to have the trial on your home world. It is decided.*

Johanna felt a moment of nausea and realized she had unexpectedly been whisked through the portal to another library. She recognized the structure of the executive boardroom, and knew she was on Terroria when she saw the oily mist swirling in the air. It resembled the atmosphere inside the residence in which she found Jackson. Even here, shelves filled with obelisks of all shapes and sizes lined the walls. She looked around the room to see who had accompanied them to witness the proceedings. The twelve overseers were there, as well as Jackson, Furst, and Nero 51, but she was the only other person in the room. The Dramatican Library Council had been left behind.

🎵 *Johanna Charette, state you story from the beginning, before breaching the portals.*

Once again, she could not tell where the voice originated. She looked at Jackson, startled to see that he, Furst, and Nero 51 were suspended in what appeared to be tubes of glass.

🎵 *Do not be alarmed,"* the voice said. *"It is to*

*prevent interruption, or the accidental disclosure of
sensitive information not meant for the many.*

Johanna recounted how Jackson had discovered
a window in the cupola that would not open and how
he was sure there must be something like a safe hidden
behind it. She explained how she had been skeptical
but allowed him to try to remove the window after he
promised to fix anything he broke. She explained how
saying the word *illumination* caused the window to fly
open, and how Jackson repeating it had resulted in their
transport to Terroria. She stated she was "scared" and
her primary goal was to return home, but Jackson had
a curious mind and a zest for exploring new places. She
recounted everything that happened—from breaking the
obelisk to escaping the residence—and finished by telling
the overseers how surprised she and Jackson were to find
themselves on Dramatica, when all they wanted to do
was return home.

She revealed how Furst had explained that there
were a dozen realms, plus the home world, Lumina, and
that she came from Fantasia, Realm Eleven, which she
hadn't known.

An overseer nodded, and Johanna found herself
inside a glass tube. She watched as Jackson answered the
overseers' questions, but could not hear what was said.

JACKSON HAD A SIMILAR VERSION of what had happened,
except he gave more detail about being captured by Nero
51.

"It felt like a steel cable had wrapped around
my arms, and when I saw all the tentacles he had, I was
surprised he didn't wrap them around my legs as well,

because I kicked as hard as I could, trying to get away. But then he reached for this huge weapon that looked like a rocket launcher, threw me against the wall, and fired it at me. I found myself locked behind a force field and couldn't move. He started clicking and whirring at me, but I couldn't tell what he was saying. I just knew he meant business, considering the number of weapons he had stacked up across the room. If that guy's going to war, I don't want to be the enemy."

Jackson found himself back inside the glass tube and watched as Nero 51 approached the overseers.

"THIS IS AN outrage," the Terrorian said in a low-pitched, threatening tone. "Those two *curators*," he sneered, "invaded my library and wreaked havoc. It is against library law. I demand that they be executed for breaking the peace of a million millennia."

FURST WAS THE last person to be interrogated. He spoke about how he had first found Johanna behind the circulation desk holding the bell, and how she said she was back there because the bell was not on the desk. He stated that she spoke the truth, because he had hidden the bell after Dungen gave him a headache by ringing it nonstop.

He was mystified that Johanna did not know anything about the various realms, but said, other than that, she seemed very knowledgeable about the layout of the library and its inner workings.

He talked about his decision to ask the Library Council for permission to contact the Board of Overseers, and that once the decision was made, how Jackson helped him climb to the dial at the top of the portal. He also detailed how the teen had saved his life when he lost his balance and nearly fell to his death.

Like the others, Furst was returned to a sound-proof holding tube after his testimony.

AFTER MUCH DELIBERATION, the College of Overseers agreed their decision would depend on the testimony of Johanna's mentor, whom they instantly summoned to corroborate the information they had been given. Mal was escorted to Terroria through one of the portals.

𝕾 *Malcolm Trees?*

"Yes."

𝕾 *It is said your charge had no knowledge of the confluence of realms. Did you not teach her?*

"I did not. I thought her too young to fully comprehend the importance of the information when she first became curator of the library. She is, by far, the youngest person ever to assume that role, although it must be noted, she has admirably mastered the proficiencies necessary to run such a, shall we say, *dynamic* institution. I had arranged for the provenance of the library system to be apportioned to her within the text of my eternal diary, which I know she refers to frequently. I had scheduled it to start in her twenty-first year. She is not even nineteen years old, and I did not want her youth to influence the possibility that she might overlook the importance of our history."

𝕾 *This would bear out the testimony of Furst, who claims she entered Dramatica without knowledge of the realms or her place within them.*

"I am sorry to admit that I have been remiss."

𝕾 *The boy, Jackson, is a curator-in-training?*

"Yes. Johanna hired him to help out at the library. After I witnessed his devotion to her and to the library, I—quite unknown to them—took the necessary steps to have the young man designated a curator-in-training. Like Johanna, his background makes him highly suitable for the position. Together, I believe they will grow into all that the job demands."

𝕾 *You see them as equals, then?*

"Not exactly. The girl is intelligent and pragmatic, with excellent business sense and a love of literature. She is a natural-born leader of the levelheaded variety. Jackson, on the other hand, takes risks Johanna would never take. While this may seem foolhardy at times, his bravery, geniality, and ability to take charge of difficult situations and foresee their outcomes complement her leadership by making Johanna push her boundaries past what is comfortable. I believe they can accomplish great things together. In light of the rumored build-up of arms and unrest in some of the realms, I see them as the light of the future."

𝕾 *You have ascertained, then, the increasing possibility of conflict within the realms?*

"Yes. It is said the Terrorians are bartering ancient obelisks for weapons."

𝕾 *It would be detected.*

"Not if the obelisks were replaced by counterfeits."

There was a moment of silence. 𝕾 *That is all.*

Mal was escorted back to his point of origin.

—LOI—

4

⌘ RECOUNT THE CHARGES *against Johanna Charette.*
ᴪ *Charge: Portal Breach.*

⌘*Acquitted: She had no knowledge of their existence.*

◉ *Duly noted.*

ᴪ *Charge: Destruction of LOI Property.*

⌘*Guilty: Johanna admitted to destroying property.*

◉ *Duly noted.*

⌘*Recount the charges against Jackson Roth.*

ᴪ *Charge: Portal Breach.*

⌘*Acquitted: He had no knowledge of their existence.*

◉ *Duly noted.*

ᴪ *Charge: Trespass.*

⌘*Acquitted: As a LOI curator-in-training, it is impossible to trespass on any LOI property.*

◉ *Duly noted.*

Ψ *Charge: Illegal Entry of a Residence.*

⌘ *Acquitted: The boy was pulled inside and detained by the resident.*

☿ *Duly noted.*

♅ *Johanna must be punished for the destruction of property.*

★ *Extenuating circumstances existed. Nero 51 ignored her communication, thus inviting the use of unorthodox methods to get his attention.*

◍ *She broke the obelisk to save the boy, not knowing what fate awaited him, due to her ignorance of the realms.*

⌘ *She must pay for her transgression. She is from Fantasia, based on Earth. It is decreed she work the equivalent of three Earth days on Terroria to repay the loss.*

Σ *Nero 51 will condemn the judgment as too light.*

⌘ *Nero 51 is not an overseer.*

π *Johanna Charette will not like the judgment.*

⌘ *Johanna Charette must pay for willful destruction of library property. And we need her to serve time on Terroria.*

✳ *Your decision, perhaps, is based on the boy's testimony about weapons, as well as other rumors that have come to light ...*

§ *Ahhh ... the counterfeits.*

⌘ *You are correct.*

⇌ *And the electromagnetic waves?*

⌘ *We continue to monitor them.*

◍ *And the boy, Jackson?*

⌘ *He must remain on Earth to curate the Fantasian library.*

Ω *Shall we seal the portals?*

⌘ *No. Johanna Charette must be able to return to*

her realm.

■ *What if Nero 51 uses them to wage war?*

⌘ *That is to be expected, and countered.*

The tubes vanished, and the four curators stood before the College of Overseers.

⌘ *All charges have been acquitted, save one.*

Nero 51 took a threatening step forward. "How could all charges have been acquitted? I demand retribution."

⌘ *All charges, save one.*

"And what charge is that?" The Terrorian sneered.

⌘ *Johanna Charette, you have been found guilty of the willful destruction of LOI property. You are sentenced to work in the service of the library on Terroria for three Earth days.*

"No!" Nero 51 roared. "I do not want her on my world. She is a spy and must be executed!"

⌘ *Nero 51, Johanna Charette has been sentenced to a period of service on your world. As a ward of Terroria for that given period of time, you must guarantee her safety, or lose all rights as curator of your realm.*

Nero 51 huffed and puffed like he was about to explode.

"If she's going there, I'm going with her," Jackson interjected. "It's my fault she broke the obelisk."

⌘ *No. Jackson Roth, you have been acquitted of all charges. In the absence of Johanna Charette, you must assume the duties as curator of the Library of Illumination in the realm of Fantasia.*

"You can't let her go to Terroria alone."

⌘ *It is the finding of the College of Overseers and cannot be overturned. Johanna Charette, you have an equal amount of time to prepare for your sentence: three Earth days. We will send an escort to accompany you to Terroria when the moment has arrived.*

The College of Overseers stood in unison.

♄ *Johanna Charette, Jackson Roth, Furst, accompany us. We will return you to your home worlds before we seal the portals,* the overseers said in unison.

"This is an outrage!" Nero 51 screamed at their retreating number. "I will not stand for it!"

JOHANNA AND JACKSON found themselves back in the alcove of oddities. "Do you think we're really home?" Jackson asked.

Johanna stooped and retrieved a chunk of their window frame from the floor. "Yes."

"You can't go to Terroria alone."

"I have to. You heard what the College of Overseers said."

"That Nero guy has it in for you. He wants to execute you."

"He can't without losing his curatorship, and I have the feeling that it's something he doesn't want to lose. So I'll be fine. I'll polish a few obelisks. I'll wash a few windows. Whatever."

"Who's that guy they brought in at the end?"

"Mal."

"That's Mal? Really? He looked so different."

"That's because you met him when he was only one hundred forty years old."

Jackson took a moment to think about what she had just said. "Why do you think they called him there?"

"I don't know, but I have every intention of asking

him ... or at least his diary."

"Are you going to do that now?"

"Right now, all I want is a slice of pizza."

"Since I got you into this, I'll treat."

She linked her arm in his. "Let's go." She refrained from telling him how safe she felt while they walked arm-in-arm. If she did, he would argue with her about going to Terroria. Instead, she secretly welcomed the warmth and security that holding his arm offered, if only for a little while.

PICCOLO ITALIA DID not seem very busy for a Friday night. "Where is everyone?" Jackson asked.

Dante wiped his hands on his apron. "Been and gone. We close in fifteen minutes."

Jackson looked at the clock on the wall. "Do you believe it's already eleven fifteen?"

"Time flies when you're on trial," Johanna murmured.

"We can still get slices, can't we?" he asked.

"I've got three plain slices left and one mushroom."

"Ugh, I hate mushrooms." Jackson made a face.

"I'll eat the mushroom slice," Johanna offered.

"Okay." He turned to Dante. "We'll take them all. And a couple of colas."

Dante slipped the slices in the oven, while Johanna and Jackson slid into a red leatherette booth across from the counter.

"Anyway, I was thinking," Jackson started, "that once I tell—"

"Stop."

"What?"

"You're dangerous when you think."

"I'm going with you."

"You have school."

"I'll just tell Old Man Benson that you need me to go with you."

"To another world, where the beings have tentacles for arms and alien eyes? I don't think so."

"You can't go alone."

"I *will* go alone. And you *do* need to ask Mr. Benson for three days off from school, because you have to run the library while I'm gone."

"They should have sentenced me to hard labor on Terroria, instead of you. You were there because of me. Besides, I don't know how to run the library."

"Yes, you do. Nobody is asking you to do any bookbinding or to research special exhibitions while I'm gone. All you have to do is open the mail, save the bills for me, and process the requests to borrow books. The list of approved borrowers is on the computer. I'm sure you know where to find it, because you're the person who entered all that information. That's all you have to do for three days, besides answer the phone. Tell anyone asking for me that I was suddenly called out of town and that I'm expected back on Thursday. What could be easier?"

"I still think—"

"Pizza's up," Dante shouted.

"Get our food. Then tell me all about the project you and Logan have planned for this weekend."

THAT NIGHT, JOHANNA's dreams were peppered with nightmares about all the horrible things that could happen on Terroria. She slept fitfully, and it was after nine by the time she woke up. She checked her messages, prepared two book deliveries, and grabbed her camera before heading out.

When she arrived at Mrs. Caruthers's house, Jackson and Logan, along with what looked like half the neighborhood, were already busy scraping old paint off the siding and chopping up the broken sidewalk. Cassie walked around the house with a clipboard in hand, jotting down ideas for plants. Brittany and Chris painted new shutters, so they would be dry enough to handle when it came time to attach them to the windows.

Johanna walked over to Jackson's mom, who stood with Ava in their adjoining yard. "So what does Mrs. Caruthers think of all this?"

"She doesn't know. Jackson made a deal with someone over at the senior center to get her out of the house. She's apparently a gifted quilter. They asked her to give a class in quilt making and offered to pay her fifty dollars, so she happily agreed."

"That's pretty amazing. Where did the money come from?"

"It's from a senior-center program. They have a grant that pays experts to teach classes. I hope it goes well."

"Me, too. I'd better start shooting video. I promised Jackson I'd edit it to music so he could post it online."

Mrs. Roth sniffed back a tear. "They're really something, these kids. They did the same thing for me last year, and I was overwhelmed. I'm so proud of them. But don't let me keep you. Go take pictures."

It turned out to be a long day, but Ava supplied everyone with lemonade and water, and the Students for a Better Society club at the high school brought sandwiches and brownies for the crew. It turned into more of a celebration than anything else, and the camaraderie made everyone work a little harder.

By late afternoon, Chris and Jackson had finished attaching the shutters to the house, and stood back to admire their work. The only thing they had overlooked was how long it would take the new concrete sidewalk in the front yard to dry.

"I hope Mrs. Caruthers has a key to the back door," Chris said. "I'd hate to have to break a windowpane to get her inside her fixed-up house."

The crowd cheered when the senior-transit van pulled up in front of the house. Everyone waited anxiously for Mrs. Caruthers to get out of the vehicle, but after a very long interval, only the driver emerged.

"Is everything all right?" Mrs. Roth asked.

"She's crying. She wanted to know why all these people are standing in front of her house, and when I told her, she became very emotional. She needs a moment to compose herself."

Slowly, Mrs. Caruthers climbed out of the vehicle, her eyes bright with tears. Mrs. Roth pulled a tissue out of her pocket and offered it to the elderly woman.

"Thank you, dear." Mrs. Caruthers sighed deeply and made her way toward the front door.

Jackson reached for her arm. "I'm sorry, Mrs. Caruthers, you can't go in that way, for now. The cement is still wet. Do you have a key to the back?"

She nodded, and then her head movement changed from up and down to side to side. "Why...?" She could not finish her thought.

Jackson turned on the charm. "You know, you're a pillar of this community." He slipped his arm around her shoulders. "And you've always watched out for us. This is just a gesture from your friends and neighbors that we're watching out for you, too, and we're here to help you. If you need help ..."

A giant tear rolled down the old woman's cheek. "Thank you, Jackson. This is the nicest thing anyone has ever done for me."

"Let me introduce you to everyone who helped out." Jackson called out each volunteer by name. He told her about every person's contribution to the project, and Mrs. Caruthers shook hands with each and every one of them, to thank them personally.

Johanna captured it all on video, glad that her tears did not splash onto the camera lens and blur the images.

JOHANNA STAYED OUT late with Jackson and his friends, celebrating the success of their community project, but in the back of her mind, she couldn't shake the fact that her sentence would begin in forty-eight hours.

It was after two in the morning when she finally crawled into bed. She yawned with exhaustion, but her looming incarceration prevented her from getting much sleep. Finally, she gave in to her insomnia, brewed a pot of coffee, and grabbed Mal's diary.

"Mal, why were you on Terroria?"

She waited. After several minutes passed with no word from her mentor, she felt abandoned. Then, the pages riffled to a section near the end. The diary outlined how Mal had been summoned to appear before the Library of Illumination's College of Overseers to testify on behalf of Johanna, who had admitted to destroying Terrorian property. According to his diary entry:

I had initially thought the punishment too harsh, but then I discerned an undercurrent of deep concern among the overseers. It began when I testified about reports that I had heard about obelisks being counterfeited so the originals could be sold to finance weaponry. The overseers dismissed me, but more importantly, they did not dispute my testimony. I am sure the College of Overseers needs Johanna to serve her sentence on Terroria, so that she can act as its eyes and ears on that world. I am quite certain she is being planted as a spy.

Johanna gasped when she read Mal's words. *Counterfeits. Weapons. Spy.* She would have to keep her eyes and ears open for any indication of warmongering and subterfuge. Well, maybe not her ears, not unless the overseers reinstated her ability to understand the Terrorians. *They'll have to, or else how am I supposed to know what Nero 51 expects of me?*

Three days. She planned to travel light. Nothing fancy—just a change of clothes, a toothbrush, and protein bars in a backpack. And water. She would need to bring her own water. She didn't even know if they *had* water on Terroria. She spent the rest of the day trying to find out as much as she could about the realm. She didn't expect it to be easy, but when she plugged Terroria into the library database, listings for it came right up. Finding them would be another matter. They were located on sub-level fifty-six. *Could that be in the basement?*

She picked up Mal's diary and consulted it again. "Where's sub-level fifty-six?"

The diary opened to a section she had never seen before. It contained page after page of detailed floor plans, starting with the cupola and ending with sub-level 1,311. The plans for most of the sub-levels looked the same. They were made up of countless rows of stacks filled with every book, pamphlet, drawing, musical composition, letter, treaty, mathematical equation, and other tangible collection of words, numbers, symbols and ideas the realms had ever known.

"How do I get down to sub-level fifty-six?" The pages shuffled again, and a picture of an archaic hand-crank elevator appeared. *Hand crank—for fifty-six levels? Going down might not be so bad, but coming back up would be a bitch.*

"Mal, do you know if it's hard to crank?"

A new entry by Mal appeared.

The original apparatus has been upgraded many times. The container was last replaced in the mid–nineteenth century with an open cage elevator that may look old but is in good working order. It is easy to operate. The hand crank has also been replaced, and the device is nuclear powered, just like everything else in the library.

Johanna breathed a sigh of relief.

"Are you okay?"

She jumped. She hadn't heard Jackson come in the back door. "I'm fine. I located books on Terroria on sub-level fifty-six."

"Where?"

"My thought exactly. If you come with me, we can find it together."

She led him down into the basement to the area where Mal's diary had indicated the existence of an elevator. A large cabinet containing library castoffs stood where the elevator should be. An old adding machine, a broken postage meter, and other obsolete office equipment that had seen better days filled the shelves.

"Look for a lever," she said.

They inspected every shelf, removing the junk and piling it on the floor so they could spot the lever more easily.

"I don't see any," Jackson observed, while pressing on the backs of the shelves, looking for a way to get them to swing open.

"It's too dark in here." The absence of windows made it hard to see in shadowy corners. "See if that light still works."

Jackson inspected a tarnished brass frame encasing an old-fashioned light bulb. "I don't see any switch. Maybe I just need to tighten the bulb ... if I can get my fingers through these stupid bars." The frame made reaching the bulb difficult. "I wonder if this thing comes off," he said, twisting it. As he did so, the cabinet pivoted open, sending up a cloud of dust.

"You're like an accidental genius," Johanna said, with a smile.

"Thanks ... I think."

They found an ancient cage made of brass bars hidden behind the cabinet. It had a bronze medallion affixed to the front of it: *LOI*. Johanna pulled the door open and pushed aside an inner scissor-gate. She tentatively entered the elevator, and Jackson followed. They looked at the massive panel of numbers. The number *6* was already lit. The button for the lowest level said *1311*. She found the button for sub-level fifty-six and pushed it. The elevator lurched as it started its descent.

—LOI—

5

JOHANNA DIDN'T KNOW what to expect on sub-level fifty-six, but envisioned something dark, dirty, and in disrepair. Instead she found a comfortable space filled with abundant soft lighting and climate-controlled air. She located the section where the computer catalog system said she would find books on Terroria, and she soon chose one that looked promising.

"That was easy," Jackson said, as they headed back to the elevator.

"All things considered," she agreed, "we got off lucky."

They hopped on the elevator, and Jackson studied the buttons. "What floor? I've never seen an elevator in the library. Do you think there's a door hidden behind one of the shelves?"

"I'm pretty sure the basement is level six. Press that button. We can look for an elevator on the main floor after this is all over."

The cage made a creaking sound as it started to ascend. Jackson gazed at the staircase that wound around the elevator as it climbed. "Could you imagine if we had to walk up all these stairs to get back? There must be thousands of them. Tens of thousands, if the library really does go down to"—he inspected the button panel—"sub-level thirteen-hundred and eleven."

The cage suddenly stopped between floors, and the lights went out.

"No, no, no, no, no." Johanna huffed.

The lights suddenly turned on, and the elevator began moving again.

"Frit. My heart dropped to my stomach when that happened. I wouldn't want to be stuck down here. No one would even know where we were. We would starve to death. Maybe even have to kill one another for food." He thought about that for a second. "Don't worry, I could never do that to you. You could eat me first."

"Uh-huh." She left it at that.

"You're supposed to say that you would do the same thing for me."

"It grieves me to say that you would have to die alone, because the College of Overseers is coming tomorrow evening to escort me to my sentence, and I get the feeling that they would find me no matter where I am."

"That's probably true. You don't think they would leave me down there, do you?"

The elevator stopped. Johanna opened the scissor-gate and stepped out. "I guess we'll never know."

They sat together on the sofa. "Be prepared in

case the Terrorians appear."

She opened the back cover and immediately inspected the bottom of the endpaper. "It's a zero. We're safe."

"How do you know?"

"Mal's diary. I saw a section about how the library's collection has a hint about the book levels camouflaged in the endpapers." She turned the book and showed him a minute *0*.

"That could come in handy. When were you going to tell me?"

"I just read it this morning," she replied.

She paged through the *History of Terroria*. It gave details on Realm Twelve from its earliest days through the present, and included the curators who had overseen it. There was a section on Terrorians' major contributions to music, art, and literature, and a detailed geographical outline of the world and its natural resources. The book also touched upon the portals, and how all the libraries had full use of them for communicating with the other realms, until the Two Millennia War.

> *Terroria's impatience with some of the other realms, as well as its unbridled thirst for power, resulted in a scheme to take over the entire library system. The Terrorian Realm formed alliances with Adventura and Mysteriose to overturn the Council of Twelve (now defunct), a governing board formed by the curators of each of the realms. In a well-planned coup d'état, the three rogue curators seized control of the Council of Twelve and commanded their troops to use the*

portals to invade each library and take over its operation. The population of each realm resisted the invaders, but could not break the defenses of the well-protected libraries. The nine realms that refused to join with the Terrorians, Adventurites, and Mysterians suffered severe deprivation at the hands of their captors. The population on some worlds decreased by more than two-thirds.

The College of Overseers moved to seal the portals, isolating the rebels in nine separate battles. The overseers immediately convened the First Inter-Realm Peace Council. Rebel leaders agreed to attend, but as soon as the portals reopened, Terrorian curator Claff 8 ordered new troops to transport into the war zones and push for victory. He took two of the overseers prisoner and had them executed in a demonstration of power.

The remaining overseers escaped and sealed the portals again—scrambling their configuration so anyone breaching a portal would never be sure where he or she might emerge.

The war raged on until the overseers secretly built a one-way portal to a containment cell in Lumina. In a stunning use of reverse propaganda, the overseers leaked information that the portal doors would be opened so a secret emissary could travel between worlds, but in fact, no such visit had been planned. Instead, all the portals were reconfigured to lead only to the Luminan cell. In a stunning victory, all newly recruited rebel fighters, along with Claff

8, were captured. The Terrorian curator turned his weapon on himself, rather than become a prisoner. Many of the other fighters broke down and told the Luminans everything they knew about the military operation. Claff 8's allies were taken into custody and, after cross-examination, found guilty of treason and put to death.

Special Luminan troops traveled to each realm to restore order. A substantial amount of blood continued to be shed during the following half century, while Lumina battled to regain control of all the Libraries of Illumination. Once peace was established, new curators who swore loyalty to the College of Overseers were put into place, and the portals sealed. The Two Millennia War had ended, but would never be forgotten, especially by those realms that suffered the deepest losses. (For more information, refer to "The New Epoch" by Summeria 15.)

"Do you think the Terrorians still hold a bit of a grudge against the overseers?" Jackson asked.

"It's possible, although that was a very long time ago."

"Nero 51's living room had piles of stuff that looked like rocket launchers. They were huge."

"Did he say anything when he put you behind the force field?"

"Ik, ik, glug."

"Helpful."

"You asked."

"Mal is pretty sure they're counterfeiting obelisks

to buy weapons, which would give credence to your observation of a stockpile of heavy artillery. Did you get a peek into any of the other rooms of the residence?"

"No. He slammed me inside that force field pretty quickly. And a moment later, you began banging on the door. Except, now that I think of it, I did see something that looked like a TV screen on the wall that he momentarily 'ik, ik, glugged' into. It may be some sort of communications device."

"I wonder if there's a book downstairs on the Terrorian language."

"Why? Are you planning to say 'how do you do' in Terrorian?"

"I'd like to know how they say words like *weapons*, *war*, *counterfeit*, and *invasion*, so that I'll know if they're talking about something other than literature."

"Well, if you're going to use the elevator, I'm going to stay behind. And if you're not back within a half-hour, I'll lasso the hook in *our* cupola and dial up the College of Overseers."

"Maybe I'd better take a flashlight and Mal's diary with me."

"You think Mal has a better chance of helping you than I do?"

"No. But I think he's an excellent backup plan."

Johanna checked the computer for a book on Terrorian language and syntax and found one listed on sublevel fifty-six. "Fifty-six must be the Terrorian level."

She grabbed what she needed, and Jackson followed her down to the basement and watched as she twisted the light fixture.

"The way I figure it," Jackson reasoned "it should

only take you one minute to get down there, three minutes to find the book, and another minute to get back up. After that, I'm calling in the troops."

"You gave me a half-hour just a few minutes ago."

"Just hurry."

Johanna entered the elevator. Before she could slide the scissor-gate shut, the lights blinked.

"See what I mean?" Jackson said.

"I'll be back before you know it."

A REALM AWAY, a society of select Terrorians met in secret. One member of the group, Zor 114, discussed how they might be able to hack into the portals and take control of their operation. He attempted a demonstration, but after a promising flash, it failed.

During that attempt, the power on twelve different worlds … blinked.

JOHANNA FOUND THE language primer quickly and hurried back up to sub-level six. Jackson awaited her there, as promised.

"Four minutes. Not bad. Let's go back upstairs. For some reason, this place is giving me the creeps."

Johanna cracked open the book, thankful for another Level Zero designation. Jackson sat down next to her and read aloud from the middle of the page. "Ik, ock, uk: *I am; you are; he, she, or it is*. What are all these funny symbols?"

"The conjugation of ik, ock, uk, written in Terrorian."

"While you were down there, you should have looked for a Terrorian-English dictionary."

"Yeah. Why don't you just go download one on the iPad while I study this."

"Good one." He sat back and closed his eyes.

Johanna turned to the back of the book to see if a word list or glossary existed. She found what she wanted and looked up *weapons*. "Ergat."

"You gargling?"

"I'm saying the word for *weapon*. Ergat."

"That's an easy one. Wyatt Earp carried a gun. Mobsters called a gun a gat. 'Er' for Earp, 'gat' for gun."

She marveled at Jackson's ability to make anything sound simple. "Cru."

"What's that?"

"*War*."

"Okay, war is cruel. Just cut off the end. What's it say for 'counterfeit'?"

"Nothing. There's no listing in here for fake, phony, or even bogus."

"There's got to be some equivalent."

"Noh."

"There has to be."

"I didn't say 'no'—n-o—I said 'noh'—n-o-h— which means 'copy' or 'reproduction.'"

"Oh. That's a 'noh'-brainer."

She sighed, even though the corners of her mouth turned up just a little. "Guz."

"Does that mean they're going to cut out your gizzard and guzzle your blood?"

"Close. It means 'invade.'"

"What's the future tense of 'ik, ock, uk'?"

Johanna turned back the pages. "Iki, ocko, uku, ikin, ockon, ukin."

"Rhymes with ..."

"Stop it."

"Okay. If you hear someone say, 'Ikin guz,' it means we will invade."

"Porg."

"We will invade pork?"

"Porg means 'portal.'"

"How do you say 'takeover'?"

She turned the pages. "There's nothing listed for 'takeover,' but there is 'seg.'"

"What does that mean?"

"'Seize.' So if I hear anyone say, 'Ikin seg porg,' I'll know they're planning to seize the portals."

As Johanna tried to commit words to memory, Jackson made up little mnemonic devices to help her absorb them. She laughed at his attempts because they sounded goofy, but had to admit they actually helped her learn Terrorian.

"Do you know this one?" he asked. "Bli z' Bril."

"Cold?"

He smiled. "If you're talking about your answer, it *is* cold. 'Bli z' Bril' means 'Library of Illumination' in Terrorian."

WHEN THE CLOCK struck nine, Johanna kicked Jackson out. "Go home. You've got school tomorrow, and I've got to rest up so I can spend the day learning about Terroria and tying up loose ends here at the library."

"I'm thinking of taking tomorrow off."

"Don't. I need the time to get stuff done."

"I can help you."

"You can help me after school. We didn't get back

here until around eleven on Friday night, so they won't be coming for me until late tomorrow. If you come straight after school, we'll have plenty of time to go over everything you'll need to do here while I'm away."

He made a face at her.

She pulled him over and kissed him. "Really, it's going to be all right."

"I hope so."

NORMALLY, JOHANNA DIDN'T mind Monday mornings, but this one filled her with anxiety. She dressed quickly and made herself a huge breakfast. She would be taking protein bars to Terroria to help her keep up her energy, but she wanted to make sure that she ate several hearty meals before leaving Exeter. Earth. Fantasia. Realm Eleven. *Whew.* Everything she had learned in the past seventy-two hours boggled her mind.

She crammed everything she thought she'd need in her backpack, and placed it by the circulation desk. She packed Mal's diary, but then unpacked it to ask a question.

"Mal, if I leave Jackson my diary, will he be able to read it the way I can read yours, and ask questions?"

His words crawled across the page: *A curator has the ability to read the diary of either a mentor or a protégé.*

She grabbed her diary and quickly scanned it. Mal had given it to her when she became his protégé. She placed it on the circulation desk.

"How will I know if Jackson asks a question? Will I be able to see it?"

You will sense it. And once you consciously think of the answer, it will appear in your diary. It will be a mostly

61

*one-way conversation, however, because Jackson will have
no way of knowing if you are trying to reach him.*

"Thanks, Mal." She closed his diary and slipped
it in her backpack. She kept busy for the rest of the day
by doing chores around the library and memorizing as
much Terrorian language and lore as possible.

"How's it going?"

She jumped when she heard Jackson's voice. "Is it
that late already?"

"I had to ask Old Man ... uh ... Mr. Benson for the
next few days off to take care of the library, and I asked
if I could leave an hour early so you could *mentor* me.
He's so happy about all the positive feedback he's getting
about our community-service project that he was happy
to oblige. It's like being a superstar. I can get anything I
want right now."

"Help me with my Terrorian. Even better, sit
down, relax, and think back to when Nero 51 grabbed
you. I need you to tell me everything. What you saw,
what you felt, what you smelled, what you heard."

"I thought we already went over all that?"

"You said he spoke to someone. Can you recall
what he said?"

"I'll need to close my eyes for this."

Jackson sat on the sofa and put his head back. He
envisioned the tentacles pulling him into the residence.
He recalled the acrid, metallic smell—like a chemical
lab—and while most of the Terrorian library was merely
hazy, he remembered the residence contained an oily
mist rising from the floor.

"It smelled really bad, like a solvent mixed with

rotten eggs. I could actually taste it when I inhaled, but then he picked up a weapon and shot me, and I didn't really think about it after that."

"You didn't tell me he shot you."

"He didn't shoot me with bullets or arrows or anything like that. He shot me with a force field that locked me in place."

"What did the weapon look like?"

"Like all the other weapons piled up against the wall."

"How many were there?"

"A hundred, maybe? Didn't you see them?"

"I was too focused on getting you out of there."

"Yeah, well, if we hadn't made a run for it before Nero 51 returned, he would have probably used the same weapon on you."

"So their weapons can immobilize any enemy without killing them?"

"Yeah."

"Which means they want them alive."

"Yeah."

"Why?"

"Dinner? Slavery? Maybe they want people to work the mines. Or maybe, they want to brainwash them and turn them into soldiers, so their own people don't get killed on the front lines."

"The front lines ..."

"Yeah. I think they're planning something big. I didn't know what 'cru' meant at the time, but I'm sure Nero 51 said it to the communication device."

"Did he use the word *tec*?"

"Maybe. I don't remember. What does it mean?"

"'Spy.'"

"Did you learn anything touristy, like 'I'm thirsty' or 'where is the bathroom'?"

"No." She looked them up. "There is no word for 'thirsty.' Apparently Terrorians absorb liquid from the air." She thumbed through the book for several minutes while Jackson quietly looked on. "Ewww. They don't have bathrooms, either. That thick, hazy vapor is their 'waste product,' which is discarded through their feet. We walked through that stuff."

"Everyone walked through that stuff, including the overseers."

"This is going to be the longest three days of my life."

"You'd better pack a roll of toilet paper."

Johanna slumped back against the cushions.

Jackson picked up her hand. "I'll be with you every step of the way. I won't stop thinking about you until you return."

"Oh." She jumped off the sofa to fetch her diary. She handed it to him. "This is my diary. It has a lot in it about how things work in the library. If you're stuck and need to ask me a question, write it in the diary on the last page. I'll sense it and can tell you the answer if I know it. Check it often, even just to ask how I'm doing, so I can answer you, or else there's no way I can stay in touch with you."

"What about Mal's diary?"

"I'm taking it with me."

"What if they take it from you?"

Her eyes widened with alarm. "Do you think they'll do that?"

"If they think it's important to you, they might. If they think they can get secret information about our library, they might."

"I never thought of that. Maybe I should leave it here."

"Why don't you ask Mal?"

WHEN JOHANNA POSED the question, Mal did not reply, but she felt the diary shrinking in her hand. It finally stopped when it was a half inch wide and three-quarters of an inch long. A small, metal loop grew out of one corner, and a little glass peephole appeared in the front. She raised it to her eye and saw her last entry. "Mal, do you hear me?"

She peeked inside and saw the word *Yes*.

"I'll be right back." She practically flew up the stairs and went straight to her jewelry box. She returned with a gold chain that she attached to the book and then placed around her neck, slipping the tiny tome under her tee shirt. She smiled at Jackson. "I feel better, now."

He picked up Johanna's diary and slipped it in his back pocket. "Don't worry about me. I don't need a shrinking diary. I'll just carry you around au naturel."

The clock struck eight. And Johanna's stomach rumbled. "Pizza?"

"Okay. Relax. I'll run out and get it. You're getting a little jumpy."

"I'll call it in" she said, picking up her cell phone. As soon as Jackson left, she stuck the phone in her pocket. She sat on the sofa and closed her eyes.

* * *

Ω *THIS IS NO time to sleep, Johanna Charette. Your sentence has begun.*

—LOI—

6

A MOMENT LATER, Johanna and Overseer Plato Indelicat stood in front of the circulation desk on Terroria. Nero 51 was nowhere in sight. The overseer rang a large brass bell attached to the front of the desk.

"Uk infi," Nero 51 stated as he entered the area. The overseer waved his hand to enact a translation enchantment. *You're late.*

Ω *I have delivered Johanna Charette to you at the appointed hour. She is here to work off her sentence under the rules of the Arkan Peace Treaty, ratified after the Two Millennia War. She is to be treated in a civilized manner in accordance with her species, which is human. I will inspect her quarters, now.*

Nero 51 led the overseer to a small storage room toward the back of the library. It was empty except for the oily mist rising from the floor. The overseer waved his hand, and the mist vanished. A cot appeared, as well as a small sink and a toilet.

"You give preferences," Nero 51 shouted at him.

Ω I am giving her the minimum accommodations necessary for her species.

He turned to Johanna.

Ω This room will serve you for one-third of every twenty-four hour period that you are here. You may spend seven consecutive hours here in repose, and one full hour dividing the workday for your meal break. You have merely to say the word 'sustenance,' and a meal made up of foods common to Fantasia will appear on this table.

He waved his hand again, and a small table and a single chair appeared.

"You coddle the spy. Call me when she is ready to begin serving her sentence." Nero 51 left them alone.

Ω As you can tell, I have enacted a translation enchantment, so that you can understand what Nero 51 and his minions expect of you. I will be back in seventy-two hours to escort you home. Be Illuminated, Johanna Charette.

She dropped her backpack on the cot. The overseer disappeared, and Johanna found herself transported back to the front of the circulation desk. After waiting a moment, she rang the bell.

"You dare summon me."

"My sentence has begun."

A tentacle extended the width of the library to a utility closet and withdrew a rag and a jar of oily paste. "Polish the obelisks. If you dare to break one, you will be punished."

"I will need a ladder to reach the higher shelves."

"Find one," he snarled.

"I didn't want you to think I was snooping around."

"Look in the utility closet."

"Thank you."

JOHANNA STARTED WITH the stacks to the right of the front door. She planned to work from top to bottom, but she wanted to determine what she was in for first. She selected an obelisk from a lower shelf. It was heavy, which she expected. The one that she had smashed had been just as heavy. As she opened the jar of paste, the noxious fumes nearly caused her to swoon. The odor resembled a cross between putrefied flesh and rotten fish, with a biting quality that stung her eyes and made them tear. She pulled her tee shirt up over her nose to filter the air, and did her best. The paste made the obelisks slippery, and she was afraid of dropping one, so when she climbed to the upper shelves, she tucked the obelisk inside her belt. She also learned a drop of polish went a long way, so she used as little as possible.

Johanna worked mindlessly, but the constant climbing to retrieve crystals made her back and knees ache. It didn't help that the Terrorian day started just when her day should have been ending. She had been at it for hours, and relief washed over her when she heard a voice out of nowhere say, Ω *Johanna Charette, you may take a one-hour meal break.*

She returned to her room and lay down on the cot. It turned out to be more comfortable than it looked. She thought back to Nero 51 accusing the overseer of coddling her, and wondered if it was true. It took a while before she felt her back muscles relax. She remained on the cot for a half-hour, then sat at the table and said, "Sustenance." A plate filled with carrots and peanuts appeared before her, as well as an old-fashioned tankard. She picked up the cup and sniffed. *Apple juice.* She consumed everything the overseers provided, and slipped a protein bar in her pocket.

Hardly a moment had passed when a voice said, *Ω Return to work.*

By the end of the day, she had polished most of the obelisks along the outer walls of the first story. It had been a massive effort, but hardly enough to make a small dent in the number of crystals in the building. She silently kept track of how many times she saw Nero 51. He spent a great deal of time in the antechamber and the residence, and she only saw him every couple of hours, when he would cross from one space to the other.

At the rate she was polishing obelisks, she would never reach the second level, or the curator's residence. She hoped to get a peek inside, or at least to eavesdrop on some snippet of conversation, but she may as well have been on an iceberg off the coast of Siberia, for all the good her proximity to the Terrorian war effort was doing.

BACK ON FANTASIA—as Jackson now liked to call it— sudden demands on his workload kept him on his toes. It started when the president of the library's board of directors called and demanded to speak to Johanna.

"She's out of town," Jackson explained.

"What do you mean, 'out of town'? We have no record of a request for time off."

"Her grandmother ... is dying," the teen fudged.

"Oh. Well. Who's taking her place?"

"I am, sir."

"And who are you?"

"Jackson Roth, Johanna's assistant." He paused. "You must know about me. I'm her curator-in-training. Just ask any of the overseers of the Library of Illumination ... uh ... foundation."

"Aren't you just a kid?"

"I'm the curator-in-training."

"Well, *Mr. Curator-In-Training*, some of the libraries in our neighboring communities are impressed with our facility's new information retrieval system. I've invited about two dozen of them to view a live demonstration of it on Thursday evening."

"No," Jackson said.

"Yes," the president of the board of directors stated emphatically. "I'm sure you can find money in your budget for some coffee and cookies. If we play our cards right, we could be named 'Library of the Year.' It's an honor that I would hate to see snatched away from us by a less prestigious facility that's still operating in the dark ages. We would be forced to *cut jobs* if that were to happen, if you get my drift."

"Right. A demonstration for a couple dozen people, with snacks, on Thursday evening," Jackson confirmed.

"At seven."

"Gotcha."

Click.

How hard can it be? He had helped Johanna set up evenings like this before. Clear out the furniture, set up some chairs, call the gourmet food shop in the village for coffee and cookies. *Easy peasy.*

71

He thought about the demonstration. How would he show all those people how easily the system worked? A large-screen TV would allow him to illustrate his workflow.

He called the president of the board of directors back.

"What is it?" The man sounded a little snarky.

"This is Jackson Roth, the curator-in-training at the Library of Illumination. There's the matter of a large-screen TV. I need one to stream our new digitized system, so your guests can see how well it works. Unfortunately, the library board rejected our request last fall. I'm so sorry, but that oversight will prevent me from demonstrating the system."

"What?"

"No TV, no ability to live stream my digital demonstration."

"That is not an option. Order the damn TV."

"Plus installation, of course."

"Just do it."

Jackson smiled. *This management stuff is easy.* He called The Guys Next Door—an appliance store in the village—and explained what he needed.

"What's the P.O. number?"

"We don't have a P.O. box. I'll give you the street address."

"Not post office—*purchase order*. What's the purchase-order number?"

"I'll have to get back to you." Jackson put down the phone and began to pace. It helped him think. Unfortunately, he lacked the experience or knowledge necessary to continue. *Johanna's diary.* It was right there in his back pocket. He dredged up a memory of her using it to contact Mal. He wrote down the words as he said them. "Johanna, how to you get a P.O. number?" *It stands for purchase order,* he added, just in case she was confused.

JOHANNA HEARD JACKSON'S voice in her head.

She said aloud, "Why do you need a purchase order?"

After a minute she heard Jackson reply, "The president of the library board told me to get a TV for a demonstration that he's scheduled here. The Guys Next Door asked for a P.O. number."

"There's a pad in the top right drawer of my desk that says 'purchase order' on it. They're pre-numbered. Fill out the next blank page. Take the top copy to the president of the library board for his signature, then give it to The Guys Next Door."

"Thanks," she heard him say. "How are you doing?"

"It's okay. The overseers are making sure I'm treated humanely."

"Anything you need?"

"Diet Coke with ice."

"Right."

Her evening meal seemed astonishingly similar to chicken soup—at least, she hoped it was made out of chicken. It contained meat and a variety of vegetables, accompanied by something that looked like bread that had been run over by a truck. Surprisingly, her tankard held beer. She had never been much of a beer drinker, but after the day she had endured, it quenched her thirst.

She lay down on the cot to contemplate her next move, and felt something poking her—her cell phone. She switched it off and stuck it in her backpack. She would have no use for it here. The next thing she knew, the voice in her head warned her that her workday would begin in twenty minutes.

Day two seemed tediously comparable to day one. After her midday break, Johanna saw Nero 51 go up to the second floor, followed by several other Terrorians. *I believe I'll continue polishing obelisks on the outer walls before working my way in to the interior stacks. Since I'm done down here ...*

She climbed up to the next level and began working on the crystals that lined the shelves next to the residence. She couldn't hear a word they said, which was really disappointing. *Maybe when they're done.* With luck, they would continue their conversation as they exited the apartment, and she would learn something of value.

Johanna's stomach growled. She pulled a protein bar from her pocket, but before she could remove the packaging, the door to the residence slid open. She shoved the bar behind the obelisks and grabbed a rag, polishing the closest crystal.

Nero 51 fumed when he saw Johanna near his residence. *This Fantasian is nothing but trouble.* He wished he could delay his meeting until after she left, but the very fact she was on Terroria was the only thing keeping the portals from being sealed. *We must be ready by tomorrow.* He cursed the overseers for putting a translation enchantment on his library. He would have to contact his followers and demand a night meeting at an outside location. They must prepare. He would be forced to leave the girl alone on the premises; however, anything she learned would not matter once they claimed victory.

He waited until she retreated to her room for the evening. Once he heard her door latch into place—a precaution taken by the overseers—he walked to the front entrance and hit a switch on a control panel. Giant fans that blew warm, humid air into the library stopped running. *No use wasting precious humidity on the Fantasian.*

JOHANNA'S SUSTENANCE CONSISTED of a fish cake and a hill of beans. *Edamame.* She thought of the protein bar that she had left on one of the shelves outside the residence. She held her breath as she opened her door, praying Nero 51 was not out inspecting her work. She popped her head out just in time to see him disappear out the front door.

Something struck her as odd. The mechanical sound that droned day and night suddenly stopped. She wondered what it meant.

NERO 51 ENTERED Building 7, a neighboring structure at the end of the block. Almost everyone he contacted had already assembled there. "Where is Heil 66?"

"Printing maps of the realms. They must be ready by morning."

Nero 51 nodded. "Before dusk tomorrow, our teams should be ready to amass outside each portal. They must be indistinguishable from the library patrons I have invited to a special fundraising event in the cupola. There should be no reason to question anyone being there."

The gathering had originally been organized as a bona fide meeting, and it proved to be fortuitous planning after the teenagers from Realm Eleven breached the portals. Nero 51 decided at the outset that the Fantasians were too young and stupid to be spies. His accusations were deliberately intended to keep the portals open, until Terrorians could use them to invade the other libraries. He knew the overseers would impart *justice*.

"You could not have planned better," Opel 29 stated. "If we had dialed the overseers as originally planned, they may have suspected our motives. Instead, we are reacting to an external intrusion, and the element of surprise will be ours."

Operation Final Darkness would begin in less than twenty-four hours.

THE LEVER TO the residence was missing, just like when she had tried to rescue Jackson. She crossed her fingers. "Illumination." Nothing happened.

She took a deep breath. "Delumination." The door remained sealed.

She had never been within hearing distance when Nero 51 entered his apartment, yet something poked the back of her brain. For some reason, she conjured up an image of Jackson grinning. *What did he say?* She closed her eyes for a moment and scanned her memory for something he had said, which she should have known, but didn't.

Ahhh ... "Bli z' Bril."

The door vibrated as it slid out of the way. She tentatively entered the residence. The thick, oily mist

inside the private quarters made her gag. She remembered what she had read about it and hated having to wade
through it. A light would have been helpful, but she dared
not use one, for fear of being caught. The building across
the courtyard was lit, and let in just enough of a glow to
illuminate the cache of weapons stacked against the wall.
She did a quick count and moved into the next room. It
also appeared to be filled with weapons, although it was
difficult to tell because they obscured the window, eliminating it as a potential light source. The only reason why
she could see at all was because the entry door remained
open and the library proper was still illuminated.

She returned to the living room and looked for
a desk. She found a short column shrouded in the haze
that held several obelisks. It did not appear to have any
drawers, and while she had taken the time to learn some
Terrorian words, she had not learned the symbols that
went with them, so she could not read the obelisks.

The room dimmed. Johanna glanced through the
window and noticed the light from the other building
had gone out. There was nothing more she could learn
here. She slipped out the door, but it did not automatically close. "Bli z' Bril," she said aloud. As the residence
door whooshed shut, the main door to the Library of
Illumination creaked open. Nero 51 had returned, and
Johanna stood immobilized—trapped—on the residence
floor.

The Terrorian passed beneath her on his way
to the curator's staircase. Johanna slipped to the front
shelf that separated the apartment from the balcony
overlooking the main reading room. If this library was a
duplicate of her own, she'd find a tiny space between the

end shelf and a front window. She scurried to it, pressed herself into the space, and held her breath.

"Bli z' Bril." *Swoosh.*

She waited for a second swoosh that would tell her the door had closed. She heard the latch snap into place, and quietly released her breath. *I just need to get to the staircase.* She waited a minute before stealthily sneaking to the spiral stairs. She had not paid attention to whether they squeaked, and prayed with each step she took. Downstairs, she hurried back to her room and heard the door latch loudly click into place. She wondered if Nero 51 heard it as well.

Johanna picked up Mal's diary. "What should I do if I found several rooms filled with weapons?" she whispered. She held the tiny book up to her eye and waited. After several minutes, a single line of type appeared.

Nothing. You are only there to serve out your sentence.

Johanna's face wrinkled. She thought the overseers wanted her to learn as much as she could about the Terrorian plot, but now Mal stated that she must merely serve her sentence. She slumped. *Did Mata Hari have to go through this?*

JACKSON ROLLED HIS shoulders. Even with the help of the dumbwaiter, removing enchanted books from the most accessible stacks turned out to be a back breaker. He had worked well into the evening, and had conked out on the sofa in the main reading room.

He spent most of the following morning re-populating the shelves with the old unenchanted books they had stored in the basement. *Good thing we never sold these back to Bebe's Bibliothèque.* He was almost done when he heard someone banging on the front door.

"Are you from The Guys Next Door?" It was a dumb question. Their uniforms had the company name emblazoned across them, and they stood next to a huge box decorated with a full-size picture of a sixty-inch flat-screen TV.

"Yeah. Where do you want it?"

Jackson surveyed the library. In the back of his mind, he had always thought it would be cool to have a TV rise out of the back of the circulation desk, but that would require special cabinetry. And a budget (he had learned about the importance of budgeting when he opened the petty-cash box the day before and found only $11.45 for coffee and cookies. The bill was actually four times that amount, and he ended up paying the difference with his own money). Regardless, the circulation desk seemed like the most logical place for a TV. "Put it here, facing those chairs."

"You got an antenna or cable hookup back here?"

It was another one of those questions he didn't know the answer to. "You go ahead and unpack it while I find out." He consulted Johanna's diary in the antechamber. He didn't want the repairmen to think he was some kind of nut when he asked it a question.

OUTSIDE THE TERRORIAN library, Heil 66 lumbered along, hidden in the shadows of the building across the way. He had been delayed making maps for the war effort, and needed to leave them for the troops gathering in Building 7. He saw Nero 51 reenter the library and knew he had missed that night's meeting. Seconds later, he saw a fleeting shadow in a second-floor library window. Nero 51 was strong, but not necessarily quick. Heil 66 doubted his compatriot could have reached the upper level so swiftly. He watched, waiting. The shadow appeared a second time, several minutes after the first darkening. The mapmaker waited to see if anyone would emerge from the Library of Illumination. Anyone trying to escape the building would have to use the front door, because the rear entrance had been sealed shortly after the start of the Two Millennia War and had never been reopened. The night was raw, and Heil 66 wrapped his unoccupied tentacles around his body to keep his moist emissions from evaporating.

An hour elapsed. There had been no further shadows nor disturbances of any kind, so the Terrorian continued on his journey. *It's probably nothing.* Still, as he hurried along to Building 7, he made a mental note to mention the shadows to Nero 51.

—LOI—

7

JOHANNA SAT AT the edge of her cot staring into space. Jackson's voice broke the silence. "Do we have a cable hookup or TV antenna near the circulation desk?"

She had no idea, but she knew where to find the information. She asked Mal's diary. She waited several minutes for an answer.

No need. Any device inside the library will wirelessly absorb any transmission signals. Just plug it in and let it warm up. No further setup is required.

She relayed the message to Jackson, wondering what she would find when she returned to the library. *My library.*

That night, Johanna slept restlessly. Her only solace was that at the end of her sentence, she could burrow beneath the blankets of her own bed.

Finally she fell asleep, but could not escape her dreams.

She worked feverishly in the cupola of the Terrorian library, trying to clean obelisks. Every time she reached for one, it floated away. Nero 51 had ordered her to clean them all, or she would not be allowed to leave the Twelfth Realm. With her future at stake, Johanna chased the crystals around the cupola, trying to grab them, but as soon as she wrapped her fingers around one, it fell to the floor and shattered.

She panicked, sweat oozing from her pores. She tried picking up the broken pieces, but could barely see them through the hazy mist. Perspiration made her hands slippery, and the shards she found slipped through her fingers, cutting her hands and making them bleed. She managed to push the pieces off into a misty corner where she hoped they would not be discovered. She reached for another obelisk, but again, it eluded her. Try as she might, she could not grab on to it.

"Did I hear an obelisk break?" roared Nero 51.

She was so startled by his sudden appearance, her arm hit the shelf, and several of the crystal manuscripts crashed to the floor.

"She is willfully destroying library property," he shouted. "Off with her head."

Two other Terrorians appeared behind him, their tentacles snaking toward Johanna, *to take her into custody. She tried to grab an obelisk to hurl at her captors, but the crystals continued to evade her grasp. Finally, she snatched one out of the air and hurled it at one of the Terrorians, but it bounced off his chest and dropped to the floor, where it bounced again, but didn't break. Amazement overcame her. Instead of continuing her attack, she dove for the unbroken obelisk. It was fashioned out of a plastic-like material that looked like the crystal obelisks but was indestructible. "Counterfeits," she screamed. "Fakes. Noh-nohs."*

"Kill her now!"

Johanna felt a tentacle wrap around her throat. Another held her wrists while a third bound her feet. She gagged.

Ω*THE WORKDAY WILL begin in twenty minutes.*

Johanna's eyes flew open. She reached for her throat. The chain attached to Mal's diary had tangled around her neck. She pulled it loose, got out of bed, and splashed water on her face. *It was a dream.* She dropped down onto the chair. "Sustenance." A bowl of cold gruel and an apple appeared. The gruel had no taste, but it filled her stomach and stopped it from growling. The apple, at least, had flavor. She also received a tankard of weak tea, but no honey or sugar to sweeten it. She drank it to quench her thirst, knowing she had only one bottle of water left.

The dream haunted her. She thought of the obelisk that would not break. If the Terrorians had counterfeits, where would they be? Not on a shelf where anyone could find them. More than likely, they would be on a shelf that no one looked at. *The Cupola?* True, it was a seldom-used area of the library, but it meant carrying heavy obelisks up five flights of stairs. The least likely place would be among the main-floor stacks, the ones closest to the back wall, by the antiquities.

She berated herself for being so predictable. The obelisks she had polished were the most visible ones. Maybe today she would pick up a clue by investigating the ones buried in the stacks.

She exited her room. Nero 51 stood at the circulation desk, placing glass microscope slides into a box. *That can't be right.* They looked like microscope slides, but Johanna had a hunch they were documents of some sort.

She went to the utility closet and grabbed a rag and the jar of oily paste. She could feel Nero 51's eyes boring into the back of her head as she walked to an interior shelf and started polishing.

THE CURATOR SLIPPED the last bit of glass into a padded box. Time was of the essence, and he could not stop to bother about the girl, even though she was a nuisance. *Let her clean obelisks. She's not going to find anything. Even if she does, it's too late.*

He picked up the box and walked out the front door, switching off the humidity fans as he passed by. Terrorian soldiers awaited the information he carried— detailing the different realms, their curators, and the conditions rebel troops might face on each world. They had less than twenty-four hours to review maps and other forms of intelligence and complete their war preparations.

Nero 51 had grown up learning about the Two Millennia War and dreaming about the part he could have played in it. He imagined winning the war and being proclaimed "Grand Guardian of all the Libraries," a master of twelve different worlds—thirteen if you counted Lumina, the home of the Board of Overseers. He desired ultimate rule, and he would not allow some insignificant human female from Fantasia to disrupt his plans. *Johanna Charette, curator of the Eleventh Realm, I will make sure you are taken alive. I want to watch you being tortured. Yours will be a slow, painful death that will give me great pleasure.*

JACKSON ENTERED JOHANNA'S apartment. He felt uncomfortable being in her residence without her. He had debated asking her diary where he could find a blanket and a pillow, but didn't want to write something that might distract her—in a bad way. He knew they had to be there. Casanova had used them.

He stopped in front of two closed doors. He'd seen them during his previous visits to her home. He selected the one on the left and entered her private sanctuary. A four-poster bed dominated the space, and the comforter that topped it looked so fluffy, Jackson knew if he lay down on it he would sink halfway to the floor in a cloud of goose down. He looked around the room. Additional closed doors beckoned him. He pulled one open and found an en suite bathroom with a huge built-in tub. Creamy-white pillar candles decorated the back ledge, and he imagined them flickering, their light reflecting on the polished marble walls and mirrored surfaces while Johanna soaked in a mountain of bubbles. *No blanket or pillow in here.*

He pulled open the second door. It contained an L-shaped walk-in closet filled with very few clothes. Johanna dressed nicely, but he knew she didn't splurge on clothing the way Cassie and Brittany did. He sniffed. Her closet smelled just like her—baby powder and roses. He looked at an empty hanging rod. *If I ever move in with Johanna, there's plenty of space for my stuff,* he thought, then shook his head. *Talk about a pipe dream.*

He walked back into the hallway and opened the other door. It was a linen closet, and sitting on the upper shelf, right at eye-level, he found a blanket and pillow. In the back of his mind he knew they would be there, but if he had opened that door first, he would not have had an excuse to explore her bedroom. *Tour over.* He grabbed the linens and carried them downstairs.

Jackson stretched out on the sofa. All he had left to do was test the visual presentation he had created for the group of visiting librarians, but that could wait until morning. *I've got it all under control,* he thought, before rolling onto his side and falling asleep.

JOHANNA NOTICED THE sudden silence when Nero 51 exited the building.

She continued polishing obelisks, but soon realized if she wanted to find what she sought, it would make more sense to pick the crystals up and hope the fakes felt different. She calculated fifty or sixty obelisks on each shelf, and hundreds of shelves. Thousands, even. She also had to consider the private book rooms, antiquities, erotica, periodicals ... she rubbed her temples as she felt the beginnings of a headache. *What if they're on a sub-level?*

She heard the front door open. She dipped a rag in the wax and polished another obelisk.

"Nero 51, are you here?"

"I told you he wouldn't be here," a second voice said. "He's probably already at Building 7."

"Where's the Fantasian creature? Shouldn't she be here? I want to get a look at her. I hear she's hideous."

Johanna could hear the Terrorians flat feet slapping against the floor. She continued polishing.

"Oh. Here she is."

"What a pathetic little beast."

"I know. But she's the key to our victory. The portals wouldn't be open if she weren't here."

"Shhh!"

"She can't understand us. I doubt she can speak Terrorian."

"Just hold your tongue. Anyway, there's nothing for us here. Let's go meet the others."

Johanna focused on their words. *The portals are open because I'm here. And I'm the key to their victory.* When she heard the door open, she peeked around the edge of the stacks and watched them leave. She began grabbing obelisks at random, hoping to find one that would prove to be false. She wanted to be able to give the Board of Overseers the proof they needed. Unfortunately, the obelisks all looked alike, so she had to pay very close attention to make sure she made progress.

Ω *Johanna Charette, you may take a one-hour meal break.*

She finished the shelf she'd been working on and left her cleaning supplies there, so she would know where she left off. She needed sustenance, and she wanted to tell Mal what the Terrorians had said. She choked down dense, grainy bread with some kind of vegetable mash, and followed it with orange juice. *This cuisine will never earn a Michelin star.*

She detailed what she had heard in Mal's diary. "What should I do?"

She waited quite a while before a reply appeared.

Nothing. You are only there to serve out your sentence.

She gritted her teeth. Her jaw clenched so tightly it gave her a headache. *I should have brought aspirin.*

Johanna left her room and looked around the library. It didn't look like anyone was there. She grabbed the rag and paste and climbed up to the second level. She placed her ear against the door of the residence, listening for any sounds coming from within. She heard nothing, and quietly said, "Bli z' Bril." The door opened, and she ducked inside.

The light of day brightened the room, and she tried to estimate the number of weapons. They were piled everywhere. She grabbed one from an inconspicuous area and left, but froze outside the door to the residence, her mind racing. The quickest way to her room was down the curator's staircase, but if Nero 51 walked in, he would surely take those stairs. Her intuition told her to take the stone steps by the front door. They would provide more cover once she got there, and she could ditch the gun behind the steps if she heard anyone enter. Using them, however, would force her to run around the very visible second balcony to the opposite end of the library, and then past the circulation desk on the main floor. That would be too much time out in the open. The Terrorians would not think twice about killing her.

Stop wasting time. By now she could have run down the stairs and been safely back in her room.

She heard a noise in the outer vestibule. She sprinted down the spiral stairs with the weapon raised above her head so it would not bang against the handrail. As she reached the bottom step, the front door screeched open. *The "juvenile" stacks should shield me from view.* She prayed she wouldn't be seen darting past the gaps that allowed light to flow throughout the space.

When she got into her room, she threw the weapon under her cot, sat down, and said, "Sustenance." A bowl filled with yogurt appeared, a ripe peach and a cup of coffee beside it. She bit a huge chunk out of the peach and felt its juice run down her chin as her heart pounded. She could hear it quite clearly, even if it wasn't as loud as the pounding on her door.

—LOI—

8

"COME IN," SHE CALLED OUT, as she stuffed a spoon of yogurt in her mouth.

"You're supposed to be working." Nero 51's eyes darted around the room.

"If the overseers told me my break was over, I would have heard them." Even as she said it, she racked her brain trying to remember if the message might have been drowned out by her escapade.

Ω *Johanna Charette, your break period has ended.*

The announcement came as if on cue. She bit into the peach again before standing up. "I guess I'll save this for later."

"You will not," Nero 51 said, grabbing the uneaten food in a tentacle and stretching it out the door and across the main reading room to dump it in a trash bin. "Get to work."

Johanna glared at him, but did not defy him. He

took one last look around the room, which made her heart pound. Plato Indelicat had removed the mist that might prevent Nero 51 from seeing the weapon, yet he did not comment on it. She worried that he *had* seen it but failed to mention it because he wanted her to lapse into a false sense of security. She had no recourse but to get back to polishing obelisks.

The hairs on the back of her neck suddenly stood on end. She had left the cleaning tools upstairs by the ladder. If Nero 51 saw them, he would know she had been snooping near the residence. She disappeared behind a stack and wondered what her next move should be.

JACKSON SHOT OFF the sofa when the television turned itself on at sunrise. He stumbled and then realized where he was. He looked to see if he had rolled over on the remote control, but found it on the circulation desk where he'd left it the previous night. He shut off the TV and walked around the library to make sure everything was secure. The main level seemed fine, and the public portions of the other levels appeared to be clear. Up in the cupola, he inspected the portal window he and Johanna had used. It looked sealed, but how could it be if Johanna had to use it to return home? The notion that Nero 51 and his pals could come flying through it at any given moment made him shiver. *Thank God Johanna's coming home tonight and the portals will be sealed.*

His imagination shifted into overdrive. What if a few Terrorians slipped through with her when she returned and held them hostage? Would the College of Overseers even know if that happened? *They would have to know. One of them will probably escort Johanna home.*

The Terrorians would have to take the overseer hostage as well, and then everyone would know what had happened, because it would mean the beginning of a revolutionary multi-world war.

Stop it. You're making yourself crazy. Although, craziness might explain his sudden desire to buy a gun—*just in case.*

"HAVE YOU LOST your mind? Who do you think is going to sell a gun to a seventeen-year-old?" Logan bellowed over the telephone.

"Lots of people our age get guns. I hear about them all the time."

"It's illegal."

"All right. Forget I ever mentioned it."

"No. I want to know why you need a gun."

"What part of 'just forget it' don't you understand?"

"All of it."

"I've got to get back to work." Jackson disconnected the call. The phone rang almost immediately, but the teen ignored it when he saw Logan's name on caller ID.

Jackson spent the next hour perfecting the details for that night's presentation. Johanna would probably walk in, right in the middle of it. He froze. If the Terrorians were planning anything, all those poor little librarians would get caught in the crossfire. Talk about rotten timing. In his estimation, the library board had picked the worst possible night for a demonstration. *Maybe if I call the president of the board of directors, I can appeal to the man's better sense.* Jackson dialed the number and waited for the president's secretary to put him on the line.

"Is everything ready for tonight?" No *Hello, Jackson, how are you?* No small talk of any kind—just a command disguised as a question.

"Sir, I'm thinking tonight is not the best night for the presentation."

"Tonight is the perfect night for it. And it's the only night for it. Tell me, Jackson, do you *like* working at the library?" The teen shivered when he heard the thinly veiled threat with an icy-cold delivery.

"I only mentioned it because Johanna is returning tonight, and as curator, she'll be very disappointed she wasn't part of the event."

"That's what she gets for leaving town without notice." *Click.*

Jackson did not have time to react to the click, because someone started banging on the door. He checked the security camera and sighed. *Logan.* "Illumination." The door slid open.

"I had a devil of a time finding this place," Logan said. "I was sure I knew how to get here, but the streets all seemed to lead me in a different direction."

"Yeah, that happens," Jackson answered.

"So, why do you want a gun?"

"There may be some trouble here tonight. The library board wants me to give a demonstration, but some ... uh ... unsavory characters may show up."

"'Unsavory characters'? At this library? I think you're reading too many of these books and not spending enough time in the real world."

"You can't repeat that to anyone, you know. My job is on the line."

Logan knew how much Jackson's family depended

on his paycheck—not that he made a lot of money, but every little bit helped. "Marcus Hurble."

"What about him?"

"I heard he has a couple of guns he wants to sell. That was last week. I didn't pay much attention, because I'm not interested in buying one. But he may still have one to sell. Do you want me to find out?"

"You can't tell anybody."

"Right. How much do you want to spend?"

Jackson counted the money in his wallet. It contained every cent he owned. He wanted to buy a car, and hoped by the time he turned eighteen he might be able to scrape together enough money to get a used one. He hated parting with his hard-earned cash, but if trouble broke out tonight and he wasn't prepared, he might not even be around for his eighteenth birthday. He counted out five hundred dollars. "Do you think this is enough?"

"How do I know?"

"Just make sure the gun works."

"I'm not shooting it."

"Well ... don't buy something you haven't heard of, you know?"

"So you want an UZI ..."

Jackson didn't answer.

"Fine. I'll be back as soon as I can."

"Ammo," the curator-in-training blurted out.

"You know if you load it, you can hurt someone."

"That's the idea."

JOHANNA HEARD NERO 51's footsteps fade as he headed toward the antechamber. She waited a few minutes, to allow him to become totally engrossed in whatever he was doing, before dashing up the spiral stairs and grabbing the cleaning supplies. She then scurried up the ladder to retrieve the protein bar she had hidden the day before.

"Looking for something?"

The sound of Nero 51's voice gave her chills. "Yes. I forgot my protein bar up here yesterday, and since you wouldn't let me to finish my lunch today, I need it to relieve my hunger."

He stared at her hands. "I don't see any such thing."

She reached behind the obelisks and pulled out the bar. "This."

"You are here to work, not to eat." He grabbed the protein bar and put it in his pocket. "I believe you were working downstairs."

"Yes."

"Take the ladder with you."

He obviously did not want her working on the second floor. *Maybe this is where he's hiding the fakes.*

JACKSON PACED IN wide circles around the circulation desk. It seemed like hours since Logan had left. The curator-in-training's stomach growled, but he didn't want to leave the library to get lunch, in case his friend returned while he was out. *Instead of a car, I should get a cell phone. Then I could text him.*

"Argh." He hit himself in the head for being so stupid. He picked up the phone on the circulation desk and dialed Logan's cell number. "Where are you?"

"Piccolo Italia. A guy's gotta have lunch."

"Good. Bring me a meatball hero. I'm starving. Did you have any luck with ... you know?"

"Yeah. I'll be there soon."

"Okay. Hurry."

The ticking of the grandfather clock drove Jackson crazy. It was still early, but he felt like every minute stretched into an hour. He had practically worn a groove in the floor by the time he heard Logan banging on the door. His friend carried two bags, a white one from the pizzeria and a brown one, which must have held the gun.

Logan handed him the white bag. "Eat while I tell you about my little jaunt into the world of handguns."

Jackson ripped the wrapper off his sandwich. "Spill."

"Marcus Hurble has been arrested."

"While you were there?"

"No. Last night. The cops say he robbed a church poor box. Mrs. Krebs, that little old lady who lives across the street from the rectory, told police she heard a gunshot and thought someone killed Reverend Blake. She claims she saw Hurble leaving the church. Reverend Blake is fine, but Hurble had a gun on him when the cops picked him up, so they charged him."

"I thought you said you got me a gun?"

"I did, but not from Hurble. I got it from Larry at Once A-Pawn A Time."

"That guy's a nut job. You didn't tell him it was for me, did you?"

"I told him I needed it for target practice. He took down all my info ... or I guess I should say, my older brother's. If you ever shoot someone with this gun, he'll be the one they send up the river, and my life won't be worth a damn."

"So show me."

"Oh. And by the way, you owe me twenty bucks."

"It cost that much?"

"No," Logan answered, sliding a black case out of the bag and unlatching it. Inside, a 9mm Glock and an empty magazine sat embedded in the box's foam lining. "The gun was four hundred ninety-nine dollars. The ammo is what put you over the top."

Jackson inspected the Glock. "Did he show you how to use it?"

"It's a pawn shop, not a firing range. So no, he didn't show me how to use it."

"Did he at least show you how to load it?"

"No, because he didn't have any nine-millimeter rounds in stock. I had to go to Buy-Mart for that."

Jackson tensed. "Anybody could have seen you getting bullets at Buy-Mart. That's where my mother shops."

"It's Wednesday afternoon. Your mom is working. Everybody's mom is working. So you can stop working ... up a sweat. Can I use the computer?"

"Why?"

"So we can find out how to load a gun you shouldn't own with bullets you shouldn't have."

"Go ahead."

Twenty minutes later, the gun was loaded and the safety was securely in place.

THE COLLEGE OF Overseers sat in an ancient chamber, considering their options.

⎋ *The girl has confirmed the existence of weapons.*
⌘ *Yes.*

■ *Do we have evidence of the sale of antiquities?*

Ψ *No counterfeits have been reported.*

Σ *Our hands are tied.*

☿ *The Terrorians will strike.*

π *We cannot prevent them from taking action.*

✸ *We do have options.*

§ *Yes.*

☋ *We must turn on the resonator.*

★ *A visit to each of the realms is essential.*

⦿ *We will begin immediately, with the exception of Terroria. Plato Indelicat will travel there at the appointed time and escort the girl back to her own world.*

Ω *I do not see Pru Tellerence. Who will visit Dramatica?*

⌘ *I will go to Dramatica. Stay illuminated, my brethren.*

IT WAS TIME for Johanna's seven-hour rest period. Upon its completion, she would be escorted home. *Why can't they just let me go home now?* She thought it, but she didn't really mean it. She needed the time to look for counterfeits.

She listened carefully for the telltale signs of Nero 51's departure. She could barely hear the squeak of the front door from her room, but when the giant humidifier stopped churning, she knew for sure he had gone. She asked for sustenance, and quickly ate the potato-and-bean soup provided. The tankard contained lemon-flavored water, which she was glad of, because beer would have slowed her down. She noticed a light go on in the building across the courtyard. *That must be Building 7.* She would have to keep checking to make sure the light did not go out while she investigated the residence floor.

* * *

Two hours later, Johanna yawned. She had examined thousands of obelisks, and still hadn't found anything. Suddenly, she heard the humidifier fans sputter to life. She glanced across the vast opening in the center of the library and out the window. The light in Building 7 still burned. She dropped to the floor just as the front door opened, and dozens of Terrorians entered the library and headed toward her quarters.

Johanna did not hesitate. She stuffed the rag and paste in the back of the shelf and wriggled across the floor on her stomach. She heard feet slapping against steps as the Terrorians climbed the curator's staircase. Johanna rolled across the floor as fast as she could, straight into the old, stone stairwell adjacent to the front entrance.

She heard someone say, "Bli z' Bril." They were apparently more interested in Nero 51's residence than her quarters.

She crept down the stairs, but remained hidden in the stairwell. If she crouched in the dimly lit corner, she could watch the main part of the library, unobserved. Before long, she saw a parade of Terrorians carry weapons out the main entrance. They walked in unified precision, as if one brain commanded everyone's movement. Only one Terrorian at the end of the line marched a hair out of step. *He won't last long,* she thought. *They'll probably execute him for missing a beat.* By the time the last of them exited, those who had been at the front of the procession returned to transport even more weapons. She knew the retrieval of arms had ended when the humidifier again went silent.

Johanna wanted to contact Mal, but first, she

needed to clean up loose ends. She climbed the stairs, and tried to remember which shelf she had hidden the rag and paste on. She grabbed them in haste, clumsily knocking over an obelisk. If anyone had been in the library, they would have heard her gasp. She could not afford to break another crystal and incite the wrath of Nero 51. She looked at it lying on its side, unbroken. *Curious.*

She picked it up. It felt as heavy as the others, but not in the same way. She picked up a second obelisk and immediately knew it was real. The crystal was uniformly heavy. But all the weight of the unbroken figurine was in the base. *I'm such a fool.* She had probably picked up dozens of fakes, but disregarded them because they had felt as heavy as crystal. She took the counterfeit back to her room and got out Mal's diary.

"Mal, I found a fake obelisk. It looks like crystal, but I knocked it over by accident and it didn't break. What should I do?"

His answer did not arrive for more than an hour.

Nothing. You are only there to serve your sentence.

Mal could be so exasperating. Surely she could do something. She grabbed her backpack and looked for her cell phone. Her battery had lost a lot of its juice, but she only needed enough power to take a few pictures. She photographed the obelisk from several different angles, so she could describe it in her diary, which she knew Mal read regularly. She also took several pictures of the weapon she had ... uh ... confiscated. *Stolen is such an ugly word.*

She didn't know what else she could do. She looked at her phone—6:00 a.m. In two more hours, it would be time to return home.

JACKSON SLIPPED THE loaded gun in his waistband, just like he had seen on TV. *I hope I don't shoot off any body parts. That would be embarrassing. And painful.* Everything was ready to go.

R-R-R-I-I-I-N-N-N-G-G-G! He answered the phone. "Library of Illumination."

"Yeah. I'm from Delectable Comestibles. You placed an order?"

"Yes."

"Could you open the front door? I've been standing here for fifteen minutes and still haven't figured out how to get in."

"Illumination." The wall slid open. "Right in here," Jackson said, leading the man to a table he had dragged up from the basement. He had considered using the circulation desk for serving coffee, but the television took up a lot of space.

While the man set out the refreshments, Jackson switched on the TV to warm it up.

"That's it. Sign here." The caterer handed Jackson the invoice.

"Thanks." Jackson took a ten-dollar bill out of his pocket and tipped the guy. He was going broke as curator-in-training, and wished he had never pried open that stupid window.

THE SCREECHING SOUND of metal upon metal disrupted the silence in Libraries of Illumination on each of eleven worlds. Curators looked up to find their cupolas opening, and stared at the blinding light shooting up from their

LOI medallions—straight through the sudden openings in their roofs. A moment later, the light went out as a member of the College of Overseers greeted each world's steward. Most of the curators expressed outrage when they learned Terrorians had stockpiled weapons and the threat of war was imminent.

HUNDREDS OF TERRORIAN soldiers amassed outside Building 7. They had been training all year for this moment, and were fired up. Nero 51 had promised them they would be handsomely rewarded for helping Terroria establish itself as the prime sovereign of the twelve literary worlds.

Inside Building 7, a quartermaster outfitted each Terrorian with a weapon and two crystals, one with their orders on it and another with a map of the library they were assigned to seize. The return of the Fantasian to her own world meant all the portals would be in a specific alignment, allowing the Terrorians to know which realm each portal would lead to.

In the courtyard, soldiers assembled into twelve flanks, with three leaders at the head of each. Nero 51 emerged from Building 7 and stood in the middle of a wide loggia facing them.

"Terrorians. For many millennia, our realm has waited patiently to reclaim its position as prime sovereign of the Libraries of Illumination. It is an honor we held for two millennia, only to have it snatched away by a united force of rabble-rousers who refused to recognize our indomitable spirit and natural ability to lead. Nine worlds against our one forced us to sacrifice our position of power, if not our dignity.

"It has long been my dream to restore our great world to its true destiny as leader of all Libraries of Illumination." Nero 51 smiled in the strangled way in which Terrorians contorted their faces to impart any semblance of benign cordiality. "To succeed in our endeavor, we must do something that at first may seem reprehensible, but is ultimately necessary. Your primary objective is the destruction of every piece of documented literature in each of the libraries, as soon as you have secured the site. Once the other library systems have been wiped clean of all knowledge, their outlying books and papers will cease to exist. Their records will be eradicated. They will be devoid of all facts, fiction, figures, histories, music, art, plans, manuals, maps—any and all information that has ever been recorded will cease to exist for them. The compendium of universal literature on Terroria will be the only surviving resource for all our worlds, and will provide us with the ultimate power to rule the others—consummate knowledge.

"Maul 232, take our 'fundraisers' to the cupola, immediately. May I remind you that this is supposed to be a social event, so mingle amiably. When the time comes, you will find weapons inside my residence.

"Advance teams, prepare to take your places. We are moments away from glory. Use your weapons' force-field initiators to prevent our adversaries from detaining you. Humane conquest is the key to obtaining support. Those who yield to *our* ways will be *conditioned* to serve Terroria. However, there may be some who prefer to spill blood rather than accept the magnanimity of our governance.

"If you must, do not hesitate to use the Omicron

Key." He turned a key on the side of his weapon and took aim at Heil 66. A black-and-white beam shot out of the armament, disintegrating the Terrorian. "Heil 66 claimed dedication to our cause, yet delayed giving me crucial information about a spy planted by the overseers in our library until just moments ago. He disregarded the prime directive, and has paid the ultimate price.

"If you must, eradicate all who resist."

—LOI—

9

OVERSEERS, EXCEPT PRU Tellerence and Plato Indelicat, arrived at their designated realms carrying large, flat boxes containing translucent screens. The overseers did their best to calm the librarians by discussing their precautions against the possibilities of what might occur, but without overwhelming success.

"How could you allow this to happen?" most curators asked.

꙾ *We did not allow this to transpire. We simply did not prevent it.*

Their answer confused the curators. The overseers sought to distract them by asking their help to position the screens across from the portals. The shiny, paper-thin attachments easily adhered to the walls, and once in place, could not be detected.

"What will that do?" one curator asked.

꙾ *It will make the Terrorians reflect on their*

actions.

"From what I've read about Terrorians, they're not a species that embraces reflection. They have more of a 'kill first, ask questions later' attitude."

𝕊 *That, unfortunately, is accurate.*

JACKSON MOVED OUT of sight when he heard the cupola screech. Having witnessed it on Dramatica, he knew it meant the portals were opening. He should have been excited at the prospect of Johanna returning, but it was much too early. *If Terrorians are invading the library, I'm not going to be an easy target.* He slipped inside the coat closet and held his breath. Relief washed over him when he saw an overseer approach the circulation desk. Jackson walked out to greet him. "Where's Johanna?"

◍ *I am Selium Sorium. I'm here to assist in Johanna Charette's return.*

Someone pounding on the front door interrupted them. The overseer waved his hand, and the door slid open. The president of the library board of directors was on the other side, with his wife and a pair of librarians from a nearby village. The president stared at the overseer, then grabbed Jackson by the arm and pulled him out of earshot. "What the hell is this, a masquerade ball?"

Jackson pulled his arm away. "That man," he said, nodding at Selium Sorium, "is a very important member of this library's College of Overseers, and I suggest you don't insult him."

"If he's so important, why haven't *I* ever met him?"

Jackson felt momentarily bewildered until the answer formed in his consciousness. "You're in charge of development for the management and growth of the library. However, Mr. Sorium oversees its *literary* endowments. After all, there would be no library if there was no collection of literature."

As far as the board president was concerned, the word *endowment* was spelled M-O-N-E-Y. He glared at Jackson before he walked over to the elderly man in the odd costume and introduced himself.

Jackson smiled. *That should keep him out of my hair.* He turned to see a librarian lean over the top of the circulation desk and pick up a slender volume of *The Strange Case of Dr. Jekyll and Mr. Hyde.* It was a Level Two book that had just been returned that afternoon. "Excuse me," he said, as he rushed to her side and pulled the small book out of her hand before she could open it. "If you start reading that," he joked, "you'll never pay any attention to me. Why don't you find a seat up front? We'll be starting in just a minute."

"I was just looking for a little something to occupy my time."

Oh, it will keep you occupied, he thought. He stuffed the book in his jacket pocket and continued greeting guests, while keeping an eye on the crowd to make sure *curiosity* did not *kill the cat.*

NERO 51 CHECKED his timepiece. It was time for Operation Final Darkness to commence. He raised his weapon into the air while pulling a sliding lever on its side, a feature not included on most of the other arms. Suddenly, everyone's weapon glowed with an eerie purple light.

"To the portals!" he cried.

*   *   *

THE LIBRARIANS IN the Fantasian reading room settled in for the presentation.

Selium Sorium nodded at Jackson.

The teen took his cue. "Good evening, everyone. Are you ready to see how to convert your system into one that's designed for the twenty-first century?"

Some of the librarians applauded. One man shook his head and said out loud, "I hope this isn't a waste of time, because our system is already computerized." Other librarians whose organizations had also converted to computer nodded in agreement.

"I know most of you have already switched to online public-access catalogs. That's not what we're discussing. We're here to talk about wirelessly retrieving information from anywhere—a car, your back yard, or even a cruise ship at sea. Tonight, we're talking about serving our communities with cutting-edge technology. In today's society, the keyword is 'instant gratification.'"

Jackson used a remote control to bring the giant TV screen to life. It showed banks of library tables filled with sleek computers—with nary a book in sight. "These computers will access our library's full array of knowledge, as well as connect to online creative editing programs for video, photos, music, and text. We like to call it our 'digital hub.'" He took a deep breath. "And if we're very lucky, maybe we can talk the president of our board of directors into approving this." An image of a three-dimensional printer filled the screen.

Jackson saw the board president scowl, but forged ahead. "With our wireless and online capabilities *and* a 3-D printer, we can become *research central*—a think tank that fosters creativity, invention, and innovative solutions to take us into the future."

"What happens when your hard drive fails?" someone asked.

"Lock the doors," another person called out, inciting giggles and snickers.

"Here at the Library of Illumination, we save all our information to multiple cloud servers, and retrieve it wirelessly using these." He waved an iPad in the air.

"Does that work when you've got no electricity or modem?" someone asked.

"It does if you have a mobile hot spot—which is easy enough to get."

The audience buzzed. Jackson grinned as he changed the slide and pointed to the screen. An image with a graphic about cloud computing appeared, and then pixilated before changing to video of a scary-looking alien with a huge weapon. Everyone laughed except Jackson and Selium Sorium, who immediately recognized a Terrorian soldier.

JOHANNA SAT ON the edge of her cot, wearing her backpack. Inside, she had packed the fake obelisk. She rebalanced the stolen Terrorian weapon, now braced against her shoulder. She almost abandoned her choice to use it when it started emitting a purple glow, but changed her mind when she heard the humidifiers roar to life.

The Terrorians embraced precision. Johanna had witnessed it when they marched in unison to recover the weapons stored in Nero 51's residence. It would not surprise her if the curator activated all the guns at the same time, resulting in the subtle purple light.

She took a deep breath. If anyone entered the

room, other than an overseer, she planned to immobilize that person and everyone who followed. She didn't really know how the weapon worked, but it looked fairly straightforward; it had a wider end, a narrower end, and a double ring that reminded her of a partial eclipse, which she surmised was the trigger. She shivered not because she felt cold but because she was anxious. *What if this thing doesn't shoot? What if they execute me? Who will take care of the library? What about Jackson? Is that why they made him a curator-in-training, because they already knew I wouldn't be returning?*

Her door suddenly opened, and without thought she pulled the trigger, and the weapon fired.

ON EVERY REALM, Terrorian advance teams dove through the portals with their weapons at the ready. A scout on each team stepped forward to survey the open space that exposed each library's aboveground levels, looking for signs of resistance. A second member of the team covered the scout, while the third warrior stood guard over the portal. On the other side of the openings, troops began amassing, ready to launch into battle. They stood poised, awaiting the go-ahead from the advance teams.

In most cases, the libraries were quiet. However, some exceptions existed.

OPEL 29 WAS motivated by the possibility of confrontation. Like many members of his species, his eagerness manifested itself as secretions from overactive glands—much like sweat. He signaled his Terrorian partners that they should hold their positions until he got an idea of what they might be up against. He leaned over the cupola walkway and was instantly stunned by what he saw. *How can this be?* Below sat an army of Fantasians, waiting to take them on. He wiped excess secretions from his brow with a tentacle, which sent a hail of minuscule droplets onto the people below. One of them turned to look up, and Opel 29 immediately jerked back.

"Do you have a sprinkler system in here? I think it's leaking," a librarian said.

Jackson took a deep breath. "I'll go see what it is."

"Wait," the overseer said in a normal voice, rather than transferring his thoughts inside everyone's head. "These people are interested in what you have to say. I will check on the upper level."

"No," the president of the board of directors declared. "If anyone's going to check on the condition of this library, I'll do it." He pushed past the overseer and headed toward the cupola stairs.

◍ *Oh, dear.*

Jackson could hear the overseer's thoughts in his head.

◍ *This has "catastrophe" written all over it.*

THE FORCE OF the blast from the Terrorian weapon threw Johanna forward. She collided with Plato Indelicat, who grabbed the young woman to steady her. The wall behind the cot glowed. The overseer moved to touch it.

Ω *You have enveloped the wall in a force field.*

"Delumination," Johanna stated. The force field continued to glow.

Ω *The Terrorians have obviously reconfigured the key to their force fields.*

"Bril," Johanna tried.

Ω *Bril means "illuminate," not "deluminate." Dril.*

The overseer's attempt failed.

Ω *As I have said, they have altered the code for deactivating the shield. Little matter. The Terrorians will deal with it when they come back. It is time to go to the portal.*

Johanna picked up the weapon and turned it around. "At least now I know which end to aim."

Plato Indelicat warily eyed the young woman.

Ω *Be illuminated, Johanna Charette. There will be Terrorians on your world.*

THE LEADER OF the Terrorian advance team assigned to Dramatica descended to the main floor of the library. He could hear Furst humming in the antechamber. He twirled a tentacle in an upward spiral, motioning the others to begin moving through the portals to the cupola. A dozen soldiers had crossed when the Terrorian scout heard Furst push back his chair. His tentacle suddenly dropped, and the troops stilled, awaiting further instruction.

The team leader stepped back behind a shelf.

Furst's humming got louder as he approached the main reading room, but then ended in a series of sniffs.

The team leader readied his weapon.

Furst rounded the corner, and then he spotted the Terrorian. His red, curly hair pulled into tight, wiry corkscrews, and he flexed his knees.

The Terrorian aimed his weapon.

⌘ *That is ill advised.*

The words he heard did not deter the soldier from pulling the trigger.

* * *

ON EACH OF the worlds, curators experienced similar events. They had been instructed to go about their normal routines, while the overseers used an enchantment on themselves to shrink to the size of one of Johanna's protein bars. At that height, they looked more like figurines than people, and could often observe what was going on undisturbed. Even the curators disregarded the overseers' presence.

JACKSON FOUND IT difficult to concentrate as he continued his presentation to the librarians. He could hear the president stomping up the cupola staircase as it rose like a patinated metal helix through the five uppermost levels of the library. Every so often, the footsteps stopped as the president paused to catch his breath.

High above him, the Terrorians watched and waited, ready to suspend their first victim behind an impenetrable force field.

JOHANNA BEGAN TO exit her quarters but stopped when she heard countless troops of Terrorian soldiers stomping up the cupola stairs. She slammed the door to her chamber, with Plato Indelicat and herself still inside. "The Terrorians are all heading to the cupola. How will we get past them to the portals?"

Ω We will wait. Terrorians are an impatient breed. They will waste no time traversing the portals to force their will on beings from other realms. Once they have done that, we will return to Fantasia.

"But they'll already be there, doing lord knows what to my library."

Ω I suggest you leave the weapon behind. There is the possibility that other Terrorians will follow. Being caught with one of their weapons could mean certain death. You would be perceived as a spy and never be allowed to leave this place. Without the weapon, you are merely a Fantasian who has served a sentence and is being escorted home. They will allow the charade to continue until you reach your home planet, just so they can relish your sudden realization of domination rather than escape.

"How nice of them."

Ω Come. The footsteps have ceased.

They climbed to the cupola and made their way to the portal to Fantasia. They saw no sign of the Terrorians. The troops had all transported to the other libraries. Johanna took a deep breath and said, "Illuminate." When nothing happened, Plato Indelicat repeated the command, and the pair immediately transported to the other side.

ON TERRORIA, NERO 51 lifted a tankard of fermented merk. "T' cra!"

Members of his inner circle echoed his toast. "T' cra." *To victory.*

It would not be long before reports filtered in from the troops, declaring their positions and successes. Nero 51 used a tentacle to wipe the foamy head of the sudsy spirits from his mouth. His plan had been perfectly executed. Every man had been thoroughly trained and appropriately dispatched. One member of each advance team was fluent in the language of the realm being invaded. The timing had been perfect. The only imperfection scratching the smooth surface of his plan was Heil

66. He had been a member of the inner circle, and yet had withheld information about a spy. Nero 51 wanted to believe the shadow Heil 66 had seen belonged to Johanna Charette, but the information had come too late to interrogate the girl. *What if someone else spied on me?* It made Nero 51 uneasy.

"I am going to withdraw in preparation for victory," he told the others. He handed them a small black box with three buttons. "Please buzz me when you have heard from our soldiers on every world. Press the white button for total victory, the purple button for partial victory, and the red button for retreat."

"So fancy, Nero 51. Why not just have us meet you at the library when we hear from the troops?"

"I will be contemplating victory and fine-tuning our plans for the future—in a place of meditation. It will be easier to contact me in this manner." He raised one of his right tentacles. "T' cra!" He worked his way toward the exit, entwining tentacles with each member of his inner circle in a show of solidarity.

Back inside his library, Nero 51 descended to the basement and moved the bookcase leading to the sub-levels. Like all the Libraries of Illumination, his had been designed with 1,311 floors, most of them underground. However, he had taken the initiative to create a secret passage on level 333 that led to a living compartment only he knew about. He had used it as his personal residence for years, and had stocked it well, with everything he could possibly need. He preferred to use his official quarters on the residence level as a command post. It was the perfect place to store munitions and pertinent information about the invasion, to keep them close at hand.

He settled into a comfortable position and looked at the bank of lights near the ceiling, white, purple, and red. He could relax here, undisturbed, while remaining informed about Terrorian exploits on distant realms. He closed his eyes and sank into deep meditation.

—LOI—

10

"WHAT THE ...?"

Even before the president of the board of directors had finished his sentence, a Terrorian trooper took aim and fired his weapon. The blast caused a high-pitched squeal that reverberated throughout the library and caused the president, as well as Jackson and their guests on the main floor, to slump over or drop to the ground, cover their ears, and suffer the pain. The pitch of the audio signal had a much different effect on the Terrorian who fired his weapon. It caused the weapon to reverse action, locking the shooter in a force field.

The other soldiers did not immediately comprehend what had happened to their team leader. Instead, they saw the president of the library board still moving, so several of them took aim and fired.

Terrorians began freezing in place, unable to move after firing their weapons. One of the remaining

117

soldiers threw his weapon down and raced down the stairs, intent on strangling any Fantasians he met with his bare tentacles.

JACKSON STRUGGLED UP from the floor, even though his ears continued to ring. If Johanna returned now, he feared she would get caught in the crossfire. He raced up the stairs to the cupola, only to find his way blocked by a Terrorian. The soldier extended his tentacles, as Jackson stepped back and reached into his waistband. The teen removed the gun and fired a shot before the Terrorian knocked the Glock out of his hand and it clattered down the long staircase. The bullet hit the Terrorian, and a spray of blood covered Jackson in a purple haze. The soldier squealed in pain, but did not give up.

Another tentacle snaked toward Jackson. He stuffed his hand in his jacket pocket, looking for a screwdriver or pen—anything he could use as a weapon. His fingers closed over the slender volume of *The Strange Case of Dr. Jekyll and Mr. Hyde*, and he pulled out the book.

The Terrorian knocked it out of his hand, but Mr. Hyde suddenly sprang from the pages of the open book, carrying a heavy cane with a blood-covered handle. He used it to beat the startled Terrorian until the soldier went limp. Jackson ducked, grabbed the book, and quickly closed it. He slipped it back in his pocket before he climbed over the inert soldier and continued up the stairs.

THE LAST FEW troopers on Fantasia realized their weapons had been turned against them and tried to retreat, but the portal suddenly flashed, and Plato Indelicat and Johanna appeared.

Without thinking, one of the soldiers fired his weapon, causing Johanna to drop to the ground, writhing from the pitch of audio feedback. The warrior immediately found himself locked behind a force field. His fellow soldiers dropped their weapons, grabbed the overseer, and jumped back through the portal to Terroria. They dragged Plato Indelicat through their library, out onto the toxic streets of the Twelfth Realm, and into Building 7—a location that they felt would give them greater control over their hostage.

Members of the Inner Circle grew disturbed when they heard about the defeat of their plan, but remained hopeful that a hostage would aid their negotiations with the College of Overseers.

TROOPS ON OTHER realms reported similar outcomes. Soldiers found themselves suddenly immobilized by force fields. A warrior in the Numericon library switched on his weapon's Omicron Key and was vaporized when he fired at Pi, curator of the Tenth Realm. The few Terrorian troopers who managed to retreat all had similar tales to tell.

JACKSON QUICKLY RECUPERATED from the second earsplitting blast, and reached the cupola in time to see Johanna recover from the effects of the Terrorian weapons. He helped her off the ground and slipped his arms around her, glad to see she was okay.

She pushed him away. "I've got to save Plato Indelicat," she screamed, and disappeared back through the portal.

His mouth hung open—just for a moment. He leaned over the cupola railing and yelled to the crowd below: "Tonight's demonstration has been canceled due to unforeseen technical difficulties. Please exit in an orderly fashion." Then he jumped through the portal.

ON TERRORIA, JOHANNA's footsteps pounded down the cupola stairs. Jackson followed as fast as he could, often taking two steps at a time to catch up to her. He saw her run into a utility closet and reemerge with a weapon.

"You can't shoot that," he said. "You'll end up caught in a force field."

Johanna studied the gun. "Did the overseers do anything strange before the Terrorians arrived?"

"Yeah. They stuck a bunch of shiny white papers on the walls by the portals, but they had nothing on them. You couldn't even see them."

"That high-pitched tone ... did you hear that when Nero 51 grabbed you outside his residence and put you in a force field?"

Jackson shook his head. "No."

"Okay. I'm thinking those shiny white papers had something to do with the way the guns backfired. But I'm also thinking the overseers wouldn't have bothered sticking them here on Terroria, where they might have been discovered. So this weapon is probably going to work just the way we expect it to."

"If you say so. Do you think the overseer is here? I don't hear anyone."

Johanna ran to a window and looked over at Building 7. "No, but I bet I know where they took him.

Follow me."

The two of them ran into the street, but immediately retreated, coughing and gagging. "What is that smell?" Jackson moaned.

"I don't know. I never strayed outside of the library. I only know that every time the Terrorians entered, they'd turn on a blower that makes a real racket. That's how I knew when Nero 51 was in residence."

"Is there some kind of secret passageway to the building you want to go to?"

"Nope. We've got to go out there, but it's just across the courtyard. We can hold our breath that long."

"Right. We deplete our oxygen supply while we run into a building that's full of armed Terrorians, with a weapon that may backfire."

She nodded. "Pretty much."

"Okay. Let's do it."

They both took a deep breath and headed out.

SELIUM SORIUM MADE sure everyone who had attended Jackson's presentation left the building safely. The president of the board of directors babbled about being attacked by some "armed monstrosity," but the overseer convinced everyone that the man had hit his head when he fell. He encouraged the president's wife to have her husband checked for a concussion.

Finally alone, the overseer closed his eyes to commune with his brethren. Ten of his colleagues gave positive reports on the worlds they observed; however, they now knew Plato Indelicat had been taken hostage.

Ω *That is a setback.*

The overseers possessed supernatural powers that

enabled them to communicate, transport themselves, and alter the perception of their appearance. They had also undergone a special longevicus ritual to extend their lives a thousandfold. As the guardians of all knowledge, they relied on those gifts to maintain their existence. However, the overseers were not immortal. The Original Thirteen, save one, had passed on. Overseers could be fatally injured, and Plato Indelicat would have to use his wits wisely to continue his state of being.

JOHANNA AND JACKSON heard the pandemonium erupting inside Building 7 before they even reached the door. They hid in the shadows as someone exited, and saw a cloakroom just inside the vestibule. A diminutive Terrorian, possibly a woman or a child, appeared to be in charge of it. The discussion in the main hall became more and more heated, and the tiny Terrorian got up and joined the crowd to get a better look.

"Come on." Johanna pulled Jackson inside the grimy cloakroom.

"It smells almost as bad in here as it does outside," he whispered.

"Yeah. This is what Terrorians smell like. And if we smell like them, they may not notice us." She grabbed a cloak from the corner and threw it over her shoulders, covering the weapon. She pulled the hood over her hair and tugged it down to conceal her face.

Jackson did the same. "There are no arm holes."

"Look again. There are four on each side—they're just smaller—for tentacles."

The teens moved out of the coatroom but stayed in the shadows near the door. Most of the Terrorians, by contrast, pushed forward to get right into the middle of the discussion.

"Did you learn any more Terrorian here?" Jackson whispered.

"No. Plato Indelicat performed a translation enchantment so I would be able to understand the Terrorians when they ordered me around."

"So everything was in English?"

"Everything except the passphrase to get into the residence."

"Did you figure it out?"

"Lucky for me, someone taught it to me before I started my sentence."

"Who did that?" he asked, amazed.

"You."

The roar of the crowd increased, and a pair of Terrorian soldiers marched Plato Indelicat to the front of the room.

Jackson leaned toward Johanna. "It sounds like a freakin' cricket convention."

"I wish we knew what they were saying." She stared at Plato Indelicat, trying to read his face. A moment later, an English translation enchantment took effect.

"What did you do?" Jackson whispered.

"He knows we're here. He must have read our thoughts."

MANY OF THE younger Terrorians called for Plato Indelicat's execution. Older residents claimed they needed him as a hostage to use as a bargaining chip. With Plato Indelicat incarcerated on Terroria, the possibility that they could exchange the overseer for the troops who remained immobilized in force fields on distant worlds still existed. But more importantly, the portals might remain open, keeping the hope of a future victory alive.

A Terrorian soldier interrogated the overseer about why their weapons had backfired. Plato Indelicat did not answer his questions. A nearby soldier picked up a weapon and swung it at the overseer. He swung high, and the weapon knocked Plato Indelicat's hat off his head.

The overseer suddenly grew agitated, and struggled to pull away from the soldiers who held him in place, but they kept a firm grip on him. Another soldier stuck his weapon inside the hat and raised it above his head—a symbol of their small victory in capturing the overseer. The crowd cheered, barely noticing that Plato Indelicat had started to wither.

Johanna turned to Jackson. "We've got to do something before the Terrorians tear him to pieces."

"What do you suggest?"

"I don't know, but we'd better act soon."

Someone shouted a command from the center of the crowd. "We must take him to Nero 51. He'll know what do."

"Where is Nero 51?" a soldier asked.

"Planning our future path to victory in the Library of Illumination. We must take the prisoner to the library."

"Let's get out of here," Johanna said. "We've got a better chance of saving Plato Indelicat in the library than we do here."

"How do you figure that?"

"We know the lay of the land. They'll be afraid to shoot their guns in there. And the portals are nearby."

"So all we've got to do is run up five noisy flights

of ancient stairs with an old man in tow? Piece of cake."

They slipped out of Building 7 with the crowd and made their way to the library. Inside, Johanna grabbed Jackson and dragged him into the corner of the stone stairwell.

"We'll be safer in here," she whispered.

On the other side of the wall, the mob got restless when Nero 51 did not answer the bell they used to summon him.

"The box," a member of the Inner Circle said. "Where is the box he gave us?"

Another member held it up. "I have it right here."

"Good. Press the button."

"Which one?"

"Well, we weren't completely victorious, so don't press the white one."

"Do you think I should press the purple one for partial victory?"

"Uhhh ... We haven't really taken control of any of the libraries. The few troops who have returned—retreated."

"So you think I should press the red button?"

"That would be the most accurate assessment of what has happened. He deserves to know that."

The Inner Circle member pressed the red button, and almost immediately Building 7 exploded, blowing out the windows on one side of the library and shaking the structure to its core. Stunned Terrorians squealed as they dove for cover.

"Now!" Johanna said, and ran into the fray, grabbing Plato Indelicat and dragging him to the cupola steps.

Jackson followed close behind her. They began running up the stairs, but the overseer's robe, his advanced years, and his delicate condition slowed them down.

"Can you carry him?" she asked. Jackson threw the overseer over his shoulder like a bag of laundry, and Johanna pushed him ahead of her. "Run," she cried.

A RED LIGHT blinked on sub-level 333. Nero 51 rose in a rage. What could his troops have done to lead to total defeat? He felt the subterranean cavity he had built shudder. *Building 7 has been destroyed. It serves them right for ruining my plan.*

THE EXPLOSION STUNNED the Terrorians. Some were knocked unconscious by the percussion, but a few raised their heads in time to see *aliens* grab the overseer and drag him away. Many Terrorians felt defeated and did not rush to pursue the interlopers, but a few seized the moment, believing the aliens had bombed Building 7 and were now escaping with Terroria's hostage. They clambered up the stairs, their fat, flat feet slapping the metal treads.

JACKSON WAS STRONG, but rushing up five flights of narrow, spiral stairs carrying a man over his shoulder took its toll. He could feel the Terrorian pursuers. Their added weight on the staircase made it shudder. He hoped that whatever held the stairway in place had been designed to withstand the weight load.

"They're gaining on us," Johanna shouted. "Can you go any faster?"

"No." He knew it wasn't the answer she wanted to

hear, but he had to tell her the truth.

"Here goes nothing," she said, as she turned and raised the Terrorian weapon to her shoulder. She barely had time to aim before she pulled the trigger. A force field encased the closest Terrorian, blocking the ones who followed. She turned and ran, catching up to Jackson and Plato Indelicat at the portals.

"Illuminate," Jackson yelled.

Nothing happened.

Johanna echoed his command. "Illuminate!"

The portals remained closed.

"Plato," she cried. The overseer was unconscious. She gently tapped his cheek. "Please, Plato, you've got to help us. How do we open the portals?"

The overseer's eyes fluttered. He mumbled something difficult to understand.

"What is he saying?"

Johanna looked confused. "I think he said, 'The key is in the might.'"

"What does that mean?" Jackson asked.

"I don't know, but I hear them coming up the stairs, so they must have gotten around the soldier I shot.

"Please, Plato," she begged. "There must be a word that will open the portals."

He looked at her through clouded, gray eyes.

Ω *Totalis illuminatio.*

Instantly, they transported to their own world, where Selium Sorium met them.

◍ *Totalis tenebris.*

The portals slammed shut.

"We saved him," she cried triumphantly.

◍ *He will be laid to rest with those who have come*

before.

"What are you talking about?" Jackson gently placed Plato Indelicat on the floor.

◍ *He is no more.*

"You mean, he's dead? He can't be dead. We saved him," Jackson stated.

Johanna's face clouded over. "How could he die?"

◍ *We are grateful that his body has been returned to us. You have provided a great service, Johanna Charette. And you, Jackson Roth.*

"How can you say that? Why don't you help him?" She suddenly felt empty inside.

◍ *You have provided us with information about Terrorian arms and confirmed violations against the Library of Illumination through the illegal trade of precious artifacts.*

Jackson looked around at the Terrorians still suspended behind force fields. "What about them?"

◍ *They will be taken to Lumina for trial.*

"So the portals are still open?"

◍ *We have effectively sealed them for now.*

Johanna's brow furrowed. "How will you get to Lumina?"

◍ *Like this.*

Selium Sorium, the body of Plato Indelicat, and more than a half dozen Terrorian soldiers disappeared.

Johanna and Jackson looked around in astonishment, and then at each other.

"It's over," Jackson said, as he wrapped her in his arms and gave her a bear hug. "It's over," he repeated, "and you're home."

Tears streamed from her eyes, and she began to

sob.

"Don't cry." Jackson rubbed her back. "You helped avert a war. You did everything in your power to rescue an overseer. You survived! You should be overjoyed by your accomplishments. And then there's your crowning achievement."

"What's that?" She looked up at him.

"I will never, ever again say, 'I bet there's something hidden behind this wall.'"

She smiled, but she could not shake the sensation of doom she felt. The Terrorians had been planning an all-out war, and she didn't think they would easily abandon their plan.

To THE CONTRARY, whatever Johanna and Jackson had unwittingly become embroiled in had just begun.

—LOI—

THE OVERSEERS

11

"THAT'S THE LAST OF THEM," Jackson said with finality, as he pushed a stack of books toward Johanna. "Once you've read these, you'll know everything there is to know about the realm of Terroria. Although, why you want to become an expert on planet evil is beyond me."

Johanna shook her head. "That's why I'm the curator of the Library of Illumination and you're just my assistant."

"Hey, hey, hey, didn't you hear what they said when we stood trial for breaching the portals? I'm a 'curator-in-training.' I'm the one waiting in the wings to pick up the pieces."

"Well then, you'd better read some of these, too," she said as she pushed the pile of Terrorian history books she'd already read in his direction. "Then we'll both be prepared."

"Prepared for what?"

"I'm not sure." She felt her nerve endings jitter. "But it never hurts to be prepared. You never know what can happen."

As if on cue, the middle of the venerable library began to wobble and shimmer, like the air that hovers above a hot roadway on a steamy summer day. Suddenly, a twenty-second-century time machine appeared. Johanna's predecessor, Mal, had used the same vehicle to transport Casanova back to eighteenth-century Venice after the legendary lover suddenly popped out of a book in the library and stayed. Mal smiled as he stepped out. His appearance had changed dramatically in the short weeks since Johanna and Jackson had last seen him.

"Are you growing a beard?" Johanna walked to her mentor and gave him a hug. Mal had been in charge of the library for nearly four hundred years, and had only relinquished his stewardship after he personally trained Johanna to deal with the intrusions, oddities, and after-maths of living literature.

Mal stroked his face and smiled. "It itched a little at first, but I'm getting used to it now."

"It makes you look older," she observed.

"Yeah," Jackson said. "You used to look four hundred and thirty years old, and now you look four hundred and thirty-one."

"Don't listen to him." Johanna placed her arm protectively around Mal's shoulder. "You don't look a day over eighty."

Mal smiled. "I come with sad news and happy news."

"I think the actual saying is, 'I have some good news

and some bad news,'" Jackson quipped.

Mal drew in a long breath. "Sadly, we will say our final goodbyes to Plato Indelicat tomorrow. He'll be enshrined following a celebration of his life and a memorial to his death. On a more positive note, his replacement will be inducted into the College of Overseers on the following afternoon."

"Will anyone ever be able to take his place?" Johanna wondered out loud.

"Where do overseers come from anyway?" Jackson asked. "Is there a special place filled with them, like Overseers-R-Us? Do they have to supply their own hats? I know Plato Indelicat really lost his cool after the Terrorians knocked his pope hat off his head."

Mal's eyes grew more focused. "Can you tell me what became of Plato Indelicat's headpiece?"

Jackson shook his head. "Not really."

"We were too busy trying to stay ahead of the crowd," Johanna said. "They had turned into a lynch mob, and we didn't want to become hostages, too."

"So it remains on Terroria," Mal said.

"Unless the explosion obliterated it," Johanna replied.

"Yeah," Jackson chimed in. "The last place we saw it was in the building around the corner from the library, and that place was blown to smithereens—which was really good for us, because that's how we escaped."

Johanna took Mal's hand. "So what's the happy news?"

"I've been selected as one of the candidates for the vacant overseer's position."

"One of the candidates!" Johanna smiled broadly.

"Who are the others?"

"Well, you wouldn't know them all because they're from other worlds, but there's Prophet IAN c. from Adventura, who is the current library curator there. You may have met Torran, the head of the Library Council on Dramatica. He declared himself a contender, although I don't think his chances are very good. Then there's Dame Erato, the former curator of Romantica, who relocated to Lumina many years ago and has reinvented herself as something of an inspirational insider. She and Prophet IAN c. are both strong competitors."

"Do you think you have a chance?" Jackson asked.

"I have my strengths. But ultimately it will be whoever the overseers believe brings the most needed assets to the college at this point in time. Whether that resource is political, administrative, militaristic, or inspirational remains to be seen.

"There will be a challenge among the four of us, and any others who choose to declare themselves by noon tomorrow. I'm hoping the two of you will remain after the memorial service to cheer me on."

Johanna grabbed Mal's arm. "We're invited to Plato Indelicat's memorial service?"

"Of course," Mal answered. "That's why I'm here."

Jackson nodded solemnly. "Cool."

"But I'll have to stay behind to take care of the library, Mal." Johanna sighed. "Both Jackson and I can't be gone at the same time."

"The library will be closed. All the Libraries of Illumination will cease operations for two days as a sign of respect for Plato Indelicat, and will not reopen until a new overseer has been sworn in."

Jackson slapped his hand on top of the circulation desk. "That seals the deal for me."

"Where is this all happening?" Johanna asked.

"Everything takes place on Lumina."

She felt surprised that she and Jackson were invited. "The overseers sealed the portals after the Terrorians tried to take over the libraries. How will we get there if the portals are sealed?"

"I will escort you both."

"In that?" Jackson asked, not trying to hide his excitement.

"Absolutely. There's nothing like traveling in a time machine." Mal wiggled his eyebrows and grinned.

Jackson entered the time machine and looked around. "It's like standing inside a bubble." There appeared to be no floor, nor doors, nor any visible controls. He touched the surface. It felt firm and warm, as smooth as glass, yet undulated when he touched it.

Johanna idly straightened out the circulation desk. "Why do we need a time machine if we're traveling in the present?"

"Because it will take us back to a time when the portals were open, so we can travel to Lumina and then zigzag back to the present." He tapped on the outside of the bubble twice, then exchanged places with Jackson. "I'll be back tomorrow morning at ten sharp." He pointed a finger at the curator-in-training, then laughed and shook his head, lowering his finger. "You won't be late."

"You've got that right," Jackson answered. "I'll get here by nine so I don't miss a thing."

Mal waved. The air around the time machine seemed to melt for a second before the apparatus disappeared.

"Lumina," Jackson said in awe. "We've been to three realms, including our own, and now we're going to Lumina. I'd never even been out of the country before we discovered the portals, but tomorrow I'll travel off world for the third time. How cool is that?"

"We're going to a funeral and then to Mal's challenge. You're acting like we're the guests of honor at the Grammy Awards."

"I know, but this is the most amazing thing that has ever happened to me." He shrugged one shoulder and leaned over to kiss her. "Actually, you're the most amazing thing that ever happened to me. If you had never come to school and asked me if I wanted to work in the library, I'd probably be tossing pizzas at Piccolo Italia. Free pizza is nice, but not as nice as traveling to other realms with you."

He pushed the books on Terroria aside. "Do you think we have any books downstairs on Lumina? I think I'd like to study up on that world before we leave tomorrow."

"Sometimes you surprise me." Johanna laughed.

He winked at her. "Refreshing, isn't it?"

PLENTY OF BOOKS ABOUT LUMINA lined the shelves, as well as folios of pictures, and Jackson grew more captivated with every new detail he learned. "I can't believe most of their world is covered with water."

"I don't know if it's most of the world. The cities are built on numerous outcrops that jut way above the surface."

"Yeah, look at this picture of the capital. The bottom of the giant outcrop looks like it rests on legs—kind of

135

like a huge molar. The middle is open, and I bet you can sail a tanker right through it."

"Like a subway traveling under a city."

"No, this is way cooler than a subway. Besides, anyone riding in a subway would drown unless by subway you mean submarine."

"The golden city on top of the rocks makes it look so ethereal." She ran her finger across a picture in *Lumina: Past and Present.* Instantly a miniature three-dimensional version of the capital city of Lumi appeared, complete with clouds above and water below.

Jackson moved closer and stared at one of the rock legs supporting the outcrop. "Look. This one has a door."

Johanna studied the scene. "I would have loved this as a kid. It's better than a dollhouse. I never owned one, but I once saw one in a museum and I thought it looked like the most wonderful toy in the world."

As they watched, a round wooden tub with a dozen oarsmen sitting around its radius rowed up to the tiny entrance. One of the oarsmen unlocked the door, and a group of tiny Luminans disembarked and disappeared inside, allowing the door to slam shut with a resounding thud.

"Can you believe this?" Jackson laughed.

Johanna laughed as well, but it changed to a gasp when she saw a group of men appear from under the surface of the water and begin pulling the oars and tossing them away so the oarsmen couldn't row. The tiny sailors grappled with their attackers, but one by one many of them were pulled into the water. A few others managed to hang on to their oars and moved into the middle of the tub, where they used them to fight off their assailants.

One of the attackers hoisted himself onto the vessel, soon learning he had made a big mistake.

"Holy … frit. Look at him," Jackson cried. "He's a fish!"

Johanna squinted. "I think the correct term is merman."

"Like Ethel Merman—the singer some of those guys at the Comedy Club impersonate?"

"No. Like the male equivalent of a mermaid."

"I knew that."

"Um-hmm."

While Johanna and Jackson talked, the oarsmen beat the brazen merman to a pulp and pushed his body overboard—an example of what other underwater creatures could expect if they thought about hijacking a boat. That ended the attack, and in a single blink, the bodies of the fallen oarsmen and beaten merman disappeared under the surface of the murky water.

Johanna slammed the book shut. "I could have done without that."

"Yeah. But this isn't a storybook. It's a textbook that describes how things are on Lumina. And apparently everything isn't fun and games in the golden city."

"Let's just hope we don't have to travel anywhere on the water while we're there."

B-R-R-R-I-I-I-N-N-N-G-G-G!

A phone call from Book Services informed them they had just received a scholarly request for research information and ancient texts. The order kept Johanna and Jackson busy for the rest of the afternoon. When they finished, Johanna sent Jackson home. She needed time to get ready for their impromptu trip. Besides, she didn't want to start talking about Lumina again. She still felt uneasy about the attack they had witnessed when the book came to life, and it reminded her of the potential for an attack by Terrorians if any of them were actually invited to the memorial service. She hoped not, but that wasn't her decision to make. The thought of running into Nero 51 again turned a trip that might be meaningful and interesting into a duty that filled her with dread.

THAT NIGHT, AS SHE NESTLED under the duvet in her bedroom, Johanna opened Mal's diary and asked him if Nero 51 would also be on Lumina. Except for the time when she served her sentence on Terroria, Mal's answers to her requests had always been immediate; but tonight she dozed off waiting for his reply. When she awakened in the middle of the night, he still hadn't answered her. She glanced at her clock. It was two in the morning—more than three hours after she asked the question. He had never taken so long to answer before. Johanna dozed off again, but continued to wake and check for Mal's answer every hour or so. At seven she threw off the covers and arose for the day. A quick check told her Mal still hadn't responded.

To take her mind off Mal, she focused on her wardrobe. She selected a long tan-and-black chevron-print sweater and paired it with a short black skirt and black boots. She examined herself in the mirror. Funeral attire. She added a belt and a scarf. Stylish funeral attire. She packed something more festive for the induction ceremony as well as comfy clothing to relax in. She

brought her bag down to the circulation desk. It was still

too early for Mal to show up, but Jackson should be on his way.

She grabbed Mal's diary to see if he had answered her question, but the last page of the diary remained blank. She threw the book in her bag and sighed. Sometimes she hated being efficient. She had officially closed the library and packed her bags for their trip to Lumina, but it was still early. While she waited, she did the only thing she could think of that felt natural—she paced.

A HALF-HOUR LATER, THE back door flew open and Jackson breezed in. "I know I'm late, but I really needed to eat something, so I stopped to pick up some coffee and donuts. Unfortunately, everyone in town had the same idea. I thought of saying 'screw it,' but who knows when we'll get to eat again?"

Johanna stared at him. "Is that a tie?"

"Yeah. You like it?" He stroked a narrow strip of black leather with pride. He wore it over a light blue shirt and khakis. Everything else he needed he'd stuffed in the backpack slung over his shoulder.

"I don't think I've ever seen you wear a tie before."

"I don't think I've ever owned a tie before. I bought this one on my way home last night. It's real leather."

She gently touched the black leather and then straightened out the knot. "You look very nice. I like it."

He grinned. "I couldn't have done it without you. My salary bump for being elevated from assistant to curator-in-training made it all possible.

"Now all I have to do is make sure I don't spill any coffee on myself. Just to be safe, I didn't buy any jelly or cream-filled donuts. Why take chances?"

"Why indeed." She removed a plain cruller from the bag of treats.

They chatted amiably until the grandfather clock struck ten. Johanna gulped down her coffee and used her hand to sweep the donut crumbs into the paper bag. "Mal will be here any second."

Jackson refused to rush through his morning meal and took his time as Johanna fussed. The minutes ticked by. When he finished, he threw his coffee cup and crumbs in the trash bag and took it out to the dumpster. The clock chimed the quarter hour when he returned.

Johanna's smile faded. "He's late."

"So the guy got hung up. Maybe he had to make an under-the-counter deal for the transport of human cargo.'"

Johanna didn't answer.

"That's what Mal said when he picked up Casanova. Don't you remember? He said he had to bargain with the people at Lloyds of London."

"You don't understand. Mal is always punctual. He's very reliable. His schedule usually runs like clockwork. But last night he didn't answer a question I asked his diary. And now he's late. Something's wrong."

Jackson studied Johanna's face. Her eyes had a glassy sheen, like she was on the verge of tears. He pulled her into a hug. "Don't worry. It won't matter if he's late. He's got a time machine, and no matter what time he gets here, we can travel back to the perfect moment to pass through the portals."

He rubbed her back to calm her down and felt her start to relax, but she grew tense again when the clock chimed the half-hour.

—LOI—

12

π *THIS IS ABSURD.*

⊕ *I agree.*

⌘ *While your opinions are highly valued by us all, they have no bearing on this argument. Under the Ultimium Codi, the curator of any realm is welcome to enter the challenge for overseer.*

Σ *Plato Indelicat lost his life at the hands of the Terrorians. That is irrefutable. Nero 51 announcing his challenge for Plato Indelicat's position is a mockery of everything we hold dear. Instead, Nero 51 should be charged with our fellow overseer's death.*

⌘ *Nero 51 cannot be charged. There is no evidence of his signature at the locations where the Terrorians either captured or later attacked Plato Indelicat. Nor did his signature materialize in the library when the Terrorians stormed the portals.*

π *Terrorian soldiers captured in their own weapons'*

force fields have independently claimed he led the rebellion.

⌘*It matters not. The absence of his signature during the attack and abduction clears him. It is his word—a curator sworn in four hundred thirty-two years ago by our own ruling council—against the word of overzealous soldiers who may have been working on their own and had decided in advance to blame Nero 51 if they lost the battle. Without tangible proof against him, his challenge cannot be denied.*

PROPHET IAN C., DAME ERATO, and Mal had been summoned to the overseers' chamber but were not allowed to attend the discussion. They knew neither the reason for the overseers' emergency meeting nor the reason for being detained outside of it, which forced them to speculate about why they were there. Prophet IAN c. reckoned it was part of the challenge. Dame Erato pointed out, if that were true, Torran of Dramatica would also be there. That led her to deduce the overseers had eliminated Torran from the competition, narrowing the field to three. Mal guessed that another challenger may have entered the race, causing some kind of controversy.

Dame Erato smoothed the folds of her silk gown. "Why would they call us here for that? We already knew that the potential for other candidates existed."

"That is why I'm sure this is part of the challenge," Prophet IAN c. answered. "They have taken the three strongest challengers and eliminated the fourth, knowing we would try to determine why. The overseers must wish to ascertain which of us has the most finely honed deductive skills."

A moment of silence followed. Dame Erato smiled

at Prophet IAN c. as she jerked her head toward Mal. "Our fellow challenger obviously has no idea why we've been called here, nor the wits to reason it out."

Mal answered with two words: "The Terrorians."

"Don't be ridiculous," Dame Erato replied. "The overseers would not stand for it."

"I quite agree," Prophet IAN c. concurred. "The Terrorians caused Plato Indelicat's death. The overseers would never invite them to participate in either the memorial or the challenge."

"The Terrorians are not a race that waits for an invitation to do anything," Mal replied.

They each paused when they heard the same voice inside their heads.

♪*Honored guests, please join us in the chamber.*

The three challengers filed into the room and stood at the open end of the horseshoe-shaped dais.

⌘*There has been a change in the field of challenge.*

Dame Erato lifted her chin and addressed her competitors. "I told you Torran is no longer part of the challenge. I don't know why you doubted me."

⌘*Torran is still very much a part of this challenge— as is Nero 51.*

"No," she cried.

Φ*We have gone over his entry in minute detail.*

⌘*If any of you can produce tangible proof why he should not be allowed to participate, now would be a good time to provide it.*

Prophet IAN c. stepped forward. "He killed Plato Indelicat."

⌘*Tangible proof.*

"Would proof of the commission of any crime

against the realms be enough?" Mal asked. "Or would it have to apply specifically to the tragedy on Terroria?"

♪*You have something for us, Malcolm?*

"Not at the moment, but I may know where to get it."

⌘*Go then, with great haste and retrieve it.*

AS THE MINUTES TICKED AWAY, Johanna kept busy behind the circulation desk. Nearby, Jackson idly paged through a volume of the Codex Atlanticus. As he flipped through it, various three-dimensional body parts floated in the air. He didn't really pay attention until the *Vitruvian Man* stood above them, slowly rotating in a large circle.

"Jackson."

He looked at Johanna and saw her staring, red-faced, at their naked visitor. "Sorry." He quickly closed the cover and selected a different volume from the collection of Leonardo Da Vinci's notes and drawings. Various tanks and war machines invaded their space.

"Jackson!"

"This stuff is so amazing. He drew these in the sixteenth century, but nothing like them appeared until hundreds of years later. And when we did produce weapons like these, they were just as Da Vinci had pictured them."

"Did you learn that in school?"

"The History Channel."

"Right. I should have known. If you weren't my curator-in-training, I'd recommend you for a job there."

"Don't go getting me jobs anywhere else. I'm very happy right where I am."

She smiled. "Now that the overseers have authorized

a hefty pay raise, I'll never get rid of you."

He grew serious. "You want to get rid of me?"

"Don't worry. I don't think I have it in me to break in another new assistant."

"Another assistant would never be like me. I'm one of a kind."

"We can only hope."

THE CLOCK STRUCK ELEVEN AS Mal and the time machine appeared in the main reading room.

"Thank God." Johanna rushed to him and gave him a hug. "I know how punctual you are, and when you didn't show up, I thought something terrible had happened."

"Something terrible could happen," Mal answered, "and you may be the only person who can stop it."

"What can I do?"

"You sent me pictures of a fake obelisk. Would you be willing to testify in front of the College of Overseers that the obelisk is a fake and explain how you found it?"

"Of course."

"If the photos you took and your testimony can convince them the obelisk is a replica, which is against LOI bylaws, we may be able to prevent Nero 51 from joining the challenge for the position of overseer."

Jackson's mouth dropped open. "No way! He's a challenger?"

"Yes. And as a library curator, he's a strong challenger. But if Johanna's testimony and photos discredit him enough, he may have to stand trial for counterfeiting, the illegal sale of library property, and possibly even treason."

"I can do that. I want to do that. I have to do that," Johanna said.

Mal smiled at her. "That's my girl. I knew you were right for this job, and you prove your value more and more each day."

"Hey, what about me?" Jackson half joked.

"I can honestly say, Jackson, that without you, we wouldn't be standing here like this today."

Jackson stared at Mal for a moment. "You're saying I got you into this, aren't you?"

"The Terrorians got us into this. You helped flush them out."

Jackson snaked his arm around Johanna's shoulder and squeezed. "See. I'm your Watson."

"Which Watson?"

"What do you mean, which Watson? Dr. Watson, from *The Hound of the Baskervilles.*"

"So you don't mean Thomas Watson, Alexander Graham Bell's assistant?"

"There may be two Watsons," Jackson admitted, "but I bet neither of them ever got to ride in a time machine."

"You're entirely right, young man," Mal said. "I'm sure neither of the Watsons have traveled through time, with the exception of visiting this library, of course."

"Of course." Jackson pointed to the bubble. "How does this thing work anyway?"

Johanna wriggled out from under Jackson's arm. "I'll be right back, I forgot something," she said, as Mal and Jackson embarked on a discussion about twenty-second-century physics.

"It's guided by the light waves that pass through this crystal." Mal held out one of his hands, on which lay a tiny semitransparent gemstone with flecks of multicolor minerals embedded in it.

"So do you put it in a hidden compartment somewhere?"

"No. I simply think of where I want to go on a particular date, and then I join it with this." Mal reached into his pocket and removed a second crystal, which emitted an ethereal glow. "The synergy of the two crystals together causes a reaction in the time-machine generator—and poof."

"Is that crystal, too?"

"Completely," Mal answered.

"Do you think the Mayans knew about this?"

"Undoubtedly."

"Some people believe the Mayans were extraterrestrial."

"Travelers from other worlds."

"Yeah."

"Or realms."

"Yeah!" Jackson's excitement mounted.

Johanna rushed back to join them. "I'm ready now." She entered the time machine. "What time is the memorial service?" she asked. "We're not going to be late, are we?"

"Not at all. This is a time machine. We're going to travel back to the last moment the portals were open, pass through to Lumina before they slam shut, and shoot forward to the morning of the service. It doesn't start until midiodi, the Luminan equivalent of high noon. My plan is to get there early, so I'll have time to show you to your quarters, where you can leave your bags, and give you a quick tour of the capital."

"Cool," Jackson said.

"I hope it's not too cool," Johanna replied. "I'm not bringing a jacket."

"Don't worry. Lumina is surrounded by a climate-controlled atmospheric layer. The city of Lumi is always seventy degrees, with a humidity level of thirty-five percent."

"Is that why the boats are open? Because it's so mild?" Jackson asked.

"The boats? Why would you ask about the boats?"

"Because we were looking at a text about Lumina and it came to life. We saw a tub full of people attacked by a bunch of mermen. Does that happen a lot?"

"That is a very real but unspoken problem on Lumina. It's one of the issues I'm hoping to address if I'm appointed overseer. Let me suggest that you don't speak of it while we're there. It has a tendency to upset people, and we wouldn't want to take away attention from Plato Indelicat's memorial."

"Okay," Jackson replied. "Just don't sign us up for any cruises."

—LOI—

13

THE ENTIRE PROCESS PASSED QUICKER than Johanna or Jackson had anticipated. Their stomachs roiled as they were propelled back in time through a wormhole, then ricocheted forward to the present.

At their destination, Mal jumped out of the time machine and turned to them. Neither of them moved. "You both look a little green. Are you all right?"

Jackson groaned. "Remind me to never to eat breakfast if I'm going to travel through time."

"It is a little unsettling," Mal admitted. "I should have warned you."

"I'll live. But I'm not so sure about Johanna."

She clutched Jackson's arm with a vise-like grip. She stared up at him and then inhaled deeply through her nose. "I'm trying not to get sick," she half whispered.

"I've got just the thing." Mal reached into his pocket and removed a small tin container. He deposited a dark pellet into Johanna's palm. "Suck on this. It will take the nausea away."

"Can I get one of those?" Jackson held out his hand. He made a face when he tasted the tablet. "Ugh ... licorice. I hate licorice."

"Are you still nauseated?"

Jackson thought for a second. "No. But still ..."

"Trust me," Mal said, "it's better than feeling sick."

It took Johanna only a moment to recover. She gazed in awe at the buildings surrounding them. The structures had intricately carved sparkling walls, topped by gold onion domes. The sky above was a vivid bluish-purple, and lush greenery spilled out of troughs lining the walkways. Tall, graceful Luminans dressed in flowing fabrics that looked like liquid silk glided past as they made their ways to one of the many palaces within the capital city of Lumi.

"Everything looks so beautiful," Johanna gushed.

"Too beautiful," Jackson added. "It's all a little too perfect. I feel like if I reach out my hand, someone will slap it and yell 'don't touch that.'"

"I've been in Lumi only a short time," Mal noted, "but you'll find most of the people here are quite pleasant and amiable."

"'Most'?" Jackson asked.

"There are a few strong personalities, but it takes strength to run the Prime Realm."

"'The Prime Realm,'" Johanna repeated Mal's words. "It makes Earth sound like a trailer park."

"Not Earth," Jackson corrected her, "Fantasia."

"What do you think of when you hear the word 'Fantasia'?" she asked.

"A Mickey Mouse film."

"I know. And I can't get past that. I'd rather be called Realm Eleven or Earth." Johanna turned to Mal. "What are the other realms called?"

He ticked them off on his fingers: "There's Romantica, Adventura, Educon, Scientico, Juvenilia, Dramatica …"

"That's where Furst comes from," Jackson observed.

"Comedia," Mal continued, "Inspiracon, Mysteriose, Numericon, Fantasia, and Terroria. And, of course, Lumina is the Prime Realm."

"I'll bet Comedia is a fun place," Jackson said.

"That's understandable, considering its name. Just remember, it's a complex world, like any of the others, with its own politics, religions, and cultural tastes. And like any other world, there are differences of opinion among the inhabitants. However, it is a bit more laid-back than some of the other realms."

"Like Terroria?" Johanna asked.

"Terroria is in a class all by itself," Mal answered.

"Aw, c'mon," Jackson said, "is that all you can say about Terroria?"

A passing Luminan looked at them with distaste. "We'll talk about that more in private," Mal said in a low voice. "Let's move along to your lodgings."

They walked into an ornate building containing a large light-filled atrium. At its center lay a flat, glassy circle lit from below. Mal guided Johanna and Jackson onto the center of the disk, which began to move on an angle.

"Kind of like surfing," Jackson commented, "but smoother."

The disk stopped and then rotated its occupants until they faced a door. The entrance sprang open automatically, and a soft disembodied voice announced, "Johanna Charette, welcome to your retreat in Lumi."

"Wow." Jackson's face lit up. "We didn't even have to check in or anything. It just knows who you are."

"Would you like some time to freshen up?" Mal asked. "Or do you just want to leave your bag here and continue on with us?"

"I really should unpack, or everything will be wrinkled."

"All right," Mal answered. "We'll come back for you in a few minutes."

"Thanks."

The door slid shut, leaving Johanna alone in a glass palace. She slipped the leather backpack off her shoulder and removed the outfit for the Overseers Challenge. She looked around the elegantly furnished room but did not see a bathroom or a closet. "So where am I supposed to hang this?" she murmured aloud.

A section of wall slid open, and inside she found a silver torso, a looking glass, and a tower of shelves. Johanna slipped her outfit over the torso and placed the other items she had brought on the shelves. When she walked away, the wall slid closed.

"Is there a bathroom?" she asked aloud.

A different section of wall retracted, and behind it she found a crystal-soaking tub flanked by little fountains of falling water. When she approached one of them, a small compartment opened, revealing a collection of creams and lotions. She picked up a bowl of exotic petals. The front of it wavered as the word "soap" appeared. She replaced it and picked up a vial of creamy pink lotion and the word "moisturizer" materialized on the front surface.

She looked around. "Toilet?" she asked. Another door opened, revealing a private commode. "Excellent."

The disembodied voice that had welcomed her to her quarters announced, "Johanna Charette, Malcolm Trees and Jackson Roth are seeking your company. Do you wish to reunite with them?"

"Yes," she answered, then paused. "How do I let them in?" The door slid open, and Mal and Jackson walked in.

"This place is something, isn't it?" Jackson contemplated the inside of her quarters. "I wish my mother could see it. She'd love this place."

"What did your mom say when you told her you were going to another world?" Johanna asked.

"I didn't. That's not something you tell your mother. She thinks I'm just spending the night at Logan's house."

"Interesting," Johanna replied.

"Would you have told your mother?"

A shadow of sadness flickered across Johanna's face, but her voice remained strong. "No mother to tell."

"Trust me, if you had a mother, you wouldn't tell her because, first of all, she wouldn't believe you."

Johanna thought about it for a second and then smiled. "True."

Not far in the distance, deeply resonant bells pealed. "It's time," Mal said, then led the teens out of the room.

The transport disk awaited them, and once they stepped on it, the circle glided across the atrium and out the front door. Johanna held on to Mal's and Jackson's arms as they traveled along the walkways of Lumi. An impressive building marked the end of their journey.

"What is this place?" Johanna asked.

"It's the University of Lumi, the home of the College of Overseers. The memorial will be held in the rear courtyard, outside the chantry."

Their disk came to a halt in a sunny area surrounded by walls covered with flowering vines of varying hues. The pavement sparkled like diamonds, and the center of the space featured a high altar topped by the body of Plato Indelicat.

Jackson rubbed the toe of his shoe against the surface. "What is this stuff? It looks like diamonds."

"It is," Mal answered. "The entire planet is one big diamond."

"Is that what all the buildings and walls are made of?" Johanna asked.

"Indeed. On Fantasia, you have buildings made out of limestone and granite cut from the earth. Here, the buildings are also fashioned out of indigenous materials. However, in this case, it's diamond."

Jackson stooped down and rubbed the surface with his fingers. "It must all be worth a fortune."

"Diamond is no more valuable here than stone is on Earth. Some diamonds are worth more than others, depending on the grade of the material. And they do dazzle the eye. But they're plentiful enough and don't have the same allure here they would have on Fantasia."

"So if I picked up a diamond here and brought it back to Earth, it would still only be worth as much as a rock?"

Mal raised a finger in warning. "If you picked up

a diamond here and tried to take it back to Fantasia, you wouldn't survive the trip. The Ancients created an atmospheric ring around Lumina countless millennia ago, to prevent this world's bioengineered air from evaporating. It also prevents other natural resources, like diamonds, from leaving the system. Once our time machine breached that ring, the diamond would explode, terminating us all."

"Yikes!"

"Exactly."

"Who are the Ancients?" Johanna asked.

"According to legend, they're a superior race who created the realms on twelve different worlds. When they looked for a thirteenth planet to host Lumi, they couldn't find a suitable one for their purposes. So they chose this planet, which is almost entirely composed of graphite and diamond."

"But everything else is like Earth … or Fantasia," Johanna noted. "The water. The atmosphere …"

"All bioengineered by the Ancients," Mal explained. "This place was uninhabitable before that, at least by beings like ourselves, who need an oxygen-rich atmosphere. The Ancients introduced the necessary ratio of water and vegetation to this planet to produce a habitable environment."

Jackson nodded. "So the Ancients created the mermen."

Mal shook his head, almost imperceptibly. "No."

"Then where did they come from?"

Music began playing, signaling the beginning of the service. "The mermen are mutated Luminans, which is a controversial topic here," Mal whispered. "So let's not talk about it again until we're alone. And that excludes our lodging, because it's mind controlled."

—LOI—

14

JACKSON'S EYES NEARLY BUGGED OUT of their sockets. "What do you mean 'mind controlled'?"

"How do you think the transport disk knows where you want to go?" Mal asked.

"I didn't think it was mind controlled. Now, every time I get on that thing, I'm going to have to be careful about what I'm thinking."

"It's not that bad," Mal consoled him. "Besides, you're standing on one now."

Jackson twisted from side to side, looking for an open space that he could escape to.

Mal shook his head and pulled Jackson back. "This disk isn't a problem," he whispered. "It's talking about sensitive subjects inside the lodging and public places that we have to be careful."

Jackson looked down warily. "You're sure?"

Mal began to answer, but his whispers were

drowned out. The choir raised their voices in tribute to Plato Indelicat, forcing Mal to nod his head.

The memorial service seemed to go on for hours. The overseers had nothing but praise for their fallen colleague and dozens of anecdotes about him. After each one, the Luminans would raise their right hands and rotate their forefingers in an upward spiral, a silent indication that they appreciated what had just been said.

Just when it looked like the last overseer had finished speaking, a new overseer appeared. But unlike the others, this one had no beard. She took her place in front of Plato Indelicat's body.

★ *Plato Indelicat was one of our finest philosophers.*

"He's a woman," Jackson said, amazed.

A nearby Luminan glared at the teen.

Mal spoke quietly. "That's Pru Tellerence. She couldn't attend your hearing on Terroria because she was away on private business."

"She doesn't look as old as the others," Johanna observed.

"Right now, she's the most recently appointed overseer and the youngest, although that will change tomorrow."

"I thought all the overseers were men," Jackson said.

"No. At one time, the majority of deans were women. But as they died off, men were selected to replace them."

"What do you mean by 'dean'?"

"It's the honorific used for the overseers, just like we might say 'doctor' or 'professor' on Fantasia. Although here, their scope as deans is a lot more encompassing because it means they are in charge of entire realms."

"Who's our dean?"

"Selium Sorium."

"And this woman … dean?"

"Pru Tellerence is the dean of Dramatica."

"And she's the only woman?" Johanna asked.

"The inequality of the board's gender is the reason why Dame Erato is such a strong contender and is generally favored to win tomorrow's challenge."

Johanna took Mal's arm. "I'm hoping you'll win."

"Thank you, Johanna. But we must be realistic."

★ … *leaves us all with empty hearts over the passing of such a great dean.*

Pru Tellerence turned to the other overseers, who nodded in unison. She stood silently as a procession of two dozen children in flowing white robes surrounded the altar. Each carried an enormous bunch of crystal-clear balloons. The remaining overseers took their places between pairs of children and helped them attach the balloons to small hooks decorating the pallet that held Plato Indelicat's body. After they fastened the last balloon, everyone stepped away and a musician played a hauntingly beautiful song on a flute-like instrument.

Pru Tellerence began to sing the Luminan song "Musi Morti" in a strong, clear soprano:

★ *As we unite our spirits soar,*

★ *Together we're perfection …*

Mal tilted his head toward Johanna. "I'm told this is one of the most revered hymns of Lumina. It's been sung to memorialize the passing of each overseer since the beginning of the realms."

★ *But when one cherished breathes no more*

★ *Our sweet, fragile connection*

★ *Evaporates, leaving all we*
★ *Once held dear—behind*
★ *Until we may unite again*
★ *I fear we travel blind.*
★ *For it is wisdom that we seek*
★ *Yes, tolerance and peace*
★ *We search out one whom, like the lost,*
★ *Can help our grief release.*
★ *We celebrate your being, we voice*
★ *Sorrow at your death*
★ *But know that we will love you ere*
★ *Until our dying breath.*

Mal and Jackson turned and stared at Johanna, who had quietly sung the last two lines of the song with Pru Tellerence.

"What?" she asked, embarrassed.

"You're singing," Jackson replied.

She blushed.

"How do you know the words to that song?" Mal asked.

"I don't know. I just do." She shrugged.

"Curious," Mal said.

"I bet you saw the lyrics in one of those books about Lumina you studied," Jackson guessed.

"Maybe."

"That wouldn't explain how you knew the melody," Mal continued to probe.

"Oh, come on, Mal. It's really a simple tune," she argued.

"I just find it curious."

The locking device holding Plato Indelicat's pallet snapped loudly as it disengaged. The crowd chanted a gentle "ooh" as the overseer's body rose into the air, carried upward by the crystalline balloons. The bottom of the pallet had a design etched into it.

"Is that the logo of the miter hats the overseers wear?" Johanna asked.

"It's the constellation Illumini."

Jackson lowered his gaze from the pallet to Mal. "Illumini?"

"Yes. It's an asterism of the twelve Libraries of Illumination and their positions around Lumina. The different realms form the design of the overseers' miters. If you look at each dean's hat, you will see that each one has a significantly larger diamond embedded in one of the points of the design, indicating which realm that overseer represents."

Jackson shook his head. "How come those diamonds don't explode when the overseers travel to different worlds?"

"Because the overseers travel a path that's different from the one you and I travel. When new overseers are inducted, they take part in an enrichment ceremony that gives them special powers. Not a lot of magical hocus-pocus, mind you, but simply the powers of longevity, transmogrification, and time travel."

"Simply?" Jackson huffed. "That doesn't sound so simple to me."

Mal's expression changed with sudden realization. "Oh dear. Oh dear. How could I have forgotten to tell you?"

Johanna stared at the little twitch that developed over Mal's right eye. She grasped both his hands and asked in a calm voice, "Tell us what, Mal?"

"About the Curator Orientation and Longevicus Ritual. All the other curators were subjected to strenuous testing when they were appointed, but I didn't submit your names for it because you were both under the age of twenty-one and did not have any knowledge of the other Libraries of Illumination. Selium Sorium arranged for a special dispensation for you. However, Master Ryden Simmdry now requests that you go through the ritual since you're here on Lumina. I am so sorry I forgot to tell you."

"Strenuous testing?" Jackson croaked.

"You two will do fine on the operational part of the exam. It's the section on historic knowledge that I'm afraid you're unprepared for, but I think if we go off to a quiet place this afternoon I can give you a crash course that will help you get through it."

BOOM!

Lumi vibrated from the shock waves.

Jackson grabbed Johanna and pulled her close. "What was that?" He looked around, but none of the other people seemed phased by the explosion.

"The balloons contain diamonds, as did Plato Indelicat's new miter hat. They reached the atmospheric ring put in place by the Ancients and were obliterated."

"Ahhh ..." the crowd gasped collectively.

Johanna looked up and saw the spectacle. Diamond dust rained down, and flash rainbows appeared everywhere.

"No wonder the streets sparkle," Jackson muttered.

"Oh, that won't reach the streets," Mal said. "It will disintegrate momentarily."

Jackson sighed. "I hope that's on the test. At least I'll

be able to answer one question."

"I guess with preparing for your own challenge you just forgot to tell us," Johanna reasoned.

A group of musicians began playing a lively composition in the corner of the courtyard. Johanna turned away from Mal and watched as people danced. "That was sudden. I guess the funeral is over and a new party is starting up."

"This is a celebration of Plato Indelicat's life. His passing may be sad, but his accomplishments were many and his very existence was a gift to all he served. By dancing, these people are acknowledging his rich legacy."

"Are we supposed to dance?" Jackson asked.

"I think it would be better if we have some lunch. Afterward, I can prepare you for your orientation." Mal led them into the chantry, where more than a dozen tables of delicacies originating in all the realms awaited them.

Jackson stopped in front of an undulating chartreuse blob. "What is that?" he asked without moving his lips.

"That's bornivor heart from Comedia," Mal replied.

"I think I'll pass on that."

Johanna accepted a beverage from a passing waiter. "This is delicious."

"Herg wine."

"Where does it come from?"

"Dramatica."

Jackson snagged a glass of Herg wine and chugged it down. "It's good to know that we have something like grapes in common with Dramatica."

"It doesn't come from grapes," Mal said.

Johanna stopped sipping and looked warily at Mal. "What does it come from?"

"It's juice extracted from the brains of tzen-tzalis, small animals similar to the aardvarks on Fantasia."

Jackson's face paled. "You gotta stop telling me this stuff. You're ruining my appetite."

Mal led them to a far table.

"What is that?" Jackson pointed to a platter of meat surrounded by vegetables.

Mal smiled. "It's something the Fantasians call roast beef."

"Yes!" Jackson pumped his fist.

"Um-hmm," Johanna agreed. "Everyone's entitled to a last meal."

"You two will do just fine. Let's enjoy the overseers' hospitality. Then I'll tell you everything you'll need to know to get through tomorrow morning's ritual."

"When is your challenge?" Johanna asked.

"Midiodi."

Jackson imitated a cowboy drawing his gun. "Like the *Gunfight at the O.K. Corral.*"

"No," Johanna answered.

"Sure it is," Jackson rebutted.

"Historically speaking, the gunfight at the O.K. Corral happened at three p.m. I think you're confusing it with the film *High Noon.*"

"Whatever," Jackson conceded.

They finished eating and stepped on the nearest transport disk. It took them to a park at the edge of Lumi. During the journey they passed many buildings, each as grand as the next one.

"People around here are not very original," Jackson observed.

"There are several reasons for that. Lumi doesn't

have a lot of natural resources, although they could be imported from other cities. Then, there's the governing council. They have long felt that, as the capital, Lumi must set an example by exhibiting only the finest taste. The capital's keywords are 'stately' and 'elegant,' and the governors have imposed strict building codes to make sure it stays that way."

Johanna pointed to a rock outcrop in the distance, dotted with colorful structures. "What's that over there?"

"That is Ranbi, a city renowned for its artistic pottery and glassworks."

Jackson created a spyglass with his fist and looked at Ranbi through it with one eye closed. "It's a lot more colorful than this place."

Mal was impressed. "You can see that far?"

"Sure, I just blocked out everything else so that I could concentrate on one little area. It has red buildings with bright green roofs, and royal-blue buildings with orange roofs. And it has trees. You called this place a park—it has lawns and flowers—but it doesn't have any trees. What if you want to put down a blanket under a tree and have a picnic?"

Mal laughed. "Thank goodness there are no trees here, because if you did decide to have a picnic, the Lumi authorities would take you into custody for eating in a public place."

"You can't eat in public here?"

"No."

"What else can't you do?"

"Litter, loiter, shout, sing, skip, dance ..."

Jackson threw his hand up, palm facing outward. "Hold it. I just saw people singing and dancing."

"That was at the university, which is privately owned. I'm talking about public walkways, parks, and squares owned by the city of Lumi."

"They should call this the Land of No."

"I don't know, Jackson." Johanna laughed. "Maybe you should have asked Mal what you *are* allowed to do."

Jackson raised one eyebrow and turned to Mal. "So?"

"You can transport from one place to another. Quiet conversation is allowed. But no raucous laughter, yodeling, swearing, and no advertising of any kind."

"It doesn't sound like much fun. And I really feel like yodeling my heart out right now."

"Lucky for us," Johanna said, "we just have to take a test, watch the Overseers Challenge, and then go home, where you can yodel in the street."

"Lucky us," Jackson repeated.

The transport circle floated to a half wall by the water. Mal removed a small cube from his pocket and inserted it into a square at the top of the wall. A tiny screen opened up, and Mal placed the pad of his thumb against it. The front of the wall unfolded into a bench. Mal squinted at the screen, where he had left his thumbprint.

"We have been approved for a half-hour of time. I suggest we start our lesson."

—LOI—

15

"AS YOU ALREADY KNOW, THERE are twelve realms plus Lumina." Mal reached into his coat and pulled two booklets entitled *Illumini Primo* from an inside pocket. "Here, I suggest you study this tonight. It covers each of the realms with a short history, the names of its overseer and curator, and the properties of that realm's library. Each realm is self-sufficient and operates independently. In return for the guidance of an overseer, the realm pays a tithe—not money but the inclusion of all its new literature, art, math, and music into all the Libraries of Illumination. That way everything that's newly created on an individual realm automatically becomes part of the entire library system on all of the realms."

Johanna's excitement mounted. "Are you saying that we have every bit of knowledge from all twelve worlds in our library on Earth?"

"Fantasia, Johanna," Mal cautioned. "You have to

remember to call it that. A cult faction that split off long ago started referring to your world as Earth in defiance of the realms, but the overseers do not recognize it. It has been known as Fantasia far longer than it's been called Earth, and you will need to remember that during the Curator Orientation and Longevicus Ritual."

"Will we need to know who all the overseers are?" Jackson asked.

"Yes, and all the curators. And you'll need to know the approved description of the Two Millennia War, which is in the booklet. There have been some attempts of revisionist history over the years, but it's usually discovered and purged." Mal tapped a finger against Jackson's booklet. "Go by what's written in here."

Johanna slipped the booklet into her purse. "What else will we need to know?"

"The day-to-day operations of the library. You already know how to re-energize the library reactor, and how to summon the overseers in an emergency. Those are two things that some curators who have been taking care of their libraries for centuries are still unfamiliar with.

"The two of you may be young, but you have a lot more practical experience than many of your more seasoned colleagues. Most curators never travel to other realms, except when they come to Lumi for the Orientation and Longevicus Ritual." Mal paused. "Come to think of it, only the three of us and the overseers have set foot on four or more worlds. We've been to Fantasia, Dramatica, Terroria, and Lumina. Some deans only travel between Lumina and the world they oversee. Stepping foot on four realms is an extraordinary accomplishment for two young people like you.

"Then there are the sacrosanct tenets of library law, first set forth in the *Ultimium Codi*."

Jackson paged through the booklet. "Is that in here?"

"No, but I'm going to teach them to you right now.

"First, with the exception of Lumina, no one library is more important than the others. They have all been created equally, although they share different properties. The libraries were created to assess, inform, illustrate, and entertain. Romantica, Juvenilia, and Mysteriose are all class-V Libraries. They entertain. Their visitors actually enter into the books they read and become auxiliary characters. Adventura, Dramatica, and Numericon are class-R Libraries. They were designed to inform. Their books rearrange themselves daily in the order of their importance to current events in that realm. Educon, Comedia, and Fantasia illustrate. They each have books that come to life and are class-L libraries. And finally, Scientico, Inspiracon, and Terroria are all class-G libraries. Their books each have a presence that appears and determines the reader's true intention for selecting it.

"Originally, the libraries were all designed to work together, allowing users to travel among them through the portals. However, the portals were sealed after the Two Millennia War, as you well know."

As they continued their discussion, the bench they were seated on began to glow.

"Look," Jackson said, "it's lighting up because it's getting dark."

Mal shook his head. "We had better stand. And quickly."

They rose and watched the bench rapidly intensify

in brightness. A moment later, the seat retracted faster than a gunslinger going for his weapon.

"That's kind of rude," Jackson said. "If we hadn't noticed the light, would we all be sitting on the ground now?"

"Yes. And if we didn't get up immediately, we'd probably be detained for inappropriate behavior. It's the Lumi government's way of preventing loitering."

Johanna surveyed the park. "That's the second time you mentioned loitering, but it doesn't look like Lumi has any bums or derelicts hanging around."

"Let's head back to our lodging." Mal led them back to their transport disk. As it moved, he kept his voice low. "Lumi, like any other city, has its ups and downs, but doesn't tolerate any display of poverty. So as soon as residents stumble upon hard times, they are relocated to a benefit center."

"What's that?" Jackson looked at Johanna, but she shook her head to indicate she didn't know.

"They are located on rock outcrops much farther to the south," Mal explained. "You can't see them from here. They're in the Toro Zone."

"Ah, Toro." Jackson mimicked a matador, and almost lost his balance on the moving disk.

Johanna grabbed his arm to steady him. "I don't think it has anything to do with bullfighting."

"Yeah, me neither. But thanks for saving my life." He brushed her cheek with his lips.

Mal laughed. "I believe I previously mentioned that if you step off the transport disk, it stops. I think you're just looking for an excuse to kiss Johanna."

"Don't laugh," Jackson said, joking. "You'll get

arrested."

Johanna dismissed their levity and picked up the thread of their conversation. "So what's the Toro Zone like?"

"Let's just say you'd rather watch Jackson fight a bull than be assigned to the Toro Zone."

"Jackson would be mauled if he ever tried to fight a bull."

"No," Jackson said, defending his prowess.

"Yes," Johanna responded, "and if you ever tried it, I wouldn't watch."

"That being said," Mal continued, "you would rather watch someone get mangled by a bull than watch Luminans wither to death in the Toro Zone."

The color drained from her face. "How could such a beautiful place have such an ugly … zone?"

"Lumina is not just Lumi, its pretty capital city," Mal replied, his voice barely above a whisper. "It's an entire world. It's Ranbi, and Hypo, and Meccan, and Fridi, and dozens of other rock outcrops. And as beautiful as Lumi may be, it is in direct contrast to how awful the Toro Zone is."

"Not keeping secrets now, are we, Mr. Trees?"

The three of them looked up, startled by the unexpected interruption. A tall man who would be gaunt except for his very round face and the protrusion of a very noticeable potbelly stood right next to them.

"Governor Tare," Mal said cordially. "I wouldn't think of keeping secrets here in Lumi, knowing how the city council frowns on it. To explain, let me introduce Johanna Charette and Jackson Roth. They are the curators of the Library of Illumination on Fantasia, and tomorrow is their Curator Orientation and Longevicus Ritual. I'm just instructing them on the history of all the realms. We tried to be as quiet as possible so our lesson wouldn't disturb any of your citizens."

"Carry on, then. I wouldn't want to be responsible for these two fine curators having a difficult time during their orientation." He smiled widely and circled his right forefinger in the air in approval.

"Close one, Mal," Jackson whispered after the governor left.

"You have no idea," Mal replied gravely.

—LOI—

16

"I'D LIKE YOU BOTH TO STUDY the pamphlets I gave you, that way if you have any questions, you can ask me about them later when we get together for dinner," Mal said.

"Okay." Jackson grinned. "Johanna and I can study together."

"No. It would be highly inappropriate for you to be seen in each other's rooms without a chaperone. And illegal."

"Land of No," Jackson mumbled.

"This is not the time to defy authority. Just accept it during your relatively short stay here."

Johanna disappeared inside her chamber, and Mal escorted Jackson back to his room.

It irked Jackson that they had to be so careful about everything they said and did. "Mal, are we like prisoners here?"

Mal's face remained noncommittal. "Let's just say if you abide by Lumi's somewhat irrational regulations, you'll avoid becoming a prisoner here."

JOHANNA REREAD THE *ILLUMINI PRIMO* Mal had given her—several times—hoping to commit all facts about the realms to memory. She wished she and Jackson could study together, because she knew he would come up with mnemonic devices to help them remember everything. He was probably doing that right now, alone in his room.

Some connections were easy to make, like Pi being the curator of Numericon. Others were a little more random. *How am I going to remember that Zenith Fullova is the dean of Juvenilia?* She started reading the pamphlet a fourth time, testing herself as she read, but found it hard to concentrate because she kept thinking about Jackson. Maybe she could call him. She looked around for a telephone but didn't see anything that remotely resembled one. "Telephone?" she said aloud, hoping a little door would slide open somewhere, but no such luck.

As it turned out, it didn't matter. "Johanna Charette, Malcolm Trees and Jackson Roth are outside your door requesting your company."

"Open the door," she replied as she grabbed her bag and slipped the booklet inside.

"Dinnertime," Jackson sang as the door slid open. His face widened into a grin as he kissed Johanna hello. He suddenly jerked away and looked at Mal. "Am I allowed to do that?"

"I'm your chaperone, and I'm not filing a complaint. But I would keep displays of affection to a minimum."

"I can't wait until we get home. This place is starting

to give me the creeps."

Johanna nodded and looked at Mal. "What happens when two people fall in love here?"

"They don't. All marriages in Lumi are arranged."

"Is it that falling is love is frowned upon, or are the Luminans incapable of feeling love?"

"Let's focus on Lumi. The people in the capital city—the Lumites—have worked for millennia to subdue their emotional and carnal instincts.

"There are people who fall in love on some of the other rock outcrops," he continued, "but not here in the capital city."

"What if two young people here did fall in love? Could they run away to another rock outcrop?"

"They could." Mal paused. "But they would never be able to return to Lumi. Leaving the city without the approval of the city council would be tantamount to breaking the law. And then there's the problem of trans-portation. There is no mass transportation to other rock outcrops. To travel between cities, all Luminans must go through a lengthy process to secure preapproved travel orders, which they then use to arrange for transpor-tation." He lowered his voice. "And as you have already noted, traveling to other rock outcrops by sea can be extremely dangerous."

"There's no place like home," Johanna murmured.

"You got that right," Jackson agreed.

Their transport disk stopped inside a building bathed in orange light.

"Juice bar?" Jackson asked.

"This is one of the most popular restaurants in Lumi. The color orange stimulates the appetite and aids digestion, and its bright hue apparently hasn't hurt business here at all," Mal replied.

A host led them to a table in the center of the room. Jackson squirmed. He looked around at the other diners, and they all seemed to be looking back at him. "I feel like we're the main attraction. I wish they had seated us in a corner."

"The corner tables and those along the walls are considered less desirable. The closer a table is to the center of the room, the more important are the people who are seated there."

"But *we're* in the center of the room."

"I'm a candidate for overseer. You are visiting curators. That makes us very important people."

Johanna pulled the booklet Mal had given her out of her bag and looked at Jackson. "I'm having some trouble remembering which curators and deans go with which realms. Can you help me figure out a way to remember them?"

"Who's giving you a problem?"

"I keep thinking Dr. Infinitis is Scientico, but he's Educon and that doesn't make sense to me."

"It would if you think of doctors as college professors who teach in educational institutions. As for Scientico, Galon Senter's first name sounds almost like Galileo, a fellow scientist who seconded Copernicus in saying the sun is the center of the universe."

"How do you make it sound so easy?"

"Just talented, I guess. Anyone else giving you trouble?"

"Yes, Comedia. I've got Abbello Abbato committed to memory because his name sounds comedic. But I'm having trouble remembering the dean."

"Think of a comedian who makes you groan. You just want to take a bag of rice and bean him with it. Instead of rice and beans, we have Reichel Bean. Or, as I like to call him, Dean Bean."

Johanna grinned. "Got it."

MAL ORDERED DINNER WHILE JACKSON helped Johanna with a few more troublesome associations.

"You two never cease to amaze me," Mal told them a moment later. "You balance out each other's strengths and weaknesses. Together, you're the perfect mix of practicality and innovation."

Johanna grinned. "Women just love being told they're practical."

"That makes me innovative. I like it," Jackson said.

"I could have said 'the perfect blend of beauty and brains,' Johanna, but they both apply to you, and I didn't want Jackson to feel slighted."

"I'm happy with 'innovative,'" Jackson remarked. "And if you would have said 'beauty, brains, and innovation,' we would have both been happy."

Bing ... bong ... bung.

The triple tone came from the center of their table. A second later the middle of the surface retracted and a turntable filled with food rose. Mal turned the lower shelf. "This roasted vegetable soup is especially delicious, but the salads and meat pies are equally good." He raised his hand to turn the smaller middle shelf. "This fruited wild game looks wonderful, as do the medallions of veal, and the grilled lobster with lime butter. And I've been told the vegetable risotto is an excellent choice. Let's leave the postprandials on the top shelf for later."

"'Postprandials'? Do I even want to know what that means?" Jackson asked, remembering the herg wine and bornivor heart.

"Dessert."

"Why didn't you say so? Do we just help ourselves?"

"That's the idea. Other restaurants in the capital have full wait service, but a lot of visitors prefer to just help themselves rather than sit through a traditional four-hour Lumi dinner."

Jackson picked up his fork. "How much food do they serve at one of those?"

"Not any more than they serve here, but full wait service is intentionally slow to give individuals time to digest each course."

"I prefer instant gratification." Jackson stabbed a piece of meat and promptly ate it.

"Me, too," Mal said, doing the same.

Johanna ladled soup into a bowl, but swirled her spoon around it instead of eating it.

"Is there a problem, Johanna?" Mal asked.

"Is there anything we need know, like if any of these foods come from the body parts of rodents?"

"Don't worry, I told our server that we would be dining Fantasian tonight."

"Thank goodness." She tasted the soup and savored the flavor. "This is so good."

"That's another reason why this is one of the most popular restaurants in Lumi. The food is excellent."

DAWN BATHED THE CITY IN shades of lilac.

"Johanna Charette, it is time to prepare for the

Curator Orientation and Longevicus Ritual."

Johanna marveled at how efficiently the hotel's artificial intelligence catered to her needs, but at the same time resented the disembodied voice for being intrusive. She dressed quickly, then studied the booklet Mal gave her one last time.

"Johanna Charette, Malcolm Trees and Jackson Roth are here to escort you to the ritual."

She grabbed her backpack and walked to the door, but it remained closed. "Are you going to open the door?"

"You did not command me to open the door, Johanna Charette. Do you wish me to open the door?"

"Yes."

It slid open on her command.

Jackson winked at her. "Hey, Mal, I won't get in trouble for just winking, will I?"

"Don't worry. I'll tell them you have a nervous tic."

"That's big of you."

Johanna couldn't help but smile at their banter.

After breakfast, their transport disk took them to an amphitheater on the north edge of the city. Inside, a ring-shaped table with thirteen seats sat in the center of a grassy field surrounding a diamond disk embedded with the Illumini constellation.

"Heads up," Mal whispered.

Jackson turned to see a dozen overseers file out of the structure. Eleven deans took their seats, while Master Ryden Simmdry approached Johanna and Jackson.

⌘*Please accompany me.*

The two teens followed him through an opening in the round table, to the marble disk in the middle.

⌘*Take your place on the disk.*

They did as they were told. A railing immediately encircled them as the disk rose several feet into the air.

Ryden Simmdry took a seat with the others.

⌘*Answer the questions to the best of your ability. Dean Proteus Bligh will begin the first round.*

Ŧ*Johanna Charette, who is the curator of Juvenilia?*

And so it began. The overseers alternated their questions between Johanna and Jackson for more than an hour. The teens stumbled only once.

✗*Jackson Roth, who quelled the second uprising of the Terrorians?*

Jackson stood speechless for a long, uncomfortable moment as he tried to envision the page in the booklet where the answer to the question could be found, but his mind went blank. He had no recollection of reading any information about a second Terrorian uprising.

Johanna intertwined her fingers with Jackson. In a clear, strong voice she answered for him: "We all did."

During another long pause the overseers' hats glowed as they communicated silently among themselves.

♪*Jackson Roth, what provides the Libraries of Illumination with illumination?*

"Ahhh, that would be the blue orb, a nuclear reactor that needs to be recharged every half millennium."

The overseers changed topics and drilled them on day-to-day operations and procedures related to the libraries' unusual properties. The teens' answers came quickly and easily.

Another period of silence followed their second hour of questioning, while the overseers again communicated internally.

Suddenly, the platform Johanna and Jackson stood

on began to descend, but did not stop when it became level with the surface. Johanna gripped Jackson's hand tightly as they dipped below ground level. They found themselves surrounded by triangular diamond bars inside a glowing chamber. The disk turned, causing the light in the room to shower the teens with the entire spectrum of color. Centripetal force held Johanna and Jackson in place as the disk turned with dizzying speed.

A medicinal odor permeated the room as the disk began to slow down. Johanna found it strangely soothing. Finally, the disk stopped rotating, and a moment later it began to rise. As they rose above ground level, the teens found themselves inside a tight circle of overseers, who were standing nearly shoulder to shoulder, with just enough room between them to allow them to raise their right forearms and rotate their forefingers in upward spirals. Johanna smiled as she remembered Mal describing the action as a sign of appreciation.

§*Johanna Charette, you have successfully completed your Curator Orientation and Longevicus Ritual. Go forth and illuminate.* The overseers changed focus and said the same thing to Jackson. They then formed a single line and slowly made their way to a door leading inside the amphitheater walls.

Mal's smile reached from ear to ear. "I'm so proud of both of you. There had been speculation that the overseers might approve only one of you because there have never been two curators at the same library before, but that all changed with the question about the second uprising. My heart stopped when you stalled answering the question, even though I knew it was designed to see how the two of you would react to something unexpected."

He looked at Johanna. "Taking Jackson's hand was brilliant. It's a bond that most Lumi residents wouldn't approve of, but I could hear the overseers as they deliberated afterward, and they interpreted it as unity and strength." He turned to Jackson. "If Johanna had just answered the question without taking your hand, she alone would have been allowed to go ahead with the Longevicus Ritual. But the simple act of joining with you showed that she was not trying to triumph over you, but to fortify you, and that impressed the overseers."

"If I didn't get to go through the ritual, would that have meant I couldn't work at the library anymore?"

"You would have remained a curator-in-training, and may have been able to reapply for the Curator Orientation and Longevicus Ritual in another ten years, but it would have delayed the blessing."

"What blessing?"

Mal rubbed his head. "I guess I forgot to explain to you the benefit of the Longevicus Ritual." He sighed. "This may be hard to explain to your friends and loved ones, but Longevicus delays aging. For every ten years a normal person ages, you will only age one year. In another ten years, your friends will be in their late twenties, but you two will still be teenagers. You'll have the accumulated knowledge of someone older, but your physical age will have slowed dramatically. How do you think I got to be over four hundred years old? Longevicus! And it's even more dramatic for overseers. They undergo a ritual that allows them to age only one year for every thousand years. It provides continuity in the governance of the libraries.

"You'll both go down in history as being the first

curator team, and you're already in the history books for helping quell the second Terrorian uprising. You're quite a pair."

Jackson grinned as he looked at Johanna. "I can't believe we're equals."

Mal groaned. "That's not entirely accurate."

"What do you mean?"

"You're a full curator, but Johanna is curator primo. She has seniority because she is the chosen curator, and she's been in the job longer. You're a curator because she chose you as her second-in-command."

"Okay. I can see that. Besides, 'curator' still sounds better than 'assistant.'" Jackson picked up Johanna and swung her around. When he put her down, he whipped his head in both directions to see if anyone was watching. "I don't think anybody saw that. We're good, right, Mal?"

"I'll just confirm it's that nervous tic."

—LOI—

17

JACKSON'S STOMACH GROWLED. "THE LONGEVICUS Ritual really makes you work up an appetite. Lunch, anyone?"

Mal led them to the transport disk. "There's a small place right around the corner that has delicious Fantasian food. Or would you prefer something from another realm?"

That piqued Johanna's curiosity. "Is there food from other realms ... similar to Fantasian food? Veggies? Grains? Hold the eyeballs ..."

Jackson shook his head. "Let's just stick with Fantasian food, thank you."

"Why can't we just try something new, if Mal says it's not so bad?"

"You won't even eat squid, and that's Fantasian. What makes you think you're going to like something totally foreign?"

"I want to open myself up to new things."

"Buy a pair of Luminan shoes. Have you noticed how the toes curl up, like something Aladdin wore in *One Thousand and One Nights*?"

"All right. We'll eat at the Fantasian place. C'mon, Mal."

"I can't go, it's almost midiodi."

"Oh!" Johanna grabbed Mal's arm. "The Overseers Challenge. I got so caught up in our orientation this morning I almost forgot. We're not going anywhere. We're staying right here to support you."

Mal smiled. "I don't want you two to starve. You hardly ate a thing at breakfast."

"Nope, it's fine," Jackson said. "We're staying put."

"Where's the best place to watch?" Johanna took Mal's arm and started walking toward the amphitheater.

"Lucky for you, now that you've successfully completed orientation, you can sit in the special section reserved for curators. You may see your new friend Furst there, since Torran is a competitor. And Natalia Dalura, the curator from Romantica, may be there in support of Dame Erato. Nero 51 and Prophet IAN c. are curators, but anyone who might accompany them would not be allowed to sit in that section."

"At least we won't have to worry about creeping tentacles," Jackson remarked, only half in jest.

A flourish, similar to the sound of baroque trumpets, came from the amphitheater.

Mal took a deep breath. "It's time. Let's go inside."

JACKSON EXPRESSED SURPRISE OVER THE massive crowd of people vying for seats in the stadium. "Where did they all come from? We were just in here and it was empty. I didn't see anyone outside."

"They came via the inter-fare," Mal stated.

"They're going to interfere with the challenge?" Jackson tensed, ready to defend Mal.

"No." Mal chuckled. "The inter-fare is an inter-borough thoroughfare. It's a fast way for transport disks to travel across the city underground. The disks magnetically interlock so they can travel at an even speed and not bump into one another. It's really an ingenious mode of transportation."

Jackson traced an imaginary number one in the air. "Chalk one up to the Luminans."

Mal stopped abruptly. "This is where I take my leave."

Johanna kissed his cheek. "Good luck."

Jackson snaked his arm around Mal's shoulder. "May the best man win—which is you, so just go out there and do it."

Mal smiled before walking through what appeared to be a black screen on the wall.

Jackson walked to it and tried to stick his hand through it, but yelped when he smashed his fingers against it. "It's solid!"

A nearby official said without emotion, "That entrance is preprogrammed to admit only the genetic coding of the challengers. All others will be turned away."

"I guess that explains it," Jackson said, massaging his fingers.

Johanna took advantage of the official's proximity. "Could you tell us how to get to the curators' viewing area?"

The official looked them over. "You're the Fantasians." He pointed to an entryway on the left. "The entrance is right there. Your seats are in the first row abutting the field. When you're stopped and asked for identification, show them your left palm."

"What good will that do?" Jackson asked, twisting his hand palm up.

Johanna gaped at his palm, and then turned over her own hand. They both had the Illumini constellation embedded in their palms, and Fantasia sparkled like a diamond chip. "Where did these come from?"

"I don't know," Jackson said.

The official noted their sudden distress. "That is a symbol that you've completed the Curator Orientation and Longevicus Ritual. It will stay with you always. Once bestowed, it can never be taken away, even if you are stripped of your duties as a curator."

"You know, I saw Mal's symbol when I shook his hand," Jackson said, "but I thought it was some weird tattoo."

Johanna smiled. "I don't think of Mal as the tattoo type."

"Me neither," Jackson admitted.

When they entered the curators' viewing area, they found Furst already seated. He rose when he saw them and bowed.

Jackson greeted the Dramatican curator: "Hey, Furst." He gave him a playful punch on the arm.

Furst looked at his arm with trepidation as his curly red hair pulled into tight wiry corkscrews. "A concern, do you have, to take up with me?"

"Concern? No. Just saying hello."

Johanna explained. "That's just Jackson's way of playfully saying hello. It's how we greet our friends on Fantasia."

"Friend, yes." Furst nodded, relaxing. Jackson had saved Furst's life by pulling him to safety after he lost his balance while trying to summon the overseers. The teen was the only person among a crowd of Dramaticans willing to risk his own safety to help the curator.

"Do you have one of these?" Jackson asked, holding up his left palm.

"A curator, I am," Furst said, revealing his own constellation.

"I heard one of your friends is running for overseer," Johanna said, joining in the conversation. "That must be very exciting for you."

Furst's hair tightened into wiry corkscrews again. "A countryman, Torran is. A friend, Torran is not."

"Oh." Johanna didn't know what else to say.

They barely noticed her sudden silence, for at that moment a parade of musicians marched onto the field and formed a colossal circle around the perimeter. Each wore a coat with a different jewel tone embellished with gold arabesques.

"There must be hundreds of musicians out there," Jackson said.

"On pageantry, Lumi thrives," Furst noted.

"That's what I love about it," said a voice behind them.

Johanna, Jackson, and Furst turned to find a beautiful woman seated directly behind them.

Johanna tucked a stray hair behind her ear. "Where did you come from?"

"I'm Natalia Dalura, the curator of Romantica. My kinswoman Dame Erato is a challenger, as is Malcolm Trees and Torran. I believe we will be the only curators in the viewing box, considering the last two challengers are curators themselves."

"I'm Jackson Roth." He reached for her hand and, for a moment, looked at it like he was going to kiss it. He gave it a squeeze and then introduced Johanna and Furst.

Natalia gave them a dazzling smile. "It's a pleasure to meet all of you."

Jackson moved to the seat next to Natalia. "Have you been to one of these before?"

"Only once," she replied, "when Pru Tellerence won the challenge. It was my first year as a curator."

"I heard the overseers were all males before that," Jackson said.

"Yes, and some challengers were angry that the tradition did not continue."

"Were …" Jackson paused and laughed. "I was going to ask if the challengers were anyone I might know until I realized they probably aren't around anymore." He gave it some thought. "Unless it happened recently. How long ago was the last challenge?"

"Pru Tellerence became an overseer three hundred seventy-seven years ago."

"Gee, is that all?" Johanna's tone had an uncharacteristic edge to it.

Jackson stared. "You look really good for your age. But what's really amazing, is that you speak the same language that we do. And I'm surprised that you said 'years,' because even though we measure time in years on Fantasia, I didn't think people from other worlds would."

190

Natalia laughed. To Jackson it sounded like the tinkle of crystal wind chimes.

"I'm quite sure we don't speak the same language, or use the same system of measurement. However, Lumi has a translation enchantment, so that everyone here can understand everyone else."

Jackson blushed. "I knew that. I don't know what possessed me when I said we spoke the same language."

JOHANNA KNEW EXACTLY WHAT POSSESSED JACKSON. Lust. Natalia Dalura was an exquisite beauty. She had an abundance of blond waves, high cheekbones, sensuous lips, and eyes the same shade of violet as the Luminan sky. Her floor-length ice-blue dress had a plunging neckline and was fashioned out of a diaphanous material that both molded to her curves and floated in the wind. To make matters worse, the Romantican curator's voice was as soothing and hypnotic as her laugh was lyrical.

Johanna considered her own outfit: tan slacks, brown boots, a brown silk shirt, and a burgundy scarf looped around her neck. It had seemed low-key yet sophisticated when she packed it, but now she felt plain and brown next to the Romantican curator. She sighed deeply, suddenly realizing how Jackson must have felt when she had shown an interest in Casanova.

Johanna stared at the center of the amphitheater. It had changed since that morning when she and Jackson had taken center stage. Now, even though the circle of overseers remained, Master Ryden Simmdry stood in the center of the Illumini constellation, and five podiums had popped up, encircling him.

She turned to Jackson. "Are you going to move up?"

She patted the seat next to her.

"I'm good here," he answered quickly, before asking Natalia about her home world.

Each of the candidates spoke about themselves and their particular talents and explained the benefit their strengths would bring to the position of overseer. Johanna heard Jackson laugh at something Natalia said. The only thing that prevented her from sliding into a deep funk was suddenly seeing a giant three-dimensional hologram of Mal's head floating above the center podium. He was the fourth candidate to take the podium, and Johanna realized she had been so obsessed with Jackson's reaction to Natalia Dalura, she'd missed hearing what Torran, Dame Erato, and Prophet IAN c. had said.

Get it together, she told herself. She concentrated on Mal's words rather than Jackson's infatuation.

"… but there is so much more to take into consideration," Mal said. "So allow me to discuss a matter that came to my attention a few weeks ago and plays into what is going on here today. It all starts with counterfeit library books."

Furst suddenly jumped up from his seat and left the curators' viewing area without a word to anyone else. An odd sense of vulnerability swept over Johanna as she sat alone in the front row of the viewing box.

—LOI—

18

LIKE A SWARM OF BEES, THE crowd buzzed at the possibility of a chink in the library's armor. They quieted when Mal began speaking again, hanging on to his every word. As Mal spoke, some of the Luminans discreetly looked at Nero 51 while covering their mouths, so he couldn't read their lips.

"What some of you might not be aware of," Mal's voice rang out, "is a recent breach of the portals brought on, innocently enough, by my own protégés."

Suddenly, all eyes were on Johanna and Jackson, as their three-dimensional images replaced Mal's and slowly rotated above the central podium. Jackson, engrossed in his conversation with Natalia, remained oblivious, but Johanna could see her humiliation etched on her face after being called to task by Mal.

"That rather unfortunate event," Mal continued, "resulted in my handpicked successor having to submit to three days of servitude in another realm. During that period, a counterfeit was discovered. I humbly ask the overseer's permission to enter a picture of the offending literary offering and an excerpt from Johanna Charette's own diary: 'Mal, I found a fake obelisk. It looks like crystal, but it's not. I knocked it over by accident and it didn't break.'

"This observation by a young curator"—Mal's voice increased in strength—"obviously begs the question"—Mal's voice increased in volume—"why does the Terrorian library have counterfeit literature on its shelves?"

THE CHALLENGER'S PODIUMS WERE POSITIONED according to the realms that they came from, placing Nero 51, Realm Twelve, right next to Mal, Realm Eleven. The Terrorian's tentacle snaked around Mal's neck in an instant. Everyone watched as Mal's holographic image turned blue. Ryden Simmdry raised both arms in the direction of the Terrorian curator. Nero 51 felt the overseer willing him to release his grip on Mal's neck, and as he fought the interference, he felt himself strangling. One of his tentacles had wrapped around his own throat, mirroring the pressure he put on Mal. He reluctantly released his grip, standing there—glaring at Ryden Simmdry.

"Lies!" the Terrorian curator spat out. "The Fantasians seek to discredit me to promote their own candidate into the role of overseer. Let us see this fake obelisk of which he speaks. Can he produce it?"

All eyes turned to Mal. "No, I cannot." There was defeat in his voice.

* * *

194

Mal's statement stunned Johanna. She had brought the fake obelisk to Lumi. Just before leaving Fantasia, she had run back up to her apartment while Mal and Jackson discussed the time machine and had thrown the counterfeit in her bag. Even though she had inserted pictures of it in her diary, she had never admitted taking it, nor had she shown the actual object to Mal. She rummaged in her bag for her diary, and wrote on the end page: *Mal, I have the obelisk here on Lumi.*

Mal turned to stare at her, as did all the overseers, who sensed what she had written in her diary. They stood as a group and faced her.

§ *These proceedings will be postponed for an hour, in light of the charges made by Malcolm Trees against Nero 51.*

The crowd grumbled discontentedly about the delay but, in true Lumi spirit, dared not publicly complain.

§ *Johanna Charette, because you specifically insti-gated the charge, we would like to see you in our chamber.*

Two Lumi officials instantly stood over Johanna, waiting to escort her inside.

Jackson shot up. "I'm going with her."

"No. Just the girl," one of the officials said.

"I'm a curator as well," he insisted.

§ *Jackson Roth, you were not sentenced to serve time on Terroria. Your presence is not warranted.*

The officials took Johanna's backpack and led her away, while Jackson remained behind.

Johanna felt her blood run cold. She had stolen a book from the Terrorian library. She had done it willfully, while being punished for destroying another Terrorian artifact. The only bright spot in the whole sordid affair turned out to be Jackson demanding to accompany her. He might be attracted to Natalia Dalura, but he still wanted to protect Johanna, and that gave her a small measure of warmth.

The overseers' chamber formed a circle, just like everything else at the amphitheater. Officials led her to the center of the room, where she stood and waited. Except for the guards at the door, she remained alone. Fifteen minutes passed; then a half-hour. Her legs were starting to ache from standing in one place for so long. She began pacing, relieved the guards did not try to stop her.

Finally, the overseers entered the chamber. A Lumi official handed Johanna her backpack.

They're sending me off to jail somewhere. Please don't let it be Terroria, she prayed. Then she realized another place might be even worse: the Toro Zone.

OUTSIDE, THE CROWD WHILED AWAY the delay by speculating about what might be going on inside the overseers' chamber. They were confused. Officials declared the delay after Malcolm Trees lodged a charge against Nero 51, yet both curators still stood in position at their podiums. Only Johanna Charette and the overseers had left the field.

Jackson tried, unsuccessfully, to talk to Mal about the strange turn of events. He knew only that Johanna had disappeared. He had been too busy flirting with Natalia to know why, and he couldn't ask Furst because the Dramatican had disappeared.

* * *

THE OVERSEERS TOOK THEIR PLACES around the chamber.

⌘ *Johanna Charette, show us the obelisk.*

Johanna dug inside her backpack, and pulled out the counterfeit. She weighed it in her hand, to make sure someone in cahoots with Terroria hadn't replaced it with the real thing. Confident it was the same obelisk she had taken from Terroria, she trembled as she handed it to Pru Tellerence. The woman calmly looked her in the eye, without a hint of what might be coming, and nodded almost imperceptibly as she took possession of the object. Like Johanna had done, she weighed it in her hand before telekinetically transporting it to Ryden Simmdry.

As Ryden Simmdry inspected the obelisk, the other overseers began nodding their heads. They all sensed the inferiority of the object and knew they faced a monumental task. If the Terrorians were selling library artifacts to buy weapons, merely replacing the Terrorian curator might not be enough to stop the mounting war effort. The overseers needed a strategy that would give them time to prepare for what might be coming.

⌘ *Johanna Charette, please wait here. If you wish to view the remainder of the Overseers Challenge, you can do it from this location.*

A screen showing the amphitheater appeared, as well as a chair.

The overseers filed out and returned to their positions on the field. Mal looked at the curators' viewing area expecting to see Johanna—and raised his brow at seeing only Natalia Dalura and Jackson in the section. He looked at the overseers, but they averted their eyes— with the exception of Pru Tellerence. She looked at Mal as calmly as she had gazed at Johanna, but it did little to lesson his anxiety for his protégé.

"What has been decided here?" an agitated Nero 51 shouted.

Ryden Simmdry opened his arms. ⌘ *The findings are inconclusive. A possibility exists that the Fantasian curator manufactured the obelisk she presented to us.*

Mal's head jerked back as if slapped. Inside the chamber, Johanna screamed, "Nooooo!"

NERO 51 MANAGED A SMILE. The unerring desire of the overseers to remain fair and impartial in all decisions had once again worked in the Terrorian's favor.

⌘ *Because of the uncertainty created by the charge of counterfeiting, Malcolm Trees and Nero 51 are eliminated from this challenge.*

It was Nero 51's turn to scream: "NO!"

Lumi officials approached both men to escort them away. Nero 51's tentacles struck out, knocking both officials away. Using his tentacles like rotors, he fled the field without looking back and disappeared. Lumi officials pursued him, trailing him to the Terrorian compound.

Countless millennia ago, the Terrorians had paid handsomely to have a secure embassy erected, citing their need for a high-humidity, low-oxygen biosphere that would support their unique life form on Lumi. Terroria was the only realm to have an embassy in the capital city, and no one dared enter it because of the unusual force field defending it. The overseers had chosen to not dismantle it, knowing there were occasions when Terrorians would have business in Lumi and would need a place to stay. And so the stronghold had remained through the ages, untouched. Now, it provided Nero 51 with a fortress as he planned an alternate strategy for library domination.

⌘*CHALLENGERS, THE FIELD OF COMPETITION HAS grown smaller. However, your answers are just as important as they were before. Selium Sorium will present the first scenario.*

Φ*A problem of catastrophic proportions overwhelms a realm. It could spell annihilation for that world and its civilization, but could be averted if the portals were opened to allow people to relocate. Debate the wisdom of such an undertaking.*

Torran jumped right in, stating that, of course, the portals should be opened. "Why let people perish when an alternative exists?"

Prophet IAN c. cut Torran off, claiming there was insufficient information. "What is this sudden catastrophe? Would it affect every living creature, or just a portion of the population?" The Adventuran went on to outline different levels of catastrophes and how he would react to each.

Dame Erato waited patiently before chiding both of them. "Under no circumstances should the portals be opened. Not only does such a move make other worlds susceptible to the same catastrophe—be it plague or nuclear cataclysm—but it opens the realms up to invasion as well." She then launched into a tirade about how the Terrorians nearly overwhelmed them all when the portals were recently breached.

Upon the conclusion of her remarks, the trio of challengers looked to Ryden Simmdry for their next question.

⌘*Galio Abbingdon, I believe you have our next*

scenario.

♪*In a closed-portal system, the scientific strides of some worlds may not benefit other worlds. What is your opinion?*

And so it continued until each overseer had presented a scenario and the contenders had answered to the best of their abilities. Normally, the overseers would retreat to their chambers to make their selection, but they telepathically determined that would be unnecessary because they all agreed.

LUMI GUARDS ESCORTED MAL TO the overseers' chamber. Johanna flew into his arms for solace.

"I'm so sorry," she cried, "for stealing the obelisk. It never occurred to me that doing so would put your chance to become an overseer in jeopardy."

Mal patted her back. "Everything happens for a reason. We must be content in knowing our actions are decided by the Fates."

"But you're losing something you worked very hard for, and I'll probably get sent to do hard time for grand theft on Terroria—or worse, in the Toro Zone. I've ruined both our lives."

THE PODIUM ON WHICH MASTER Ryden Simmdry stood slowly rotated, giving him an uninterrupted view of the crowd. The amphitheater was filled to capacity, with many additional spectators lining the walkways.

⌘*In a perfect society, educated contemplation and the careful weighing of all sides of an issue is desirous.*

Prophet IAN c. smiled, knowing his answers had encompassed that exact approach.

⌘*However, in these current times, the College of Overseers has a duty to all of our realms to coalesce into a unified and decisive front. We have carefully considered all the answers put before us, and after careful deliberation there is only one choice. It is our great pleasure to introduce to you our newest dean: Dame Erato.*

Several arms, forefingers raised, circled toward the heavens, but a larger number of spectators remained unmoved, for varying reasons.

"How wonderful!" Natalia Dalura cried as she threw her arms around Jackson.

He gently pushed her away. "Congratulations and all that, but I've got to find Johanna and Mal."

"Of course," she replied, but he barely heard her as he escaped the curators' viewing area. He asked every official he encountered where he could find Johanna and Mal. No one seemed able to help him.

★ *Perhaps I could have done more to prevent this from happening.*

Mal and Johanna both turned and stared at Pru Tellerence.

"I don't understand." Johanna wiped away tears with the back of her hand. "What could you have possibly done?"

⌘*A decision has been made.*

Johanna heard Ryden Simmdry and spun around looking for him, but he wasn't in the chamber. She turned back to Pru Tellerence for clarification. The overseer, who had seemed so forthcoming just a moment before, now appeared guarded.

The door opened, and the remaining overseers entered the room and again took their places around the circle. Johanna watched as Dame Erato took a seat next to Selium Sorium. The teenager bowed her head as a sign of respect to the new overseer, but couldn't stop the tear that escaped out of empathy for Mal.

⌘*Johanna Charette, stealing valuable artifacts is a crime of the highest degree, and is punishable by death.*

Johanna felt her stomach hit the floor and her skin chill. The sound of her heartbeat nearly drowned out the remainder of Ryden Simmdry' statement. *They're going to execute me.* She stared at the floor. She could not face the overseers.

⌘*We have determined that an obelisk of the same description is currently missing from Terroria, reportedly destroyed in a sudden explosion that Nero 51 blames on you and Jackson Roth.*

Tears ran down her cheeks. She didn't want Jackson to suffer for her actions. She couldn't let that happen. She looked up at Ryden Simmdry to defend her curator-in-training. "You have to let me explain …"

SWEAT BEADED ON JACKSON'S BROW, and he felt his underarms grow damp. No one could tell him where to find Mal and Johanna. He wouldn't be surprised if Mal had left the stadium after being disqualified, but Jackson refused to leave without Johanna. He spotted the guard who had helped them earlier, and explained his dilemma.

"Wait here, and I will inquire about your companions." The guard left Jackson cooling his heels in the hallway and disappeared behind a door that said "No Admittance."

* * *

Inside the overseers' chamber, Ryden Simmdry continued dispensing his ruling.

⌘*Further investigation indicates the technology used to create the counterfeit obelisk is beyond your realm of expertise, and therefore could not be attributed to you. Considering the object you presented to us is obviously a fake, you cannot be held liable for stealing an artifact. This obelisk is only a poor imitation of the real thing and is not held in high regard. Once again, Johanna Charette, you have done the Library of Illumination a great service by casting light on the nefarious deeds of the Terrorians and eliminating any possibility of their leader entering the rank of overseer.*

Remorse replaced a momentary feeling of relief. "You eliminated Mal from the challenge because of me, and that should not have happened."

⌘*Malcolm Trees's disqualification stands and will not be revisited.*

Jackson watched the official reemerge from the closed door. The guard escorted him to the black screen. "You may enter."

Jackson flexed his fingers, which were still sore from his previous attempt to navigate the black screen.

"It is all right, Jackson Roth. You have been approved to enter, and the pathway has been programmed to accept you."

Jackson gingerly felt the screen with his finger. He watched as it disappeared into the black abyss. He edged closer to it, sticking his whole arm through. "Okay. Here goes nothing."

He stepped through the screen and found himself in a hallway identical to the one he had just left. A guard stood at attention in front of a closed door. "I'm looking for Johanna Charette and Malcolm Trees. From Fantasia," he added, just in case the guard didn't know whom he meant.

The guard pressed a symbol on the wall, and a door slid open. He waved Jackson inside.

JOHANNA'S MISERY INCREASED. SHE FELT too ashamed to look at Mal, but couldn't stop herself. Then Jackson walked in, and she rushed into his arms. "I've ruined everything," she sobbed as Jackson wrapped his arms around her.

"It will be okay," Mal said to Jackson.

"It will not be okay," she exclaimed, surprised to see Mal smile at her and wink at Jackson.

Mal addressed the overseers. "We'll need a guard to escort us back to our hotel."

"To protect us from the Terrorians?" Jackson asked.

"No," Mal replied. "To protect Johanna from her Lumi fans who are so fascinated that a young woman had the power to stop Nero 51 from bullying his way into the position of overseer that she is achieving rock-star status as we speak."

"Rock star, huh? You know this means I'm still going to be the one at the library stuck with doing all the dirty work," Jackson said. His words got a half smile out of Johanna.

A pair of guards escorted them to a closed transport vehicle.

"Let's go back to the lodging and freshen up for the

new-overseer celebration," Mal said.

"Do we have to go?" Johanna whispered. "Can't we just go home?"

"Let's compromise. We'll freshen up and go to the celebration but stay only long enough to congratulate Dame Erato and show the college there are no hard feelings. And then we'll head straight back to the time machine and return to Fantasia."

"Okay, if that's really what you want to do."

"I knew you would do the right thing."

A HALF-HOUR LATER, THEY stood on a small line waiting to speak to Dame Erato. When their turn finally came, the newest dean took Johanna's hand and smiled.

Φ*I have you to thank for this honor. If it weren't for you and your foresight in taking the counterfeit obelisk, Nero 51 may very well be standing here right now.*

"For just a moment, I thought you were going to say my name rather than his," Mal said, laughing.

Φ*He would have bullied, and threatened, and found a way to flout our time-honored traditions.* She patted Johanna's hand. Φ*This young woman is very special, and I wouldn't be surprised if she were to become an overseer herself one day.*

★ *That would be magnificent.*

Pru Tellerence laid one hand on Dame Erato's arm and the other on Johanna's shoulder.

Johanna looked at the two women—the two most highly revered women on thirteen worlds. Her gaze settled on Pru Tellerence. "You never finished what you started to say before …"

Pru Tellerence held up a finger to stop Johanna.

★ *That … is a conversation for another day. Today, we celebrate the introduction of our new dean.*

Johanna sighed. As they walked away, she leaned over and quietly asked Mal, "Can we go home now?"

"Of course." He took her arm and gripped Jackson's shoulder, just before the young man popped a morsel of food in his mouth. "I distinctly remember you telling me to remind you not to eat anything before time traveling."

Jackson looked longingly at the food, and then put it down. "I guess I could hold out for some lasagna later on."

They returned to the Grand Illumi Hotel to pick up their possessions, then headed to the transport center where they had left the time machine.

As the disk carried them to the edge of the city, Johanna once again gave voice to her regret. "I'm really sorry, Mal."

"You've got to stop saying that. My chances of being appointed overseer were only one in five, and I may very well have lost.

"Meanwhile, you continue to demonstrate your value to the realms. Being told by the overseers that they can see you joining their ranks one day is a very strong recommendation of their trust in you. And being your mentor, some of that glory naturally rubs off on me. Besides, my value to the college has not gone unrecognized."

"What do you mean?"

"I can't talk about it right now. Suffice it to say that the results of this … let's call it an adventure, have not been in vain."

* * *

THEY ARRIVED AT THE TRANSPORT center to find officials swarming all over the place.

"What's going on?" Mal asked.

A small blue-haired man came running out of an office waving his finger in their direction. "That's the man who brought it here. That's Malcolm Trees," he exclaimed.

"I *am* Malcolm Trees, and at the risk of repeating myself, what is going on?"

"Your vehicle has been illegally appropriated."

"Appropriated?" Jackson questioned. "You mean stolen?"

"Taken without authorization," the little man cried.

"But who would do such a thing?" Mal asked.

"Nero 51," Johanna answered, without needing further proof. "I can smell him." She pointed to a wisp of mist rising from an oily spot on the ground. "Terrorian … uh … residue."

They turned and stared at her.

"And now," she continued, "he can travel back to a period in time when the portals were open. He'll carry out his plan to wage war against the Libraries of Illumination on all twelve worlds—thirteen including this one."

"We're doomed," Jackson groaned.

"He's been planning this war for a long time, and with the time machine, we'll never know when or where the Terrorians will strike." Johanna's shoulders slumped. "For all we know, he may have already launched his first attack."

—LOI—

207

MYRDDIN'S MEMOIR

19

THE NEWEST ROCK STARS AMONG the Library of Illumination curators found themselves stuck in the capital city of Lumi, or as Jackson liked to call it, the *Land of No.*

"Now what?" he asked. "It's not like I can call my mom and tell her I'm not coming home for dinner, *ever*, because our time machine has been stolen on a distant world."

⌘ *We will make sure you are safely returned to Fantasia.*

"Thank you." Johanna felt her shoulders relax—just a little. "It doesn't change the fact that the Terrorians have the time machine."

⦾ *That is a wrinkle in the fabric of existence.*

Jackson's eyes lit up. "Wow. Can I use that? It sounds amazing."

Pru Tellerence smiled.

★ *I'd like to escort them back to Fantasia.*

⌘ *That is the duty of Selium Sorium.*

★ *Please. I would love to see the library where these two fine curators work.*

◍ *It is not my place to say, but I have no problem with Pru Tellerence escorting Johanna and Jackson back to their library.*

⌘ *It is highly unusual for overseers to handle duties on realms other than their own. However, we are faced with unusual circumstances. It is decided. Pru Tellerence will accompany our young curators home. But first, we must convene the others. All must be apprised of the situation and allowed to contribute before the next step is taken. Mal, please see to your protégés' needs until Pru Tellerence returns.*

JOHANNA, JACKSON AND MAL BOARDED a transport disk and traveled to the park at the edge of the capital city. Johanna remained oddly silent during the ride, while Mal and Jackson discussed Luminan architecture and culture. Once they reached their destination, Johanna spoke. "If Nero 51 took the time machine, he can invade any of the realms whenever he wants by going back to a time when the portals were open. It may be as recently as last week, but he could choose an earlier time—perhaps before the Two Millennia War—and armed with the knowledge of what is to be, take steps to insure the Terrorians take over all the libraries and control all knowledge."

"You're right, of course. It's a very prickly situation."

"If only it were yesterday," Jackson said and sighed.

"If it were yesterday," Johanna reasoned, "we'd be all nervous about preparing for the Curator Orientation

& Longevicus Ritual. So what good would that do?"

"I don't know. I'm brainstorming here."

Mal laughed. "And rightly so. We do need to put our heads together if we want to find a way to thwart Terrorian tactics."

"'Thwart Terrorian tactics,' I like it. Wish I had said that."

Johanna groaned. "Between that and 'wrinkle in the fabric of existence,' I'm sure you can impress all your friends."

Jackson swung around and looked her in the eye. "Feeling a little snarky?"

"Yes. And I'm sorry if I offended you, but I need you to give this *all* of your attention. I know you're capable of analyzing situations, and it bothers me that you're more interested in saying *cool* phrases to your friends."

"Hey, I'm the one who wanted to brainstorm."

Mal intervened. "I think we need to allow everything that's happened here over the past two days—to percolate in our subconscious a while longer."

"You're right," she said. "I'm tired. I apologize."

Jackson put his arm around her shoulder. "Me, too." He kissed her neck.

★ *May I interrupt?*

Mal stood when he heard Pru Tellerence. "Of course. Have arrangements been made for transporting Johanna and Jackson home?"

★ *Yes. Are you ready to go?*

Johanna looked at Mal. "Will you be coming with us?"

"I'm afraid not," he answered. "My place is here."

She threw her arms around him. "I always hate

saying goodbye to you."

"I'll miss you, both of you. But as long as you have my diary, you'll always be able to stay in touch with me."

Jackson nudged Johanna. "And as long as I have your diary, I'll be able to stay in touch with you.

"Use your cell phone. I need my diary back."

"I don't have a cell phone."

"I still need you to return my diary."

"Why?"

"Because I journal the day-to-day events in the library. Whoever comes after us will need that information."

"Oh."

Mal shook Jackson's hand. "The next time we meet, I'll present you with a diary of your own. You each have unique experiences in the library and see events from different perspectives. It will be beneficial for both of you to journal independently."

"Thanks."

★ *It is time. Give me your hands.*

As soon as they joined hands with Pru Tellerence the trio disappeared.

Johanna and Jackson had only been away for two days, but it felt like ages. The lights in the Fantasian library turned on automatically and warm air penetrated the vast space.

"Honey, we're ho-ome," Jackson said in a singsong voice.

"Too bad there's no one here to welcome us, like a fluffy little kitten."

"You want a kitten?"

"I hadn't thought about it until I saw Mal again. When he first talked to me about being the curator, he took me upstairs to the residence and there was the cutest little kitten there named Ophelia. I think she was one of the reasons why I didn't fight Mal tooth and nail about taking over his position. I really wanted a kitten of my own and sought the unconditional love we could have shared. But then when I moved in, there was no kitten. I guess she was a prop of some sort to illustrate what *could* be. And we've been so busy, I haven't really thought about her. But now, I wish she had come with the library."

★*I had a kitten when I lived here.* Pru Tellerence had a dreamy far-away look in her eyes. ★*She was a silver miniature that went by the name Cassiopeia. I could swear she read minds, because she came before I called her, and led me to whatever I needed to find. She was the sweetest little thing.*

"When you lived here?" Johanna raised her eyebrows. "Do you mean when you were a curator, because Mal had been the curator here for hundreds of years before we came along."

★*Of course. I meant when I was a curator. The libraries are all very similar.*

Jackson's curiosity got the best of him. "How long ago was that?"

★*Before either of you were born. Please, I would love for you to show me around.*

"One guided tour coming up." Jackson held out his arm and Pru Tellerence gladly accepted it. "Right this way." The teen led the tour with the overseer at his side, and Johanna behind them. Whenever Jackson stumbled for a word, Johanna supplied it and would continue

212

speaking until Jackson took over again. They delivered their dialogue seamlessly, as if rehearsed, and showed Pru Tellerence all the aboveground levels of the library. As they stood on the seal directly beneath the cupola, Jackson asked, "Do you want to see the basement and sub-basements as well?"

★ *No. That's quite all right. Most of the libraries are identical in many respects, and this one is no exception.*

"If you want to see an exception, you should go to Terroria, where the ground is covered with oily mist. Or Dramatica where the floors are made out of glass."

"She's an overseer, Jackson. I think she knows."

★*For the most part, you're right. I represent Dramatica, and I've been to Mysteriose and Lumina. However, I've never been to Terroria. I was unable to attend the hearing when Nero 51 accused you of spying. From your description, it's not a library I look forward to visiting.*

"Mal mentioned most of the overseers hadn't been to all the libraries."

★*Correct. Most overseers have only been to their home worlds, the realms they represent, and Lumina.* She gazed off into the distance. ★*And now—with the exception of myself—Terroria. Any curator or overseer who's seen more than four worlds is very well traveled.*

"We've seen four realms," Jackson said, "but aside from that, I've never been out of the country. My country."

★ *I'm sure that will change. I have a feeling that you and Johanna are destined for greatness. Mark my words.*

"Greatness sounds good." The grandfather clock chimed the hour. "Uh, I don't want to seem rude or anything, but I think I should check in at home to see how my family is doing." He looked at Johanna. "Is that okay?"

She nodded. "Of course. I'll see you Monday."

"If you need me, call me at home."

"Will do."

★*Goodnight, Jackson. I look forward to seeing you again.*

"Will you still be here on Monday afternoon?"

★*That will depend on whether Johanna asks me to leave.*

Johanna gasped. "I would never do that."

PRU TELLERENCE LAUGHED. SHE WAS interested in getting to know Johanna better. There was something intriguing about the girl, and the overseer wanted to learn about her motivations and ideals. And there was a place she wanted to visit. A place someone had offhandedly mentioned years before that Pru Tellerence never forgot about. Fantasia could hold answers to questions she had kept dear for a very long time.

THE LIBRARY PHONE RANG. The mail carrier on the other end told Johanna he'd left a package for her in the vestibule. She immediately retrieved it and inspected the wrapping, but she didn't open it.

★ *Is something wrong?*

"There's something odd about the return address."

★ *Where is it from?*

"It says, Lighthouse, Skokholm, Wales. But I think they must have meant Stockholm which is in Sweden."

Pru Tellerence closed her eyes. She swayed for a second before opening them and walking over to a reference shelf, where she removed an atlas. ★*There is a Skokholm lighthouse in Wales.*

Joann walked over and looked at the entry. "I wonder if the same explorers who named Stockholm named Skokholm?

★*I believe so. Are you going to open the package?*

"It's probably just a book that needs rebinding. I'll wait until Monday when Jackson is here so we can work on it together. Bookbinding isn't his strong suit and he needs more practice. If I open it now, I'll just start working on it myself and that won't help him develop his skills. This way, we'll both be surprised by whatever literary treasure awaits us."

Pru Tellerence merely nodded. She, too, might be around on Monday to learn what secret the package held.

JOHANNA'S STORY ABOUT GROWING UP in a foundling home intrigued Pru Tellerence. It was a tale of woe she knew only too well—the loss of those closest to us, before we've had a chance to know them. In turn, she told Johanna how she had been a curator on Romantica before becoming an overseer. ★*At that time, there were no female overseers left, and when it came time for my challenge, most of the males scoffed at my chances. But I knew what the overseers were looking for and tailored my answers toward that end. You could see all the bravado and self-proclaimed superiority of my competitors deflate noticeably when the deans named me winner of the challenge.*

★*My first position was on Mysteriose, a realm ruled by high priests and priestesses. Obviously, the college expected my gender to be a huge help trying to tame the*

Mysterians, who had never fully returned to the fold after the Two Millennia War ended. They had joined forced with the Adventurans and Terrorians during the uprising, and remained unhappy about losing prominence after the war. Some of the male overseers before me had been bewitched by the priestesses and were subsequently forced into what you might call 'early retirement.' I didn't fare much better. Even though I'm female, the priestesses perceived me as weak, and they flouted library law. One of them, Magra, was curator of their library and thought of herself as more powerful than any overseer. I caught her charging patrons 50 bailon each to vacation in the library. She—

"Excuse me. Did you say 'vacation' in the library?"

★*Yes. Mysteriose is a class V library. Unlike your books, which come to life, the books on Mysteriose invite people into the story as a character. It's a popular vacation spot for Mysterians who want to live out their fantasies. But it's meant to be free. Libraries of Illumination never charged patrons for the use of their facilities. Except on Mysteriose. I told Magra she had to stop, but she refused, and there was a bit of unpleasantness. She overstepped her bounds by a large margin and lost her curatorship.*

★*I have since moved on to Dramatica, where the citizens are a delight to work with, and rules and regulations are respected. The Library of Illumination doesn't ask for much. We were established long ago to preserve ancient tales and history and have grown since then to protect every bit of knowledge that has been committed to paper, canvas, inidri, stone, bark, caspirt and various other materials on which whimsy, knowledge, and masterpieces are recorded. We serve all people in a way that protects our literary resources. I'm sure as curator of a class L library, you've wondered why your library isn't open to the general public. We've learned over the years that people in this realm aren't ready to accept living literature. You may argue that motion pictures are the same thing, however, the general public can't interact with a film. It's quite different on Educon, which is also a class L realm. Their citizens embrace a book's ability to come to life and interact with it to further their knowledge and education. Interacting with literature is in its infancy on your world.*

Pru Tellerence paused. Her use of the word 'infancy' sparked a faraway look.

"Are you okay?"

The overseer smiled at Johanna. ★ *Yes. I just remembered a promise I made to someone on my home world, Romantica. Her baby was abducted, and she believes it was brought here. Maybe you could help. Where might I inquire about a missing three-year-old child?*

Johanna drew in a deep breath. "You could try adoption agencies. If the child is only three, it's too young for … uh … slave trading, but could be too old to appeal to some couples. A lot of people here are more interested in adopting infants, so a three-year-old may have been left at a home, like the one where I was raised."

★ *Where would I find such a place?*

"I hardly know where to tell you to start looking. Every city, state, and country would have such facilities, and those are just the legal places. I'd hate to think she's a black market baby which is more likely, considering she was abducted from another realm.

"Do you have a picture of her?"

★ *Sadly, no.*

"But you do know what she looks like, and you can describe her."

★*I haven't seen her for a very long time.*

"If you haven't seen her for a while, and she's three, she may have changed dramatically since you last saw her. Does she have any distinguishing traits?"

★*She looks very young for her age.*

"Anything else?"

★*She has a birthmark behind her ear ... but nothing else that I can think of off-hand. I need to impress upon you the need to keep this just between us. The child's mother is very upset over her daughter's disappearance and doesn't want word to get out that we may be looking for the missing girl. So promise me you'll only discuss this when no one else is around. Including Jackson. Or Mal. Or any of the overseers.*

—LOI—

20

THE NEXT MORNING, JOHANNA HELPED Pru Tellerence contact local adoption and child welfare agencies to inquire about the best way to look for a missing three-year-old. Johanna helped set up appointments, but the overseer would not allow the curator to accompany her.

Nothing Johanna said could persuade Pru Tellerence to change her mind. "You'll get lost. You don't know your way around."

★*I'm an overseer. We have our own methods of transportation, which are quite accurate, and this is a personal inquiry that I must make alone.*

"You're going to stand out like a neon sign in church dressed like that. Do you have any, uh, normal clothing with you?"

★*Normal is in the eye of the beholder.*

"Yes. And there are a lot of 'beholders' out there who are going to give you a hard time if you go out in your robe and miter. Let's go see if I have anything in my closet that might work for you."

A navy blue suit with a knee length skirt appeared to be the best choice among Johanna's limited wardrobe. She had worn it the day she applied for her job in book services and again when the library board had set up a public reading that nearly ended in disaster because of a pawnbroker's greed. Johanna had purchased the suit at a second-hand store, and while well made, it was neither young nor trendy. That made it perfect for the overseer. Unfortunately, it was a couple of sizes too small. "I don't know if this will fit."

★*Allow me to evaluate and remediate.*

Pru Tellerence removed her miter hat. The long white hair that all the overseers had in common came off with it. The faux hair and hat had covered a coil of dark auburn tresses. Without the robe, the dean looked thinner than she appeared, but the zipper to the suit's skirt fought her when she tried to zip it. Pru Tellerence smiled serenely and shrunk to fit the suit.

Johanna gaped. "You don't know how many women in this country would give anything to be able to do that."

★*One of the blessings received when becoming an overseer is the ability to transmogrify, to change our appearance.*

"I hope it works for your feet, too, because you'll need to change into these shoes."

★*Yes.* Pru Tellerence's foot slid inside the pump. ★*They feel lumpy.*

"That's because the stockings you're wearing are way too thick. Have you ever worn pantyhose?"

★*I do not know what you mean.*

Johanna found a pair in her dresser and opened the cellophane packaging. She held up the shriveled hosiery for the overseer's inspection.

Pru Tellerence stared at the twisted bit of nothing.

"It stretches." Johanna slipped her hand inside and demonstrated.

The overseer didn't look convinced.

"I'll give you some privacy. Why don't you remove the skirt and see if you can slip the pantyhose on."

★*And wear only this in place of the skirt?*

Johanna couldn't hide her grin. "No, under the skirt. After you put this on, you wear the skirt over it."

★*That is yet to be determined.*

Johanna left the older woman to figure it out for herself.

PRU TELLERENCE EMERGED FROM JOHANNA's bedroom, fully dressed and sporting a different hairdo that looked modern enough to deflect undue attention.

"You need a handbag."

★*I have nothing to carry in it.*

"It doesn't matter. Women around here wouldn't be caught dead without one." She went into her room and retrieved a small red clutch. She stuffed a few tissues inside and a ten-dollar bill. "Here."

★*I have no need for Fantasian money.*

"I'd hate to see you get hauled off for vagrancy if anything unexpected occurred." She immediately thought of Lumi. "Loitering is greatly discouraged."

The older woman smiled.

"One more thing." Johanna ran out of the room and returned with an eyeliner pencil and a tube of lipstick. "I just want to make you look like … a local." She applied a little eyeliner to define the overseer's eyes and showed Pru Tellerence how to apply the lipstick.

"Wow. You kind of look like an auburn Catherine Deneuve."

★I'm not familiar with that person.

"Don't worry. It's a good thing."

★*While I am gone, you must protect my miter at all costs.*

"Your hat? Sure. No one's here but me. It'll be fine."

★*I prefer that you lock it away someplace. Do you have a strongbox? Or perhaps you could put it in the vault on sub-level six.*

"What vault on sub-level six?"

★*Don't you know? Never mind. I will acquaint you with it.* The overseer picked up the miter and walked to the panel leading to the basement stairs. Johanna followed. Pru Tellerence entered the storage room where Johanna kept extra chairs and approached the rear wall. She held the palm of her left hand against the bare stone. A low rumble preceded the lowering of part of the wall, which slid out of sight into the floor. Seven doors lay behind it.

"Where do these lead?"

★*That is a question best left for another day.* The overseer approached the door on the far right. ★*I need your assistance.*

Johanna walked over, and Pru Tellerence took the curator's left hand and placed it against the door lock. The door, much thicker and sturdier than it appeared from the outside, groaned as it swung open. Inside, Johanna saw a heavy marble and metal table, laden with very dusty books and scrolls. On the opposite side of the room, an unfathomable amount of gold ingots, shrouded in cobwebs, stood in irregular piles in a corner.

Pru Tellerence picked up a scroll and blew the dust off it. She unrolled it and scanned it. ★ *This is one of the original gospels that didn't make it into your Christian bible. It's the Apocalypse of Peter. The architects of the New Testament discarded a number of gospels just like this one.*

"Gospels … really?"

★ *Yes. Like diaries, they recorded events from the writer's viewpoint. Some were deemed fringe documents. In other realms, they appear bound as history texts on the appropriate sub-level, but here, the curators before you chose to save the original scrolls. Most curators in other realms made that same choice. The information contained herein is recorded throughout the system, but each library has its own collection of historic documents and artifacts that they choose to preserve.*

Pru Tellerence placed the gospel on top of some others, making space for her miter. She blew the excess dust away as she carefully placed the headpiece on the table. She removed a key from inside the miter and slipped in in her pocket. ★ *We can lock this room now.*

They left the vault, pulling the door closed. A series of clanks sounded as the lock moved back into place. Johanna stared at the other doors.

★ *On another day, Johanna, after I have culminated my business here on Fantasia, I will explain the significance of each door.*

Johanna sighed. "I never knew they were here. I never knew this," she swept her arm taking in the small vestibule, "existed."

★ *There is much to learn. I will assist you upon my*

return. A moment later, Pru Tellerence disappeared.

It took Johanna a second for the sudden disappearance to sink in. *I guess that's what she meant by her 'own method of transportation.'*

An afternoon delivery made Johanna spend the rest of the day wondering why the head of the library board wasted a sizable amount of money on little gold pins with 'LOI' engraved on them. Not only were they expensive, they called attention to a library that didn't want attention. He claimed they were for the library board, but only eight people sat on the board. The order she received contained one hundred pins.

Johanna didn't stop dwelling on the *pin problem* until the sun's shadows lengthened and Pru Tellerence failed to return. The woman had been gone for hours, and Johanna wondered what could be taking her so long. She held off having dinner, not wanting to seem rude by eating without the overseer.

By the time the clock struck ten, Johanna gave in to her growing hunger pangs and dialed the phone. "Hi, it's Johanna Charette. I'd like to have a platter of lasagna and a salad delivered to the Library of Illumination."

"The kid just left on a whole bunch of deliveries," the hostess answered. "By the time he gets back, it'll be closing time. Do you want to come pick it up?"

"I can't. I'm waiting for someone."

"Hot date, huh? No wonder Jackson is here without you."

"No. It's nothing like that." Johanna's mind raced. "Could you put him on the phone?" THUNK. The phone hit the counter before the voice on the other side

SECOND CHRONICLES OF ILLUMINATION

screamed Jackson's name.

"Johanna?"

She relaxed at the sound of his voice. "Hey, are you doing something important?"

"Shoveling pizza down my throat is *very* important. You never know when I'll be called upon to save the future of the realm. I need to maintain my energy level."

"Pru Tellerence went out this morning around eleven and hasn't returned yet. I don't know what to do."

"Do you want me to come over?"

"Would you mind?"

"No. I'm just about done, and those other jokers I'm with probably won't care one way or the other."

"Would you mind bringing my lasagna order with you?"

"Ahhh, the truth comes out. I'm just the messenger boy."

"No. I held off eating dinner because I wanted to wait for her. Now the delivery guy is gone and there's no one to bring my food. I need to be here in case she returns. However, I want to discuss the options with you, in case she doesn't. It's okay if you don't bring dinner."

"Yeah. Guilt me into it."

She heard his muffled voice ask, "How long until Johanna's order is ready?"

"I'll be there in fifteen," he told her before hanging up.

JOHANNA JUMPED WHEN THE FRONT wall slid open, and she frowned when she saw Jackson walk in with her dinner.

"Wow. I thought you'd be happy to see me. Now I'm

not so sure."

"I thought you were Pru Tellerence, although she didn't use the door to get out, so I don't know why she would use it to get back in. I just wasn't expecting you to use the front entrance. You usually come in the back way."

"That's when I have my bike. But Logan's got new wheels, so he volunteered to drop me off."

"I'm surprised you didn't invite him in."

"He's with Cassie and they're driving over to the pier to spend a little private time together."

"Borrowed the car from mom, huh?"

"Nope. He bought it while we were up on Lumina. Is that right? Up? If it's not here on Earth, I think of it as being up, even if it's straight out from the other side of the world, which would technically make it down."

"Up is fine."

"Anyway, his great aunt died and left him some money, so he bought a Mini Cooper."

"I guess they can't get into too much trouble in a car that small."

Jackson laughed. "You don't know Logan."

"How much do I owe you?"

"Consider it my treat—if you give me some. If you're going to hog it all for yourself, then you owe me twenty bucks."

"Let's go upstairs."

THE EDGES OF THE LEFTOVER lasagna curled up as it dried out awaiting the overseer's return. Jackson, his arm wrapped around Johanna, had fallen asleep on her couch. He woke when she jumped up to answer the phone. "He's right here Mrs. Roth. I guess we fell asleep watching TV." She handed the phone to Jackson.

"Mom? ... Sorry. ... We fell asleep in front of the TV. ... Church? ... You'd better go without me. ... Right. ... Bye."

"Everything okay?"

"She's worried because I stayed out all night. She thought something horrible had happened to me."

"I know how she feels. Pru Tellerence isn't back yet."

"She's a big girl. She can take care of herself."

"She's on an unfamiliar world and may have ended up in trouble."

"She's an overseer."

"Plato Indelicat was an overseer, and they *killed* him."

"Okay. Let's figure this out logically. Where did she go?"

"I can't tell you."

"What do you mean you can't tell me? How am I supposed to help you if you don't tell me?"

"She's doing something special for someone else and she made me promise I wouldn't mention it to anyone. Not even the other overseers."

"She may be an overseer, but they don't live forever. They can be injured and they do die. What if she's lying at the bottom of a pit somewhere? I can't help you if you don't let me. Besides, I can keep a secret as good as the next guy."

"She'll kill me."

"She wouldn't dare. Besides, I know how to hurt her. I saw what happened when they knocked Plato Indelicat's pope hat off his head. He shriveled up and died. I won't let her touch a hair on your head." He picked up a strand of her hair and rubbed it between his fingers.

Johanna pulled it away from him. "She's not wearing a hat. And don't go getting cute and sexy now, when Pru Tellerence could pop back into the room at any moment."

"Maybe she made herself doll-size, and she's hiding out on your bookshelf."

"How do you know that? I saw her shrink her size today to fit into my suit and shoes. It was weird."

"On the night the Terrorians tried to invade the libraries, Selium Sorium made himself smaller than a G. I. Joe action figure and hid out next to the pencil cup on the circulation desk."

"You didn't tell me that."

"There was so much going on while you were away. That was just a small point in a whole mess of details. I would have gotten around to mentioning it eventually."

"I guess I should take a shower."

"I'll wash your back."

"No, you won't. You'll go home and explain to your mother how we simply fell asleep after stuffing our faces with lasagna."

"She doesn't care."

"I think she does. She worries about you and that's a good thing. I've never had anyone worry about me and it's a lonely way to grow up."

"I worry about you. So does Mal."

"That's not the same thing. We're friends. We worry about each other. But it's not like a mother worrying about her child. That's a special kind of love and shouldn't be taken for granted."

"Fine. I'll go home and see my mom. Maybe I'll

change my clothes. But then I'm coming back here to brainstorm with you in case P. T. is still missing."

"P.T.?"

"She's got a freakin' long name and it sounds so formal. P.T. is just easier to say, you know?"

"Um hmm." She pushed him toward the door. "Go home."

JACKSON RUSHED TO RETURN TO Johanna, but before he could leave the house, his mother and younger sister returned from Sunday services.

Ava scowled at him. "Nice of you to stop by for a visit."

He stared at her. *Sarcasm? When did my sweet little sister turn into the enemy?*

"We were worried about you," his mother said, setting her purse on the table. "If you're going to spend the night with Johanna, at least say you'll be at the library."

"I didn't plan to spend the night at the library. She has an ... uh ... aunt staying with her and the woman went out last night and didn't return when Johanna expected her to."

Ava folded her arms. "I thought Johanna was an orphan."

"She is. It was one of the women from ... the ... home where she was raised. She calls her 'aunt' as a term of endearment." He could tell by the expressions on their faces they didn't believe him. It was the best he could come up with on the spur of the moment. "Anyway, gotta go. Johanna is waiting for me."

"You just spent the night with her Jackson Ryan Roth. You're eating lunch with us."

He had no choice. When his mother used his full name, she meant business. "Okay. Just let me call Johanna and tell her I won't see her again until this afternoon. If she thinks *two* people are missing, it will drive her bonkers."

"So she deserves the courtesy of a call, but we don't?" His sister turned with a huff and strode away. Jackson closed his eyes and his shoulders slumped in defeat.

—LOI—

21

Later that afternoon on his way to the library, Jackson stopped for a bouquet of flowers for Johanna. Confronted by dozens of varieties, he stood glued before the showcase.

"Can I help you?"

He turned to find a woman standing next to him. "I need flowers for my girlfriend, but I don't know what to pick."

"Long stemmed roses are always nice."

He frowned. "That may be a little too intense."

"What are you trying to say with your selection?"

"What?"

"What emotions are you hoping your flowers will ignite in her?"

"Ignite …." He nodded. "I want her to know I'm always here for her, you know? I want her to know I think the world of her."

"So you're looking for something more friendly than romantic?"

"No, friendly *and* romantic."

"I see." She slid open the glass door to the showcase and selected flowers. "Roses are all about romance, but the paler colors have sweeter meanings. Tea roses mean *always*—one of the words you just used to describe what you're trying to say. So let's put together a selection of tea roses." She chose some lavender stems. "These mean enchantment—."

"Enchantment is good."

"Coral for desire."

He blushed.

"Pink for sweetness. Yellow for joy. We'll round it out with baby's breath for purity of heart and add maidenhair fern which signifies a special bond of love."

"Yeah. That's good."

She wrapped everything in waxy tissue paper and tied it with a ribbon.

He thanked her and paid the bill.

JACKSON DROPPED HIS BIKE BEHIND the library and rushed through the back door to find Johanna curled up in a little ball on a reading room couch. "Is she back?"

Johanna barely moved. "I think we should contact the overseers. She's been gone more than twenty-four hours."

Jackson searched the cupola for the hook attached to its highest point. "We could do that, or we could give her another twenty-four hours just to be on the safe side. Not to mention, you said she didn't want the other overseers to know what she's up to, which is crazy considering they can all read each other's thoughts. I wonder how long she thinks she can keep a secret?"

"If she's not back by tonight, I don't think we'll have any choice."

"Here." He offered her the flowers. "I got these for you."

She managed a smile. "Thank you, they're beautiful. I'd better put them in water."

He followed her up the stairs to her residence. After she finished arranging the flowers, Jackson pulled her close. "Now that we're going to wait a little while before contacting the overseers, I know a few things we could do to pass the time." He lowered his head to kiss her.

"So do I," she answered, twisting away from him. "We received a package and I've been waiting for you to open it."

"Great," he replied without enthusiasm.

"You don't *want* to work on a book with me?"

"I didn't say that. I'd *love* to work on a book with you."

"Good, it's in the back."

JACKSON INSPECTED THE STAMP AND postmark. "So where do you think Skokholm Island WAL is?"

"It's off the coast of Wales. I looked it up with Pru Tellerence the other day."

"Hand me that iPad, so I can look for a map while you open the box." He surfed the web for a decent map and found one with a satellite view. "There's not a lot there—a couple of buildings and a lighthouse. The rest is green space and rocky cliffs."

Johanna pulled a clump of dried hay out of the

package and separated it from the treasure it protected. "The return address says it came from the lighthouse."

"Is it a bird book? This says the island is a bird sanctuary."

She examined the old book, which appeared to be handmade. The covering was fashioned out of thin hide stretched over two wood boards with a soft spine. It was no more than a container for the collection of very old papers tied up inside, but it did have one interesting detail. The front was hand-etched, "Myrddin Sóþspell," in gold.

Jackson stretched over to look at the book. "Myrddin Só… Sóbspell. Sópspell" Is that a "b" or a "p"?

"Good question."

"You ever see that before?"

"There are millions of books written in different languages. We could hardly be expected to be familiar with them all. And multiply that by all the realms."

"Yeah. But this one doesn't come from another realm. It comes from Wales." He typed variations of Myrddin Sóþspell into the iPad. "Google has no matching documents."

"Access the database and see if we have an Old English dictionary."

"What good is an old dictionary?"

"Not old as in aged, old as in *Old English*, which came before Middle English, which came before modern English—which is what we're speaking. At least, I am." She untied the leather cords holding the sheaf of papers together and pulled out a heavy piece of beautifully illustrated parchment showing a man at work behind a table laden with bowls and crockery. She stroked a corner with her finger to test the integrity of the colors. As soon as she touched it, a man appeared. He spoke in a language she didn't understand.

Jackson looked up. "This says some guy named Myrddin was the inspiration for Merlin the magician. Do you think that's him?"

The vision of the man became hazy for a moment, then re-gained clarity until he stood solidly before them. "If you summoned me in this manner, it means my life's work is in danger."

"Hey, he speaks English." Jackson said. "Do you think he knows the same kind of enchantment the overseers use so everyone understands him?"

Johanna ignored Jackson. "Who are you?"

"I am called Myrddin Emrys."

"Yep. He's the guy Merlin is based on." Jackson turned to their visitor. "So, like, can you do magic and stuff?"

"I am a bard, a philosopher, and a prophet."

Jackson held up the iPad. "This says you're a shape shifter, a sorcerer, and a wizard."

"Why did you call me here?"

"We didn't call you," Johanna answered. "We received a collection of manuscripts sent to us from Wales. When we opened it, you appeared."

"I must see the wrappings."

Johanna handed him the crude packaging. Myrddin carefully examined it until he spotted a bit of wax holding two sections together. He removed a small blade from a sheath buried within the folds of his robe and used it to carefully pry the pieces apart. He ran his thumb over a waxy red disc with a recessed seal in its center. "The

Brotherhood," he whispered. He turned the package over. "Who is Johanna Charette?"

"I am."

"Why would the Brotherhood send this to you?"

"I have no idea."

He looked at the packaging again. "The Library of Illumination." His eyes widened and his mouth opened. "I must have time to contemplate. Allow me to return to the confines of my memoir for a full sun and moon before calling upon me again."

Jackson held out the cover. "Wait."

"What is it?"

"How do you pronounce this?" He showed him the cover.

Myrddin ran his fingers over it. "Myr-thin Soth-spell. It is what you might call my memoir. But it's more. A diary. A journal. A collection of important documents and formulae. It is the history of my life's work.

"Now, if you would excuse me." He faded away.

Johanna replaced the illustration among the papers and slipped them inside the cover.

Jackson grimaced. "That's kind of sketchy, don't you think?"

"What do you mean?"

"He faded away *before* you closed the book."

"Hmmm. Does he seem familiar to you?"

"Nope. Never met the guy."

"There's something about him."

"Perhaps you met him hiking through the Middle Ages without me."

"Funny."

"Where could you have possibly met him?"

She shook her head. "I don't know. I guess everyone reminds us a little of someone else."

"Couldn't have said it better, myself."

"WE CAN'T DELAY CONTACTING THE overseers anymore." It was evening, and Johanna had just lost a not-so-rousing game of Monopoly to Jackson.

He snuggled up to her, but she pushed him away. "No."

"Why?"

"I don't want to be in a compromising position when Pru Tellerence decides to return."

"You see, that's where your logic is faulty."

"Excuse me?"

"You want to contact the overseers because you're afraid she's not coming back. But you don't want to *do anything fun* because you're afraid she'll walk in on us. If you really want her to return, you would compromise yourself—just so she can suddenly appear and catch you. I think it's the only way to get her back."

"I think you're the one with faulty logic."

"We've been together for nearly a year, but we're like a couple of twelve-year-olds. Don't you think it's time to take this relationship to the next level?"

"This is the worst possible time to do that. You'll be going away to college soon and—"

"Whoa, whoa, whoa! What are you talking about? I'm not leaving for college."

"You're graduating from high school this year. Of course you're going to college."

"I can get all the education I need right here."

"You're smart Jackson. You qualify for scholarships. You've got a great public service record. Your mom would be so proud of you. I would be proud of you. And you'd be setting a good example for Chris and Ava."

"Do you have a college education?"

"No. But I'm getting one."

"Where?"

"What does it matter where?"

"Because we're both curators and if you go away to college, I'm going to have to be here to hold down the fort."

"I'm not going away. I've taken a few courses online, and I've applied to Cranford University. I can take morning classes and still put in a full day's work at the library."

"Then, I can too."

"No, no, no, no, no."

"Yes, yes, yes, yes, yes. You can just forget about me going away to get a degree. If you want me to have a college education to work here, fine. But I'm staying in town, just like you."

Johanna changed the subject. "Do you need help carrying the ladder to the cupola?"

"No. But can I ask you something?"

"What?"

"Mal's in Lumi. Couldn't you just use his diary to ask him to contact them, rather than making me haul up the ladder and lasso the hook, et cetera, et cetera, et cetera?"

"She asked me not to tell anyone, and now you want me to bring Mal into it too."

"You don't have to tell him anything other than P.T.

is missing and ask if he can contact the overseers for you. That way, you barely tell anyone anything—until they force you to tell them something."

"Mal is going to want to know— "

"Know what?"

They both jerked around to face an intruder.

"Pru Tellerence, you're back!"

★*Are you surprised to see me back so soon?*

"Soon?" Johanna's eyes were as big as ping-pong balls. "You've been gone for a couple of days. We were, uh, discussing whether to contact the overseers because we thought something terrible had happened to you."

Pru Tellerence gazed calmly at Johanna.

★*We discussed the privacy of this matter.*

"Well. It's not like we did anything yet."

The overseer slowly turned her head toward Jackson.

"He doesn't know anything," Johanna said.

Jackson stepped back. "I know lots of things. Just … not … why you disappeared for so long and made Johanna crazy."

★*I am an overseer. I must be free to conduct business as I see fit and cannot worry about your reaction to the amount of time it takes or any secrecy it involves. If you would prefer, I could remove myself to a lodging.*

"That's not necessary. Now that I understand how you feel, I won't worry the next time business takes you away. It's just with Nero 51 running around with a time machine, I feared he might have taken you hostage."

★*That is a consideration. Now that I'm back, let us move past this issue.*

"Okay." Jackson grabbed his jacket. "I guess I'll be going. See you tomorrow after school."

Pru Tellerence nodded to Johanna. ★*Good night.*

Johanna made sure the doors were locked and the lights were out on level five before calling it a night. Something didn't feel right. The overseer had safely returned, but offered no reason for her delay, nor information about what she found on her trip. *Maybe she's just tired.* She turned in for the night, but tossed and turned for hours before falling asleep.

The following morning, Johanna woke to the smell of fresh baked pastry. She found Pru Tellerence in the kitchen eating a fragrant piece of bread studded with colorful bits and pieces.

"What is that?"

★*It's a Romantican specialty—brichi—a yeast cake flavored by flowers. As soon as I saw them, I knew we should share this for our morning meal.*

Johanna looked at the bouquet from Jackson. Pru Tellerence had decimated it. She opened her mouth to comment, but something held her back. "Will you be staying long?"

★*My business here did not provide the answers I hoped for, but I'm sure I will find the child here, somewhere. For now, I must return to my duties on Lumina and seek more information regarding the child's whereabouts.*

Pru Tellerence handed Johanna a piece of brichi. ★*Try it. It's wonderful.*

Jackson's Monday morning gym class did nothing to

help him work off steam. Afterwards, he hurled his gym shoes in his locker.

"You must hate those shoes," Logan said, punching Jackson in the arm. "Why so glum?"

Jackson shrugged.

"It's Johanna, isn't it? What's going on?"

"I feel like we're in the sixth grade."

"What are you talking about?"

"My relationship with Johanna is no more intense than my relationship with Cassie."

Logan stopped walking. "What relationship with Cassie?" His voice had lost its warmth.

Jackson turned to him. "I see Cassie, I kiss her hello. When I leave, I hug her goodbye. That's the extent of my relationship with Johanna."

"Hold on. Word is you spent the night with Johanna a couple of days ago."

"On the couch. Fully clothed."

"That sucks."

"Yep."

"What are you gonna do about it?"

"I don't know."

"Flowers?"

"Tried it."

"And?"

"Nothing."

"Maybe you need to shake her up a bit."

"How?"

Logan grabbed Jackson's arm. "C'mon."

Jackson shook him off. "We've got Sanderson's class."

"Sanderson's out sick. We've got a sub—that little

guy with the glasses. He doesn't even take attendance." Logan pulled Jackson out of the building.

Fifteen minutes later, they stood in front of Inklings tattoo parlor.

"I don't know about this."

"Chicken?"

"No."

"Then show her you're a man." Logan dragged him inside.

Behind the counter, a guy with tattoos covering every inch of his bulging arm muscles put down his cell phone. "Here for ink?"

Logan pointed to Jackson. "He is."

What kind of tat are you thinking about?"

"I don't know. Something small …"

Logan pointed to a design. "I think you should get this snake crawling up your left cheek and circling your eye."

"No." He looked at the proprietor. "Maybe something on my shoulder."

"Where she won't see it. Dude, you've gotta do better than that." Logan paged through a book of designs.

The tattoo artist checked out Jackson. "Spider on the side of your neck."

Jackson swiped at his neck.

"The design, dude. I'm suggesting we ink a spider on the side of your neck."

Jackson shivered. "No spiders."

"This look familiar?" Logan pushed the book in front of Jackson. The page was filled with different varieties of Celtic knots. "Doesn't your mother have a necklace with one of these on it?

"I'm not doing this for my mother. Besides, she'll have a hissy fit when she sees it. And she's not feeling overly fond of *number one son* right now." Jackson pulled the book closer. He tapped one of the illustrations a few times. "This is the one," he said after a long pause. "I want this on the side of my neck.

—LOI—

22

A SMATTERING OF TROOPS LINED up in the cupola of the Terrorian library. Only a small number of soldiers had signed on for this battle after learning the overseers had incarcerated many of their comrades on Lumina following their last invasion attempt. No one wanted to risk a repeat performance, however, Nero 51 had persuaded a number of his countrymen that the time machine almost assured their victory. They would travel back in time to the day Johanna Charette had arrived on Terroria, a time when the portals were guaranteed to be opened, but before Johanna Charette had any opportunity to spy on them.

Nero 51's plan called for them to start their attack on just one realm—Juvenilia—a world populated by children. He doubted they would give his troops much resistance.

They would have to be careful. Only three

Terrorians could squeeze into the time machine at one time, so Nero 51 instructed the first wave of troopers to wait in the cupola until at least a dozen of their fellow soldiers arrived before fanning out.

He inspected each team. "Once you have reached the minimum number of soldiers, use the decimator to destroy books. Complete one section before continuing to the next one. When you are engaged by Juveniles, switch your weapons to stun and capture as many of them as possible without leaving the library."

One of the troopers raised a tentacle. "What if our soldiers are captured, like during their last attack?"

Nero 51 sneered. "Whatever went wrong during the last attack can be blamed on the curator Johanna Charette. She alone is responsible for our failure. But now she won't have a chance to report to the overseers, because we're going back in time to her first hours on Terroria.

"We want to set up a power base before striking out against the rest of Juvenilia. It is important we destroy all their literature before doing that, which means disintegrating every book on 1,311 levels. It may take some time, and it's important to complete that task before the Juveniles get a chance to send out a warning."

He raised a tentacle into the air. "T'cra!"

"T'cra," the soldiers replied in unison, their tentacles raised.

Nero 51 puffed out his chest. "Team one, to the time machine," he bellowed.

JOHANNA MINDLESSLY SHELVED BOOKS RETURNED earlier in the day. She didn't want to think about Myrddin

Sóþspell. She didn't want to think about Pru Tellerence. She didn't want to think about Jackson. And yet they all elbowed each other for space inside her psyche, so she chose to think about cotton wool instead. No color, no agenda, no demands.

A crashing bicycle interrupted her state of oblivion. She turned when Jackson burst through the door. In that instant, the lights flickered and a low rumble shook the building.

Jackson stopped short. "Earthquake?"

"I don't know."

"What else could it be?"

"I'm not sure, but every fiber of my being is telling me something fundamentally important has just changed."

"Yeah, like what?

She shook her head. Aside from a gut feeling, she had no explanation why she felt the way she did. Her eyes focused on Jackson's neck. "What happened to you?"

His hand flew to the bandage. "Bee sting."

"Ouch. I would have thought it too early in the season for bees. I guess I'm wrong."

Jackson hesitated. "It could have been a wasp. Maybe even a spider. All I know is it stung like hell and it's all red and swollen." At least the end of his statement was true.

"Sorry." She heard someone pounding the wall in the vestibule. "Illumination."

The wall slid open, revealing a deliveryman. "You ordered groceries?"

"Yes," she answered, taking a bag. "I expected you hours ago."

"Flat tire." He held out the other bag to Jackson. "You need to sign for them."

"Of course." Johanna held the bag in one arm while signing with her free hand.

"Did you feel the earthquake?" Jackson asked the driver.

"You mean when my tire went flat?"

"No. Just a moment ago."

"Nope." He tucked the signed receipt under his arm. "Thanks," he replied as he did a quick about-face and hurried out the door.

"I'd better bring this upstairs before the milk spoils," Johanna said, walking toward the stairs.

"Odd that he didn't feel anything." Jackson followed her up to the residence and into the kitchen. His eyes narrowed when he spotted the vase with severed stalks and only a few flowers left. He dumped the bag on the table.

"What's wrong with you? There are eggs in there." She followed his gaze to the vase. "Oh that. I can explain."

"Don't bother." He turned abruptly and walked out.

Johanna put the groceries away, then went downstairs to find him. "Jackson," she called out. He didn't answer. She searched all the rooms before she finally pulled the back door open. His bike was gone. She closed her eyes for a few moments, exhaling slowly. *What is going on with everyone?*

JACKSON LAY ON A PATCH of grass and bounced a basketball off the back of his house. His brother Chris came out the door. "You gotta stop doing that. You're giving me a headache."

"Yeah. What do you care?"

"I care that Mom is going to blame us for all the marks on this side of the house and I'm telling her straight out you're responsible."

"Whatever you want…"

Chris's voice went up a notch. "What is wrong with you?"

"Why do people keep saying that?" Jackson bounced the ball again.

"It's Johanna, isn't it?"

"I gave her flowers, you know, like that old ad, 'say it with flowers?' She destroyed them. I guess that tells me what she thinks of our relationship."

"What do you mean—*destroyed them*?"

"She cut them up or broke them or something. I was just over there and all that's left are a bunch of dead stems and a few scattered buds."

"Maybe it was an accident."

"No. It was very deliberate. She left them on the counter where I would be sure to see them."

"Did you ask her why she did it?"

"Nope."

"Maybe you should give her a chance to explain."

"She said that, you know?" He mimicked Johanna in a whining voice. "'I can explain.'"

"So what was her explanation?"

"I didn't hang around for the answer."

"But aren't you supposed to be working there? Don't you *need* to work there to get paid?"

Jackson glared at his brother.

"I don't care what you do, bro', but Mom needs the money," Chris continued. "And I'm not making that much at The Burger Pit."

Jackson sighed.

"So why don't you just go back to work and tell Johanna you left the water running or something."

"She thinks little enough of me as it is, and you want me to tell her I'm an imbecile as well."

"Yeah."

Jackson tossed the basketball against the house. Chris smacked it away on the rebound and watched it skitter out of his brother's reach. Then he turned and went back inside.

Pru Tellerence looked at a long list of child welfare and adoption agencies. There were hundreds—possibly thousands—of them, and out of the entire realm she had only completed her search of agencies in one state of one country.

The image of the three-year-old child remained fresh in her mind, yet none of the hundreds of young children she'd seen were the child she now sought. *No matter.* The longevicus blessing meant Pru Tellerence didn't need as much sleep as normal beings, and if she searched day and night across time zones, her slow spiral around the globe should eventually reunite her with the child in question.

Finding the youngster, however, proved elusive. The overseer had gained entry to orphanages and foundling homes in various places, but could not find a child with the one distinguishing mark she knew to look for—a tiny star-shaped birthmark behind the little girl's right ear.

Her stomach sank when it occurred to her the child could very well be dead. It had been a long time, and youngsters in institutions had less access to healthcare than children with families. The child could have died in an accident or been killed by an act of war. The harder she searched the more disillusioned she became, and she wondered if she was wasting her time.

JOHANNA PULLED OUT MYRDDIN'S MEMOIR and opened it to the illustration she'd seen the day before.

Myrddin instantly appeared.

"Gōdne æfen …" His image flickered. "Good evening."

"More than a day has passed," Johanna said. "Is there anything new you can tell me?"

"Apparently, someone or something is after my life's work."

"Is this person looking for something in your history to discredit you?"

"Not exactly."

"What then?"

"I have conducted a number of experiments in my laboratory that are coveted by others."

"What sort of experiments?"

"Too many to detail. However, I believe the spells desired by the dastardly interloper have either to do with transmogrification or alchemy."

"Spells?"

"They called me a magician. I had to have *some magic* in my arsenal of tricks."

"Alchemy is changing base metal into gold."

"Yes. And there are other uses. I experimented with various alchemic elixirs to prolong life."

"What's transmogrification?"

"As the young man said earlier, it's ... shapeshifting."

"You can really do that?"

"Indeed."

"Successfully?"

"Of course successfully. There wouldn't be much reason for anyone to want my notes if my spells failed. They're quite successful."

"Why were they sent here?"

"This *is* the only Library of Illumination on Fantasia, is it not?"

"You know about Fantasia?"

He studied her face. "I know a great deal about Fantasia, as do you."

"Yes. But that's because I'm a curator."

"Yes. Well. I, too, was a curator."

"Oh!"

"And now, we must secure my memoir."

"There's a vault downstairs."

"I know."

Johanna picked up the book and the wrappings and carried them to sub-level six. Myrddin trailed behind her. She found the seven doors and opened the one on the far right.

The sorcerer walked inside and stopped in front of Pru Tellerence's miter. He stooped down to study the constellation on the front. "Why is this here?"

"One of the overseers left it here for safekeeping. I guess she forgot to retrieve it before she returned to Lumina."

"She wouldn't be able to return to Lumina without it."

"But she did."

"Impossible. She must still be on Fantasia."

"She's not. I'm sure of it."

"How can you be so sure?"

"She said goodbye."

"That means nothing. However, traveling deans do usually lodge in Libraries of Illumination, which leads me to believe, if she is still within this realm, she remains here in secret. I must find out what she's up to."

Johanna felt her face grow hot. "Is that any of your business? You're a magician from the Middle Ages, and even if you *were* a curator at one time, you aren't anymore. You have no business poking into Pru Tellerence's business."

Myrddin huffed. He placed his memoir next to miter hat and then disappeared.

Johanna closed her eyes and took a deep breath, exhaling slowly while she counted to ten. She locked the vault and returned to the circulation desk to find Jackson playing with the gong.

"Where were you?" Jackson asked. "I looked for you from the cupola on down and couldn't find you. I was just about to pound on this thing to see if you responded."

Johanna took the mallet out of his hand and placed it where it belonged. "I was downstairs, putting Myrddin's memoir in the vault."

"What vault?"

Johanna opened her mouth to answer, but didn't want to get into a long explanation about Pru Tellerence's miter hat. Instead she asked, "Why did you run out of here before?"

"You know why. If you didn't like my flowers, you should have told me. I could have given them to my mother."

"I loved your flowers. But I overslept this morning and when I woke up, Pru Tellerence had already cut the blooms off the stems and baked them into bread. I was just as stunned as you were to see them destroyed."

"The way you've been acting toward me lately, I thought *you* did it."

Johanna's stomach quivered and her heart raced, but she tried not to let it show. "Nothing has changed between us," she replied, barely above a whisper.

"Show me." Jackson pulled her over and placed his hands on either side of her face. He stared into her eyes as he rubbed her lip with his thumb.

Johanna immediately stiffened. She forced herself to snake her arms around his waist and tilted her head.

Jackson channeled a lot of emotion into his kiss, and Johanna relaxed and responded. Eventually they had to come up for air, and Johanna gasped when she noticed Myrddin standing a few feet away with his arms crossed over his chest.

"YOU'RE BACK!" JOHANNA CRIED.

"You must find whoever sent you my memoirs and ascertain the name of the person interested in stealing my work."

"How did you get out of the vault?" she asked.

"I'm a sorcerer!"

Jackson nodded. "You can't beat that."

Johanna glanced at him, before speaking to Myrddin. "How are we supposed to figure out who's after you?"

"You must go to Skokholm, to the lighthouse, and

find the *Eahta Frean fram Drycræft.*"

Jackson shook his head. "In English, please."

"*Eahta Frean fram Drycræft* is a secret brotherhood of sorcerers. It means the 'eight masters of wizardry,' and you must locate them."

"Eight, huh?" Jackson joked. "Why not seven? Or ten?"

"There are eight specialties of wizardry: alchemy, transmogrification, time manipulation, prophecy, conjuring, healing, telekinesis, and totalis pereamus."

"Right …. What is totalis pereamus, exactly?"

"Total annihilation."

Jackson narrowed his eyes. "So, like, he can get rid of someone or something that's bothering him?"

"Total annihilation, of either your realm, or if he's exceptionally powerful, *all* realms."

Johanna raised one finger. "There's no one who can actually do that, is there?"

"There was once a sorcerer who possessed that power. He chose to turn his power upon himself rather than allow others to use him for nefarious purposes. We are all indebted to him. He is the only *known* sorcerer to possess that power, but who's to say there couldn't be another? Just because we don't know of someone's existence, doesn't mean that person does not exist."

Jackson and Johanna just stared at Myrddin.

"When you find *Eahta Frean fram Drycræft*, show them this." Myrddin removed a ring from his finger and handed it to Johanna. The ring bore the same symbol embedded in the sealing wax found on the memoir's packaging. "They will recognize it and know it is mine. You need to discover whom they believe is trying to decipher my spells, and what they think the usurper's plans are. Time is of the essence. You must leave immediately." The wizard's eyes widened and he disappeared.

JOHANNA HANDED THE RING TO Jackson. "You'd better go. I have to watch the library."

Jackson shook his head and refused to take it. "I can't do this alone. Besides, he gave the ring to you. Maybe Mal will babysit the library. Or *Jeeves*. Or *Mrs. Doubtfire*."

"Do you really think Mal might do that?"

"Get out his diary and ask him."

"I think I will."

It didn't take long for Johanna and Jackson to receive an answer.

—LOI—

23

Terrorians quietly arrived in the foreign library and waited until their troop numbers reached the required minimum. They silently adhered to the plan laid out by Nero 51 and began demolishing books section by section. Within the hour, all the arcane books normally stored in the cupola had been obliterated.

One of the troopers motioned to the others to remain still while he descended to the main floor. The cupola stairs in all the libraries were built as one unbroken circular staircase that linked the first and fifth levels only. There were no gateways to the other floors. The only way down from the cupola was that single circular staircase.

The soldier quietly moved down the stairs—not an easy task for someone with big flat feet, but he had trained for stealth and made it to the main level without incident. He looked around for forms of life, but saw no one. He signaled the others to make their descent.

It was a time consuming affair. The troopers had been advised to descend one at a time so their combined weights wouldn't make the old metal in the circular stairs groan. When the next Terrorian had completed his descent, he remained in position while the first one quietly made his way to the farthest reaches of the next level and began decimating books.

Each new soldier to make the descent relieved the one before him, freeing him to work on the destruction of books. Most of the books on levels one though five had been turned into dust before the door to the antechamber opened.

Johanna and Jackson finished assembling a book that had come in for repair. The clock had just chimed the hour when they exited the antechamber. Johanna's heart nearly stopped when she heard footsteps descending the cupola staircase. She and Jackson both looked up at the same time and she grabbed his arm and signaled him to be quiet, while she slowly nudged him into the shadows of the nearest stack.

"What's going on?" he whispered.

"I don't know. But remember when the building shook and you thought it was an earthquake?"

"Yeah."

"I think this could be related to that."

"You think we're being invaded?" His volume increased.

"Shhh…"

"We're dead. We've got no weapons. We've got nothing."

Johanna's mind raced. There had to be something

they could do to protect themselves. She carefully removed a metal bookend from one of the shelves and handed it to Jackson. "Maybe we can use these to crack a skull or gouge out an eye," she whispered.

"Great. Hand to hand combat and you think this will save us."

"Have you got a better idea?"

The footsteps stopped.

"The only way to get out of here alive is to throw this as hard as you can and run out the front door," Jackson said. "On my count, one …"

"A count of what? Three? Ten?" Johanna's voice quivered.

"Three. Okay? One—"

◍ *That will not be necessary.*

Johanna's eyes widened. She peeked around the bookshelf. Selium Sorium stood beside Mal at the circulation desk.

"Hi," she said. "We didn't expect you."

Jackson walked out beside her still holding the metal bookend.

"I'm surprised at your surprise," Mal said. "After all, you did ask me to watch the library."

◍ *Without a time machine, Malcolm needed me to escort him to your world.*

"Right." Jackson looked for a place to stash the bookend.

"It's just that the whole building shook before, and it unsettled me," Johanna said. "It felt like something bad had happened."

◍ *Indeed. We felt it, as well. But we have yet to ascertain if there is a threat.*

"Still, it seemed like a good enough reason for me to visit Fantasia for a while and watch the library so you two can go off on vacation."

"Vacation? We're not going on vacation. We need to go to Wales because a magician named Myrddin claims someone is trying to steal his book of spells.

◍ *Oh dear.*

Mal leaned toward Johanna. "Merlin the magician was here?"

"We received his memoir, and he appeared when I touched one of the illustrations. He said the only reason why the fraternity of magicians he belonged to would send me the book, is if someone is trying to steal his spells."

"Did he mention who he thought the culprit might be?"

"No," Jackson said. "He just told us to go to Wales and find eight guys who can help us."

◍ *When will you leave?*

Johanna replied, "He told us to go immediately."

"But we can't." Jackson grabbed her arm. "I've got to go home and pack a few things and square things with my family. They're going to raise hell if I just disappear again."

◍ *Do it now, without haste.*

"I'll be back within the hour," Jackson called over his shoulder as he headed out the back door.

"Hold on." Mal handed Jackson a small leather diary with his initials on the cover. "Stay in touch."

Jackson flipped through the pages. "Thanks."

"And don't worry about the library," Mal said. "I think I know a thing or two about how to handle the place."

Johanna finally smiled. "It's good to have you back."

FURST APPROACHED THE MAIN READING room and immediately knew something was wrong. He could smell it. Having been to Terroria when the Fantasians were accused of spying, he knew what Terrorians smelled like, and his hair pulled into tight little ringlets as he covertly made his way to the bell tower entrance through a hidden door in the coatroom. He climbed the stairs to the bell tower and quickly made for the ropes. The sudden peal of the library bell alerted all Dramaticans that something was not right at the Library of Illumination.

The curator poked his head out of a circular window in the tower to see if anyone emerged from the library entrance. He didn't see any Terrorians, but he didn't want to take any chances. He hoisted himself through the window and jumped to the walkway below.

People hurriedly approached, but the curator prevented them from entering while he explained why he'd rung the bell. They amassed into a huge mob, afraid to go inside, but ready to defend their realm.

Dramatican conciliators—law officers—congregated off to one side, discussing a course of action. They decided they were more in need of an army, so the head conciliator went to fetch the military provost. Within a short period, Dramaticans with "special training" stood outside the library. Unfortunately, their only duty in recent history had been to march in formal parades. Consequently, they were woefully unprepared for what awaited them. As for the provost, his only area of military expertise was to coordinate the parades and rehearse his militia several times a year.

FIVE REALMS AWAY, AN OFFICIAL at a Russian orphanage ordered all three-year-olds gathered in one main room, before escorting Pru Tellerence in to inspect the children. It helped that the translation charm allowed her to speak perfect Russian in a local dialect and accent. Russia had a ban in place on some foreign adoptions, and officials wanted to be sure Pru Tellerence had no plans to facilitate an American adoption.

She used a spell to put their minds at ease and calmly went from child to child, quietly questioning them while looking for birthmarks behind their ears. One little auburn haired girl pulled away when the overseer tried to check her ear. Pru Tellerence calmed her by telling her a fairy tale. When she felt she'd gained the youngster's trust, she again asked if she could look behind her ear. The little girls eyes brimmed with tears. Pru spoke softly as she held the girls hair back. Pru Tellerence spoke softly as she held the girls hair back. She found a raw burn mark behind the three-year-old's ear as if someone had used the child to snuff out a cigarette, or perhaps, used the cigarette to disguise a birthmark.

JACKSON RETURNED TO THE LIBRARY and found Johanna packing. "You're taking a suitcase?"

"I only want to take a backpack, but we'll be gone a few days and I don't know if I can fit everything."

"Well, you can't take all that."

"I guess if I wear dress pants and a nice jacket on the plane, I can stuff my jeans and a couple of tee shirts and underwear in my backpack, and a dress for dinner, oh, and a sweater or shawl and high heels, along with some makeup and my electric toothbrush and the flatiron for my hair and my hair brushes, and a pair of sneakers ..."

"Whoa. Do you really need all that stuff? Can't you take a regular toothbrush and leave the flatiron at home? And ditch the dress."

"What if we want to go out for dinner?"

"Then wear the dress on the plane. But I think you're overthinking this packing stuff. It's not like we're going on our honeymoon or anything."

She felt her hair follicles bristle. "Fine. I'll leave the dress, heels, and flatiron home."

"Now you're talking."

She meticulously folded each item before placing it in her backpack.

"I don't know why you're being so careful. It's only going to get wrinkled in your backpack."

She inhaled deeply as she silently counted to ten. "Right." She picked up the last few items and stuffed them in her bag.

Jackson picked up a slim volume on Wales Johanna intended to pack. "Where do we get tickets?"

She took the book and zipped it into the front compartment of her backpack. "I ordered them online. That's why I'm still packing."

They heard Mal call them before he entered the residence. "I took the liberty of obtaining these for you." He handed them a pair of booklets.

"Don't tell me they're going to give us some kind of a crazy test or ritual in Wales," Jackson said.

"Passports!" Johanna gave Mal a hug. I didn't even think of them. I've never been out of the country, so I've never had to apply for one."

Jackson opened his. "Cool. And look at this. It's good for ten years."

"We won't be gone that long," Johanna said as she slung the backpack over her shoulder. She picked up her purse and stuffed the passport inside."

"And you'll want to use this." Mal handed Johanna a small plastic card with the Illumini constellation on it.

"Is this a credit card?" Johanna asked.

"Yes. You're going away on official library business since it concerns one of the books remanded to our care. So the College of Overseers is paying for all your expenses."

"Maybe we can upgrade our plane tickets to first class," Jackson said eagerly.

Johanna used her sternest voice. "We are not going to abuse our privileges. I already booked our tickets and those are the tickets we'll use."

"Whatever," Jackson said sheepishly.

"Let's go. The taxi should be out front by now."

Mal placed his hand on her shoulder. "I don't have to warn you to be careful, but I can't let you go without saying it just once. Don't worry about the library. Everything here will be fine. You two just do what you have to do." He kissed Johanna's cheek and shook Jackson's hand. "Good luck."

The taxi horn honked, signaling the driver's impatience. Johanna and Jackson said goodbye and headed out.

FURST ADVISED THE DRAMATICAN MILITARY about their invaders' multiple tentacles with far reaching capabilities.

"Be ready to spring into action, you must."

"The crowds back, we must keep," the military commander said.

"Done, consider it," Furst replied.

The Dramatican soldiers stormed the library and faced a race of beings they couldn't begin to comprehend, armed with devastating weapons. The Terrorians took aim and soon several Dramaticans were frozen in force fields before they could avoid being captured.

When Furst had advised the soldiers to spring into action, he meant it literally. Finally, a Dramatican trooper, on seeing a Terrorian take aim, leapt high over the invader's head and shot him in the back with a pistol crossbow that fired powerful, four-blade broadhead arrows. The arrows appeared to be a medieval design forged out of metal, and although their power could not rival the decimators, they still gave the Dramaticans the means to avoid total obliteration.

While this transpired, a lone Terrorian trooper continued to erase books from the shelves of the library.

"I AM TAKING THIS CHILD WITH me," Pru Tellerence insisted for a third time.

"Impossible. The child stays here." The Russian official took the little girl's arm and tried to pull her away.

★*Imperium.*

The Russian official eyed Pru Tellerence warily as he let go of the little girl's arm.

"We're going home," Pru told the youngster, taking her hand. She turned to the official. "Her birth records, please."

The official nodded to a clerk who disappeared into

a back office.

While they waited, Pru Tellerence sang softly to the child who stared at her with wide, blue eyes, but said nothing. The clerk returned with a sealed manila envelope, which Pru Tellerence immediately ripped open. She searched the documents looking for clues related to the child's birth. The record was sparse. "There's not even a mention of her name here. She must have a name." She looked expectantly at the official.

"Izabella," one of the staff members said. "We call her Izabella."

Pru Tellerence stooped until she was eye level with the child. "Izabella. What a pretty name, but such a mouthful. I think I'll just call you Bel." She returned the papers to the envelope, folded it, and stuffed it in her borrowed purse.

"Good day," she said, nodding curtly at the officials. "You can consider this child *adopted*."

JOHANNA AND JACKSON WAITED in a long line to check in at the airport. When they finally reached the ticket counter, the agent told them someone had made a mistake.

"Don't tell me we have to wait in another line," Jackson whined.

"You didn't have to wait in this one," the agent replied. "You're first class passengers and could have checked in at priority services."

Johanna glared at Jackson.

"What?" he said. "I didn't do anything."

"Would you like to tell me how we ended up in first class?" she whispered.

"You ordered the tickets. You tell me. I had nothing to do with it."

The agent handed them the new tickets. "Bags?"

"We have one each," Johanna replied.

"Yes," the agent said. "Would you like to check them?"

"No," Jackson answered. "We'll carry them onboard."

"Can I see them?"

They both held up their backpacks. "That's fine. You'll have to go through security, but you can get in the priority line. It's much shorter."

"Thanks," Johanna said as she retrieved their passports.

"Gate eighteen."

"Gate eighteen, got it." Jackson nodded at the agent, grabbed Johanna's hand and led her away from the crowded counter.

"What time is it?" she asked.

"About half past eight. Our plane doesn't board until a quarter past nine. Let's get something to eat."

"They may give us food on the plane."

"Who knows when that will be?"

They quickly got through security, and Jackson scouted out different places to eat. "This one looks good and there's a corner table open. Let's eat here."

"Let's just get something portable that we can eat at the gate. I wouldn't want to miss the plane."

"They're not going to leave without us."

"Please."

"Fine," he said. "We'll pick up sandwiches and soda and eat at the gate."

But the seating area served two different gates and was jam packed, so when they got there, they were forced to eat standing up.

Jackson struggled to balance his soda while eating his sandwich. "Isn't this fun and exciting."

Johanna rolled her eyes. "Just eat. And don't talk with your mouth full."

He didn't say another word until it was time to board the plane.

—LOI—

24

Pʀᴜ Tᴇʟʟᴇʀᴇɴᴄᴇ ᴇᴍʙᴀʀᴋᴇᴅ ᴏɴ ᴀ mini shopping spree with her 3-year-old charge in tow. Izabella had only the clothes on her back and needed various items. Once they'd purchased sufficient garments and sleepwear to clothe her for a week, the overseer took the tot into a toy store. The youngster stayed glued to her side but Bel's eyes took in everything. Finally, Pru Tellerence held out a doll and a stuffed kitten. The child touched the faux fur on the kitten and moved closer to rub her face against it.

"You're sure you don't want this," the overseer asked, pushing the doll closer to the youngster, but Bel did not reach for the doll. Instead, she clutched the kitten as if it were a lifeline.

The overseer paid for the purchase and proceeded to their next stop.

Mᴜᴄʜ ᴛᴏ ᴛʜᴇ Tᴇʀʀᴏʀɪᴀɴ ᴛʀᴏᴏᴘᴇʀs' chagrin, they did

not land on Juvenilia as expected, but on Dramatica. "Where are the docile kiddlets they promised us? What are these leaping creatures?" And they didn't expect the inhabitants of the realm they invaded to possess weapons. Terrorians excelled at inflicting pain, but not at tolerating it and would much rather be decimated than painfully gouged by a four-blade broadhead arrow.

"Do not allow them to break through our ranks. Keir 414 must have time to finish clearing the shelves."

"What good will that do?" a new Terrorian recruit asked. "They must have books and maps and manuals in their homes they can rely on."

"It doesn't matter. This is a Library of Illumination. When the information kept here disappears, the contents of their personally owned literature and documents will vanish. There will be no record of their history, their battles, and their accomplishments. Mathematic and scientific formulae will cease to exist. Thousands of years of recorded documents will be nothing more than a memory. They will become powerless."

THE FASTEN SEATBELT SIGN WENT off and Johanna's grip on Jackson's arm loosened. "I don't think I'm cut out for flying."

He rubbed the spot to restore circulation. "Why would you say that? This is so cool." He stood to stretch his legs.

"Where are you going?"

"I don't know. For a walk, I guess. I want to see the rest of the plane. You coming?"

"No. I'll stay right here, thank you."

"Suit yourself."

A flight attendant approached him. "Can I help you, sir?"

"I'm not a 'sir.' I'm Jackson." He stuck out his hand to shake hers.

She obliged him. "The lavatories are right behind the curtains." She pointed over his shoulder.

"Thanks." He disappeared into the next compartment.

Jackson looked around. The seats weren't as large or luxurious, but were generous enough. "Why does everyone complain about coach? This looks comfortable."

A man looked up from a nearby seat. "This isn't coach. You're in the business section."

"Where's coach?"

The stranger maneuvered his thumb like a hitch-hiker. "Back there, behind the partition."

Jackson made his way through the compartment and disappeared into another section of the plane. The seats were definitely smaller.

"Okay. Maybe coach is a little tight."

A woman shook her head. "If you want coach, it's back there."

Jackson saw another set of curtains and ventured past them. The next section was so crowded there was barely enough room in the aisle to maneuver past. He walked as far back as he could and found himself in one of the galleys.

A lone flight attendant stocked a cart with beverages. "Need something?"

"No. I just wanted to see what the rest of the plane looked like. I've never flown before."

"There's not that much to see, really."

"Haven't you been to first class? It's a lot different than it is back here."

"Are you a first class passenger?"

"Yeah. And I could really get used to traveling that way."

"So could everyone else."

Jackson stuck out his hand. "I'm Jackson. What's your name?"

"Beck," the attendant replied. He ignored Jackson's proffered hand and continued to load the cart with bottles.

The plane hit turbulence and Jackson lost his balance. He grabbed the flight attendant's arm to steady himself. A pinging sound rang out and the seatbelt sign went back on.

"I suggest you go back to your seat and strap yourself in," Beck advised.

"Was that turbulence? It really wasn't as bad as I thought."

They hit another pocket of unsettled air and Jackson's feet literally left the floor. He grabbed the cart to keep from falling. "Maybe you're right."

"Where are you headed?"

"Skokholm Island. It's in Wales."

"A bird fancier, are you?"

"Nope. I'm going to look for a group of magicians."

Jackson finally received Beck's undivided attention. "Magicians."

"Yeah. Have you ever heard of the Eahta Frean fram Drycræft?"

The attendant's expression froze. "Never heard of them. You'd better return to your seat now."

"See you." Jackson headed back to the front of the plane.

The flight attendant reached for more beverages. As he did, the sleeve of his shirt pulled back exposing a wrist tattoo of a dragon rampart entangled in a double eight Celtic shield.

SCORE UPON SCORE OF DRAMATICANS arrived at the library, ready to do battle.

Pleth pushed to the front of the pack carrying a bucket of pitch and rags. "Wrap this around the arrows, I will. Up their pants, this will light."

"No!" Furst shouted. "Burn down the library, you will. An option, that is not."

"More books, we can get," Dungen said. "Our world, we cannot allow them to invade."

Someone in the crowd chanted, "Fire, fire, fire …"

Pleth tied a bit of rag around the end of his arrow and dipped it in the pitch.

"No! Do this, you must not," Furst screamed, but to no avail. His fellow Dramatican lit the arrow and when a Terrorian looked out of the front door of the library, Pleth took aim and shot it into the invader's chest.

The resulting high-pitched squeal would be slow to leave Dramatican memories. The Terrorians had oiled their skin before battle to protect it from the dry air in Juvenilia. The flaming arrow ignited the oil and the Terrorian fried faster than calamari in a restaurant kitchen.

Some of his fellow troopers witnessed his distress and tried to retreat, but there was no way back to their homeland. The time machine that delivered the soldiers was far, far away and would not return for hours.

JACKSON KNELT NEXT TO JOHANNA's seat. Her eyes were closed tight and her white knuckles clutched the armrests.

"You okay?"

Johanna opened her eyes and nodded. "Where were you?"

"I told you, I wanted to see the rest of the plane. Be glad you're not sitting in coach. Those people are packed in like cattle. There's hardly room to walk."

"That's what you went to do? Check out coach?"

"Pretty much. What did you do while I was gone?"

"Pray."

"For what?"

"A safe flight."

The plane hit a pocket of turbulence and dropped several feet in a split second. Johanna's face went white. Jackson's stomach clenched. "Maybe praying isn't such a bad idea." He rubbed the side of his neck.

"Is that bee sting bothering you?"

"What bee sting?" He suddenly realized what he'd just said. "I, am, uh … pretty convinced it couldn't have been a bee. It's too early in the season." He closed his eyes, wondering why he kept up the charade. *It's my neck, and I can get it tattooed if I want.* Still, Jackson wasn't ready to show the artwork to Johanna.

He didn't have to think about it for long because their flight attendant arrived with dinner menus, and their conversation changed to what they'd have for dinner. "Steak with peppercorn sauce. That's what I'm having," he said, "with sautéed potatoes."

"I think I'll have the salmon."

The flight attendant returned. "Champagne?"

Jackson smiled at her. "Sure."

She poured them each a glass of champagne before moving on.

Jackson leaned close to Johanna and whispered, "I guess they don't realize how old we are."

"We're old enough to drink wine in the U.K."

"Oh." He thought for a second. "It was more fun when I thought we'd be drinking on the sly."

"You would think that."

After dinner, Beck stopped by Jackson's seat. "I have something for you." He handed Jackson a bottle of ale. "It's a local brew from Pembrokeshire, near Skokholm Island. Since you've never been there before, I thought I'd give you an introduction to what the area has to offer."

"Hey, thanks." Jackson chugged a generous amount of ale. "Want some?" he asked Johanna.

"I think I'll pass."

He took another pull before yawning. "Maybe I'll take a snooze." He played with the seat buttons until his seat was fully reclined.

Their flight attendant opened an overhead compartment and removed a duvet.

"Thanks," he mumbled before yawning again and sinking into a deep sleep.

"I'm glad one of us can sleep," Johanna murmured as she thought about Jackson. She knew he'd fall asleep immediately and appear innocent, even angelic, in repose. But try as she might, every little sound or movement disturbed her and she would not be blessed with a few hours rest.

She closed her eyes, but they immediately flew

open when she sensed movement in the area. The flight attendant who had given Jackson the beer was crouched down next to his seat. "You can take that beer away," she told the attendant. "He has no more use for it."

THE FLIGHT ATTENDANT NODDED AT Johanna as he removed the half-full bottle of ale and walked to the rear of the plane. He returned to the first class cabin a few times. Whenever he did, he noticed that Johanna remained keenly aware of everything going on near Jackson's seat.

THE DRAMATICANS FELT EMPOWERED WHEN they saw other Terrorians quickly fall back inside the library. "We can win this battle," Dungen shouted as he lit an arrow and headed toward the library doors.

Furst stood dumbfounded. Nothing he had encountered during his career as curator prepared him for the ruination about to ensue.

Inside, Terrorians squealed at the sight of flaming arrows. Hurl 881 spun his tentacles like a fan trying to blow the flames back at the Dramaticans, but his spin worked in reverse, drawing the heat and flames closer. He ducked back behind the stacks, but the Dramaticans pursued him and he unwittingly led them to where Keir 414 stood destroying their books. The Dramaticans became enraged.

They shot at Keir 414, but the Terrorian turned his decimator on them instead of the books, and when the men in the rear saw their kinsmen disappear, they scurried out of the building to rethink their defense.

* * *

THE NEXT MORNING, JOHANNA GRATEFULLY accepted a cup of coffee from the flight attendant.

Jackson awoke with a start and threw off the duvet as he struggled to sit up. Tiny beads of sweat covered his forehead. "I feel awful."

"Coffee, sir?"

"Do you have anything cold? I need something cold."

"Orange juice?"

"Yes. Please."

Johanna unbuckled her seat belt and bent over him. "Are you okay?"

"I don't feel so good."

"Are you sick?"

"I don't know." He closed his eyes until the attendant returned with orange juice.

Johanna got some aspirin from her backpack. "Take this. It may make you feel better."

"Thanks."

He scratched the side of his neck and the corner of the bandage came off.

"Let me take a look at that sting."

Jackson didn't have the energy to stop her.

Johanna gently tugged away the gauze and her eyes widened when she saw a scabbed-over, oozing tattoo. "Were you going to tell me about this?"

"It's a surprise."

"It's infected."

"Maybe that's why I feel so bad."

"What possessed you?"

"It's the symbol in the library."

Johanna squinted, trying to look past the infection.

She could barely make out a triquetra design with the initials L O I in the center. She shook her head. "Like I said, what were you thinking?"

WHAT COULD HE TELL HER—that he got the tattoo while overcome with depression because he thought she destroyed his flowers? Nope. It was better that she thought of him as unpredictable.

The flight attendant returned with a first aid kit. "Will this help?"

"Thank you." Johanna opened the kit and looked for an antiseptic towelette. "This might sting." She gently dabbed the tattoo.

Jackson grimaced as she wiped away pus and put antibiotic cream on the tattoo. She covered it with a fresh bandage.

He leaned his head against the airplane seat and closed his eyes.

"Did they explain to you that this might happen?" she asked.

"No. We only discussed the design."

"Maybe it will look better when it heals, but right now, it looks like a big mistake."

"Without risk, there is no reward."

"Nice platitude."

"Works for me."

"You don't have to look at it."

"I can see it in the mirror."

"When was the last time you looked at it?"

"I, uh, haven't exactly looked at it. I got it and Logan covered it up with a bandage so I wouldn't have to explain it to everyone."

"And you made up the bee sting story."

"Lame, huh?"

Instead of answering, Johanna just shook her head.

The flight attendant returned to ask about their breakfast selection. Jackson immediately chose pancakes and sausage.

Johanna smacked his arm. "I thought you didn't feel well?"

"I'm never too sick to eat."

"Just don't throw up on me."

"I wouldn't think of it."

INSIDE THE FANTASIAN LIBRARY OF ILLUMINATION, Mal conferred with Ryden Simmdry and Selium Sorium.

"We must retrieve the time machine. I'm not saying this because I'm personally liable for it—which I am—but because the Terrorians are going to use it to wreak havoc."

◍ *You are quite sure they have it?*

⌘ *Our actions would be clear-cut if you had witnessed them taking it.*

"I did not see it happen, but Johanna reasoned it out and her observation was sound."

⌘ *What was her observation, exactly?*

"She found a small puddle of oily residue on the ground near the time machine's resting place and correctly identified it as Terrorian waste product. I had a sample tested to make sure her assumption was correct, and she was one hundred percent accurate."

◍ *The Terrorians arrived by escort. They had no reason to be at the field housing the time machine. I wonder how they even knew of its existence?*

⌘ *That is a very good question.*

"I will endeavor to find out how they knew about it, but it will be difficult if I'm right in thinking there's a spy in our ranks."

◑ *A spy? On Lumina?*

⌘ *Malcolm, you have an uncanny knack for discerning these truths.*

"Maybe, but people are tight-lipped. They'll be afraid to give me information if they suspect a spy and fear retribution. Frankly, there's no way I can promise them safety.

⌘ *You must be given the ability to operate unhindered.* Ryden Simmdry closed his eyes, as did Selium Sorium, just for a moment. ⌘ *Malcolm Trees, it give me great honor to name you the Chancellor of the Exchequer.*

"The Exchequer? You're putting me in charge of collecting taxes?"

⌘ *I could name you Chancellor of War, but that would scare the perpetrator away. As Chancellor of the Exchequer, you will undergo all the blessings befitting an overseer, without the actual title. You will be advised in the ways of transmogrification and your consciousness will become attuned to our own. But do not fear, your private thoughts will remain your own. You will be trained, thusly. As Chancellor of the Exchequer, you will be free to audit the financial offices of every realm, and be privy to the gossip that abounds within their governments. And you will not need a time machine to travel, for you will have the transmogrification blessing.*

"How does transmogrification do that?"

⌘ *It will allow you travel as wind and light, sound and heat.* Ryden Simmdry clasped Mal's shoulder.

"I'm honored by your trust in me. How difficult is it to master?

⌘*As your young Jackson Roth might say, 'you'll get the hang of it.'*

—LOI—

25

THE CAPTAIN ANNOUNCED THEIR IMPENDING arrival as flight 8183 prepared its descent into Paris.

"Did he just make a mistake?" Jackson wondered aloud. "I thought we were going to Wales."

"No mistake. We have to change planes."

"So now I can say I've been to Paris."

"Barely. But you will be able to brag that you've been to Orly Airport."

"You're closer to the window. See if you can you see the Eiffel tower."

"All I see are clouds."

"Maybe when we get closer to the ground …"

But they didn't get to glimpse the tower. All they saw was the inside of the airport and the waiting area for their connecting flight. Before too long, they boarded a shuttle that took them to their plane.

"Do you think they'll offer us more champagne?"

"It's still morning. Why would you even think about drinking champagne?"

Jackson grinned. "Because it's there?"

Johanna hopped out of the shuttle and climbed the boarding stairs to the much smaller plane. Inside, the seating options were limited.

"What happened to first class?" Jackson whispered in her ear.

"I don't know. I haven't flown any more than you have."

Before long, the small plane took off, en route to Wales. The flight lasted a couple hours and by the time they touched down, Jackson was raring to go and Johanna was ready for sleep.

"You want to sleep first?"

"I haven't slept all night. I was too busy watching you."

"You watched me while I slept?"

"I tried to."

"Either that's incredibly creepy or really sexy."

Johanna made a face and pushed ahead of him. "We'd better convert some dollars to pounds before we leave the airport."

"That's why you're good to have around. You think of everything."

"And why are you good to have around?"

He squared his shoulders. "My incredible personality and good looks."

"So you're form and I'm substance?"

He smiled. "You're my very favorite substance in the whole world, and across several realms."

They exited the Cardiff Airport in search of their

hired car.

Jackson peered into the empty vehicle. "You think it's easy driving on the wrong side of the road?"

"I don't think they consider it the wrong side of the road."

"Yeah. How difficult can it be?"

"Very difficult, so I'll do the driving."

They approached the rental car counter and saw a sign listing the minimum age for drivers as twenty-three years old.

Jackson turned his back so the guy behind the counter couldn't tell what he was saying. "Now what are we supposed to do?"

Johanna approached the counter. "I believe there's a reservation for a car for the Library of Illumination?"

The clerk checked his computer and smiled. "May I have your driver's license?"

Johanna handed it over.

The clerk reviewed her license and paused. "You're only eighteen."

"Is that a problem? When I made the reservation, no one mentioned an age restriction."

"It's just that I'll have to charge you a surcharge because you're under twenty-three."

"Fine." Johanna handed him the credit card Mal had given her. It didn't take long to sign the contract and get directions to the Tafarnwyr Inn in Pembrokeshire.

Johanna yawned as she slid into the driver's seat.

"You sure you don't want me to drive?" Jackson asked.

"I'd better," Johanna answered, "even though I'm beat. I signed for the car and besides, the rental guy is watching us from the window."

Jackson threw his backpack in the back seat. "Drive on, then," he said, just before bumping his head getting into the vehicle. "This thing's even smaller than Logan's Mini Cooper." He slouched down in the seat. "But doable. Very doable."

FROM THE RELATIVE PRIVACY OF another car with dark tinted windows, an observer watched their every move. Once they pulled away, he made his way into the car rental agency.

"I just saw a couple of airline passengers whom I promised to help. Did they get their directions to Pembrokeshire?"

"I gave them a map to the Tafarnwyr Inn. They'll do fine as long as they follow my directions."

"Diolch. *Thanks.* I don't feel so bad now, knowing they'll get where they need to go." He'd been to the Tafarnwyr Inn more than once and knew one of the barmaids working there. These kids might prove to be a problem. If so, they should be easy enough to take care of.

FURST FROWNED AND SHOOK HIS HEAD. "Understand, I do not. Just disappear, how could they?"

Dungen's eyes darted nervously between the curator's face and the front door of the Library of Illumination. "A weapon, they have. Without a trace, it destroys. Gone, the provost is. Gone, Elrod and Hout are. Gone, the books are."

Furst's ringlets tightened. "The books!"

"Destroying the books, he was. Empty, most of the

284

shelves are."

Furst looked into the eyes of the gathering crowd. "Some arrows, grab. Me, follow."

One of the men who had watched the other Dramaticans disappear shook his head and backed away. Furst lunged forward and pulled the retreater's crossbow out of his hand. "An arrow, I need." The man handed him his entire quiver. "Me, follow!" Furst loaded an arrow and stormed the library with a few reluctant Dramaticans trailing behind him.

He discovered a dead Terrorian in front of the circulation desk, a weapon entwined in his tentacles. "This, take," Furst whispered, handing a friend his crossbow, so he could extract the foreign weapon from the dead invader's grasp. With it in hand, he said, "Retreat, we will," and the group quietly exited the library.

Outside, Furst played with the weapon. It had a trigger similar to the one on the crossbow pistols. He used the Terrorian weapon to shoot at tall grasses swaying in the wind. They froze in place. "Odd, it is, but disappear, it did not." He continued studying the firearm and flipped the only other moving part he saw. He aimed at the same grass and fired again. It immediately vanished. The people surrounding him gasped. He flipped the switch back and aimed where the grass had been just moments before. A chunk of earth in the immediate vicinity disappeared. Furst's eyes widened. "Destroys, it does. Reversible, it is not. Use this, I will. Come!" Once again, the band of Dramaticans, fortified knowing they had a weapon as strong as the Terrorians, re-entered the library.

PRU TELLERENCE NEEDED TO RETURN to the Library of

Illumination before she could leave Fantasia. She could not travel without her miter, so with Izabella's hand clasped firmly in her own, she told the youngster to close her eyes and transported them back to the library reading room.

The overseer felt her stomach drop when, instead of Johanna Charette, she found Ryden Simmdry, Selium Sorium, and Malcolm Trees conferring with each other about matters of state.

⌘*Pru Tellerence.* Ryden Simmdry stared at the female overseer.

She had let down her dark auburn hair, which now flowed past her shoulders. A skirt that stopped at her knees exposed her legs. And her form-fitting clothing showed the curvature of her body. His pulse quickened, but he immediately regained his composure when he noticed the child grasping her hand. ⌘*Who is your young friend?*

★*She is a Romantican child—spirited away from the loving arms of her mother. I promised that I would do all in my power to see the child safely returned to her homeland.*

◍*How odd that she came to be transported to this realm from Romantica? I would not think it possible.*

★*The portals were open for a time and obviously used for ill purpose.*

◍*Yes, of course, that must be the answer.*

Ryden Simmdry stooped down until his eyes were even with the girl's. He took both her hands and spoke out loud. "What is your name?"

The youngster stared back wordlessly.

★*Izabella. Her name is Izabella and she's had a long journey. I thought I'd take her home with me for a few days, before returning her to Romantica.*

⌘ *What would be the purpose of that if her mother is waiting for her?*

Pru Tellerence masked her feelings behind a wall of calm. ★*Her mother is a tradeswoman, and is away for a fortnight, traveling on business. Caring for the child seemed like the selfless thing to do.*

⌘*Indeed.*

Laughter interrupted their discussion. They looked at Selium Sorium who now sat beside Izabella on the floor and made a small trinket appear from behind her ear.

Ryden Simmdry returned his attention to Pru Tellerence. ⌘ *Your miter is in the vault.*

★*I know. I left it here for safekeeping. Where is Johanna Charette? I need her to open the vault so I can return to Lumina.*

⌘*She is not here. She has traveled to Skokholm Island on a matter of great importance.*

Pru Tellerence raised her eyebrows. ★ *The package. She received a package from Skokholm Island, but refrained from opening it while I was here.*

Ryden Simmdry watched the female overseer carefully. ⌘*A secret society mailed her the package to protect the memoirs of a sorcerer named Myrddin.* He saw her pupils dilate as she understood the importance of his words. They held each other's gaze, saying nothing.

Selium Sorium continued to entertain the child and did not witness their nonverbal exchange. Only Mal wondered what powerful secret passed between the two overseers.

* * *

JOHANNA AND JACKSON ARRIVED AT the Tafarnwyr Inn by late afternoon. The proprietor showed them two rooms across from each other and Johanna told Jackson to wake her in time for dinner.

So now what am I supposed to do for the rest of the afternoon? He threw his backpack on the bed and went outside to have a look around. A two-minute walk took him to the edge of the village, where all he could see were fields of grass defined by rows of trees.

Jackson returned to the inn. "Is it possible to borrow that bicycle that's leaning against the wall outside?"

"Where do you want to go?"

"Martin's Haven. That's not too far from here, is it?"

They gave him directions, and he headed out. He found the pebbly beach a couple of miles away and asked someone about boats to Skokholm.

"Are you a volunteer?"

Jackson shook his head. "No. We're looking for someone."

"So you're looking for a volunteer."

"No. We're looking for whoever lives in the lighthouse."

"No one lives in the lighthouse. It's automated."

"Someone's got to live in the lighthouse. We received a package from there."

"Well then, it's probably from the Wildlife Trust."

"No. It's from some magicians."

The man's laugh confused Jackson.

"All you'll find on Skokholm are wildlife, the Wildlife Trust workers, and some volunteers. There's not much else there, although there is a lighthouse. But like I said, no one lives there."

"Is there a boat that will take us there?"

"Not without permission from the Wildlife Trust. They run their own boat."

Jackson's shoulders sagged. "Thanks."

He walked around the beach for a few minutes, but the cold breeze blowing in from the north made him shiver, and he returned to the inn to awaken Johanna.

BARELY TWO MILES AWAY, TWO men carried a small boat down to the beach at Marloes Sands and walked it into the water. Beck hoisted himself into the vessel, while the other man pushed it until he became chest deep in water. He hoisted himself onboard as well, and they wordlessly rowed toward Skokholm Island.

JOHANNA KNEW SOMEONE WANTED HER attention but did not want to open her eyes. She moaned when someone shook her. Her eyes fluttered open and she saw Jackson's face. "It can't be dinnertime. I feel like I just fell asleep."

"You've been sleeping for two hours and I think we've got a problem."

She struggled to sit up. "What problem?" Suddenly she felt wide-awake. "How did you get in here? Wasn't the door locked?"

"No. Or else the lock doesn't work. Anyway, I borrowed a bike and rode to the beach you told me about, and a guy there told me we can't go to Skokholm without permission from some wildlife people."

"I know."

"You do?"

"I looked up how to get to the island before we left. I emailed them yesterday."

"What did they say?"

"I don't know. I was too busy driving here and then sleeping to check for an answer."

"Don't you think you ought to do that now?"

She sighed. "I guess. Could you hand me my bag?"

Once she had it, she checked her cell phone. "I haven't received anything new for hours."

"Is that normal?"

"No. I usually receive a few hundred emails a day. There's always something new in my inbox."

"Maybe it doesn't work here."

She tsked. "It has to. I'm depending on it as a way to communicate."

"You want me to ask downstairs if they've got Wi-Fi?"

She leaned back against the pillow and stared at the ceiling. "Sure." Her reply lacked conviction.

Jackson returned a moment later and said, "Let's take it outside."

"What good will that do?"

"Apparently, that's the only way to get reception."

She followed him downstairs and out to a paved courtyard behind the inn where some tables and chairs were set up.

He pulled out a chair for her. "Look now."

She checked her phone and watched the little wheel turn as it searched for a signal. *P-i-n-g.* Emails began appearing in her inbox. "Humph." It was more of a hum than a word.

"Is a 'yay' in order?"

She saw an email from the Wildlife Trust and smiled. "Maybe." She opened it up. "They gave me a phone number to call. I hope it's not too late. We *need* to go out there tomorrow."

She called the number and heard it connect. "Hi, this is Johanna Charette with the Library of—"

"…leaveyourmessageafterthetone. *Beeeeeeeeeeep.*"

"No!"

Jackson stopped studying the rocks in the stone wall surrounding the courtyard. "What's the matter?"

"Answering machine."

"Did you leave a message?"

"No."

"Then how do you expect anyone to get back to you?"

"Stop acting mature. I'm the adult here."

"What makes you the adult?"

"I'm over eighteen."

"I'll be eighteen in six months."

"Longevicus ritual. You'll be eighteen in ten years and six months."

"I don't think it works that way."

She called the number again and left a message claiming they urgently needed permission to travel out to Skokholm Island the following day. She just managed to finish saying her phone number before she got cut off.

"Feel better now?"

"No. Maybe I'd better use Mal's diary to ask him if there's anything he can do from his end."

MAL, RYDEN SIMMDRY, AND SELIUM SORIUM all stopped concentrating on defensive invasion tactics after Mal learned of Johanna's problem.

⌘*I believe I can help out. Please excuse me.* Ryden

291

Simmdry disappeared.

Mere minutes later, the master of the overseers reappeared. ⌘*It's been taken care of. Tell Johanna a boat from the Island will pick her up tomorrow morning at ten at Martin's Haven.*

Mal wrote the instructions in his diary. "I guess they'll be on their way soon enough."

⌘*We can only hope.*

⬭*Do you believe this is tied into a Terrorian scheme?*

⌘*We have no way of knowing, but we cannot take chances. Anything is possible.*

JOHANNA SHARED THE NEWS WITH Jackson when they sat down to dinner.

"Really? Ryden Simmdry set it up himself? That's pretty cool."

"We have to make sure we don't miss that boat."

"The place where we're supposed to meet it isn't that far from here. I biked it today. It's only a couple miles away. We can walk it in a half-hour."

"Okay. We'll leave here tomorrow at 9:00 just in case. That should give us plenty of time."

"Do you think we should pack some food to take with us?"

The corners of Johanna's mouth lifted slightly. "You're already worrying about lunch tomorrow?"

"From what people say about the place, it doesn't sound like there are any restaurants there."

"Fine, maybe the inn can rustle up some sandwiches and a couple of soft drinks to tide us over."

"Now you're talking."

* * *

THE FOLLOWING MORNING THEY HEADED out to Martin's Haven with a hearty lunch stashed safely in Jackson's backpack. Johanna slowed as they walked past a field of wildflowers. "These are beautiful." The purple and fuchsia blooms swayed in the breeze, and Johanna approached the field to get a closer look. A flutter of wings diverted her attention. At first, the curator drew back, startled, but then she stooped down. "Look. It's an injured bird."

Jackson shrugged. "There's not much we can do for it. We've got a boat to catch."

"Maybe they can care for it back at the inn. It's only a couple of minutes away." She carefully scooped up the bird and carried it back to the lodging with Jackson in her wake.

The innkeeper agreed to take a look at the bird and do what he could to help it. Satisfied, Johanna and Jackson set out for Martin's Haven again.

Jackson took the lead. "I'm surprised you managed to do that without being bitten."

"I think it was too scared, or too hurt, to bite me."

"Maybe it thinks you're its mother."

She made a face at him, but didn't say anything more.

They arrived at the car park. Jackson led her to the steep cliff leading down to the boat landing. Johanna struggled to keep her balance while carefully making her way down the rocky surface.

"Johanna!" Jackson pointed to a group of people boarding a small boat.

Her mouth dropped open in disbelief. *We shouldn't have walked the bird back to the inn.*

Jackson ran for the boat shouting back, "I'll tell

them to wait for you."

Johanna hurried after him, but in her haste, slipped. A sharp stab of pain shot through her ankle as she lost her footing and tumbled to the bottom of the craggy path.

—LOI—

26

"JOHANNA."

Her eyes slowly opened. Jackson hovered above her and she felt a jolt of deja vu. "I just dreamt we missed the boat to Skokholm."

"You didn't dream it," he answered, "but that boat's on its way to Skomer, so no problem. Are you okay?"

"I think so."

He helped her sit up. "What happened? One minute we're running for the boat. The next minute I returned to find you out cold on the ground."

"I slipped." She winced when she tried to stand.

"What's wrong?"

She grimaced as she tried to put weight on her ankle. "It hurts … bad. I hope I didn't break it." She tried to balance as she brushed the dust from her clothing.

"Maybe it's just a sprain. Lean on me." He supported her as she limped to the boat landing.

"I wish I'd brought a scarf with me or something."

"You're cold?"

"No. I could have wrapped a scarf around my ankle to give it support."

"Wait." Jackson dug through the pockets of his backpack until he found what he wanted. "Could you use this?" He handed her a roll of brightly colored tape.

"Neon tape?"

"Athletic tape. I injured my ankle in gym last year and I had to wear it whenever we played basketball. I stuck it in my backpack at the end of the year and forgot all about it."

"How convenient."

"It's fate. Some oracle somewhere directed me to leave it in my bag until we needed it at this very moment."

"An oracle…"

"They're pretty smart at predicting things."

"And what does this oracle look like?"

"I've never actually seen her, but I'm hoping she looks like Sansa Stark from *Game of Thrones*."

"Right."

He took the tape and bandaged her ankle. A small boat arrived as he pulled the hem of her jeans back in place. "Wait here." He checked to make sure it was their boat before going back for Johanna.

She winced as she walked.

"Are you all right?" the boat captain asked.

"Yeah. I just sprained it. It's nothing."

"You'd better hope it's nothing. Skokholm isn't an easy place to get around if you're injured."

"I'll be fine."

Jackson got into the boat first and lifted her in.

"Hold on," the captain said as he throttled up, made a U-turn, and headed out to sea.

Jackson put his arm around Johanna's shoulders.

She nestled into him and tried to relax, but all she could think about was getting around the island on an injured ankle.

BACK ON DRAMATICA, FURST AND his infantry, armed with flaming arrows and one decimator, burst through the front door of the library. A band of Terrorians stood in a semi-circle with their weapons trained on the door. Some Dramaticans proved to have faster reflexes, but not all of them, and two were vaporized on sight. Furst, however, did not falter and managed to decimate two Terrorians. Others dropped their weapons as the flaming arrows ignited their skin. Furst continued on through the library, shooting everything that moved, and the Terrorians squealed when they saw one of their own weapons turned against them.

Furst took a deep breath when he realized he stood alone in the library. He didn't know if he had successfully eliminated all the invaders or if they now hid among the few stacks they'd failed to destroy. He carefully backed out of the library, his corkscrew curls tightening as each new bit of devastation came to light.

He knocked into an antique globe of Dramatica. He believed it to be the most detailed and beautifully illustrated rendering of the entire realm—and his most cherished prize in the library. It clattered to the ground and in less than a moment, a flash of light removed it from existence. Furst quickly returned fire, and the only remnant of the offending Terrorian was the smell of his oily residue.

Another blast of light just missed the curator, taking out a bookshelf. Furst propelled himself into the air, firing down on the alien invader before landing near the front door. He returned to the courtyard and moved everyone back behind a fountain that sat in the center of the square.

Torran descended on Furst like a tanker. "Gone, are they?"

"Of knowing, I have no way."

"Are there, how many?"

"Know, I do not."

Torran raised his voice. "Kill any of them, did you?"

Torran stood a foot taller than Furst, but the curator hopped up on the edge of the fountain and looked down on the statesman. "Go in and see for yourself, why don't you."

"I will." Torran gestured toward some of the men still holding crossbows. "With me, come."

The men looked to Furst for guidance, but the curator only stared at Torran.

"Now!" Torran demanded, and the men grudgingly followed.

Furst closed his eyes for a moment of calm, before hopping off the wall and following them inside.

PRU TELLERENCE TUCKED IZABELLA INTO Johanna's bed for a nap and sang her to sleep. Afterward, the dean decided not to return to the main reading room where Ryden Simmdry, Selium Sorium and Mal discussed anti-invasion tactics. Instead, she sat on an overstuffed chair in Johanna's living room and put her feet up.

Overseers rarely needed to sleep, but the previous day had been exhausting and her mental faculties needed recharging. ★*Let the others handle the Terrorians.* She'd plan how to proceed with the child, now that she was stranded on Fantasia. Only the curator could open the vault in his or her library, and not even overseers could override that protection, which had been in place for thousands of years. Without her miter, Pru Tellerence could not leave Fantasia. Of course, Ryden Simmdry or Selium Sorium could escort her back, but then she would be stranded wherever they escorted her to. She needed her miter, and if she had to wait for Johanna to return, that's what she would do. Besides, it gave her time to think.

Skokholm Island grew larger as the boat neared, and Johanna wondered how she'd ever survive the climb from the landing to the top of the bluff. The closer she got, the more difficult it looked.

Finally, the boat pulled in and the captain jumped out. He offered to give them a hand. Jackson stood first and got off. Johanna tried to stand, but by then, her ankle had swollen and she couldn't put any pressure on it at all. She grimaced.

"Could you grab her under the arm," Jackson asked the captain as he reached under her other arm. Together, they pulled her up and out of the boat.

Once again, she tried to put pressure on her ankle and winced.

"How far is it to the lighthouse?" Jackson asked.

"About a mile. It's a long way for her to go just to get a few pictures of the lighthouse."

"We're here for more than pictures," Jackson said. "We're here to find magicians."

The captain stared at them for several seconds. His face lost all traces of friendliness. "Whatever gave you the idea you'd find magicians at a bird observatory?"

Johanna could see the change in his demeanor. She smiled. "I'm a writer and I'm writing a story about a wizard who gets marooned on the island and has to re-build his life—kind of like Harry Potter meets Robinson Crusoe. Are you familiar with them?"

The captain shook his head and turned his attention to a small vehicle slowly approaching the dock. He jumped back in the boat and pulled back a canvas tarp. Beneath it lay several crates of supplies.

The driver pulled as close to the boat as possible and then walked down to the landing to receive the goods. "Good morning, Alwyn."

"Dylan," the captain acknowledged as he handed over the first carton.

Jackson stuck his arms out. "I'll take one of those for him."

Johanna eyed her co-curator warily. "What about me?"

"I'll be back for you. You can stand there for a minute. Just balance on one leg. Like a flamingo." He carried the second crate of supplies and got a good look at the vehicle. "It has two seats."

"The dumper truck? We use it for hauling supplies."

"I'm glad to see it has two seats. My friend sprained her ankle and I thought you could take her to the lighthouse. She's, uh, researching a book. And I don't think she could walk there on her own."

"Sorry. I don't know if that's possible. I've got a lot of work to do here."

"Wait. Maybe we could rent it? Just for a couple of hours …"

Dylan shook his head. "This isn't a great place for someone with a sprained ankle. The ground isn't completely level and there are some wicked slopes where you can roll right off the bluff and crash into the sea below.

Jackson smiled. "We'll be very careful." He picked up another crate from the boat and carried it up the incline.

"Why'd she even come here if she's injured?" Dylan asked.

"She just sprained it rushing down the path at Martin's Haven. We thought we were going to miss the boat."

"I'll ask about renting you the dumper truck. It's not like you could steal it. You'd never get it off the island."

"Umm…dee-ulch?"

"Diolch—it's pronounced dee-oalk."

"Diolch, then," Jackson said with a curt nod, before returning to Johanna.

"What was that all about?" she asked when he returned. The boat had left and she was all by herself, pulling back from the spray of the waves as they broke against the landing."

"They've got a kind of golf cart-dump truck. I asked if we could rent it."

"We don't have a lot of money on us."

"Didn't you bring the credit card?"

"Who knows if they'd take credit cards here."

"I've got a couple hundred dollars, just in case."

"That's if they even let us use it."

"Have a little faith." He grabbed her waist. "Put you arm around my shoulder and make like a bunny."

Johanna used Jackson like a crutch as she slowly hopped up the incline. Once she reached the flat section at the top, she stopped to look around. "It's beautiful, but there's not much here." They followed the path and Johanna kept hopping until they reached an old stone structure. It was built into a slope and Johanna leaned against it to rest.

Jackson inspected the rocks. He bent down and peered into the opening. "Aye!" he screamed and jumped back. A snake slithered out.

Johanna didn't care for snakes, but couldn't help but laugh.

"It's not funny."

The sound of an engine stopped her from replying. It was Dylan on the dumper truck.

"The consensus is we let you use it in return for a donation to the tick jar."

"You want us to donate ticks?"

"It's a jar we make donations to every time we see a bird we haven't seen before. A monetary donation would cover the cost of the petrol in the dumper truck and help us with repairs around the island."

Johanna took out two fifty-pound bank notes. "Will this do as a donation?"

"That will do quite nicely," Dylan replied. He pocketed the money before giving them a crash course in the operation of the dumper truck and a warning to stay on the road to the lighthouse.

"Diolch," Jackson said with a smile and helped Johanna take a seat. "I'll drive."

They slowly made their way past fields awash with flowers and shrubbery. When they got to the lighthouse, they found a warden waiting for them.

"Which one of you is the writer?"

"I am," Johanna answered as she took in the lighthouse and the view beyond. "It's really quite breathtaking."

The warden grinned. "We like it. So what do you need to know exactly?"

"Uhhh ..." Johanna didn't know exactly how to proceed.

"She's writing a book about a wizard who's like Robinson Crusoe ..."

Johanna shook her head. "No. It's not like that at all."

Jackson stared at her, not sure where she would take the conversation.

Johanna reached into her backpack and removed the wrapping Myrddin's memoir had been delivered in. She handed it to the warden. "We received a very special book from this address, and we're looking for the sender."

"Well it certainly says Skokholm Lighthouse, but I can assure you no one here sent it."

"Let me see that." Before Johanna had a chance to say no, a hand reached out and snatched the wrapper.

TORRAN HOWLED AS HE BECAME encased in a force field.

A few of the Dramaticans who had followed him fled, but others trained their crossbows on the Terrorian soldiers that remained. One was vaporized while another was locked in a separate force field. Torran's bellowing could probably be heard outside, and it took all of Furst's restraint not to obliterate his countryman forever with a pull of the trigger.

The Terrorians shared no such restraint. One of them took aim and ended Torran's screams, and everything else about him.

Furst jumped up and shot the attacker, rendering him a mere collection of particles in the atmosphere, much like Torran. The curator landed on top of a bank of shelves and spun around quickly looking for Terrorians. "Out, spread, but close to the shelves stay. Secure this floor, we must. Upward then, we must move."

The Dramaticans slowly secured the library section by section, checking every storage room, closet, and behind each shelf. When they were certain there were no invaders left in the five upper levels, Furst posted guards near each portal and told them to be prepared. He positioned them on top of bookshelves, so they would see anyone emerging from the portals before being seen themselves, and gave them each a vaporizer left behind by dead Terrorians. He then locked the entrance to the lower levels and rigged up a contraption that would shoot anyone trying to bust through the basement door. Finally, he cut power to the library.

THE *ULTIMIUM CODI* WEIGHED HEAVILY on Pru Tellerence. Its regulations on the deportment of deans outlined very specific behavior, punishable by loss of position and blessings. If she dared do anything contrary to the laws—set forth at the beginning of time, and only modified because of extreme outcome—she could lose everything she held dear, even though holding things dear was not allowed, as far as overseers were concerned.

ULTIMIUM CODI

> Deans must refrain from any liaisons that may limit their abilities to act on behalf of all residents of the Illumini System.
>
> This precludes any overseer from becoming involved in any familial or intimate relationship. Sentimentality can cloud the mind. Love can color decision-making. Overseers must be free to act in the best interests of the many, therefore are precluded from falling victim to the interests of the one. All dependent relationships are strictly forbidden and punishable by loss of position and blessings. *Be forewarned:* once the majorious longevicus blessing is reversed, metamorphosis could cause one's biology and physiognomy to reflect true age and in many cases will result in instantaneous death due to old age.

Pru Tellerence got up and walked to the bedroom door to observe the sleeping child. Deep within her soul, at the base of her very being, a forbidden emotional attachment intensified. ★*How will I ever overcome this?*
⌘*Overcome what, Pru Tellerence?*

—LOI—

27

Dramaticans quickly spread the word about Furst's heroism and leadership, as well as the tale of Torran's demise. By the time Furst exited the library to bring his fellow countrymen up to speed on what had happened, a troubadour had already composed a song extolling the sacrifice and chivalry of *The Dramatican Confrontation Against Evil*. People who had never spoken to Furst before smiled at him and raised a hand in salute. Others celebrated with libations and loud chatter.

Furst's ringlets tightened.

He jumped up on the edge of the fountain and the crowd cheered.

"Over, it is not," he warned. "To protect our realm, be ready."

Not one Dramatican picked up a weapon. Instead, they gathered baskets of fruit and barrels of fermented drink to celebrate the fact that their library still stood.

* * *

"Beck!" Jackson cried out, astounded to see the flight attendant standing there, clutching the wrappings to Myrddin's Memoir. "What are you doing here?"

"You can get back to work," Beck told the warden. "I will see to our visitors."

The warden returned to the lighthouse. Beck motioned for Jackson and Johanna to follow him. Johanna got out of the vehicle and gasped, her face going white.

Beck had already cut halfway across the field and only turned when Jackson shouted, "She can't follow you. She hurt her ankle."

The flight attendant glared at them.

"Help me," Johanna whispered. She slipped her arm around Jackson's waist. "We've got to find out what he knows. Besides, he's got the paper with the wax seal. We need that back."

By the time they made it to the other side of the vehicle, Beck had returned and swiftly scooped Johanna up. Without another word, he headed back across the field.

Burrows and mounds made the terrain uneven. Jackson watched his step, careful not to end up with an injury like Johanna's. As he trailed Beck, he spotted some small animal bones, and further along their walk, a clutch of eggs. He looked up to say something and saw Johanna watching him over Beck's shoulder.

"You know, I could have carried her," Jackson called out. "Where are you taking us?"

Beck didn't utter a word. He just continued striding toward a couple of large rocks that sheltered a tiny shed. He carried Johanna inside.

Jackson stopped at the door. "Is this an outhouse?"

Beck lifted his foot and pushed it against a stone at the bottom of the wall. It slid back to reveal a steep staircase. "Watch your head," Beck said, as he carried Johanna down the stairs into the darkness.

Pru Tellerence wheeled around to face Ryden Simmdry. She steeled herself in a cloak of calm.

★*I'm concerned about the child. She's been away from her mother for a while and I'm worried there might be some psychological detachment. I hope Bel doesn't suffer repercussions from being taken.*

⌘*I can calm the child with an enchantment; even emplace feelings of trust and contentment.*

★*But those feelings would be false. I prefer the child's disposition remained genuine.*

⌘*Perhaps her mother would feel differently.*

★*Perhaps.*

Ryden Simmdry stared at the white knuckles on Pru Tellerence's hand, which clutched the front of her blouse.

She followed his gaze and let go of the fabric when she realized he'd noticed.

He gazed into her eyes, but Pru Tellerence did not allow him to see past her defenses.

As Beck passed certain areas in the stone fortified tunnel, torches recessed in wall niches automatically sprang to life, lighting the way. He neither said nor touched anything, yet the torches seemed to sense his approach, and sputtered out after the trio passed.

"Motion sensors, right?" Jackson speculated as he

followed along. The pathway leveled out and curved for a while before descending again. "How far underground are we going, anyway?"

Beck continued to keep his own counsel. Johanna remained just as silent.

"Will somebody talk to me, please?" Jackson asked.

Just then, a door slid open and Beck carried Johanna into a large cavern with a vast window carved into the face of the bluff looking out over the water. Bowls, bottles, and boxes of all descriptions littered a large slab of sandstone that topped a complex metal structure in the center of the space. A bank of computers and high tech gadgetry lined the red stone walls. And what looked like a stainless steel elevator door set in solid rock in another corner of the room made its own statement. The windows, lighting and technology appeared to be cutting-edge. However, the cavern retained an old-fashioned aura. Without question, some of the vials and vessels cluttering the countertop looked like holdovers from another century, and while some objects looked contemporary, others appeared to be medieval.

A GROUP OF DRAMATICANS SET to work removing the Terrorian bodies from the library. It took three or more men to drag the dead weight of the much larger, heavier invaders. Meanwhile, their kinsmen gathered dried twigs and branches and built a mound out of the combustible materials. Heaving the Terrorian carcasses on top of the pile took effort, and after placing the first corpse, they knew they'd need a much larger pyre.

"Ring the bell, Furst."

"Life or death, the fire is not."

"The bell, ring, or all day we'll be here," Dungen stated.

"And all night. Not over, the war is. Just beginning, it is."

"My friends, I will get," a boy volunteered. "More firewood, we will find."

Furst nodded at the boy before helping his kinsmen heave a second Terrorian onto the mound of twigs. They continued to work until evening, gathering wood and adding to the pyre, before finally putting a match to it.

In the end, it did not take much prodding for the flames to grow into a huge blaze. The Terrorians' oily skin fueled the fire as it crackled in the heat. The plume of smoke and orange glow from the flames could be seen for miles, and attracted Dramaticans like moths. But their attention was short-lived once their curiosity was sated. The foul odor made many of them sick to their stomachs, and they retreated to the sweeter air inside their homes.

INSIDE A PRIVATE PRINT SHOP, etching machines that Nero 51 used to produce his invasion maps had been moved to make space to garage the time machine. The Library of Illumination would have been more convenient, but Nero 51 did not want to be immediately linked to the stolen vehicle if the overseers paid a surprise visit.

He approached General Lethro 814, whom he had placed in charge of the invasion. "Has a second wave of soldiers been sent to Juvenilia?"

"Not yet."

Nero 51 kept his voice even. "And why is that?"

The general held up an obelisk. "This document describes the library on Juvenilia as having translucent walls in bright primary colors."

"That is correct."

"According to Ilio 22, the cupola he left our troops in had transparent floors and dull brown walls."

"Why wasn't I informed of this earlier?"

One of the general's tentacles developed a slight tremor. "You told us you wanted to meditate and not to disturb you."

Nero 51 grabbed a weapon and pulled the general inside the time machine. "I guess if I want knowledgeable answers, I'll have to find them for myself." He thrust the firearm in the general's tentacles. "And you will protect me while I do so."

Moments later, the time machine disappeared on its journey to another realm.

"WHAT IS THIS PLACE?" JOHANNA asked. Her eyes came to rest on an older man in a tattered white lab coat studying an ancient book. Johanna quickly surmised the book to be nearly as old as Myrddin's memoir, but not quite.

Beck finally spoke, but not to Johanna and Jackson. "These are the people I told you about. And," he thrust the book wrapping at the man, "they had this."

The man examined the brown paper packaging, and then scrutinized Johanna's face, as if trying to read her most secret thoughts. "Are you Johanna Charette?"

"Yes. Will you tell me what this is all about?"

Beck released her and she yelped when her foot touched with the floor. Unbidden tears made tracks down her cheeks, but her voice remained even, belying her pain. "I was asked to come here and solve a riddle of sorts, for the person who sent me that." She reached for

311

the wrapper, but Beck lunged forward and quickly pulled it away from her.

The older man walked over to Beck and retrieved the paper. He smiled at the sigil embedded in the wax seal before looking at the curator. "I sent you this package."

She narrowed her eyes. "I saw the man who claims ownership of the contents of the book, and he is not you."

"You saw Myrddin? Of course you would in a Library of Illumination. It's protected."

Jackson coughed to get their attention. "Maybe I'm missing some obscure point here, but books, enchanted ones, that come to life inside the Library of Illumination, can come to life outside the library as well."

"Did you see the book come to life or just Myrddin?"

Jackson tilted his head ever so slightly. "What's the difference?"

"Myrddin can *only* come to life *inside* the Library of Illumination. Or inside this workshop. Viviane, the Lady of the Lake, made sure of that after she turned the sorcery he'd taught her against him and trapped him inside this rock. He can't get out, but that didn't prevent him from conjuring and experimenting and noting his findings in the memoir I sent. It's quite fascinating reading, part diary, part spell book, part philosophical treatise."

"Somehow," Jackson said, "his entrapment is a little hard to believe. Why couldn't he just use the tunnel to get out?"

The older man offered his hand. "I'm Cathasach, by the way. You must be Jackson."

Jackson cautiously shook the man's hand. "You didn't answer my question."

"There was no tunnel at that time. Myrddin made

a good start of it, but could not finish it in his lifetime."

"How do you know any of this?" Johanna asked.

"From the tales passed down by the man who found him after the earthquake of 1690. They say the tremor was felt as far as London. It apparently created a chasm that was discovered by a like-minded sorcerer looking for solitude on this island. Further investigation revealed a cave like opening that led to the tunnel Myrddin had started to carve out. That sorcerer ultimately discovered this laboratory and Myrddin's skeletal remains."

"So you're theorizing," Jackson said.

"Not theory, young man, fact. You see, Myrddin's body may have left this mortal coil, but his soul lingers. He imbued the pages of his workbook with his energy, and thus lives on inside this cave where he had been banished by Viviane. His notes briefly state his belief that he could probably materialize inside the Library of Illumination within the confines of this book. He seemed to have some kind of connection with the library, although we've never been able to figure out what that is."

Jackson folded his arms across his chest. "So he haunts the place."

"I guess that is one way you could explain it." Cathasach smiled benevolently.

Jackson motioned toward Beck. "What about him? What does he have to do with all this?"

"The secret of Myrddin's lair has always been too large—too important—for any one man to protect," Cathasach said, "but we certainly couldn't let the public get wind of it.

"Following its discovery, Bradán—the sorcerer who found this laboratory—knew it would take a special

313

cadre of people to protect it. He invited his most trusted cohorts to share and protect the secret. Those eight people founded Eahta Frean fram Drycræft."

"Eahta Frean fram Drycræft," Johanna echoed. "That answers *that* question. We've been looking for you, but we didn't want to ask for you by name."

"A wise decision. There are dark forces about who would go to great lengths to discover this site and the whereabouts of Myrddin's notes."

"That still doesn't explain him," Jackson said, pointing to Beck.

"Beck is one of the *Eight Masters of Wizardry*—one of the Eahta Frean fram Drycræft."

Jackson's mouth hung half-open while his eyes darted from the airline attendant to Cathasach and back to Beck. "You're a wizard?"

Beck smiled.

Jackson folded his arms across his chest. "How do we know you're a wizard?"

"My employer doesn't serve beer from Pembrokeshire to passengers."

"You conjured that out of nothing?" Jackson's eyes grew large.

Beck grinned. "I conjured it out of my backpack. I'm from Pembrokeshire."

"So that doesn't prove anything," Jackson said.

Beck picked up Johanna by the waist and sat her on the island, swinging her around so her swollen ankle rested on the counter. He removed her shoe and sock.

"What do you think you're doing?" Jackson rushed to her side.

Beck glared at him. "I thought you said this just happened at Martin's Haven."

"It did," Johanna confirmed.

"Really? Who taped it? This was done with a practiced hand."

"A practiced hand, huh?" Jackson turned to Johanna. "See. I told you I knew what I was doing."

"He taped it while we waited for the boat," she told Beck. "He's got the tape in his backpack if you want him to show it to you."

Beck grabbed a scissor and cut the binding on Johanna's ankle.

"Ouch!"

Under the tape, her blue-tinged skin had wrinkled. Beck gently examined her ankle. Released from its bindings, it soon started to swell. "You really did do a number on it. For a moment, I thought it was a scam." He rummaged through a rack of beakers looking for herbs. He ground some using an old mortar and pestle, then added a few other ingredients before mixing it with what looked like blue sludge. He smeared it on her ankle.

The smell turned her stomach. "What is that stuff?"

"Trust me," Beck replied. "You're going to love me in the morning."

"Whoa!" A wave breaking against the window startled Jackson.

"Looks like a storm's brewing," Cathasach said. "I guess you'll be our guests for the night."

"Thanks, but that's not necessary," Johanna replied.

"We're staying at a hotel in Marloes."

"There's no boat service to the mainland when the

weather gets like this. The seas are too rough."

"We've got to go," Jackson said. "I promised Dylan I'd return the dumper truck this afternoon."

"That's easy enough to do." Beck loosely wrapped gauze around Johanna's ankle. "The cottage is only a mile from here. You can easily drive it over and walk back within a half hour."

"Forget it. I'm not leaving Johanna alone here with you. Either she comes with me, or I'm staying put."

Cathasach addressed Beck directly. "We don't want to impose on our landlords. Why don't you return the dumper truck."

"And tell them *what* when they start asking questions?"

"Don't tell them anything. Just return the dumper truck and come back before they see you."

"Right." He finished taping Johanna's ankle before heading to the door. He abruptly turned toward Jackson. "You did leave the key in the ignition, didn't you?"

"Yeah." After Beck left, Jackson sidled up to Johanna and lowered his voice. "I don't trust that guy." Another huge wave crashed against the window.

"It's not like we've got another choice."

"I just wish you could run," Jackson said, staring at her bum ankle.

"That makes two of us."

Cathasach worked on the other side of the lab where he should not have been able to overhear them. "You have nothing to fear from us."

They turned toward him, but an odd fizzy sound and a pop hijacked their attention as they were plunged into darkness.

SECOND CHRONICLES OF ILLUMINATION

—LOI—

28

IZABELLA SLEPT FOR TWO HOURS and woke up hot and listless.

"Poor Bel, I think you're not feeling well."

The youngster did not respond to Pru Tellerence's touch.

⌘*Is there a problem?*

★*I believe she's sick and I don't know what to do for her.*

⌘*Let me take a look.* Ryden Simmdry gently stroked the child's cheek.

Pru Tellerence pulled back a little, surprised at the effect that small gesture had upon her.

Izabella open her eyes and looked at Ryden Simmdry, but Ryden Simmdry did not notice because his eyes were closed. However, his lips moved.

★*Are you praying?*

Ryden Simmdry smiled. ⌘*I don't think that's what*

I'd call it, but you can refer to it in any way you want.

Izabella rolled over and scrambled to her knees, staring at the two overseers.

"You certainly look better. Would you like something to eat?"

Izabella climbed down from the bed and continued to stare. Then she reached for Pru Tellerence's hand and the overseer knew it would be incredibly difficult to part with the child.

JACKSON GRABBED JOHANNA AND HELD on tight. "What's going on?" he called out loud enough for Cathasach to hear. He saw a flicker of light in the corner and then Cathasach's face.

"The waves have engulfed the generator. Just give me a moment." The candle flicker moved across the room, and a cold blue light suddenly flooded the space.

"You have a backup generator."

"Of a sort. The light is a little more harsh, but it won't go out."

"How can you be so sure?"

"Because it's powered by sorcery, and it would take a sorcerer more powerful than Bradán to undo it. Myrddin may be the only sorcerer that powerful."

"Then why did you call on *us* to help *you*? If you're as powerful as you say you are and Myrddin haunts this place, surely you don't need our help."

"I am neither as strong as Myrddin or Bradán. And remember, even though Myrddin haunts this workshop, he is dead. The threat, as perceived by us, is very much alive. And if the person trying to relieve us of Myrddin's memoir has any power at all, he'll be able to grow it

319

substantially using Myrddin's elixirs and spells."

Johanna lowered her bad ankle from the counter and positioned herself to hop down to the floor; then thought better of it. "Tell us what you know."

"Let's wait for Beck to return. He travels a lot and has a more global scope of what's happening."

FURST COULD NOT STOP THE celebration even though he knew recruiting additional soldiers to help defend the library was more important. The Dramaticans he had posted at the portals could not stay there forever. They would need to be relieved.

Furst approached several of the men who had fought earlier in the day, but they ignored his plea. "My part, I have done," one of them said outright. The curator felt his energy waning. Only his determination kept him going.

Then he heard a voice say, "Fight, we can."

Furst turned to find an older boy and a few of his friends standing behind him. "Too young, you are. Complain, your mothers would."

"That young, we are not. If men to fight, there are not enough, prisoners of those creatures, we all would be. Fight, we can. To hunt and shoot, we've been taught. To defend our homes, we want, as much as someone older. Years ahead of us, we have. To live free of tyranny, we want."

Furst studied the boys. They were as tall as he was even if their ringlets had not fully curled. "Reach the time of full growth, when do you?"

"When the sun lowers for winter," one said.

"Also, me," another called out.

"Near in age, we are all. Fight together, we will."

"Ask your kin, you must. In agreement, if they are, fight you will."

A boy pushed through the others. He seemed small—but determined. "Only my father, I had. Today in battle, he died. For him, I must fight. In vain, his death must not be."

Furst nodded at the lad and offered him his hand. "Your name, what is?"

"Lenc," the boy replied.

"Help you, we will."

The other boys ran off to ask for permission to fight. Their families disappointed a few of the lads by not giving them permission, but a half dozen young Dramaticans returned with slingshots and crossbows.

Seeing themselves bested by younger kinsmen, other Dramaticans who had not fought earlier, also joined Furst's ranks. And slowly a new militia began to form.

WILD SURF CONTINUED TO LASH the windows of Myrddin's workshop.

"I can't believe how high these waves are," Jackson exclaimed.

"They're not that high at all," Cathasach answered. "We're deep in the bedrock, much closer to the water line than the fields above. These waves, while substantial to us, are a small indicator of the storm to come—not yet high enough to concern people on the surface. But from here, they are already menacing."

Jackson knocked on the glass window. "How can this be embedded in the rock? Won't it leak? Can it break?"

"That glass was designed by Bradán. Remember, he was a sorcerer, and a great one at that. He designed it in a way that makes it *one with the rock*. Glass is made out of silica after all, as is rock. Here, it is fused together as if nature had done it herself. And this window is impossible to detect from the outside. An enchantment makes it blend with the shadows and crevasses of the bluff, giving us a vast, invisible window on the sea."

Bits of hail began pinging against the glass just as the door slid open to allow Beck's return. "It's getting nasty above."

"Did you run into anyone?"

"They were too busy securing everything in preparation for the storm. Apparently, it came out of nowhere fast, and it's expected to be huge."

Jackson's stomach grumbled. It was late afternoon and he hadn't eaten since breakfast.

"Well, let's settle in then," Cathasach said. "I think lamb stew and Welsh cakes should hit the spot."

"Where are you going to get it?" Jackson asked.

"I'm going to make it," Cathasach replied.

The teen's eyes narrowed. "You're going to conjure it out of nothing?"

Cathasach laughed. "I going to cook it on a stove using meat and vegetables stored in a refrigerator. And you're going to help. Come on." He walked over to the stainless steel elevator door and pressed the button to open the doors.

Jackson stepped inside and noticed only a handle, which Cathasach pulled. The elevator started moving. "Are we going up? It almost feels like we're going sideways."

"You're right on both counts. We're moving diagonally. We could have built a staircase and made an opening into the living quarters from the workshop, but we didn't want any distractions in either section from the other. This separates them quite adequately."

The door opened into a stone cavern with a window similar to the one in the lab. Cathasach clapped his hands, and a fire in a stone recess sparked to life.

"Considering people don't know this place is here, what do they think when smoke pours out of the chimney?"

"There is no chimney. The fire is a complex illusion, a hologram of sorts that gives off heat and light and provides atmosphere. It's especially calming when a storm is brewing, because no matter how raw or wild it may look outside our window, it feels comfortable and cozy inside.

"I especially like the fireplace, living here full time. Beck probably couldn't care less, but then, he's a visitor who spends most of his time off the island."

Jackson looked past a polished stone counter into an unusually large kitchen. "This is a lot of kitchen for just one person."

"Not at all. We must have space to accommodate all Eahta Frean fram Drycræft and their various dietary preferences. We learned early on that touching another person's food could lead to dire consequences and installed eight separate refrigerators and private cupboards. One for each member."

"What do wizards do to get even, when someone steals their food?"

"The offender is roasted like mutton, and no amount

of personal conjuring will release him from his bonds."

"You eat him?"

"No. We prevail upon the wizard whose food was stolen to stop, and he usually allows it after we promise the offender will be banished from the Eahta Frean fram Drycræft. Finding a replacement on short notice is quite an ordeal, I assure you. We have to make sure those who take on the position are willing to die to protect this secret."

"But now Johanna and I know your secret."

"Yes, and normally we'd enact an amnesia spell to remove all knowledge of our existence from you before you leave. But it probably won't work on curators, so we implore you to carry our secret to the grave, as we will yours."

"Wow."

"Yes."

Pru Tellerence sequestered herself inside Johanna's apartment knowing it would be easier to shield her thoughts if she only met with the other overseers occasionally. But even though she chose not to leave the confines of the residence, it didn't stop Ryden Simmdry and the others from coming in.

Mal entered the kitchen and unwrapped a meal delivered by a local restaurant. Pru Tellerence entered a moment later, in search of dinner for Izabella.

"We haven't seen much of you today," Mal said as he scooped a serving of pasta into a bowl.

★*I've been taking care of Bel. She wasn't feeling well earlier, although whatever Ryden Simmdry did for her, seems to have turned the tide.*

The child held her hand out to Mal, opening and closing her fingers.

"You want some of my dinner, do you?" He put some pasta on a small plate for the youngster. "Let me get you a fork."

But Bel didn't wait and when he turned back, she had already stuffed a handful of pasta in her mouth.

"Or not," he said, laughing.

⌘*Is this meeting of the minds for everyone, or are some of us excluded?*

"Welcome to my … Johanna's humble kitchen. Would anyone care for some pasta? Bel has certainly given it her seal of approval."

In fact, the child had finished the pasta he had given her and held out her hand for more.

◍*I can't remember what it was like to be so young, or hungry.*

⌘*When you age only one year for every thousand, you need only one or two meals a year. Three if you really enjoy food. Considering we recently ate at Plato Indelicat's memorial, our need for food is low at this time.*

◍*When we swear you in as Chancellor of the Exchequer, Malcolm, you'll receive the extended longe-vicus blessing and find your need for sustenance greatly diminished.*

"I welcome the blessing and yet I'll miss the taste and texture of food and the camaraderie an evening of dining provides." He watched as Selium Sorium made animal shadows on the wall to entertain Izabella.

⌘*Perhaps, but if we do find ourselves in an extended conflict, not needing as much food to survive is definitely an advantage.*

Pru Tellerence inhaled and held her breath for a second too long as she gazed at Izabella. *Surely, this child shouldn't need to eat as often as she does.* She looked up to see Ryden Simmdry staring at her. Mal hadn't sensed her thoughts, and Selium Sorium was busy entertaining Bel, but she felt sure Ryden Simmdry had zeroed in on them. She just didn't know how much he read into them.

Johanna and Jackson were shown to separate quarters after dinner. Jackson lingered in the open door to see which room they gave Johanna. He watched her disappear into the room next to his, then pretended to close his door until he heard Beck and Cathasach say goodnight. He waited another five minutes before sneaking to Johanna's room and rapping softly on her door.

She opened it and limped back to the bed, a huge four-poster monstrosity with heavy satin panels hanging from rails.

"Wow, maybe this was Myrddin's room. My room just has a plain old bed, not much bigger than my bed at home. But this thing looks like it can sleep an army."

"Not while I'm in it," she replied.

"How's your ankle?"

"It doesn't hurt as much as it did this afternoon."

"Do you think that stuff Beck put on it actually works?"

"Who knows? Why are you here?"

"I'm here to protect you, just in case one of those guys decides to sneak back in here tonight."

She smiled. "Okay. But all we're going to do is sleep. Don't get any ideas."

"Like I said, I'm just here to protect you."

NERO 51 SET THE TIME machine for the same coordinates his troops had used to invade Juvenilia. He activated the portal and entered the library cupola, stopping suddenly. The interior of this library appeared utilitarian at best. There were books on the shelves, but they looked neglected. Dust and cobwebs covered much of the surface. This library had an air of abandonment and desolation and he intuitively knew he was not on Juvenilia.

The Terrorian gingerly made his way to the center of the cupola and looked down. Everything looked as if it had remained undisturbed for a long time. He motioned for his general to follow him and started descending the spiral staircase. It groaned under the Terrorians' weight.

Nero 51 kept his eyes peeled for anyone lurking about below, but the pair reached the ground floor without incident. He walked to the front door and pushed it open a sliver, peering out at a courtyard overgrown with vegetation.

He caught sight of a group of beings exiting a nearby building. The bluish green color of their skin and metal appendages gave them away.

He closed the door. "Adventura."

"Allies."

"Once, perhaps. Not anymore. There was a nuclear catastrophe here immediately following the Two Millennia War. Many realms blamed us for what happened, but the portals were sealed by then, so I don't know how they came to that conclusion.

"The Adventurans are responsible for what happened to their world. Still, I wouldn't want to run into any of them and have to explain why we're here."

"Where to now?"

"I think we best return home. We must figure out how to travel the portals more accurately." He returned to the portal but it did not take him to the time machine. Instead, he finally found himself on Juvenilia and realized his troops had not been there. The cupola was filled with brightly colored books, the surrounding spaces were undisturbed, and he could hear children singing gaily and having fun.

They didn't do any better on their next venture through the portals either. In fact, they did much worse.

—LOI—

29

JOHANNA WOKE TO JACKSON'S GENTLE snoring. She hopped out of bed and didn't realize her ankle felt perfectly fine until she reached the bathroom. She unwrapped the bandage, washed away the blue gunk, and put her full weight on it again to make sure it felt fully healed. *It must have been only a sprain.* By the time she emerged from the bathroom, Jackson had awakened. She hit him with a pillow. "Get up, time's a'wasting."

"That's easy for you to say." He stretched and yawned. "You weren't up half the night listening for noises."

"Did you hear any?"

"No."

"You should have just gone to sleep like the rest of us."

"How do you know what the rest of us did while you were out cold?"

"If anyone did anything nefarious, we'd know by

now."

The teens easily found the kitchen by following the smell of freshly baked bread. Two crusty loaves cooled on the counter where Cathasach whipped eggs like a short order cook. "You two are just in time for breakfast. I'm making a giant omelet, and I just took the bread out of the oven. If you were hoping for meats, beans or mushrooms, I'm sorry to disappoint you. We eat simply here."

"Whatever you have is fine," Johanna said.

Cathasach smiled and continued to beat eggs. He broke into an Italian love song and sang his heart out while cooking.

Beck walked in yawning. "That's quite a racket you're making. How can anybody be expected to sleep?"

"We've had plenty of time to sleep," Cathasach said, grating cheese on top of the eggs. "Now, it's time to eat. Later, we'll have all day to ponder who's after Myrddin's memoir.

"I can't," Beck replied. "I'm scheduled for a flight today."

"Have you looked out the window?" Cathasach waved the cheese grater in that general direction. "The storm is full-on. You're not going to be able to get off the island."

Beck slumped into a chair. "Great." The sound of defeat echoed in his single word.

"Why wait until after breakfast?" Johanna asked. "Why can't we talk now about who you suspect is after the book?"

Cathasach sprinkled herbs on the omelet. "If I knew the answer to that, I wouldn't have needed to send the book to you.

"It started innocuously," he continued. "I found it out of place one day and thought Beck, or one of the others, had forgotten to put it away. But it bothered me because we're *all* very careful with that particular book. Myrddin produced many volumes of notes and spells, but the others are fairly simple and pragmatic. The collection I sent to you for safekeeping is *special*. It's his most important life's work. The spells in that one collection—in the hands of a powerful sorcerer—could change the world as we know it."

Johanna stopped stirring her coffee. "How so?"

"He perfected a way for a man to transmogrify into sound and light and travel to other places in the blink of an eye."

"Sound *and* light," Jackson repeated, "because either one alone wouldn't do the trick?"

Cathasach placed the large omelet on a plate and cut it into four pieces. "If I wanted to travel to California right now, I wouldn't be able to do it as light, because it's still night there. But I could travel as the whisper of a breeze, because sound can travel in light or dark."

"Then why travel as light at all?" Jackson asked. "Why not always travel as sound?"

Cathasach placed the food on the table and slid into a chair. "Because, sometimes, you want to arrive unannounced."

Johanna closed her eyes for a second as she savored the omelet. "Did he also happen to come up with a spell for time travel?"

Beck suddenly looked up and stared at Cathasach.

The older man took a while to answer. "Yes. But we have never been able to prove it works."

331

Jackson's fork, filled with food, stopped in mid-air. "Were you able to prove the other spell worked? The one where you become light and sound?"

Cathasach sighed. "Not me, personally. But one of the other Eahta Frean fram Drycræft did."

"That's what he *claims*," Beck added.

Johanna carried her empty dish to the sink. "If you haven't been able to prove the spells' effectiveness, how do you know they're real?"

"Because we've seen Myrddin perform them," Cathasach replied.

"But Myrddin's a ghost," Jackson and Johanna echoed each other.

"He is, when he's here, but not necessarily when he's away from here. He once told me he was going to travel to a future time. He disappeared and an instant later he reappeared in the workroom, as a flesh and blood man, and brought me an object that didn't yet exist here on earth.

"Fant—" Jackson stopped speaking when Johanna kicked him in the ankle.

"What was it?" she asked Cathasach.

"A tiny tablet on which words and pictures miraculously appeared."

"Like a magic slate?" Jackson asked.

"Today, it's known as a smart phone. But Myrddin showed me one thirty-five years ago."

Jackson's eyes lit up. "What did you see on it?"

Cathasach's face softened as he concentrated on the memory. "Books. Pages and pages of books. Artwork. Some from grand masters, some I didn't recognize. Music coming out of the tiny little tablet in the palm of his hand."

"Yep," Jackson agreed, "It sounds like a smart phone to me."

"Except," Cathasach said, "there were no smart phones back then."

"Do you still have it?" Johanna asked.

"No. He took it back to wherever it came from. He said *we* weren't ready for it."

"So there are spells for time travel and transmogrifying into sound and light." Johanna created a mental list. "But the collection you sent me has a lot more in it than that. What else could he do?"

Cathasach used his fingers to enumerated spells. "Turn lead into gold. Change his appearance. Command the weather…"

"Heal broken bones," Beck added. "How's that ankle, Johanna?"

Her eyes widened and her mouth opened.

"I'll bet it's not giving you any trouble today," he said.

"It's not. It doesn't hurt at all. I figured it was only a sprain."

"Did it feel like a sprain yesterday when you put your weight on it?"

"No. I thought I'd broken it."

"You did," Beck said, self-satisfied. "You can thank Myrddin for your cure."

Jackson poured himself another cup of coffee. "Are you guys sure you're not just hallucinating?"

"Johanna, walk over to Jackson on your broken ankle and tell him we're hallucinating."

She smiled. "If you're having trouble performing

some of the spells, what's to say other sorcerers wouldn't have the same problem?"

"That's a chance we're not prepared to take," Cathasach said. "Besides, Myrddin said the encroachment could be coming from another dimension."

"Like Terroria," Jackson said.

"Like what?" Beck asked.

Johanna's shoe re-connected with Jackson's ankle. "He's just making stuff up. I'd like to hear what *your* ideas are concerning another dimension."

Cathasach cleared the table as he spoke. "Myrddin said he was free to wander and experiment on another world, even though here, he was trapped inside this cavern. He made it sound special, different, ahead of us in development in many ways."

Jackson opened his mouth to say 'Lumi,' saw the look on Johanna's face, and swallowed his comment.

"Anyway," Cathasach continued, "if the threat is coming from a different dimension, I fear there is little we can do to protect his work. But then Myrddin, or at least his ghost, told me to send it to the curator at the Library of Illumination. He said it would be safe there."

"I hope so," Johanna said.

IZABELLA PULLED HER HAND out of Pru Tellerence's grasp as the overseer questioned Mal about Johanna's expected return. The toddler amused herself by poking the arm of the overstuffed couch and watching it spring back.

★*Did Johanna give you any indication when she'd return?*

"No. As far as I know, she and Jackson got a request for assistance from a library patron and asked me to watch the place until they got back. They've never been to Wales before, so I wouldn't be surprised if they take an extra day or two to enjoy the culture and scenery."

She turned to Ryden Simmdry. ★*And only Johanna can activate the lock?*

⌘*A vault is a curator's safe haven. Even I, as master, do not have access.*

Cries of terror interrupted their discussion. They turned to see a crowd of people pull back in fear as a deceased rajah rose to his feet atop a flaming funeral pyre. He picked up the woman lying beside him and descended into the smoke. He carried her toward a group of men at the edge of the woods. "Let us be off," Passepartout advised Phileas Fogg, having just saved the young woman's life. They quickly mounted an elephant and rode off, but not before the people realized they'd been duped, and a bullet tore through Fogg's hat.

Ryden Simmdry closed a book the toddler had opened and handed it to Pru Tellerence. ⌘*Izabella may be a little too young to appreciate the subtleties of "Around the World in 80 Days."* The scene faded, although it took a little longer for the smoke to dissipate.

★*She's very discerning. Most three-year-olds wouldn't have chosen Jules Verne.*

"I saw the most unusual thing," Mal said, "but it must be my eyes playing tricks on me."

◉*What did you see, Malcolm, because I saw something odd, too.*

"The bodies of Terrorians roasting on the funeral pyre."

Selium Sorium nodded, but didn't need to say anything because the other overseers read his thoughts and saw what he saw.

★*I doubt Jules Verne ever came into contact with a Terrorian.*

⌘*Which means there's been some kind of rift in reality, and the changes are trying to find their place in the continuum of thirteen different realms.*

THE CALL TO ARMS STARTED slowly, but gathered speed, and Furst soon had an army of more than three hundred Dramaticans. He divided them into groups and gave them assignments. He told one group to amass all the weapons they could find—crossbows, pitch, slings and arrows. He tasked another group with stocking a school building across from the library with food and fuel. A few select men developed military fighting tactics and strategies and trained the others. Another group made sure the new provisional headquarters had cots and blankets and medical supplies. Cooks, laborers, even blacksmiths pledged to do their part, the latter forging shields, swords and helmets for the soldiers.

"Enough time, I hope we have," Furst said to Pleth. "A big battle, it will be. Well-prepared, I hope we are."

He drew up a massive schedule indicating where each volunteer should be at any given hour. He gave each person time at home as well as at the barracks. He didn't want to completely disrupt their daily lives while they waited for another attack. If each person could donate two days a week while they prepared for battle, they would still have time for work, family, and relaxation.

Some of the Dramaticans wanted to jump into fighting mode whole hog, but Furst dissuaded them. "Continue our normal existence, we will. Devote ourselves to battle when we are attacked, we'll be able to. Soon enough, it will be."

The younger men and boys trained for the front lines. They had the energy and quick reflexes to better escape Terrorian fire. The older Dramaticans planned defense strategies. They would bring up the rear in battle, firing on the enemy while their attention was distracted by the quickness of the younger troops.

One decision rankled Furst. The Dramaticans had captured fourteen Terrorian decimators and the curator claimed they would be the Dramaticans' best defensive weapons. However, an elder inventor, considered a genius in innovation, insisted on taking one of those decimators apart in an attempt to replicate it. Furst balked at first, saying they needed to keep every foreign weapon at the ready. But the inventor, Berra, insisted and the Dramatican Ruling Council gave him his way. Berra gathered a contingent of volunteers to help him and had them making gun barrels and triggers as he studied the interior mechanism and technology. The Dramaticans trailed the Terrorians in technology, but not in wisdom. Still, creating certain components took a skilled hand, and disassembling one weapon to recreate many took time.

The Terrorians had done a thorough job of disintegrating most of the popular and frequently used books in the library. However, Furst hoped the invaders had not descended into the sub-basements. There were books from other realms stored down there, and he believed they would be an excellent source of information that could greatly help the Dramaticans.

The entrances to the lower levels remained locked,

and weapons were trained on them if they opened. However, Furst knew it would be only a temporary measure. He would have to select a couple of new recruits and venture below ground. Besides, it would be better to know if any of the invaders lurked in the sub-levels, rather than to live in ignorance.

"Your ablest soldier, I need." he told the Dramatican in charge of weapons training. He made a similar request to the person developing strategy.

Together, Furst and the two soldiers prepared to descend into the basement. Another half-dozen Dramaticans gathered to guard the door. They devised a verbal signal, and Furst instructed the soldiers to shoot to kill if the door opened without being preceded by the signal. Then, with a decimator in hand, Furst opened the door to the sub-levels and the small band disappeared into the depths of the library.

⌘*I MUST RETURN TO LUMINA. IF the continuum has changed, I will be able to witness it there more accurately.*

Ryden Simmdry transported to the capital city, Lumi, in search of the slightest differences in manner or design. Nothing appeared to have changed. He entered the College of Overseers and called for a meeting of the minds. He knew it wouldn't be immediate. Some deans were in residence, however others were abroad visiting the realms they oversaw, and would need time to complete their work before returning to Lumi. Finally, they gathered in the chamber used for their meetings. The master did a quick head count. He knew Pru Tellerence remained on Fantasia, but another one among them had not yet arrived. Not wanting to waste any more time,

Ryden Simmdry called for the others to take their places at the table.

⌘*Dame Erato appears to be missing. Please tell me she's not visiting Terroria.*

✠*Why would you think such a thing?*

The door to the chamber creaked open and the last overseer appeared.

Ω*So sorry I'm late.* Plato Indelicat took his seat at the table. Ω*I had to make sure everything is in place for Johanna Charette's sentence on Terroria. I will escort her there as soon as we have completed our meeting.*

—LOI—

30

RYDEN SIMMDRY COULD CONTROL HIS expressions better than any actor, but not when confronted by an old friend he believed he would never see again.

⌘*Plato Indelicat, it is so good to see you.*

Ω*I apologize for my delay, but as I said, I wanted to make sure everything is in place for Johanna Charette's sentence.*

⌘*Yes, of course.* Ryden Simmdry took a deep breath. A temporal rift had definitely occurred, and it appeared to be significant. ⌘*What I am about to tell all of you may seem startling at first.*

◉*What can you tell us that we don't already know?*

⌘*Quite a bit actually.* He allowed his thoughts to develop unshielded.

The other overseers' faces did little to disguise their surprise.

✠*You would have us believe we are living in the past*

and don't remember anything that will happen during the next three weeks, although it's already come to pass?

◍ *It's true.*

§ *How is that possible?*

❀ *You've time traveled?*

Ryden Simmdry shook his head. ⌘ *There has been a disruption in the space-time continuum. I was on Fantasia with Selium Sorium, when we experienced the rift.*

Ω *How can you be sure it was a temporal disturbance?*

⌘ *You would not be here, my friend, unless one had occurred. You died at the hands of the Terrorians, escorting Johanna Charette back to Fantasia after her sentence.*

Ω *Oh dear.*

Ψ *Are the Terrorians going to attack us?*

⌘ *Their uprising will be quelled, however, they will steal a time machine, which is why we are now discussing the problem.*

❀ *It could create an endless loop.*

⌘ *We must stop them before that has a chance to happen.*

π *Except it already has happened.*

⌘ *True. Yet, Selium Sorium and myself were shielded from it.*

❀ *What would you attribute that to?*

⌘ *I can't say for certain, but I believe if we all arrange to be on Fantasia in three weeks when the rift re-occurs, we may all be protected.*

Ω *That is a possibility, but isn't it dependent on what other changes may be made to the space-time continuum during that interval.*

⌘ *Yes. And we have another problem. A powerful sorcerer from earth created spells that give the person casting them special properties. Someone is reputedly trying to steal his notes, and that can't be allowed to happen. I believe they're safe for now, but we need to overcome that issue as well.*

§ *If he is so powerful a sorcerer, why can't he protect them himself?*

⌘ *He is long dead.*

◍ *Johanna Charette and Jackson Roth are currently working on who may be involved in the plot to steal them.*

✂ *Is there anything else we should know?*

⌘ *We've appointed Malcolm Trees Chancellor of the Exchequer.*

✠ *To my recollection, we've never had a Chancellor of the Exchequer.*

⌘ *We do now.*

❋ *For what purpose?*

⌘ *He will be instrumental in collecting taxes. And information.*

Ψ *We do not collect taxes.*

⌘ *The taxes will be minimal. We'll say it's for the resources needed to maintain the integrity of the portals.*

♠ *Is that necessary?*

⌘ *It's a necessary feign for the unobtrusive collection of information.*

♄ *Ah.*

JACKSON MADE A FACE AND rubbed his neck.

"Is your tattoo bothering you?"

"I think the scabs fell off."

Johanna got up from her chair so she could examine the tattoo. "There's nothing there."

"Like I said, the scabs fell off." He touched his neck.

She grabbed his hand to get his attention. "There's *nothing* there. There's no tattoo."

"That's impossible."

She looked at Cathasach and Beck. "Did either of you cast a spell…"

Cathasach eyed her warily. "Who did you say you are?"

"Johanna Charette. You sent me Myrddin's memoir."

Cathasach's eyes widened. "Why would I do that?"

Jackson murmured just loud enough for Johanna to hear. "Something's wrong here…"

Johanna stood up. She grabbed Jackson's arm and pulled him up as well. Thank you for breakfast. We'll be on our way, now."

Beck shot out of his chair. "Not so fast. What are you doing here?"

Jackson squeezed Johanna's hand before he spoke. "You brought us here after we met on the plane. Don't you remember?"

Beck's eye's narrowed. "No."

"Wow, that Pembrokeshire beer really did a number on you last night if you can't even remember meeting us. Why don't you go sleep it off? Johanna and I have to get going."

Cathasach stood as well. "You won't mind if we search you first."

Jackson spread out his arms. "Search away."

Beck patted him down and then went through their backpacks. He turned to Johanna. "Okay, darling, assume the position."

Her eyes widened as she looked up at him. "Excuse me?"

"Spread your arms and legs so I can pat you down."

She bridled, but did as he said. Beck patted her down and found nothing on her.

"Okay," the flight attendant said to Cathasach. "I'm going to escort them to the landing and back to the mainland. Call for a boat to meet us."

"I will." The older man rubbed his jaw.

THE SUDDEN APPEARANCE AND SUBSEQUENT disappearance of Phileas Fogg and company frightened Izabella to the point of hysterics, and it took more than an hour for Pru Tellerence to calm the child. Even then, occasional sobs erupted from the tiny tot until, exhausted by the ordeal, Izabella fell asleep.

Mal gazed at the sleeping tot. "No wonder overseers are banned from having families. Not only could their children be traumatized by the ever-changing properties of the various libraries, but overseers—as parents—could lose focus of their duties as deans when distracted by their children."

Pru Tellerence subtly redirected the conversation. ★*You've no children of your own, Mal?*

"No. I've never had the pleasure." His memories carried him back to another place and time and he sighed. "But it almost happened. I did meet someone special a few centuries ago. Unfortunately, she lost her life in a fire."

★*What a terrible way to die.*

He nodded. "She was the love of my life."

★*I'm so sorry. I didn't mean to bring up sad memories.*

"It was long ago."

★*What was her name?*

"Elizabeth."

★*And no one else has ever come close to capturing your heart?*

"No. She was the one." He smiled. "She was very outgoing, and keeping the Library of Illumination and its gifts to herself would probably have been a burden for her. Although I'm sure she would have found a way to keep our secret if she had lived."

★*Were you already a curator then—when you met her?*

"Yes. Her father was a scholar and often borrowed books from us. I met her one day when I dropped off a collection of research materials. As soon as I laid eyes on her, I knew I wanted her to be my wife. Still, I was wary at first, because of the longevicus charm. I didn't know what she would think about getting older, while I barely aged. I never got the chance to find out."

★*It's just as well. I see you joining the ranks of overseers one day, and the attachment would have thwarted your chances.*

"It was long ago. She would be only a distant memory."

JOHANNA WANTED TO TALK TO Jackson, but not in the company of Beck. "You know, you really don't have to go out of your way to escort us. I'm sure we can find our way back to Marloes."

"I'm not going out of my way. I have to go back to Marloes, too."

"Is that where you're from," Jackson asked, "Marloes? I know you said you're from Pembrokeshire, but you didn't state where, specifically."

"Funny," Beck said, totally serious. "I don't remember meeting you two, at all. And I have a really good memory."

"You were a flight attendant on our plane," Jackson answered. When I told you I was coming to this area, you told me it's where you're from and gave me a Pembrokeshire beer."

"The airline I work for doesn't serve Pembrokeshire beer."

"I know," Jackson continued. "You mentioned that. You told me you took it out of your private stash." He nodded at Beck, hoping he would realize it was true. Beck grew silent but kept on walking. By the time they reached the boat ramp, a boat awaited them.

"You're lucky," the captain said, helping them board. "I'd just dropped off a few crates of supplies when I got called on the radio to pick you up. So I waited here, or else you would have had to wait and see if they could send another boat out. The wind is rising, so we'd best move on." He started the engine and pulled away from Skokholm. No one said a word during the return trip. Johanna thanked the captain as she disembarked and took Jackson's arm as she pulled him toward the path.

"What's your hurry," he asked.

"I want to beat Beck to the top, just in case he gets any ideas about confronting us on the cliff walk," she whispered.

Together they made record time up to the road, while Beck hung back to talk to the captain.

"That was too strange," she whispered.

"What happened, exactly?"

"I don't know, but it was enough to wipe the tattoo from your neck and end a raging storm."

"Do you think this is an alternate universe?"

She started to mock him, but stopped short. *What if he's right?*

THE OVERSEERS LOOKED UP in unison when the lights inside their chamber flickered.

✠*We just recharged the generator fifty or sixty years ago.*

⌘*I don't believe the generator is at fault. I believe the Terrorians are wreaking havoc.*

♦*Yes. But where?*

⌘*We must all make contact with our curators, immediately.*

Moments later, Ryden Simmdry sat alone in the chamber. It didn't take long for his fellow overseers to return one by on. The earliest returnees reported *no change* as far as they or their curators could tell. However, Artemus Rexana returned with worry and concern etched across his already heavily lined face. Σ*I spoke with Prophet IAN c. and he said nothing had changed, but then as we walked back to the portal, I saw, just for a moment, a pair of Terrorians who immediately disappeared through a portal. I came back as quickly as I could. It seems the portals have been breached.*

⌘*Plato Indelicat, I believe you said there has been no change on Terroria.*

Ω*None that I could see, however, I did not speak directly to Nero 51. I was told he is away on important business.*

The electricity in the air increased, fueled by the

overseers' reaction to the news that the Terrorian curator was not at his post.

§*What business would Nero 51 have on Adventura?*

⌘*None. Terroria, Adventura and Mysteriose have been banned from direct contact with one another since the Two Millennia War.*

Ω*How shall we proceed?*

☦*We haven't all returned. Pru Tellerence has not reported back from Dramatica.*

≈*Was she here before, I don't remember seeing her?*

⌘*She is on Fantasia. I will visit Dramatica in her stead.*

RYDEN SIMMDRY DID NOT IMMEDIATELY transport to Dramatica. Instead, he stopped in his personal workroom to invoke a spell that would protect him. He remembered the Terrorian debacle from a few weeks before and knew he needed protection from their weapons. It did not take long for him to complete his task and transport to the Dramatican library.

Furst's soldiers opened fire as soon as the overseer set foot in the cupola.

The master felt the energy of the firearms that bombarded him as Dramaticans targeted him with their Terrorian weapons. He raised his left hand palm out. ⌘*I am in charge of the College of Overseers. Please take me to Furst immediately.*

At first, the Dramaticans appeared confused and angry when their weapons didn't work. Ryden Simmdry quickly informed them their weapons did *indeed* work, just not on him. The Dramaticans told him Furst had gone "below" to hunt for "monsters."

* * *

THE LIBRARY ON LUMINA DIFFERED from all others in the Illumini system in its design and layout. The Ancients fabricated the massive round building entirely out of diamond, because wood was unavailable when the library was created. It was inarguably the oldest structure in Lumi but not the grandest—by choice. The rest of the capital city wore a cloak of sophistication, however, the Library of Origination, the basis for Libraries of Illumination on twelve worlds, could be called under-stated in its simplicity. Even though the shelves glinted like diamonds and reflected light in a brilliant display of color, very few people—other than the College of Overseers—knew of its existence. A high wall protected it from prying eyes on the outside and its roof did not rise into a dome like surrounding buildings—specifically to not draw attention to its existence. The deans considered the Library of Origination their most precious gem, even though the exterior of the diamond structure would not be considered extravagant or special by Lumi standards.

One of the traits it did share with the other libraries was the dozen portals connecting it to libraries on other worlds. However, instead of a cupola, this library had the equivalent of the top of a large crystal egg jutting out of the center of its main floor, and portals danced around the egg in an undulating design.

On this particular morning, the overseers gathered in the vicinity of the egg, awaiting Ryden Simmdry's return, and in their long robes with their flowing hair and beards, they seemed to compliment the design and blend in.

Visitors, on the other hand, stuck out like inflamed

pustules, so when Nero 51 popped up in the middle of the Library of Origin, he had no way to escape unobserved.

FURST, BANGOR AND MUDGE SLOWLY worked their way around sub-level six, looking for Terrorians. Furst felt certain at least one invader lurked on one of the 1,306 subterranean floors of the library, but it was an immense space to search with thousands upon thousands of stacks of books. It could take months.

Still, they had no choice. He must secure the library at all costs.

Dark corners in a labyrinthine maze did not make the search any easier, and each floor below grade possessed the same convoluted design. Shadows lengthened and crawled as the trio of Dramaticans made their way around the dimly lit space.

Furst soon adapted to the changing patterns of light and dark. He silently held out his arms to stop Bangor and Mudge when he noticed an odd shadow. It moved even when they stopped, and Furst raised his weapon in anticipation.

JOHANNA STARED AT THE PROPRIETOR of the Tafarnwyr Inn. "What do you mean you don't have our reservations? I realize we couldn't return last night because of the storm, but we didn't check out."

"You never checked in. Perhaps you're staying at a different inn and got lost? I can tell you for a fact there was no storm near here last night."

"This is the Tafarnwyr Inn, isn't it?"

"Aye. If you want a room, I do have one available, but only the one, not two like you said you had."

"Fine," she answered.

"We'll take it," Jackson agreed.

"I'll need to see your passports." Johanna and Jackson handed them over. "You can pick them up tomorrow." She showed them to their room and left.

"This place is giving me the creeps," Jackson said. "Let's get in the car and explore."

"Do you think anyone else around here would know about Eahta Frean fram Drycræft?"

"I don't know, but I'd be very careful about talking about it too freely. Something weird is going on."

They reached the car park but found their exploration curtailed when they discovered their rental car missing.

—LOI—

31

JACKSON STOOD IN THE EMPTY space where they last parked their vehicle. "You know, we're gonna get a bad rep for borrowing transportation. First the time machine is stolen, now our rental car is gone. Don't be surprised if you wake up tomorrow and find your shoes missing."

"My shoes…"

"Yeah. You use them to get around, don't you?"

"Let's get serious. Something major has happened, and we need to figure out what that is."

"Do you have your diary with you?"

"Yes." Johanna rummaged inside her backpack, removed the diary, and wrote: *Mal, something weird is going on and we don't know what it is, but a tattoo Jackson got just before we left has disappeared from his neck, the rental car we rented is gone (possibly stolen) and people we met don't remember us? Is it a conspiracy?*

It didn't take long for Mal to get back to her. *You*

must return immediately. Someone has interfered with the space-time continuum and nothing is as it was.

Jackson read Mal's entry over Johanna's shoulder. "That can't be good."

"We need to find a way back to the airport. Now." Johanna walked inside and found the proprietor of the inn. "We've just found out my grandmother is deathly ill and need to go home immediately. We won't be staying the night. Could you tell us how to get transportation back to Cardiff?"

They soon sat in a hired car en route to the airport. Johanna used her cell phone to book their tickets, and a few hours later, they boarded a flight back home.

THE RAY FROM FURST'S WEAPON did nothing to stop the advancing shadow. He wanted to retreat to take stock of the situation, but felt like his feet were glued to the floor. Fortunately, it wasn't a threat at all, but Ryden Simmdry.

⌘*Tell me what has happened here.*

"A Terrorian invasion, it is. Theirs, these powerful weapons are. Lucky we did not hurt you, you are."

⌘*When did the invasion begin?*

"Two days, it has been. Died, several Dramaticans have. Died, several Terrorians have."

⌘*Are there still Terrorians here?*

"What we are trying to determine, that is. All levels, we must inspect."

Ryden Simmdry held out his hand and closed his eyes. ⌘*The levels are all clear. There are no Terrorians here.*

Bangor and Mudge's corkscrew curls loosened as they visibly relaxed.

⌘*Where did you get these weapons?*

"Dead Terrorians, we took them from."

⌘*How many do you have?*

"Fourteen, we have. Thirteen, we are using. Taken one apart, Berra has. Replicate it, he wants to."

⌘*Take me to your leader.*

"To see the Prime Minister, you want?"

⌘*Is he in charge of the army?*

"Died in the attack, the Military Provost."

⌘*Who is leading your people in battle?*

"Found him, you have. Now in charge, I am."

Ryden Simmdry smiled. ⌘*Excellent.* He paused. ⌘*Did any Terrorians escape into the countryside?*

"No. Dead, all who came out are."

⌘*Continue to do what you are doing, Furst, to protect the library and your people. I will take word of the attack to the College of Overseers.*

"Many of our books, they have destroyed…" Furst's shoulders slumped.

⌘*We will help you replace them when the threat has ended.*

"Expect that, when can we?"

⌘*I wish I had an answer for you.* Ryden Simmdry clasped Furst's shoulder. ⌘*Carry on.*

The overseer disappeared.

Both Bangor and Mudge let out a little yelp. "That, who is?"

"A long story, it is," Furst replied as he made his way up the stairs to the main level.

BACK ON LUMINA, THE MASTER of the College of Overseers found his fellow deans gathered in a tight circle around Nero 51 and another Terrorian. The overseers grew silent when they sensed Ryden Simmdry's recount of the battle on Dramatica.

"Master Ryden Simmdry, I am glad of your return," Nero 51 stated. "I am here to sadly report some of my countrymen have taken it upon themselves to attack one of the libraries."

⌘*How did they manage to breach the portals?*

"I innocently informed some of our officials of the Fantasian's sentence. Word must have leaked out to the general population, and some of them took it upon themselves to wage a private war.

⌘*I see. Do you have proof to back up this claim?*

"Yes." Nero 51 turned to the other Terrorian. "General Lethro 814, tell them of the missing stun guns we created to capture live game for our food supply." Before the general could say a word, Nero 51 waved one of his tentacles and continued. "Wild game is unpredictable, and rather than risk one of our own getting hurt while we hunt for food, we developed stun guns that allow us to quickly capture wild animals, and keep them alive until it is time to cook them, insuring freshness." He turned, "Isn't that right, General?"

"Absolutely," the general answered. "I-I reported the missing guns to Nero 51 as soon as I discovered their absence."

"And I," Nero 51 said, "immediately came here to report the missing weapons."

⌘*And how do you know your kinsmen used them to attack a library?*

The two Terrorians froze.

* * *

A TAXI PULLED UP IN front of the Fantasian Library of Illumination, and Johanna and Jackson climbed out, glad to be home, but none the wiser about who had tried to steal Myrddin's memoir.

"Welcome home," Mal said with a smile, when the teens walked in the front entrance.

"What happened?" Johanna asked.

★*It seems the Terrorians have invaded Dramatica, and in so doing, have caused a temporal rift.*

Jackson stowed his backpack behind the circulation desk. "What does that mean, exactly?"

★*It means they have changed the past.*

Johanna dropped her backpack next to Jackson's. "I knew it. As soon as the time machine went missing, I knew Nero 51 would use it to invade other worlds."

★*Nero 51 claims some of his countrymen launched the assault without his knowledge after he let it slip that you would be arriving on Terroria to serve out a sentence.*

"But I've already served my sentence."

"No," Mal said. "The temporal rift has jettisoned us back three weeks. You're due to return home from Terroria tonight."

"How can that be?" she asked. "I'm here."

★*The original Johanna Charette is here. A carbon copy of Johanna Charette from three weeks ago is on Terroria.*

Jackson played with the gong on the circulation desk. "What if something happens to Johanna's *carbon copy*? She would still be all right, wouldn't she?"

Pru Tellerence looked from Jackson to Mal to Johanna. ★*Johanna, you must get my miter hat out of the vault at once. I need to return to Lumi immediately. But you have to do me a favor and watch Bel while I'm gone. She's protected here, but I'm afraid she may disappear if I try to take her to Lumina with me.*

"Disappear?"

"Who's Bel?" Jackson asked, before he saw a tiny face peek out from behind Pru Tellerence. He crouched down until he was eye level with the child and stuck out his hand. "Hi Bel, I'm Jackson."

The youngster retreated behind Pru Tellerence.

"She only understands Russian," Mal said.

"I guess it's time to break out the interpreter on the iPad," Jackson said, going behind the circulation desk to retrieve it.

"Is she the child you were looking for?" Johanna asked Pru Tellerence.

⌘*Yes, but now I'm afraid she may be lost once again because of the temporal rift.*

"We'll take good care of her," Mal assured the overseer.

★*I fear you may be forced into duty, Mal, because of what has happened. Johanna and Jackson may be as well. Is there someone else who can come here, someone you trust, to watch her?*

They all turned and stared at Jackson.

"What am I supposed to do?" he asked.

Johanna placed her hand on his arm. "Just how much does your mother know about the Library of Illumination?"

"Nothing," he answered, "except that you live and work here. But I never told her anything else. I didn't think you wanted me to."

"And you were right," Johanna assured him. "But

now things have changed."

"Really changed," said Mal, "because outside this library, it's probably three weeks ago."

"That's impossible," Jackson said in disbelief. Johanna fished inside her bag and grabbed the taxi receipt from their trip home from the airport. She squinted at the date. Then she grabbed the receipt from her airline ticket and checked that as well. "He's right. It's three weeks ago."

"No. I don't believe it. And I'll prove it." Jackson picked up the phone and dialed his friend Logan. "Hey buddy just a quick question. What day is that big math test scheduled for?" His shoulders slumped. "Right. I'll catch you later, there's something I gotta do…"

"Well?" Johanna asked.

"I expected him to say I was crazy because we already took it. Instead he said it's next Tuesday."

"Jackson, we need to contact your mom," Johanna said. "We need to get her in here to watch Bel. We need to bring her up to speed on the library."

He shook his head. "She's never going to leave Ava and Chris on their own. And there's not enough room for them here."

★*But there could be.* Pru Tellerence left for a moment and returned with a travel guide. ★*Follow me.* She walked into the room reserved for current period-icals and opened the book. A two-bedroom hotel suite appeared. She looked around for a hiding place and slid the open book under a piece of furniture where it would remain undisturbed. ★*Do you think they would mind staying here? Your mother, sister and Bel could share the larger room and your brother could take the smaller one.*

"This is beautiful," Joanna said. "Where is it from?"

Pru Tellerence closed her eyes for a second. ★*It's a hotel called George V in a place called Paris."*

"Nice." Jackson said. "Do you think it comes with room service?"

"Your mother could always cook upstairs in my kitchen," Johanna said.

★*Please. Contact her while Johanna and I go downstairs to retrieve my miter.*

"Here goes nothing," Jackson said, as he dialed home. "Getting her here may be easy. Explaining *why* is going to be a bit more difficult."

FURST ENTERED BERRA THE INVENTOR's workshop and saw a Terrorian decimator laying in pieces on a bench with a note next to each piece. "Made any progress, have you?"

Berra looked up from his workbench. "Easy to duplicate, some parts are. Difficult, others are. Progress, we are making, but slow it is.

"Come to visit, an overseer has. Aware of our battle, they are."

"These weapons, do we still need?"

"Yes." Furst knew the overseers would do their best to end the battle, but he had no assurances of when that might be. He thought of the Two Millennia War. It didn't get that title because it had ended quickly. Better to have too many weapons, than not enough. "Still work on them, you must."

"Doing our best, we are, but alien, this technology is. Understand it, I am trying to."

Furst picked up a piece and examined it. "Time, I hope we have. Without it, we may be doomed."

* * *

"Some right-minded citizens who knew of the rabble-rousers' plan reported them. Sadly, there's been some unrest among our youth, recently," Nero 51 claimed. "Having heard the rumors, I thought you should immediately be made aware of the possibility of an attack."

Ryden Simmdry closed his eyes for a moment. When he opened them, he stood beside Nero 51 and the general in the Terrorian Library of Illumination.

⌘*Johanna Charette, please gather your personal belongings and meet me at the circulation desk.*

A few minutes later, Johanna appeared with her backpack.

Ryden Simmdry advised Nero 51 and General Lethro 814 to remain where they were. ⌘*I will return momentarily.*

The master transported Johanna to her office in the Fantasian library. ⌘*Please wait here for me. Do not leave this room. Do not contact anyone—even Jackson. That is of the utmost importance.* The lock on the door clicked. ⌘*I'm locking you in for your own protection.* He disappeared leaving her alone and bewildered.

The master overseer found the Terrorians where he'd left them. They were busy discussing how to handle the situation when he reappeared.

⌘*Please. Show me where you kept the missing weapons that were allegedly stolen.*

"Follow me," Nero 51 told the overseer. He walked over to the curator's staircase. "I kept them safeguarded in my personal chamber to avoid having something like this happen. Obviously, someone close to me took advantage of my trust in him." Nero 51 led Ryden Simmdry and the general into his residence and closed the door. A small number of weapons lay piled in a corner. He picked one up, quickly checked it over, and handed it to the overseer.

The master carefully examined the firearm. ⌘ *You say this will stop an animal without hurting it.*

"Correct."

⌘ *How does it work?*

Nero 51 demonstrated the weapon on General Lethro 814, who was immediately locked in a force field.

Ryden Simmdry took back the weapon and switched the lever on top. He took aim at the general, whose eyes widened. ⌘ *Does this undo the force field?*

Nero 51 snatched the weapon away. "That is a design flaw that is being remedied. It's supposed to deliver a more powerful stun for larger animals, but it doesn't work correctly."

⌘ *What is wrong with it?*

The door to the curator's residence flew open and Ilio 22 appeared. "We have—"

"It is you who betrayed me," Nero 51 shouted and pulled the trigger. Dust particles that had once been Ilio 22 floated gently to the floor.

⌘ *This is no simple stun gun.*

"I did not mean to pull the trigger," Nero 51 said matter-of-factly. "He surprised me. But he's the only one who could have betrayed me by stealing weapons and starting a battle.

"As I've said, this firearm has a design flaw. The unfortunate demise of Ilio 22 is a sad consequence, but may actually be preferable to the punishment that would have been meted out to him for starting a war."

⌘ *That statement is taken under advisement. I*

will take these weapons as well. A moment later, Ryden Simmdry and all the decimators in Nero 51's residence disappeared.

Mauk 232 entered the residence. "Did Ilio 22 tell you we have moved almost all the guns to a safe place?"

"No," Nero 51 answered before releasing the general from the effect of the stun gun. "Carry on."

The soldier stared at the empty corner. "Where are the rest of the weapons?"

Nero 51 paused a second before answering. "Perhaps Ilio 22 already removed them."

"Perhaps," the soldier answered. "I'm surprised I didn't see him."

"Well, I advise you to get right on it and discover what happened to those weapons."

Mauk 232's tentacles quivered. "Yes, sir. I'll do that immediately." He fled the residence.

Nero 51 turned to the general and folded all his tentacles across his chest. "Now, General, it's time for you and I to devise a new strategy, and for everyone's sake, it had better be a good one."

If there had been any water in the chamber, it would have immediately turned to ice.

ALTHOUGH ANXIOUS TO LEAVE, Pru Tellerence waited to meet Jackson's mother, to ensure she'd be leaving Izabella in safe hands. While she waited, she exchanged her Fantasian street clothes for her overseer's robe and miter hat. By the time she finished, Naimh Fitzpatrick Roth had arrived at the Library of Illumination with her son Chris and her daughter Ava.

"Hey," Jackson greeted them.

Chris looked around. "Another party? I didn't bring Brittany."

"No. And you can't tell Brittany about this."

"Why?"

★*Perhaps I should explain.*

Mrs. Roth and her younger children gawked at the overseer.

★*I am...*

Pru Tellerence watched their faces register disbelief and confusion.

—LOI—

363

32

Pru Tellerence abandoned telepathic communication and addressed Mrs. Roth and her children aloud. "I am a dean of the College of Overseers for the Library of Illumination. Obviously, you are not familiar with what that means, which in the past has been for the best, but we are faced with a terrible threat and must make you aware of information we previously kept confidential."

Mrs. Roth looked at Jackson and then Johanna, who both nodded gravely.

Chris edged over to Jackson's side. "So what's the deal, bro'? What's going on?"

"What's today's date?" Jackson asked.

"April second, so if you're thinking of pranking us, you're a day too late."

"But it's not April second. That's the problem," Jackson explained. "It's the twenty-fourth."

"Yeah. Right."

"Look at this." Jackson pulled out his airline ticket and stuffed it in his brother's hand. "I just got back from Wales."

"What were you doing in Wales?"

Mrs. Roth had little patience for lies. "You did not go to Wales, Jackson. You've been home with us."

"Look at my airline ticket. It has my name on it. It has the date I flew to Wales on it. It says I flew to Wales on April twenty-first of this year. But you say today's date is only April second. And that's the problem." He pulled out his passport and showed it to his mother. "Look, that's me. Look at the date they stamped it in Wales. Three weeks from now. Something bad has changed time as we know it."

Mrs. Roth stared at the passport without saying a word.

Mal took over the conversation. "This library is special. The people inside its walls have been shielded from the time change. Johanna and Jackson, as well. However, we believe something bad has happened, and we may be called on to investigate what that is."

"So tell me," Chris said, "if you were protected because you were in the library, but Jackson was in Wales, how was he protected?"

"Maybe Myrddin's workshop is protected," Jackson said.

"No," Johanna answered. "Cathasach and Beck no longer recognized us after breakfast. Could the longevicus ritual be protecting us?"

Mal nodded. "That's a distinct possibility."

"What's this ritual you're talking about?" Mrs. Roth

365

asked.

"I like to think of it as the Bruce Banner treatment," Jackson said.

Chris sneered at his brother. "You were belted by gamma waves?"

"I don't think they were gamma rays, exactly," Jackson answered. "They were blue."

The brothers stared at each other for a few seconds until Johanna broke the silence.

"That's not why you're here. A little girl just arrived here this week, and we're afraid if she leaves the library, she may disappear. So we have to keep her safe. However, since we could be called away at any time to investigate the problem, we need someone who can stay here to keep an eye on Bel."

"Ava and Chris can still go to school and stuff," Jackson added.

Chris let out a low groan.

Jackson punched him in the arm. "We just need to make sure Izabella stays safe, Mom. You could do that, couldn't you?"

"Where is this Izabella that you're talking about?"

They all turned to Pru Tellerence, but she was gone, and Izabella was nowhere to be found.

BERRA FOUND FURST SWEEPING UP the dust particles of books that had once lined the shelves of the library. Even the shelves that held them were now gone or burned beyond repair.

"A lot of damage, they have done, I see," the inventor said.

"Rebuild, we must. Take time, it will," the curator

replied.

"Unless, back, they come."

"Do what we did, again, we will. Fight back, we will."

"Have a book that might help me, do you? Heard, I have, books from other worlds, this library has. Manuals for the monsters' weapons, does it have?"

Furst stopped sweeping, he took a ring of keys from behind the circulation desk, which had survived the battle unscathed. "Me, follow." The curator led Berra into sub-level six where he twisted the light housing to open the door to the elevator. "Come."

Together they rode in silence to the sub-basement that housed the Terrorian collection. Furst sifted through a large card file looking for one listing Terrorian weapons. He located a book on Terrorian military patents and another for technical weapon specifications. He handed them to Berra. "Help, this might."

The inventor opened the book on technical details and found a schematic for the decimator. His eyes lit up as he looked at the diagram. "Help, this will. But 'zalor,' I do not understand."

Furst took the book and looked at the word perplexing the inventor. He returned to the card catalog and located a book on Terrorian elements and minerals. He pulled it off a shelf and paged through it looking for 'zalor.' He nodded and then looked for another book. "To another level, we must go."

They rode the elevator up to sub-level six. Furst led Berra through a maze of hallways and stopped in front of a stone wall. He held his hand against the rock and the wall slid out of sight revealing seven doors. Furst walked to the last door on the left and place his hand bearing the Illumini constellation against the lock. The door swung open revealing a room that resembled a bank vault. Inside, what looked like tiny safe deposit or post office boxes lined the perimeter. Each metal door had a dozen miniscule lines of symbols or letters etched on it with an odd looking depression below it. Furst searched for a particular door and inserted his thumb in the depression. The door clicked open and the curator pulled out a small tray with a rock on it. Except, it wasn't a rock exactly, but a quartz-like substance with gold veining.

Berra reached for the rock and held it close to his eyes. "Recognize this, I do. From the river bed by Baerfeng, it comes."

"Zalor, it is."

Berra's mouth split into a semi-toothless smile. "Solved a problem you have. Take this, I must."

Furst snatched the rock back. "No."

"But I must," Berra said.

"The Rodo twins, send me. Show them the rock, I will. Mine it for you, they will. But leave the library, this sample cannot."

"Go, I must," Berra said. "The better, the sooner. And immediately, send the Rodo twins to you, I will."

Furst pretended to place the rock back in the vault, but hid it under his caftan instead. He couldn't let Berra have it, but he did not want to allow the Rodo twins inside the depths of the library. He would replace the rock after showing it to them.

"I SUGGEST WE RECALL THE troops immediately while we devise our new plan," General Lethro 814 said with more bravado than he felt.

"Yes," said Nero 51, "if there are any troops left to recall."

The general puffed out his chest. "The key is in the time machine."

"No, it is not," Nero 51 said. "We have already gone back to the only time in our lifetimes when we are sure the portals were open. I do not relish returning to a time, possibly eons ago at the brink of the Two Millennia War, to wage a battle against unknown entities, with others in charge of strategy. We would merely be unknown, and unwelcome, visitors."

"Then the time machine is of no use to us?"

"I wouldn't say that. We could return to a time here on Terroria before our troops first launched, and advise them of what to expect."

"What is that exactly?" the general asked.

"Recall the troops immediately. We must determine the answer to that question."

The general seethed. "I do believe I said that in the first place."

PRU TELLERENCE APPEARED IN THE overseers' chamber on Lumina, earlier than she anticipated. She stared at Ryden Simmdry. ★*Did you just pull me here without my consent?*

⌘*There have been developments.* He pointed to the pile of weapons he'd confiscated from the Terrorians. ⌘*The Terrorians have attacked Dramatica.*

Her stomach dropped. ★*How bad is it?*

⌘*I have to congratulate Furst. He handled it well. He managed to contain the fighting within the aboveground levels of the library. There have been casualties on both sides. However, the Dramaticans managed to capture some of the Terrorian weapons and use them to their advantage, which mitigated the damage. They lost a lot of books from the upper levels, but as I explained to Furst, they can be replaced. I became concerned when I learned the Dramaticans are now busy trying to replicate these weapons. It is a foreign technology and not one they developed on their own. On the other hand, it does seem to equalize the Terrorian advantage. I believe we also should replicate these weapons en masse, and provide an abundant supply of them to each realm with the warning that they should be used only in retaliation if one of the other realms attacks. I believe it's the Fantasians who say, 'Forewarned is forearmed.'*

★ *Wouldn't that result in even more casualties?*

⌘ *Not if we go back to a period in time before this latest battle started and deliver these same weapons to Terroria with the same warning. They will undoubtedly recognize their own weapons and know their surprise attack is no longer a secret.*

◍ *We rarely use our gifts to time travel. I don't think I ever have, even though I'm aware it's possible. There is always the fear that we will turn what is into something that should never be.*

⌘ *The Terrorians have already done that. We must take the risk. I feel it is our job to mitigate the damages by taking away the Terrorian advantage.*

◍ *How will we replicate these weapons?*

⌘ *Artemus Rexana, please take some of these firearms to Fridi and help them analyze and reproduce them in very large numbers. I'm sure everyone in the College of*

Overseers would agree that we should compensate the Fridians handsomely for this work.

ΩIs this the best solution to the problem? Maybe the Terrorians told the truth when they blamed the incursion on a few rabble-rousers.

⌘Then they should be just as happy as the other realms to be warned about the threat in advance—if there are any rabble-rousers other than Nero 51. If the majority of Terrorians are innocent, this plan should help them avert a coup.

Artemus Rexana picked up an armful of weapons. *ΣI will make sure our plan is embarked upon immediately.*

★If we are done here, I must get back to Fantasia.

⌘I believe your work there is done. You were, after all, only sent to escort Johanna Charette and Jackson Roth back to their home world. Now that you have your miter back, I can't see any further reason for you to return. Until this problem with the Terrorians is settled, your place is here, on Lumina.

THE RODO TWINS NODDED IN unison when Furst showed them the rock and said they could find it among the stones in the Baerfeng riverbed. "Seen it, I have," Rilli Rodo said.

"Find it, I will," Roxo Rodo added.

Rilli punched Roxo. "Beat you, I will." The two rushed out the door as they made their way to the river.

Berra entered. "Knocked me over, they almost did. To Baerfeng, are they going?"

"Yes," Furst answered.

Berra spotted the chunk of zalor on the circulation desk. Furst followed the older Dramatican's gaze and they both reached for the rock at the same time. The zalor fell on the floor and a small piece—almost like a slice—chipped off. "Perfect," Berra announced as he grabbed the sliver. "Use this, I will."

Furst cradled the remaining rock in his hand. He considered it a precious resource of the library and as curator, it was his job to protect it. He bristled when he thought about Berra taking a piece, but he knew it was for the good of the library and his countrymen, and he struggled to accept its loss.

AFTER A THOROUGH SEARCH OF the main floor, Jackson ran up the cupola stairs, just to make sure Izabella wasn't up there. He returned ten minutes later and shook his head.

"Did anyone check the residence?" Mal asked. "That's where Bel has spent the most time."

They all trudged up the curator's stairs en masse. "I'll look around out here," Jackson said, "while you check inside." They split up and worked their way through the rooms without success. They met up with Jackson in the living room. "Anything?"

Johanna shook her head. "Could Pru Tellerence have taken her?"

"Where did Pru Tellerence go, anyway?" Jackson asked.

"It's not like her to leave the way she did," Mal said.

Jackson's head jerked up. "You don't think the temporal rift got them?"

Mal didn't say anything for a moment. "She may have been summoned by the College of Overseers."

"But she wouldn't have taken Bel with her." Johanna

sat down on the couch and grabbed a pillow to hug. "That's the reason why we asked Jackson's mom to come over in the first place."

Jackson's younger sister spoke for the first time since arriving. "Maybe she went outside."

"I don't know how she could have," Johanna said.

"We'd better look anyway. Chris, Ava, come with me. We're looking for a scared little three-year-old with blond wavy hair and no adult supervision," Jackson explained as they left the residence. "Did I mention she doesn't speak English?"

Johanna, Mal and Mrs. Roth waited in silence for them to return. After several minutes, Johanna stood up. "I can't just sit here and do nothing. I'm going to search downstairs again."

Mal looked at Mrs. Roth who nodded. "We'll go with you," he said. They headed to the main floor of the library to search again.

NERO 51 TENSED, AS IF READY to launch his own attack. *How dare General Lethro 814 assume that smug attitude with me? He's merely a pawn in a game played by masters. I'll put him in his place, but later, after he has served a purpose.*

The general sent out his minions to locate the troops who had invaded the other realm. Of the original twenty-four deployed, only ten had survived and their tales of 'jumping fire shooters' were enough to make anyone think twice before returning to Dramatica.

The survivors were called to the library to testify before Nero 51 and the general.

"You told us we would be facing weak little

children," one soldier lamented. "There were no kiddlets there, just ugly red beasties firing flames in all directions. They didn't need us to destroy their books, for they surely held no reticence about burning them, themselves."

"I am familiar with the beings you engaged in battle. They are Dramaticans—much smaller than we are in stature and with only two *arms* rather than eight tentacles. They are a rudimentary civilization with crude weaponry and slow minds." The curator drew himself up to his full height and towered over the soldier, who remained seated. "Your lack of effectiveness in performing your duty disgusts me." He took a step back and looked at each survivor. "You're lucky I don't send you before an execution squad. But you may still be of use. Tell me, what weaknesses did you see?"

"They had no weaknesses. Rather than grow terrified and fear for their lives, they fought with more ferocity every time we killed one of them. They should have quaked in fear. Instead they propelled themselves to great heights in an instant and rained their fiery revenge upon us. The others were not killed by their crude weapons, but by the flames they harnessed. Our comrades burned to death."

Nero 51 tapped his tentacles together as he thought. Before they ventured into battle against Dramatica again, they would need to develop a flame retardant covering or skin coat to protect them from burning to death before they could get the job done. "That was helpful. You will not be executed. He turned to the other soldiers. "What insights do you have to give about the battle? And in case it's not perfectly clear, allow me to state, your right to live depends on the effectiveness of the information you give.

So speak up, because stating something that's already been said will not work in your favor. I will reward you with your lives—but only if you give me useful *original* information in return."

—LOI—

33

Naimh Roth turned a corner expecting to find more books, but instead found a sumptuous apartment that looked much bigger inside than the space seemed to allow. She opened a door to a huge bedroom and walked around in awe, swiping her fingertips across the rich fabrics that adorned the bed and windows. Another door led to a marble bathroom half the size of her house. She looked around. *No child here.* She walked back into the living area and pulled back the curtains covering French doors. *This is impossible.* She walked out onto a balcony high above the street. Off in the distance stood the Eiffel Tower. *I must be hallucinating.*

Johanna looked for Izabella in the bathrooms, coatroom and bindery while Mal systematically searched the main reading room and surrounding stacks.

Johanna's private office was tucked into the corner

of the bindery. She left her office for last, but when she pushed on the door, she found it locked. "Bel, are you in there?" She placed her ear to the door and listened for sounds of the child playing. She heard something move and knocked again. "Bel?" *Why is this door even locked?* She rushed to retrieve her keys from her backpack.

"I think I may have found her," she called out. "My office is locked, which it never is, and I think I heard someone inside."

INSIDE THE LOCKED OFFICE, JOHANNA'S counterpart froze. Someone was trying to get in. *Who the heck is Bel?* She hated not knowing why she had been locked inside in the first place. She removed the tiny diary from the chain around her neck and spoke as softly as she could. "Mal. Ryden Simmdry locked me in my office. Now, someone is trying to break in. What should I do?"

BERRA APPROACHED FURST IN THE square in front of the library. He carried a rough-looking replica of a decimator with him. "Ready for a test, it is," the inventor said matter-of-factly.

Furst cleared the area behind a barrel of refuse. He retreated twenty-five paces, took aim and fired.

The Dramatican decimator was not as finely tuned as the Terrorian version. Instead of turning the barrel into dust, it sent chunks of it flying in all different directions. People nearby ducked for cover, then applauded after the flying splinters settled. For them, this weapon far exceeded the tactical advantage of a flaming arrow. The only one who didn't look excited was Furst. "Messy, it is. Why?"

"The ability to finely hone the zalor, we do not have," Berra said. "Make a difference, it would. But a device to grind down the pieces, take time to build, it would. Take too long, it might. Make do for now, we must."

Furst nodded. He preferred a more precise instrument, like the Terrorian version. He didn't care about the mess Berra's weapon would create, as much as he cared about the pain that might be inflicted if a Terrorian seized it and used it on a Dramatican. Furst did not want to see his kinsmen splattered all over the street. The Terrorian-made weapon worked so quickly, there wasn't time for pain or suffering. The Dramatican version would result in a lot of both. Still, the Terrorians were the ones who started the war, and the Dramaticans had to fight back with every weapon they could get their hands on.

Berra studied Furst's eyes. He laid his hand on the curator's arm. "Worry, do not. The Rodo twins to help, I will ask. A planing device, they must create. Be done, it will."

"Good." Furst nodded. The idea reassured him, if only slightly. "Very good."

A VOICE NIGGLED AT MAL's memory. He couldn't quite place it but it sounded like Johanna. It was hard to understand what she said. Suddenly, her voice sounded clear as a bell. He turned the corner to see her rummaging through her backpack behind the circulation desk.

"What did you just say?" he asked.

"I think Bel may be locked in my office."

The words 'locked in my office' resounded clearly in his head. *That's what I'm hearing.*

Johanna grabbed her keys and headed back. Mal followed her.

Mrs. Roth had heard the tail end of their conversation and followed as well.

Pru Tellerence stiffened, but only for a moment. The idea of being told not to return to Fantasia irritated her, but she kept her thoughts shielded. ★*I promised to return the child Izabella to her mother. It will not take me long.*

⌘*The child is safe on Fantasia. It is best to leave her there for now, lest something unforeseen happens to her because of the temporal rift.*

She couldn't fault Ryden Simmdry's logic. It was the same reason why she had prepared to leave Bel on Fantasia in the first place. But now that the master overseer had unexpectedly intervened, she felt like she had abandoned the youngster. ★*I'll just go back and explain that I need to leave her there for a while.*

⌘*You need to go to Dramatica and assess their needs. That realm is your responsibility, and an entire realm is more important than a single child.*

Pru Tellerence's shoulders sagged, but she drew them back to a position of confidence. ★*Yes. Of course. I'll leave for Dramatica immediately.*

⌘*Wait.* He closed his eyes a second and murmured a few odd words before touching her shoulder. ⌘*A small precaution—a protective charm. The Dramaticans are shooting* foreigners *on first sight. We wouldn't want you turned to dust.*

★*Thank you.* She saw him relax but couldn't do the same. ★*I'd better attend to them immediately.*

She stopped by her chamber first and retrieved an ancient book from a locked cabinet. She paged through it for several moments until she found what she wanted and committed it to memory.

JACKSON, CHRIS, AND AVA ENTERED the library just in time to see Mal and their mother head toward the bindery. "Where's everybody going?" Jackson asked as the Roth siblings trailed their mother like ducklings.

Inside the bindery, they gathered around Johanna and watched as she inserted a key in the door lock.

Johanna pushed the door open and called out softly, "Bel?" Everyone else filed into her office behind her. They looked behind the door and under her desk and in blind corners.

"She's not here," Jackson said.

"I thought for sure I heard someone," Johanna replied.

Mal rubbed his beard.

"Any ideas, Mal?" Jackson asked.

"It's odd, but I hear a far off voice inside my head saying 'in the closet.'"

"That's the only place left," Johanna said. She grabbed the doorknob and gave it a tug. It moved slightly, but felt like someone inside was hanging onto it to keep the door from opening. "Bel," Johanna said. "It's okay. It's me and … Uncle Mal." She tugged harder, but still met with resistance from the other side. "She's a strong little thing."

Jackson nudged her aside. "Here, let me." He pulled the knob with all his strength. The door flew open and Johanna's three-week-younger self tumbled onto the floor.

They all stared down at her, their mouths agape.

Nero 51 walked into a packed room in Building 16. It was not as convenient a location as Building 7 had been, nor as well-equipped, but he'd blown up Building 7 after his troops failed to take over the libraries during their previous attempt. He saw General Lethro 814 standing off to the side, surrounded by a group of military and political leaders. By now, everyone in this gathering had heard that their latest assault had failed. He needed to regain their confidence and ensure he still had their support before he could continue. This was it. He needed to *inspire* them. He inhaled deeply.

"My fellow Terrorians, as you well know, we are embarking on another extensive operation to take back our rightful place as the prime realm.

"I commend those of you who worked so hard to remove our weapons from my residence and store them in a safer place. I knew the College of Overseers would come snooping around here, and that precaution assures me we still have the weapons necessary to complete our mission.

"I have personally traveled through the portals to ascertain the damages and immediately recognized a scheme by the overseers to scramble the portals' directions, so travelers never know where they will end up. It gave me insight into what we are up against, and it allowed me to study some of the other realms as they are today."

He watched as General Lethro 814 whispered to a soldier standing next to him.

"We have seen our share of what lesser minds might construe as setbacks," Nero 51 continued, "but every step we have taken thus far has provided us with intelligence and reconnaissance." He raised his voice. "We are stronger because of them. We must now throw off our mantle of caution and attack the realms simultaneously as originally planned. Our previous battle only ended badly because of the overseers' interference. Now that we know what to expect, our mission will not fail. Be reminded, we can use the time machine to pinpoint the best moment to invade." He studied the faces in the crowd searching for signs of agreement before he continued. "But not right away. The eyes of the overseers are upon us. Outwardly, we must appear calm, but covertly, we will pursue our goals." He spoke with more force. "We will train. We will strategize. We will prepare to the ultimate of our abilities. And then, when their oversight wavers, we will attack!"

The room erupted with a roar of appreciation and renewed vigor. Nero 51 stretched out his tentacles as far as they would go, as if to embrace the entire crowd. He nodded in acceptance of their enthusiasm. *I have them firmly in my grasp.* And then he gave them a strangled smile and allowed them to congratulate him on his vision for a new Terroria.

JOHANNA GOT UP AND DUSTED herself off. She gave Jackson a playful shove. "Are you happy now? Ryden Simmdry told me not to let anyone in."

She looked around at the others, astonished to see Jackson's family and Mal standing there. "What's going on? What's everybody doing here?"

No one answered. "What are you all staring at?" she

demanded. "Is there something spellbinding behind me?" She turned quickly and froze. Both Johannas crumpled to the floor as soon as their eyes locked.

MULTIPLE GUNS PELTED PRU TELLERENCE the moment she appeared on Dramatica. She silently thanked Ryden Simmdry for casting a spell to protect her.

"No! No!" Furst screamed.

★*It's all right, Furst. The master took precautions.* She looked at the cavernous space. A lot of the debris had been cleared out. Only shelves lining some of the walls still stood, plus a couple near the cupola stairs. The others had been vaporized or destroyed by fire.

"Much destruction, we have," Furst said.

★*The College of Overseers will make sure all is set right, as soon as the threat passes.*

"Still possible, is it?"

★*I'm afraid so, although we're doing all we can to stop it. According to Nero 51, some rebellious youth on Terroria took it upon themselves to launch the attack.*

"Well trained for rebellious youth, they were. Military precision, they had, and powerful weapons. Lying, I think Nero 51 is."

★*I'm told you now possess some of those weapons, with more being made.*

"Not as efficient, ours are. Much damage, they cause."

★*Don't worry. We will do whatever we can to help. Is there anything you need right now?*

"A transparent front wall, I wish we had. That we can see through the floor, it is not enough. What is going on inside, I would like to see from outside, to prepare."

Pru Tellerence smiled. ★ *That's more than I can help you with.*

"Daydreaming, I am."

★ *You're thinking ahead, and that's to be commended. If there's nothing else I can help you with, I'll be on my way.*

"Stay for lunch, won't you? See our encampment, you can."

★ *I will return soon, I promise you.*

Before the Dramatican curator had an opportunity to say more, Pru Tellerence was en route to Fantasia.

"WE NEED SMELLING SALTS," Mrs. Roth said with conviction. "Jackson, do you have a first aid kit with smelling salts here?"

"Umm …" He thought of his brush with Dracula. "Yeah." He found the first aid kit behind the circulation desk, right where Johanna had left it.

His mother found ampoules of spirits of ammonia, inside. She broke one open and held it under Johanna's nose. The curator turned her face to get away from the odor.

Her eyes fluttered open. "What happened?"

"You passed out when you saw your alternate self," Jackson answered.

"What?" she asked, twisting around. As soon as she saw the other Johanna, she passed out again.

"Maybe, you should try reviving the other one?" Jackson told his mother.

Mrs. Roth moved over and revived the other Johanna. The exact same thing happened. She seemed to revive, asked what happened, and fainted as soon as she saw herself.

ALTHOUGH MAL WASN'T AN OVERSEER, nor had he yet been given the blessings he'd been promised as Chancellor of the Exchequer, he still had one ability few others possessed. He could commune with the College of Overseers without needing to shinny up a rope to the curator's key at the top of the cupola. He could simply use his diary, which was similar to the one used by Johanna to contact him. He immediately informed Ryden Simmdry there were two unconscious Johannas in the library, and he wasn't quite sure what to do with them.

Within a minute, the master overseer appeared.

⌘ *This is exactly what I had hoped to prevent.* He looked at the people surrounding him. ⌘ *When Nero 51 appeared and said someone had stolen weapons from his library, we immediately went to Terroria. It's three weeks earlier there than it is in this particular library, so I made sure I returned the Johanna serving time on Terroria to her office. I took the precaution of locking her in to prevent this from happening. Who opened the door?*

"Johanna did," Mal answered. "We were searching for Bel, and Johanna thought she heard someone inside her office. She thought the youngster may have locked herself in."

⌘ *And where is the youngster now?*

"We don't know. We were looking for her when the two Johannas met. That's when I contacted you."

⌘ *I see. Jackson, please take the visiting Johanna up to the residence and place her on the bed. We must separate them. When that is done, I will revive this Johanna and work with her to reunite her two selves.*

"You can do that?" Jackson picked up the visitor.

"Of course you can. You're the main man."

Jackson's family watched, dumbstruck, as Ryden Simmdry prepared to make Johanna a single entity.

The overseer went into the bindery and looked for some gold leaf and a mortar and pestle. He knew both would be there for gilding pages and mixing compounds. He selected a few other necessary supplies and returned to the office.

He reached into the folds of his robe to retrieve herbs and powders from within various pockets. Upon Jackson's return, he used the spirits of ammonia to revive Johanna. He asked the others to wait in the bindery and locked the office door so he could confer with the curator in private.

"What's going on?" she asked.

⌘ *You may not realize it, but you've been weakened by the temporal rift. There are two Johanna Charettes roaming around and I need you both to unite. I have the knowledge to create a charm that will do that, however, only you can cast the spell on your two selves. There is one caveat though.* He took her hand and pierced her fingertip with a sewing needle. He allowed a few drops of her blood to drip into the potion. He took a small piece of muslin, placed the concoction in the center, and tied it into a little bag with the same cord Johanna used to sew quires together. ⌘ *Take this.* He handed her the poultice and another spirits of ammonia ampoule. ⌘ *I told Jackson to place the other Johanna on your bed. Before you walk into the room, take a whiff of the spirits of ammonia, but don't inhale too deeply or you may pass out before you can cast the spell. Take hold of her hand and hold the poultice between your left palm—the one with the Illumini constellation—and hers. It will make the charm stronger. Then recite this.* He taught her two short sentences in the Luminan language. ⌘*Do you think you can remember that? It's important that you get it exactly right.*

She nodded and headed toward her residence. She didn't answer anyone's questions as she passed through the bindery. She wanted to make sure she didn't forget the Luminan chant.

Upstairs she inhaled the smelling salts before she stepped into her bedroom. Without delay, she grabbed her double's hand with the poultice between them and recited the spell. Everything went black as she hit the floor.

—LOI—

34

NERO 51 DRANK WITH HIS supporters, and noted that
General Lethro 814 kept his distance. The curator
would have to do something about that, but not right
away. His speech had stirred up a lot of nationalism, and
he wanted to keep the fervor at a fevered pitch. Still, he
kept his eye on the general and tensed when one of the
general's minions broke away and headed his way.

Nero 51 maintained an outer calm as the younger
Terrorian barked, "Where is Ilio 22? The general said
only you could answer that question."

Terrorians in the near vicinity craned their necks to
search for the missing soldier.

The skin on Nero 51's tentacles rippled. He felt quite
sure the general had informed his compatriots of the fate
of Ilio 22. Whatever he chose to say would be his word
against the general's. "I can understand why the general
wouldn't want to tell you himself. Your friend's fate was

quite nasty and unexpected.

"I had asked the general to accompany me while we surveyed the war zone. He brought a weapon because I asked him to protect me. We found no need for the weapon while we were off world, but the general was on heightened alert. As soon as we returned, Ilio 22 burst into my quarters in an effort to finish removing the weapons stored there. His sudden appearance quite unnerved the general, who fired. His weapon was set to decimate. I'm sure Ilio 22 didn't suffer. He probably never knew what hit him. I took the weapon away from the general and told him to confess what had happened. I can see he chose instead to implicate me to save his own hide.

Nero 51 sighed as if the weight of the world sat on his shoulders. "I'm afraid you'll have to take General Lethro 814 into custody. His lies are treasonous and will hurt our cause. You believe Terroria deserves to be the prime realm, don't you, soldier?"

Everyone within earshot of Nero 51 stared at the soldier as they awaited his answer.

"Yes," he replied, fearing he, along with the general, would be tried for treason if he answered any other way.

"Then do your duty. Arrest the general and arrange for a tribunal and execution."

Another Terrorian asked, "Isn't it a little premature to arrange for his execution?"

"What else would you have me do?" Nero 51 asked. "Who can we trust, if not the military commander in charge of our welfare?"

The inquirer nodded and others followed suit. They all looked to the soldier, who backed away.

The young Terrorian retrieved a weapon before

returning to apprehend the general.

The military leader's pitiful squeals over his unanticipated arrest made the collected crowd cringe, until Lethro 814 was finally removed from the room.

JACKSON FOUND JOHANNA UNCONSCIOUS ON her bedroom floor. He shook her gently. "Johanna?" She did not respond. He shook her a little more forcefully. No answer. He gently slapped her face a few times. She was out cold. When a splash of water from the bathroom sink didn't work, he ran to find Ryden Simmdry.

"I'VE NEVER SEEN ANYTHING LIKE it," Mrs. Roth exclaimed. "It's like a dream apartment out of a magazine. And I could see the Eiffel Tower from the balcony!" She stopped speaking when her son ran into Mal and almost knocked him over.

Jackson's eyes darted about. "Where's Ryden Simmdry?"

"He's gone," Mal answered, "now that everything has calmed down. Where's Johanna."

"I can't revive her!" Hysteria tainted Jackson's voice.

"It's probably a delayed reaction." Mal's own words of assurance didn't stop him from rushing upstairs.

Everyone followed, although Mrs. Roth told Chris and Ava to wait in the living room. If anything dreadful happened, she didn't want her younger children to be traumatized.

Mal did many of the same things Jackson had done to rouse Johanna with no luck.

Mrs. Roth felt for Johanna's pulse. "Get the smelling salts from downstairs, Jackson."

"We have some right here," Mal said, pulling a crushed ampoule from Johanna's right hand.

"What's this?" Jackson asked. He removed the poultice from her left hand.

"Could be the work of Ryden Simmdry," Mal replied.

A trembling voice asked, "Is she gonna die?" They all turned to look at Ava, who had not followed her mother's orders to stay in the living room. The girl's eyes were glassy with unspilled tears as she awaited an answer to her question.

"Take her inside, Jackson," Mrs. Roth ordered.

"I'm not leaving Johanna."

"I'll do it," Chris said, leading his sister away from the room.

The spent ampoule did nothing to revive Johanna.

Jackson pushed his mother away. "I took a CPR class in school." He performed chest compressions, trying to remember exactly what he learned. He doubted her airway was blocked, but tried mouth-to-mouth just to be on the safe side. "C'mon Johanna," he begged as he returned to doing chest compressions. He imagined Johanna's reaction if she were to suddenly come to and find him with his hands on her chest. At this point, he would welcome her outrage. "Come on, Johanna. Stop fooling around."

Naimh Roth felt as badly as her son did, but was far more practical. "We need to call an ambulance." While she fumbled with the telephone in Johanna's kitchen, Mal used his diary to inform the overseers that Johanna could not be revived.

* * *

JACKSON COULD NOT BELIEVE JOHANNA was
unresponsive. "Now you've done it," he scolded her.
"They're going to cart you away and I'm going to end up
the primo curator. I hope I can find someone as cute as
you to be my underling. I bet she'll think I'm her hero."
With each word his chest compressions got more and
more powerful.

His mother pulled him away. "Jackson, stop."

He couldn't hold back his tears. "I can't stop, now.
She may die."

"She's not breathing, honey. You did everything you
could…"

"No!" he shouted as he slipped his arms under
her limp shoulders and lifted her partway off the floor,
touching his forehead to hers."

PRU TELLERENCE CONCENTRATED ON BEL'S location
as she transported back to Fantasia. Her jaw dropped
when she ended up in a dark enclosed space. There, she
found Izabella asleep in a corner, curled up in a tiny ball.
The overseer, who could see in the dark as a perk of her
majorious longevicus blessing, scooped up the youngster
and cradled her. She kissed Bel's forehead and whispered
the spell she had looked up on Lumina—one that would
protect the child from disappearing back into the past.

Stress over the youngster, as well as a lack of fresh
air in the closet, took its toll on the overseer who, like her
young companion, soon fell asleep.

FURST CAUGHT SIGHT OF THE Rodo twins en route to
Berra's workshop, pushing a wheelbarrow laden with
stone. One of them waved when he saw the curator.

"Plenty of stone for weapons, we have. Work on making them more accurate, we will."

Furst motioned for them to stop and hurried to their side. "Zalor, you have?"

"No," Rilli Rodo replied.

"Gerylli, we have," Roxo Rodo explained, "for grinding stones."

"Many grinding stones," Rilli added. "Last long, they do not."

"Quite nicely, it grinds zalor," his twin said, "but two or three zalor chips, they are only good for. So many, we need."

Furst nodded. "Keep you, then, I won't. Important, your work is."

Rilli picked up the handles of the wheelbarrow. "Hurry, we must."

Roxo walked quickly beside him. "Important work we do, Furst said."

"More important, I am. Pushing the stone, I am," Rilli stated.

Roxo wrestled him for the handles to the wheelbarrow. "More important, I want to be."

"No!" Rilli said, not giving up his claim. The scuffle made the wheelbarrow tip over, its contents tumbling to the ground.

"Not important now, you are," Roxo exclaimed.

"Spill it all, you made me. Not important, *you* are."

"Am."

"Not."

Berra came out of his workshop to see what the twins were shouting about and spotted the rocks on the pathway.

"Done, what have you?" the inventor asked.

"His fault, it is," both twins said simultaneously, pointing to the other.

"The rock, bring in. Now," Berra threatened, "or payment, neither of you will receive."

⌘*ALLOW ME.*

Ryden Simmdry's reappearance surprised everyone except Mal.

"What did you do to her?" Jackson cried, rocking back and forth with Johanna in his arms.

⌘*Nothing that would harm her, I assure you.*

The overseer's robe puffed up like a beanbag as he squatted down next to the young curators. He picked up Johanna's left hand and studied the Illumini constellation.

⌘*See, here.* Ryden Simmdry showed Jackson Johanna's palm. ⌘*The light of illumination is faint, but if you stare at Fantasia, you will see it still shines. Her body is in stasis. She is reuniting. It's just taking a little while because she's so young.*

Jackson didn't buy into Ryden Simmdry's statement. "Usually, people our age recover more quickly because we're stronger and healthier."

⌘*Your bodies heal more quickly, but your minds aren't as mature. It takes longer for your neuro-pathways to reason out what has happened in each of the time lines and reconcile it with what it already knows as the truth.*

"So, you're saying she'll be okay?"

⌘*Yes.*

"And she's gonna be mad at you," Chris said from the doorway, "when she finds out her chest is all black and blue because you had your grubby paws all over it."

Mrs. Roth glared at her younger son. "I told you to wait in the living room."

"It's okay Mom," Chris replied. "Professor Dumbledore says Johanna's gonna be all right."

"She is?" Ava peeked out from behind her brother. Mrs. Roth sighed. Her children were growing older and had minds of their own.

Ryden Simmdry looked at Mal. ⌘*Professor Dumbledore?*

"A character created by J. K. Rowling for her book "Harry Potter and the Sorcerer's Stone.""

"That's just one book," Ava announced. "There were seven."

⌘*Do you enjoy reading?*

Ava squinted at Ryden Simmdry. "Are you a ventriloquist?"

The master laughed. "You could say that," he said aloud.

"I love to read. But all I ever get anymore are Jackson's hand me downs. I've read everything in the library. At least, everything in the juvenile section. Mrs. Keller won't let me sign out anything from the adult section. She says I'm too young."

"How old are you?" the overseer asked.

"Fourteen," Ava replied, "and a half."

Ryden Simmdry thought back to a time when he was fourteen and a half. It seemed so long ago he could scarcely recall it. It had been a different universe back then—young and growing quickly, much like himself. Little did he know how his life would turn out as time went on or how a simple rock from a distant place could have such a profound effect on him.

"Mrs. Keller is right. You don't want to grow up before your time. It all passes so quickly. Remain young and innocent for as long as you can."

"I think it's too late for innocence," Ava replied.

"Ava!" her mother gasped.

"What did you expect, Mom. I've got two older brothers and they have long, meaningful conversations when they're outside shooting hoops—right below my bedroom window. If you ever heard what they talked about, you'd be struck dumb for all eternity."

Mrs. Roth stared at her daughter, too astonished to speak.

Chris laid a hand on Ava's shoulder. "And if I ever hear that you leaked the contents of any of those conversations—thereby endangering our dear, beloved mother's future ability to speak—there would be very severe consequences to pay."

"Very severe," Jackson echoed.

"I want you all to stop this conversation this very minute," Mrs. Roth demanded.

"I wouldn't worry," Mal advised her. "If your younger children are anything like their older brother, you have nothing to worry about."

A low moan signaled Johanna's awakening. "Johanna, can you hear me?" Jackson asked, kissing her.

"How can I help but hear you," she mumbled. "You're shouting in my ear."

He kissed her forehead and then her eyes, nose, cheeks and lips.

She giggled. "You're slobbering on me."

"I thought I lost you."

"I'm right here." She struggled to sit up. "What

happened? My chest aches. Did I get hit by a car?"

"No, no, you're fine," he answered, kissing her some more. "We'll talk about your chest later."

"We will not," she said indignantly.

"You're in trouble now, bro," Chris teased.

"Right." Jackson kissed Johanna one more time. "We won't discuss it at all. Ever." He glared at his brother.

Chris and Ava laughed, while their mother cringed.

⌘*Now that we've averted one crisis, there's a second one to attend to.*

"Which one is that?" Mal asked.

⌘*The mystery of the missing child.*

The overseer closed his eyes for a second and nodded. Then he got a peculiar look on his face. He walked over to Johanna's closet and pulled the door open. He found Pru Tellerence sitting on the floor, asleep, holding Bel who was also asleep, their arms wrapped around a stuffed kitten.

The light from the doorway roused Pru Tellerence.

★*You found us! Where are we?*

⌘*In Johanna Charette's closet. What are you doing here? You're supposed to be on Dramatica.*

★*I've already been to Dramatica. Furst has every-thing firmly in hand. So I decided to make sure Bel was all right.*

Ryden Simmdry pulled the door closed and shielded their communication from the others. ⌘*I can't believe you defied my wishes and came here.*

★*I had to come. Bel is special.*

⌘*What's so special about a child from Fantasia?*

★*She's not from Fantasia. She was born on Romantica.*

⌘*And that makes her special?*

★*She's my child.* She looked at the other overseer defiantly. ★*Our child!*

—LOI—

35

RYDEN SIMMDRY LOOKED AT PRU Tellerence and the child she clutched with disbelief. ⌘*That's impossible. Overseers don't have children. The Ultimium Codi bans it.*

★ *That doesn't mean we can't have children. It means we're forbidden to. It's an ancient, outmoded law and it's time it changed.*

⌘*I can't be the one to change it. I'm the one who enacted it. It's for our own good.* He closed his eyes and recited the regulation. ⌘*Deans must refrain from any liaisons that may limit their abilities to act on behalf of all residents of the Illumini System. This precludes any overseer from becoming involved in any familial or intimate relationship. Sentimentality can cloud the mind. Love can color our decision-making. Fear for the safety of our loved ones can immobilize us. We must be free to act in the best interests of the many, therefore, we are precluded from falling victim to the interests of the one. All dependent relationships are strictly forbidden and punishable by loss of position, and blessings. Be forewarned: once the majorious longevicus blessing is reversed, metamorphosis could cause your biology and physiognomy to reflect your true age, which in many cases, could result in instantaneous death due to old age.*

★*Maybe you should have thought about that before you told me that you loved me.*

⌘*This cannot be my child.*

★*Are you saying you think I became involved with someone else after pledging my love to you?*

⌘*That was ages ago—three or four millennia at the very least.*

★*I see. Your feelings have changed. It was okay to fill my head with romantic ideas while I was a young, vital, impressionable curator even though you broke your own law, but now that you realize there's a consequence, I ...* she looked down at Bel, ★*we do not merit your consideration.*

⌘*That is* not *what I said.*

★*It's what you mean.* She clutched the child to her breast and disappeared.

THE RODO TWINS PICKED UP the grinding stones that had spilled and carried them into Berra's workshop. The inventor provided individual corner workspaces for each of them because their spirit of competition proved to be too much of a distraction for them to work together. However, each worked well when they had different tasks. Roxo chiseled chunks of abrasive stone into wheels, so they could be mounted on an axle and used to polish zalor. Rilli polished the zalor chips for the weapons Berra built. It took them a while to settle into a routine, but once they did, they accomplished a lot.

RYDEN SIMMDRY WALKED OUT OF Johanna's closet alone.

"Did I hear Pru Tellerence inside the closet?" Mal asked.

⌘*She is no longer there.*

"Oh." Mrs. Roth sighed. I thought we'd finally found Bel."

⌘*The child was inside the closet. Pru Tellerence has taken her away.*

"Is that safe?" Mal asked. "Or perhaps there's been a change in the temporal rift?"

⌘*Neither. I'm sure if anything happens to the child, we'll hear from Pru Tellerence.* He turned. ⌘*Are you feeling like your old self, Johanna?*

"Yes and no. I feel fine, and I know what day it is and all. And what you're all doing here. But part of me is having a hard time believing the past three weeks have already taken place.

⌘*Give it a day or so. Your second psyche will soon blend in.*

"You have a second psyche. How cool is that?" Jackson exclaimed.

"Totally cool," Chris confirmed.

Jackson looked at his mother, sister and brother. "I guess you can all go home now, considering Izabella's not here."

"What if she returns?" his mother asked.

"If she does, you'll be the first to know. Well, maybe not the first, more like the fifth or sixth. I'll call you."

Mrs. Roth picked up her belongings. "I was actually looking forward to staying in that room with a view of

Paris."

Johanna lifted her head in surprise. "It has a view?"

"I walked out on the balcony and off in the distance I saw the Eiffel tower. I bet it looks stunning at night." Mrs. Roth no longer seemed fazed by the oddity of a Parisian penthouse suite located on the first floor of the library.

"This place is so cool. Can't we stay?" Ava asked. "Just one night."

Jackson looked at Johanna and Johanna looked at Mal.

"I think it might be a good idea," Mal answered, "in case you're suddenly called away tonight. It will give you time to acquaint your family with some of the other fine points of the Library of Illumination and the importance of maintaining its secrecy."

"You mean I can't tell my friends?" Ava whined.

"No." Mal shook his head. "If some of the world's more unsavory characters learned about the charms of the Library of Illumination, it would no longer be a safe place for Johanna and Jackson. People would take advantage of the library's assets and possibly try to drive Johanna and Jackson away. We're facing a similar problem now on other realms and…"

"Realms?" Chris asked. "What does that mean?"

"Other cities," Johanna said at the same moment Jackson replied, "Other countries," and Mal answered, "Other libraries."

Chris narrowed his eyes suspiciously. "You guys really need to work on getting your stories straight. Which one is it going to be?"

No one spoke until Mal said, "Other libraries in

various cities and places."

"If something like that had happened," the younger Roth boy said, "I would have heard about it on CNN."

"You don't watch CNN," Jackson replied.

"I would if I knew people were attacking realms."

Jackson gave his brother a playful shove, but it appeared to be too rough for Mrs. Roth.

"Jackson, don't attack your younger brother that way. You might hurt him."

"Yeah, Jackson," Chris taunted. "You might hurt me."

Jackson gently brushed off his brother's shoulder. "Aw, did my itty-bitty brother get a boo-boo," he raised his voice, "because he's such a baby?"

"Boys, enough," their mother exclaimed. She grabbed her two younger children by the elbows and walked them to their bags. "In your rooms, now. Grab your stuff."

Jackson walked over and picked up his mother's bag and Ava's. He gazed at his brother. "Here." He shoved the bags in Chris's arms.

They were interrupted by a knock on the door.

"Illumination," Jackson and Johanna said in unison.

A deliveryman handed Jackson a shipment of books and Johanna the paperwork.

"Can you check those in?" she asked him. "I need to look at something downstairs."

"Sure."

"Before you go, I want to say goodbye." Mal shook hands with Jackson and his family and kissed Johanna on the cheek. "I'm hitching a ride with Ryden Simmdry. You know how to get in touch if you need me."

* * *

THE TERRORIANS LITERALLY BUZZED ABOUT the fate of General Lethro 814. A lot of older citizens sided with Nero 51, claiming Lethro 814 cared more about his career than the citizens of Terroria. However, younger Terrorians looked up to the general as a gifted military leader and derided Nero 51 as a librarian and politician. They felt a great injustice had been done. There were whisperings among them about forming a coalition to oust the curator. They wanted Terroria to become the prime realm, but didn't fully understand the importance of the Library of Illumination or what it meant to the realm, because everything about it was cloaked in secrecy.

The leader of one such faction, Kat 111, quickly gained popularity as a worthy opponent of Nero 51. Kat 111 was smart enough to never be heard in public talking about the curator's 'failings,' but his views quickly gained momentum behind closed doors.

Meanwhile, Nero 51 internally debated having general Lethro 814 executed. Nero 51 believed it could force his detractors to band against him, and he didn't want to give them that opportunity. The general had trained many soldiers and, in doing so, had forged a personal connection to many of them that Nero 51 did not have.

No, Nero 51 told himself. *It is not in my best interests to publicly execute the general. I will pardon him, instead.*

RATHER THAN RETURN TO LUMINA, Pru Tellerence materialized in the Library of Illumination on Romantica. She waited in the cupola until she knew the curator would be preoccupied with her midday meal and then headed to the residence where she exchanged her overseer's robe for a Romantican gown. She hid her hat on a high shelf in the back of the closet and snuck out of the library with Bel. Her stomach churned with apprehension over leaving her miter in an accessible place, but she had little choice. Besides, if Ryden Simmdry remained true to his word, she wouldn't need it much longer. Her primary mission was to find protection for Bel and then separate from the child. If Pru Tellerence lost her longevity blessing, so be it, but she couldn't bear the thought that Bel might lose her's as well, and die in the process. The child of two overseers would most likely inherit their longevity blessings and age only one year for every thousand. So a three-year-old child would essentially be three thousand years old. Izabella did not appear to have the intellect and maturity of someone so old, but her brain would have only developed as much as any other toddler's. Plus she had spent a good part of her life in an orphanage without the benefit of loving parents to stimulate her learning and developmental processes. Loving parents. It looked like Izabella would not be gaining that benefit any time soon.

Pru Tellerence carried the sleeping child through the bustling central market square and continued on to the Maroqi District on the far edge of Romantica's capital. That's where the realm's most powerful white witches lived and worked. Josefina Charo, who originally promised to raise Pru Tellerence's child, was long dead. But the overseer knew which cottage would now be inhabited by a witch with many of the same attributes as Josefina. Indeed, the cottages in the Maroqi District were bestowed more like political offices than personal property. She headed to the home of the most powerful

405

white witch in the realm.

DRAMATICANS GUARDING THE PORTALS FOUND themselves getting bored and took it upon themselves to divide into two groups, so half could watch over the portals while the other half played Zedax, a centuries old game challenging two players to capture the other's pieces while vying for control of a grid. Playing Zedax could be called the Dramatican national pastime. Teams of onlookers would often bet on players and call out what moves *they* would make.

Downstairs, Furst walked around his near empty library, creating a list of the supplies needed to rebuild the interior. He propped the library doors open because the weather was perfect and he wanted to feel connected to what was going on in the community.

Outside, a company of soldiers drilled in the square, while Dramaticans with storefronts and business dealings carried on as usual. Their commands and ripostes sounded distant, like the cries of youngsters playing in a park.

Until they didn't.

Furst looked toward the door when he sensed the silence and reached it just in time to see the soldiers break into shouts and applause as Berra walked across the square with a new weapon in his arms and the Rodo twins trailing behind. Furst walked down the steps of the library and met him at the edge of the square.

The inventor held out the weapon. "A new one for you to test, I have. A polished chip, it has. Test it, will you?"

Furst took the gun. "Yes." He waved away everyone

standing near a pile of rocks. When the area cleared, Furst took aim and fired.

The stones exploded, but disintegrated in mid air before the debris could rain down on spectators.

"Close, it is."

"Make adjustments, we will." Berra took the weapon and spoke to Rilli. "Finer, we must make the chip."

"Not as good as mine, your work is," his twin retorted.

"Not perfectly round, your sanding stones are."

"Are too."

"Are not."

"Stop!" Berra walked back to his workshop. The twins followed, nudging each other out of the way, until they got jammed trying to enter the front door at the same time. Finally they both fell into the workshop and each scrambled off to his own corner.

JOHANNA WENT DOWN TO THE vault to look at Myrddin's memoir. She opened the book, but Myrddin didn't appear until she stroked the plate with his picture.

"What have you found?" he asked.

"Not much. I don't think Cathasach and Beck trust us very much, especially after the temporal rift."

Worry etched its way across Myrddin's face. "There has been a temporal rift?"

"Yes. Some Terrorians—beings from another realm—have stolen a time machine and are wreaking havoc across all the realms."

"Terrorians." He nodded. "The Two Millennia War. I'm not surprised they're causing trouble." He closed his eyes and remained quiet for more than a minute.

Johanna grew impatient. "I have nothing more to tell you."

"It does not appear the threat to my work is coming from outside the realm."

"From whom then?" she asked.

He took a deep breath. "I fear it is coming from within—a member of the Eahta Frean fram Drycræft."

"One of the eight masters of wizardry?"

"You must find out which one."

"How am I supposed to do that?"

"You are the curator of the Library of Illumination. I do not doubt that you will determine who the suspicious party is and stop him. It's what curators do."

"I don't even know who the eight wizards are. I only know of Beck and Cathasach."

"There is a book that magically updates whenever one of the eight is replaced. It is the *Master Compendia of Sorcery*. It's either on sub-level 1,311 or in your vault. I'm not sure which."

"Is it written in English?"

"Of course."

"Modern English."

He closed his eyes for another minute. She yelped when he unexpectedly grabbed her hand before his eyes sprang open. He chanted something in a foreign language, touched his forehead to her hand, and then dropped it. "You will be able to read it."

"Thanks," she murmured, and unobtrusively wiped her hand on her pants.

"Whoever he is, use whatever means you have in your power to stop him," he commanded, "even if it requires ultimate force."

"Define 'ultimate force.'"
"Kill him."

—LOI—

36

THE ROTH FAMILY COULDN'T STOP marveling over all the amenities and eccentricities of the hotel room. From the view of Paris to the artwork hanging in the toilets, it all seemed like a wild dream.

Jackson understood why his family was impressed. The Roths had always been poor, scraping together what little money they could to get by. It's the reason why Jackson's school recommended him for the job at the Library of Illumination. School officials knew his family was in need and offered him the job so he could help out at home. As co-curator, Jackson had just started pulling in a decent wage, but for too short a time to make a real difference, so the poshness of this hotel suite absolutely astonished his family.

"Mom, can we eat dinner on the balcony?" Ava asked.

"Dinner? In all the commotion, I hadn't even

thought about it."

"Call room service," Jackson said.

His brother chided him. "Very funny."

"No. I mean it. Call room service."

Chris eyed Jackson warily as he picked up the phone. A look of surprise crossed his face when they asked him what he wanted to order. He asked for a hamburger and french fries and hung up. "They're not really going to deliver food here, are they?"

"Time will tell," Jackson answered.

"Time will tell what, Jackson?" their mother asked.

"Whether Chris's room service order will actually be delivered."

A half hour later, there was a knock at the door.

Jackson waved at his sister. "Open the door, Ava. It's probably Johanna."

"Bonjour, Mademoiselle."

"Uh … hi. Jackson!"

Jackson got up and nodded at the waiter.

"I will set the table, no?" the waiter asked. Within seconds, the table was set for one with a hamburger, french fries, a glass of ice and a bottle of cola. There were individual bowls of condiments, a linen napkin, and silverware. "Will there be anything else?"

"Can I get one of those?" Ava asked.

"You'd better send up three more of those."

"What about Johanna?" Mrs. Roth asked.

"Make it four," Jackson said, handing the waiter a twenty-dollar bill.

"Twenty dollars is an awful lot to spend on one burger," Mrs. Roth said.

Jackson handed her the room service menu. "That

was just a tip. The burgers, plus a cola, cost about sixty euros each."

His mother blanched.

"Don't worry about it." He winked at her. "The Library of Illumination is picking up the tab."

"Really?" his sister asked.

"Really," he answered.

"Then can I have dessert?" She gave him her most charming smile.

EVEN THOUGH INGUR'S FACE WAS creased with age, the old witch's eyes were bright with the accumulated wisdom of her years. She held up her hand in greeting. Pru Tellerence did the same. The witch's eyes took in the Illumini constellation embedded in the dean's palm. "What have you brought me, Overseer?"

★*A child in need of protection.*

"What atrocity pursues this bittle?"

★*She has special powers and someone seeks to take them away.*

"Is the seeker a witch?"

★*A wizard, it is true, so substantial precautions must be taken.*

"What do you offer in trade?"

Pru Tellerence looked around the cottage. Her eyes came to rest on a bunch of purple flowers laying on a table. The overseer performed an alchemy charm and turned the blossoms into gold.

The old witch walked over to the table and picked up the now-metal bouquet. She bit into it with the few teeth that still populated her mouth. "This will do, for now." She looked at Izabella. "Wake up child. We must

412

proceed immediately."

Bel's eyes opened. She stared at the witch, but tenaciously clung to Pru Tellerence.

★*Her name is Bel. Izabella.*

"Not anymore. If you wish her to be shielded, her name must change. I will call her Selestra."

★*Selestra. It's a beautiful name.*

"I suggest you wipe it from your consciousness immediately, so no one knows whom to seek. Just ask for 'the child' when you visit here next year to pay another tribute. I suggest you provide something more substantial, so you can decrease your visits. Every time you visit here, the possibility of the child being discovered increases."

★*Then I must take precautions now.* She focused on a plate of biscuits sitting on a counter and turned it into gold. She spotted a scuttle by the hearth. Soon, each individual lump of coal and the scuttle that held them, glowed like the precious metal they had become. ★*That should take care of the near future.*

"Now you must disapparate. You cannot risk being seen leaving here without the child."

★*I can't.* She had forgotten her *key* in her mitre.

"You have to."

★*There must be a way I can avoid being seen.*

"You could wait until after the sun sets, but there's no guarantee you will not be noticed."

★*It's a chance I must take. Besides, it will allow me to stay with Bel a ...*

"Selestra. Bel no longer exists."

The overseer sighed. She gently stroked the young-ster's face. ★*You have a new name, and it's a very pretty one. Selestra. It's the most beautiful name in the universe.*

The old witch brought out a basket filled with balls of yarn. "We will finger weave, Selestra, for you must learn a trade early on. It is the way on Romantica, even though I sense you are not Romantican. Still, you are fair enough to pass for a citizen and we will introduce you as my great grandchild from the Wellendra region. Your mother is gravely ill, and I have taken your care upon myself." She kissed the child's forehead. You will call me *natta* because I am now the matriarch of your family." She picked up both the youngster's hands. "Say 'natta,' Selestra."

The newly named child said, "Nada," in an extremely low voice.

"That will work just fine," the witch replied as she took Selestra's hand and taught her how to weave yarn using only her fingers.

TERRORIANS COULDN'T MOVE FAST ENOUGH when a public announcement stated Nero 51 had important information to share regarding the detention of General Lethro 814. The news traveled like wildfire, and within the hour, the square outside the library overflowed with Terrorians. They lined the surrounding streets and hung out of building windows surrounding the area.

Nero 51 kept them waiting, feeling empowered by their uncontrollable interest in what he had to say. They might be disappointed by his initial speech, which would be short and sweet. However, his follow-up speech would be more in-depth and political. He patted himself on the back for his stroke of brilliance, before striding out of the library and standing at a podium one of the soldiers had erected on the top step. He tested the microphone and heard the rubbing sound of his tentacle against the metal.

The abrupt sound caused the crowd to quiet.

"My fellow Terrorians, I have searched my heart—without abandoning intellect—concerning the incarceration of General Lethro 814, and I have determined he is not morally responsible for the death of Ilio 22. His crime is withholding his culpability from you and trying to cast blame on me. Many of us would prefer that our mistakes remain hidden and I cannot, in all conscience, condemn a man for a shortcoming we all possess. There is also his more blatant crime of trying to cast aspersions on me. That was willful and unfortunate. While I believe he brought his tribunal upon himself, in a spirit of magnanimity, and because he possesses incomparable strategic acuity, I am dismissing charges against General Lethro 814, effective immediately." He nodded at a contingent of military police. "Release the general."

A roar from the crowd clearly indicated the general possessed many supporters.

"While we're waiting for the general to reappear, I'd like to once again map out my plans for our future. As you well know, we have …" For the next half hour, Nero 51 droned on about expanding the current war against Dramatica until it encompassed all the realms.

DUSK HAD SETTLED AROUND THE Dramatican Library of Illumination, and the air had rapidly cooled. In the square, soldiers built a bonfire to warm themselves. Berra's appearance darkened Furst's doorway, which remained open even in the chill. Furst hoped it would reach the soldiers guarding the portals and keep them alert.

"Another weapon, I have." Berra delivered the

words in a taunting singsong manner.

"Test it, then we must," Furst replied, happy for the distraction. He followed Berra to the square and looked for something to shoot. The only obstacles in the square, besides soldiers, were the bonfire, the fountain, and an outhouse that had specifically been built for the troops. The curator knew he couldn't destroy the fountain or the outhouse, so he targeted the bonfire as soldiers scattered. He took aim and fired. The bonfire disappeared. The crowd gave out a roar of appreciation. They had done it. The Dramaticans had crafted a weapon that worked as well as the Terrorian decimator.

Furst grinned at Berra. "Very good it is. More, we need."

Berra nodded. "More, we'll have. Soon."

THAT NIGHT, PRU TELLERENCE LEFT the witch's cottage under cover of darkness. She stealthily made her way through the streets, most of which were quiet, and avoided the squares where denizens of the dark plied their trade.

The Library of Illumination on Romantica sat in the center of a verdant park. Rose-like bushes surrounded it and glowed in the moonlight. Small clusters of trees were spaced widely apart with benches for rest and contemplation. Many locations on Romantica looked like settings out of storybooks, but there were just as many neighborhoods that had dark cottages clustered together without space for gardens.

Pru Tellerence snuck into the library's vestibule and hoped the curator had settled down for the night. She whispered "illumination" and the door slid open to the dimly lit main reading room. A spill of light came from the vicinity of the curator's residence on the second floor, and the dean chanced making her *getaway* rather than waiting until the light went out. She tiptoed to the cupola stairs and noiselessly crept up the spiraling treads, careful to step lightly. It was only when she reached the top that she realized her miter and robes were in the curator's closet. It would be a long night, although in relation to the span of an overseer's life, it wouldn't be bad at all.

She had two options. She could wait until the light went out and curator Natalia Dalura had sufficient time to fall asleep, and then sneak into the woman's bedroom closet to retrieve her possessions. That option seemed too risky to consider. The second option required her to wait until after Natalia had risen and dressed the following morning and became so engrossed in a task, she wouldn't notice the overseer sneaking into the residence.

Once she had her miter back, Pru Tellerence could transport off world, but it looked like she would have to settle in for the night to get to that point. She prayed nothing troublesome had occurred on Dramatica in her absence.

JOHANNA LOOKED THROUGH THE VAULT, but didn't see the *Master Compendia of Sorcery*. She locked up and made her way to the elevator when she heard Jackson shout her name. "I'm downstairs," she called out and ascended the stairs to meet him. "We've got a job to do."

"That can wait."

"Tell that to Myrddin."

"The burgers will be ready any moment, and we have one for you."

"Your mother cooked dinner already? That was fast. Did she use my kitchen?"

"Not exactly."

"You ordered take-out."

"You're getting warmer."

"Jackson." She used her *don't mess with me* voice.

"We ordered room service."

"You're able to do that?"

"Apparently. Come on. I'll help you right after dinner." He led Johanna up to the room, where they found the waiter setting the table for everyone's meal.

"Good. Johanna's here," Chris said. "Let's order dessert."

The Roths had already committed the dessert menu to memory and knew what they wanted. Jackson and Johanna ordered the same sweets as Chris and Ava and settled in for dinner.

"Best hamburger ever." Chris pushed his dish away. "That white sauce was really good."

"What white sauce?" his mother asked. He pushed a small white ceramic bowl towards her. She dipped her fork in the sauce and tasted it. "This is good."

"What's it called?"

"I don't know, we'll have to ask the waiter when he returns."

"I didn't get any," Jackson complained. He tasted it. "And I'm glad I didn't."

"Why?" Johanna asked as she tasted it too. She grinned. "Its Béarnaise sauce."

"How do you know?" Jackson asked.

"Because I had it once at Le Chat and *loved* it. I never thought of having it with a burger."

"Suit yourself," Jackson said. "I'm not having any. When it comes to burgers, I'm a purist."

"You don't know what you're missing," Chris said.

"I'm with Jackson," Ava said. "I'm not having any stinky old Béarnaise sauce." She bumped fists with her brother.

Johanna enjoyed every bite of her Béarnaise burger, and for just a while, Myrddin's request faded into the background. After dinner, Johanna and Mrs. Roth took their coffee out onto the balcony. The lights of the Eiffel Tower glowed in the distance.

"I don't understand how that can be there," Mrs. Roth said. "Although Jackson once told me he couldn't talk about the library because it's very *special*, and now I'm starting to understand why."

Johanna sipped her coffee as she gathered her thoughts together. "This is not like a neighborhood library. It's not open to the public, and it's not easy to find, unless you're invited to be here. When I first saw it, I remember being surprised, because I thought I knew about every library in the area. I worked for a place called LOI Book Services, and we sent books all over. Then one night, I was told to pick up some books here and deliver them to a client. That's when I met Mal. I made more and more deliveries for him and over the course of a year he taught me all about the library, and bookbinding, and the very special *charms* this place holds.

"When he decided to retire, he left me in charge. I was young. Still am," she said with a smile, "and it seemed like an awfully big responsibility, but I had nowhere else to go. I had no family. My friends had deserted me, because I abandoned them first. I'd just lost my job. And my home.

419

And Mal literally handed me the keys to a new home, new friends, and a new career. It was a lot to take on, so I asked the high school if they could recommend someone for part-time work, and that's how I met Jackson.

"This place has been such a blessing." Johanna sighed. "But it also makes unusual demands on us, and we never know when that's going to happen." She shivered.

"It's getting chilly," Mrs. Roth said. Let's go inside. They entered the living room and heard a blood-curdling scream coming from the library.

Johanna ran to the main reading room and found the back of the library engulfed in flames. The heat stunned her.

Ava stood immobilized in the center of the room, screaming.

"Oh my God!" Mrs. Roth ran to grab her youngest child. "We have to get out of here."

Johanna stooped down and picked up a first edition of Margaret Mitchell's *Gone With the Wind*. She closed it and the flames disappeared, although the heat and smell of smoke remained.

Mrs. Roth turned when the roar of the flames suddenly went dead. "The fire? Where did it go?"

"As I was saying on the balcony, the Library of Illumination is a very special place, where books *literally* come to life." She showed her the cover of the book. "That was Tara burning." She reopened the book, just for a second, to illustrate what she meant, and then closed it again.

Mrs. Roth's eyes grew wide, but not as wide as Ava's. The girl reached for the book, but Johanna moved it away, and in a very calm, even voice said, "We do not open books in here unless we—one—know what to expect and—two—have a very good reason. Many of them are old and valuable and meant to be treasured, and we must treat them with the respect they are due. But most importantly, we never speak about what these books are capable of, outside these walls."

"But …"

"So I must ask you to take the library oath."

"What's that?" Ava asked.

Johanna placed *Gone With the Wind* on the circulation desk and grabbed the keys to unlock the Gutenberg bible.

She looked at both Mrs. Roth and Ava. "Place your right hands on top of the bible." She half-turned, "Come on, Chris, you too."

"An oath," Chris said with a hint of sarcasm. "Really?" But he put his hand on the bible.

"Raise your other hand and repeat after me." Johanna raised her left hand and the Illumini Constellation glowed. "I solemnly swear …"

"I solemnly swear …" three voices repeated as their owners stared at Johanna's palm.

"To keep the secrets of the Library of Illumination …"

"… to treat every book with the respect it is due …"

"… and to protect the wealth of knowledge that lives within these walls …"

"… so help me God."

Chris smirked. "So now do we get decoder rings or something?"

Johanna held up one finger as a gesture for him to wait. She unlocked the drawer where she had stashed the library board president's gold 'LOI' pins and removed three. She pinned one to each of the Roths. "You're now sworn protectors of the library. If anyone sees the pin and asks what 'LOI' stands for, you can tell them it stands for the Library of Illumination. But you've just sworn yourselves to secrecy, and I beg you not to tell anyone anything more."

"What happens if we do?" Chris asked.

"I'll beat the living tar out of you. And then we'll watch in horror as the greatest library in the world falls apart, because you're a stupid twit who broke his oath." Jackson grabbed a book off the circulation desk that he had checked in earlier and opened it to a page he had bookmarked for later perusal. A lion roared to life. Jackson closed it just as quickly, but not before he had scared the devil out of his brother. "These books are very real and very special and must be treated as such. But don't think I won't use one against you if you ever shoot off your mouth about the place."

Mrs. Roth was aghast. "Jackson!"

"Just making a point, Mom, just making a point. Did you get the point, Chris?"

"Yeah," his brother said.

"Good." Jackson yawned. "It's time to turn in."

"What kind of book is that?" Chris asked.

Jackson opened it up to the title page. "*Circus Life and Circus Celebrities* by Thomas Frost. It was written in 1897. You'll be happy to know that lion is long-dead."

"He looked pretty alive to me."

"As long as you don't needlessly open books, you don't have anything to worry about."

"I don't know if I want to sleep in the same room

with you."

"Not a problem. Besides, I think I should sleep on the couch, in case Johanna and I get called away on a mission."

"A mission?" Chris asked. "Now you're spies?"

"Called away on a *work emergency*."

"So it's not like you're going anywhere," Chris pointed out. "You work *here*."

"Not always," Jackson replied. "Sometime we need to work … elsewhere."

"Fine. I'm not going to mess with you as long as you're holding that book," Chris said.

"And I won't mess with you, as long as you don't mess with these books," Jackson answered. "Good night."

"You're not sleeping on the couch," his mother said. "Your brother is a sound sleeper, Lord knows, it's nearly impossible to wake him up for school some mornings. You'll sleep in a bed."

"Whatever. See you later."

"Aren't you coming inside with us?" his mother asked.

"Not right now. Johanna and I have something we need to do."

—LOI—

37

Pru Tellerence sat at the top of the cupola stairs and watched through the railing as Natalia Dalura disappeared into the bindery. The overseer quietly made her way to the main floor and headed toward the other staircase when the front door slid open. Pru Tellerence flattened herself against a stack of books that separated her from the circulation desk.

"What can I do for you, Dame Erato?" Natalia's voice floated like a melody on a breeze.

"The binding on my copy of *Baladantic Prophecies* needs repair. I may have once had the skills to fix it myself, but I ran out of the supplies necessary to make such a repair a long time ago. My eyesight has also dimmed with time. Would you be so kind as to help me out?"

"Of course."

The older woman looked up alertly and searched the surrounding area.

"Is there a problem?" Natalia asked.

"Not that I can see," the older woman answered, "yet I sense we are not alone."

Natalia looked around. "There is no one here, Dame Erato, except us. And, as you know, the library has a way of protecting itself. Come with me into the bindery. I'm sure we can repair this quickly, and no one will be the wiser that it was ever damaged."

Dame Erato lingered. She sniffed, as if smelling an intruder. She lowered her voice to a whisper. "We are not alone."

A LONE OFFICER OF THE military police force emerged from the Terrorian jail and made his way to the library steps where he stood off to the side of Nero 51 as the curator finished his speech.

"What is it, Captain?" Nero 51 asked. "Where is the general?"

The captain approached Nero 51 and whispered something in his ear. "Impossible!" The curator abruptly left the podium and strode forcefully toward the jail, disappearing inside.

Members of the crowd speculated wildly about the delay in the general's release, as well as what Nero 51 could have declared *impossible*. Several minutes passed before the curator returned.

He clutched the podium with all eight of his tentacles. "Citizens, it is with great sadness that I must inform you that General Lethro 814 is dead. We can only surmise that the shame of incarceration took its toll upon him. The general was found hanging in his cell by the military police dispatched to inform him he'd been

C. A. PACK

pardoned. I've been told the most strenuous life-saving efforts have been exhausted. My core, like I'm sure many of yours are, is heavy with grief, but we cannot allow this to detract us from our plans, which the general fully supported." Nero 51 sighed heavily before continuing. "We must channel our sorrow into victory for our realm. It's what the general would have wanted. And, forevermore, I declare this day be known as Lethro 814 day so we never forget that even in the darkest of times, we must stay optimistic, for a solution to our problems may be right around the corner.

"Let us commemorate the general's great achievements together. I decree that all places of nourishment and drink open their doors at no charge to the public and allow patrons to gather in celebration of a military genius. The Library of Illumination will take care of all expense. It's important to honor the general's passing." The curator hung his head for a moment of silence before retreating inside the library. The crowd broke into groups, each migrating toward their favorite watering hole or eatery, ready to comment on the benevolence of Nero 51 and the unfortunate death of General Lethro 814.

The curator withdrew to his secret living compartment on level 333. He poured himself a cup of absynale and relaxed. *That turned out perfectly. The guards didn't know what to think when they went to his cell to inform him of the reprieve, only to find him dead, an apparent suicide victim who couldn't face the shame of incarceration. And right after I exonerated him. I will appear to be strong and fair. Lethro 814 will appear to be weak and guilt-ridden.* Nero 51 threw back his head and downed the contents of his cup, before pouring another

426

drink. *Here's to me and the execution of another perfect plan.*

JOHANNA AND JACKSON HEADED DOWN to level 1,311 to look for the *Master Compendia of Sorcery*. They chatted about the advantages of having a hotel room inside the library, so they scarcely noticed the deeper the elevator traveled, the slower it moved until it ground to a halt.

"Here we are," Jackson said. "Lead the way."

"We're only on level 1,310." Johanna pressed the button for the lower level. The elevator didn't budge. "I wonder why it won't go down any farther?"

"C'mon, we can take the stairs," Jackson said, grabbing her hand as he pulled the brass scissor door to one side. Together, they descended the stairs that wound around the elevator like a huge spiral. "Whoever designed this place loved spiral staircases. I'm surprised the elevator doesn't spin around like a giant screw as it moves down the shaft."

"Probably because it would nauseate the passengers," Johanna replied.

"That's what I love about you. You're always able to see past the obvious."

"Do you love me, Jackson?"

He stared at her a moment, speechless, then smiled. "Well, maybe you can't *always* see past the obvious or you'd know the answer to that."

She pulled him toward her and looked up. They kissed deeply, but a few seconds later, the elevator crashed to the lowest level raising a huge cloud of dust.

They broke apart. Johanna pulled her scarf over her nose and mouth and Jackson did the same with his

T-shirt. He looked forlornly at the elevator. "How are we supposed to get back up 1,311 levels?"

"Slowly."

They backed away from the elevator, closed their eyes to keep the dust out, and struggled to breathe until the dust settled. Finally, they looked around, examining their surroundings. Level 1,311 was different from the other levels. The other sub-floors were clean and modern. This level had rock walls and floors and niches chipped out of the walls with bundles inside of them.

"What do you think these are?" Jackson nodded toward one of the bundles.

"We won't know unless we open one."

"If Superman were here, he could see right through them."

"If Superman were here, he could push the elevator back up to sub-level six. I don't suppose you've got a Superman comic book on you?"

"Nope ... talk about groan-worthy."

She reached out toward a parcel and allowed her hand to hover over it for more than a minute.

"Well, are you going to unwrap it or what?"

"I'm working my way up to it."

"I know what you're thinking. What if there are bones in there? Or an early overseer's petrified head? Am I right?"

"I was thinking more along the line of what if the contents are protected by an enchantment that turns me to stone if I unwrap them?"

"Okay. I could see how that might stop you."

"Except I'm the curator, so here goes nothing." She grabbed the bundle and when nothing diabolical happened to her or her appendages, she unwrapped it.

"Big surprise, huh? It's a book."

She opened it. The pages, browned and brittle, had withstood the vagaries of time. "This is old. Really old. It's not even printed on paper. The pages are a thin skin of some kind."

"Vellum?"

"If it is, I've never seen vellum like it. It's a little cruder."

"Is it the book we're looking for?"

"I don't know. I can't read it."

Jackson walked over to the next niche and unwrapped the book inside. "Hmmm …I can't tell if this is the right book, either."

"We'd better check the other cubbies." Johanna rewrapped the book and replaced it. Then moved on to the next niche. "Same thing, different location."

For the next two hours they moved through the lowest level, checking books.

Jackson took a deep breath. "I'm surprised we haven't died of asphyxiation yet."

"There's probably oxygen traveling down the open staircase from the upper levels."

"That's a plus. Too bad you didn't ask Myrddin how we're supposed to recognize the right book when we find it."

"I think he knew that we'd know when we found it."

"Yeah. Except that's not working."

"Oh. I wouldn't say that." She held a book in her hands that glowed from within.

Jackson walked over. "You think that's it?"

She stared at the cover. The letters and glyphs

floated into a new pattern across the top that read, *Master Compendia of Sorcery*. "Yes." She opened the cover and found a drawing mirroring the constellation embedded in her palm. Intuitively, she placed her hand over the image and eight people appeared—four men, three women, and a young girl. "Are you the Eahta Frean fram Drycræft?" she asked.

"Gese," they answered simultaneously.

"Geese?" Jackson repeated.

"It's like *yes* in old English."

"It is so," one of the women said.

"I'm Johanna Charette." She tilted her head, "And this is Jackson Roth. Myrddin told us we could find a list of the current Eahta Frean fram Drycræft in the *Master Compendia of Sorcery*. However, you don't look very current."

"Myrddin spoke to you? He is long dead. Are you one of his disciples?"

"We're curators of the Library of Illumination," Jackson answered.

"I can tell you who they are," the young girl said. "I have the power to see the future."

"You mean, like, you can tell us where and when the Terrorians will strike?"

"I can only tell you what Myrddin wants you to know," the girl replied.

"So, you don't know," Jackson said.

"I know. But I refuse to impart that knowledge."

"But knowledge is power." Jackson interjected. "Ask Francis Bacon."

"Power corrupts."

"Yeah, yeah, and absolute power corrupts

absolutely," he replied. "I know that one, too."

The girl turned to Johanna. "The names you require are Cathasach Caird of Scotland; Robert Birk of Sweden; Zendali Zendaga of Zimbabwe; Mateus Ferrari of Brazil; Alianessa Anjou of France; Brychan Rhydderch of Wales; Edmund Beasom of England; and Veronika Veselov of Russia."

"Wait a second. There's no one named Beck?" Jackson asked.

"The young girl stared into space for a moment. The man known as Beck is Brychan Rhydderch."

"Oh. For a second, I thought we'd found our guy," Jackson said.

"What guy is that," the girl asked.

"The guy who's trying to steal Myrddin's memoir."

"It is not Beck."

"Figures. He would have been the easy one to find. Who is it then?" Jackson asked.

"I have already imperiled the parameters of my power by telling you who it is not. The rest is up to you."

"We'll have to travel halfway around the world to find some of these people," Johanna said.

"Unless you wait until Ides, when they will all meet in Prague."

"Prague, huh?" Jackson looked at Johanna and raised his eyebrows. "Road trip."

"Yes," she murmured.

"That gives us a couple of days," Jackson replied

"No," the girl answered. "It gives you one day."

He did the math. "The Ides of March is on the fifteenth. Today is the twelfth."

"According to the calendar of Numa, March was

a long month with the Ides falling on the fifteenth day. However, this is April, a short month, in which the Ides falls on the thirteenth. You must be in Prague tomorrow by sunset to intercept them at their meeting place."

"Where are they meeting?" Johanna asked.

"In one of the chambers beneath Old Town Hall."

"There's more than one?" she continued.

"Beneath the buildings of Old Prague lays a labyrinth of cellars, chambers and tunnels, all interconnected in some way."

"Figures. I'll bet there are catacombs down there too," Jackson said.

"I don't believe there are any beneath Old Town Hall, but you may find a connecting tunnel to one of the churches and there could be catacombs or a graveyard, there."

"Great." Jackson replied. "There's nothing like skeletal remains to keep us on our toes."

"There's a problem," Johanna said.

"What's that," he asked.

"It's probably too late to get a flight out tonight."

"Not if we hurry."

"Up 1,311 flights of stairs?"

"Oh."

"That is not necessary," the girl said.

"Look at the elevator," Jackson said. "It crashed to the bottom from the level above us."

Once again, the girl stared off into space. "Ascend the stairs to the next level and press the button for the elevator."

"It's not going to work," he claimed.

"It is enchanted to ensnare trespassers. Are you a

trespasser?"

"No."

"Then it will come for you. However …"

"I knew there had to be a catch," he muttered.

"The book Johanna is holding cannot leave this level. If it does, there are dire consequences."

"I'll put it away," Johanna said, wrapping the book. She stuck it back in the niche. When she turned back, the Eahta Frean fram Drycræft were gone.

Jackson grabbed her hand. "Here goes nothing." He pulled her up the stairs and pressed the button for the elevator.

DUNGEN WASTED NO TIME TAKING over Torran's spot as head of the library council and immediately called for a meeting, sending an underling to fetch Furst.

Furst bristled at being called to a 'meeting of the minds,' which he felt would be long on rhetoric and short on practicality. His place was in the library, but he knew Dungen would make his life miserable if he didn't attend.

Furst arrived at the town hall to whispers of discontentment as Dramaticans voiced their anger over rumors Dungen was about to propose a *weapons tax*.

"Ridiculous, it is," one woman muttered.

"Collect everything, the Rodo twins did. Grinders, they built. Pay for their services, we must," a pro-tax board member stated.

Commerce on Dramatica was conducted by direct barter. A tax implied that people would be promising goods and services *to a cause*, without necessarily receiving something tangible in return. There would be powerful guns for protection, but they would go to the fighters and not the individuals paying for them. And, yes, the voluntary militia needed to be fed and compensated for lost trade. But what if the general public sacrificed their goods and services for a war that didn't materialize? The Terrorians were gone and the soldiers in the library already had weapons taken from the invaders. Now that the Terrorians had seen how fiercely Dramaticans protected their realm, they might decide not to return.

Dungen called the meeting to order as he uncovered a sign he had made. It listed 'Volunteer Compensation, Weapons, Militia Meals, Uniforms, Fuel, Barracks, Supplies, Maintenance, Training, and Administration.'

He faced the crowd and put both hands on the table in front of him. "Comes at a price, defending ourselves. Compensated, volunteers must be. Paid for making weapons, Berra and the Rodos must be." As Dungen stated each *need*, he pointed to it on the sign.

The volume increased dramatically when he said a barracks must be built.

"A barracks, we have," Furst pointed out.

"A school, it is," Dungen stated.

"Closed, it was," another man said.

"Need it soon, we may. Permanent, a barracks would be."

But the Dramaticans weren't buying it. A permanent barracks meant an ongoing war, and they were a peaceful people at heart. They weren't afraid to fight if they had to, but they preferred to think peace would endure.

"Our tithes back, would we get, if no war, there is?" someone called out.

"No," Dungen replied. "For preparation, the money goes."

"Ridiculous, it is," a dissenting board member said. "No wisdom, there is, for goods paying, we may not need. Waste, it is. Suggest this, Torran never would."

Dungen's ringlets noticeably tightened at the mention of his predecessor. "Dead, Torran is, which is why a prepared militia, we need. Maybe then, dead, he would not be."

"Lining your own pockets, you are. Powerful you want to make yourself," an elder pointed out.

"Take sides, we must. Bar the door. Win, the side with the most votes will."

"No," someone else yelled. "Only one vote per family, we must consider."

A younger citizen who had volunteered as a soldier raised his voice. "Fight, my father will not. Fight, I will. Get a vote, why should he, over me?"

"Enough," Furst shouted. He walked to the front of the room until he stood face to face with Dungen. "What you started, simple, it is not. No vote tonight, there should be. Reason this out, we need to. Vote, everyone of the age of majority must, to make it fair."

Dungen hissed. "Fair, that is not. Many votes, big outskirt families have. Fight, they would not choose to do. Outvote the voice of reason, they would."

"The voice of reason, you are? Not, I think," the curator countered.

"Then pay the tax, everyone who gets a vote must."

"Fine. Agreed, we are. He grabbed Furst's hand and asked the elder to break the connection. When it was done, Dungen smiled, smugly. "You, it is, who their money, wastes."

"No. Outvote it, they will, so no taxes, there will be."

Dungen turned so red you couldn't tell his skin from his hair. "Vote tomorrow, we must," he shouted, "and with you, bring your pledge."

—LOI—

38

On Romantica, a full minute passed before Dame
Erato followed Natalia Dalura into the bindery. Pru
Tellerence wasted no time getting to Natalia's closet where
she exchanged the curator's cloak for her own robe.

EEEaaaarrrrrrrk.

The stairs! Pru Tellerence fumbled as she buttoned
her robe.

"Is anyone in here?" Natalia sounded like she was
in the living room.

The overseer reached for the corner of the top shelf
and grabbed her miter, slapping it firmly on her head.

A moment later, she appeared in the meditation
room of the College of Overseers in Lumi.

ΩPru Tellerence, are you quite *all right?* Plato
Indelicat couldn't help noticing the untidiness of the
female overseer. In her haste to get away, Pru Tellerence

had missed a fastener on one side of her robe, causing it to bunch up and appear sloppy. Besides that, she had slapped the miter on her head so quickly, it failed to cover all her dark auburn hair. Instead, it had knocked some strands loose, which now stuck out from beneath the tall hat.

★*I'm fine, Plato Indelicat. A touch of joint stiffness is making it difficult for me to manipulate my hands. I'll be straightened out soon enough, if you'll excuse me.* She zipped out the door, and narrowly missed running into Ryden Simmdry.

"I never thought an elevator ride could make me this happy," Jackson said to Johanna as they exited the conveyance on sub-level six.

"I'll check flights to Prague. Maybe there's one later tonight." She looked for flights on her office computer while Jackson searched on an iPad. "I'm not having much luck here," he said, placing the tablet on top of the desk. He rubbed his face. "Now what are we gonna do?"

Johanna yawned. "I don't know. I wonder if the first flight out in the morning will get us there on time?"

Jackson closed his eyes while he listened to the click of her fingernails against the keyboard. "Let me know when you find something."

Johanna searched for several minutes. "It's no use. It's already early tomorrow in Prague. A morning flight won't get us there in time."

Jackson snored lightly. Johanna tilted her head back and rested it against the back of her desk chair. She closed her eyes, but soon realized it would be much better to sleep in a comfortable bed. "Wake up." She shook Jackson's shoulder.

"You found something?"

"No. And since we're not flying out tonight, you might as well sleep in a luxurious hotel room instead of here on a chair."

Jackson forced his eyes open. "I'm almost too tired to move, but now that you mentioned that plush bed that's waiting for me inside, I guess I can find the strength."

He stood up, but wavered a bit. Johanna put her arm around his waist to steady him.

"Want to sneak into my bed with me?" He kissed the top of her head. "We can say we spent the night together in Paris."

"Oh my God, that's it!"

His eyes opened wide. "You're gonna sleep with me?"

She returned to the computer and renewed her search. "There's an early afternoon flight leaving Paris that will get us to Prague by 3:00 p.m. All we have to do is leave from your room tomorrow."

"And how are you planning to get out?"

"The door…"

"Leads you right back to the Library of Illumination."

Her thoughts raced. "You're right. We need to be somewhere with multiple exits. If we can have a Parisian hotel room here, there's no reason why we can't open a book showing the lobby of a Prague hotel."

"What if the exits lead back here?"

"Okay." She paused. "What if we open a book to Charles de Gaulle Airport. We can fly to Prague from within the airport and not actually exit through the door we enter from. We just need to follow the other passengers onto the plane."

"That might work."

"Okay. We each need to get a good night's sleep, and we'll leave early tomorrow."

"Does this mean you're not going to sleep with me?"

"You are so astute. I'll see you in the morning."

BACK IN HER PRIVATE CHAMBER on Lumina, Pru Tellerence pulled herself together. Everything would be fine. Izabella was ensconced on Romantica. The Dramaticans had fought off the Terrorians and were taking precautions against them. And now that Ryden Simmdry knew her secret, she had nothing to fear from him. *He can't expel me without casting guilt upon himself, and the chance of that is extremely low, especially now that the Terrorians are sharpening their tentacles.* She knew an upset in the balance of powers among overseers would be like opening the door to the Terrorians, who would attack at the first sign of weakness. Finally, she could put her personal life aside and get on with her duties.

THE NEXT MORNING, DRAMATICANS BEGAN queuing up early. The line of voters wrapped completely around town hall and down the Steppingstone to Illumination past the library. The town coffers would either soon overflow, or Dungen's tax would be roundly defeated. Dungen's idea wasn't without merit, but the way he proposed it— ramming it down citizens' throats—left Furst hoping the new director would lose this round, and with it, his position as head of the library council.

A similar tax proposal would undoubtedly follow, but by then, people would have had time to think about it and get used to it. Whoever created a follow-up plan might temper it, so it pointed out the benefits for everyone, while not placing an onerous burden on those who didn't have much to give.

How did Dungen become the new head of the library council? Furst wondered. Dungen irritated a lot of people, although many Dramaticans respected his father, Pondor, one of the five judges in the commonwealth court. Furst suspected Dungen abused his father's position to get whatever he wanted. The new director's caftan now flaunted heavier embroidery and more jewels than ever before, but Dungen, aside from being a self-proclaimed *scholar*, had no concept of the word *work*. He hadn't earned the conspicuous signs of prominence he displayed on his garments. His only vocation appeared to be forcing his unpopular opinions on anyone within earshot. *If he's so educated*, Furst asked himself, *why doesn't he hold tenure in the local university?*

The curator tried to focus on his work, but his thoughts kept returning to the vote taking place a few blocks away. A half-hour later, he packed up his pencils and left a soldier in charge of the library, before he made his way to the polls. He hated wasting precious time waiting in line, but knew unless he did, he wouldn't have a say in the outcome of the tax. He couldn't let Dungen win this first round, or the new director would become a tyrant. Furst only had one vote to cast, but fervently hoped everyone who felt the same way he did, voted.

PRU TELLERENCE FOUND IT DIFFICULT to shield her thoughts, so she remained in her chambers meditating. It would not do to run into Ryden Simmdry before she had her thoughts under control. When she relaxed enough to compartmentalize her thinking and work out her emotions without broadcasting them, she considered her relationship with the master of the overseers. They had pledged their love to each other long ago and had been companions ever since. The only time they ever separated was when she had claimed to suffer from a nervous condition and had sequestered herself on Romantica. During that time, their baby was born and surrendered to the care of the witch, Josefina.

She didn't think a time would ever come when she'd confess the child's existence to Ryden Simmdry, but deep inside, she'd always known the possibility existed. Now, her secret was shared. She wanted to know what the master might have revealed to the others. That meant opening her mind, but keeping it blank so she could hear their thoughts while moderating her own. She settled into a comfortable position and cleared her head. Her fellow overseers were discussing the retrieval of the time machine. They did not know where the Terrorians had hidden it. Yet. But once they did, they planned to act immediately to retrieve it.

★*Yes. That would most likely reduce the threat.*

ℌ*Pru Tellerence, it's nice to have you back.*

★*Am I correct in believing the Terrorians have not extended their aggression past Dramatica?*

⌘*They have not. How are the Dramaticans faring?*

She tensed for a millisecond before answering. ★*I'm returning to Dramatica immediately to offer further assistance. Furst is obviously upset over the loss of so many of their books. I would like to teleport clones of the works they lost from their first five levels. I believe it will help re-establish a sense of normalcy in the library and let them know we are here to support them.*

    ♫ *Yes, of course. They all agreed.* ♫ *Make it so.*

    ★ *Excellent. I will leave at once.*

NERO 51 PACED INSIDE THE private quarters he had carved out for himself on sub-level 333. Surely there was some way to step up his invasion plan even though he previously announced they would suspend it until they reassessed their strategy. He believed his original plan to invade Juvenilia had been a good one. He mulled over it for a while. Yes. He would only need to accompany the troops to make sure they landed in the correct realm. It might be beneath him, but he needed someone he could rely on, and he only trusted himself. Once again, they would return to the day the Fantasian had started her sentence.

He pulled out his old plans. He'd lost some good soldiers on Dramatica. He couldn't fathom how those wretched, springy devils ever bested his soldiers, but that was past. Terroria would have a much better chance against the kiddlets on Juvenilia, and once he conquered their world and held them hostage, there would be no stopping his soldiers. A new idea seized him. They could also invade Romantica—a realm overrun with female creatures. *Our troops could easily overcome a bunch of useless females from the flighty realm. Overwhelming women and children will give us the edge we need to cut a swath through the rest of the realms.*

He considered an incentive—something he could propose to attract more soldiers—some menial title with an impressive sound. *Provisional Governor.* That should do the trick. He would offer the title to the primary soldier who delivered a realm. And each of the troopers serving under him would be named Lord Mayor of one of the various communities within that realm. Conquered worlds would naturally need supervision anyway. Normally, he would just put a soldier in charge, but that did not sound *alluring*. Giving them the opportunity to become a governor or mayor appeared much more enticing. The soldiers' duties would be the exact same as before, but now they would have fancy titles. Still, he would keep that to himself. *Teasing their egos should bring in a healthy number of new recruits.*

He composed an outline of his revised invasion plan and new incentives. He made it sound lucrative, but feared some Terrorians might call his bluff. *I have to increase the stakes.* It wouldn't be enough to appeal to their conceit, he had to appeal to their greed. He'd offer an additional gold ingot for governors' salaries and an extra silver one for mayors'. On the surface, it would appear generous, but if he taxed each realm, more riches would flow in than out. Besides, any added expense would be small payment for the capture of two realms to use as stepping-stones to Terrorian dominance of the Illumini system.

—LOI—

39

JOHANNA MULLED OVER SEVERAL LEVEL zero travel books until she found one with a good photograph of the terminal she needed at Charles de Gaulle Airport. She looked for the same book with a higher physical property level and opened it while standing in the door to the Executive Boardroom. She noted the *exit* back to the library before stepping into the terminal.

"Wow, you did it." Jackson stood just behind her.

"I don't know where to leave the book."

"Can't you just leave it under a seat or something?"

"Someone might take it." She shut the book and the terminal disappeared.

"What are you doing?"

"More research."

"We don't have a lot of time. Why can't you just put the open book in your backpack? It's not that big."

"What if the airport follows us everywhere we try

445

to go?"

"That would be a problem."

"Give me a few minutes. Did you tell your family you have to go away?"

"No."

"Why not?"

"I'm afraid Chris or Ava might try to follow us."

"That's why we're using the Executive boardroom. I can lock the door before we open the book. Go tell you mother you have to leave."

"Okay."

While he was gone, Johanna looked online for lockers at the airport. She couldn't find any, but did discover a service that provided short-term storage. She ran upstairs to get a ratty little suitcase she'd once found in the basement of Peakie's Foundling Home and had used for her meager possessions when she ran away. She grabbed some clothing from the *donation* box in the corner of her closet, enough to stuff around the open book once she packed it, to make sure it stayed open. Johanna carried the suitcase down to the board room.

Mrs. Roth eyed it warily. "Jackson says you're going away."

"We have to," Johanna answered. "Someone's trying to steal something important, and we need to find out who that person is."

"Is that dangerous?"

"It could be, but we're the only people who can do it." She held up her left hand with her palm facing Mrs. Roth. "Library business."

The older woman hugged her son. "Promise me you'll be careful."

"Don't worry, Mom. I don't want us to get into trouble any more than you do."

"I'll make sure we don't do anything rash." Johanna hugged Jackson's mom. "We're locking the door behind us."

"Yeah, just to make sure Chris and Ava don't get any bright ideas."

"They're at school," his mother replied. "If I don't tell them where you've disappeared to, or from, we shouldn't have a problem."

"Love you, Mom." He kissed her forehead. "We gotta go."

Johanna set the lock and stepped into the boardroom with Jackson, pulling the door closed behind them. She opened the guidebook, and they suddenly found themselves inside the Paris airport. "I've got to pack this," she said, opening the small suitcase and placing the open book inside. "I wish I had a lock for it."

"There must be a store in here that sells stuff like that for travelers."

"Okay. Could you go look for one, while I go get our tickets? Let's meet back here when we're done."

Twenty minutes later, they were together again. Jackson handed her the lock. "I guess we're set."

"Not quite. You need to check in. I didn't have your passport. They want to make sure you're you."

"My passport," Jackson said in alarm, patting his pockets.

"No," Johanna moaned.

"Gotcha," he said smiling, as he pulled it out of an inside pocket. He headed across the terminal to check in, while Johanna got directions to the luggage storage place.

They checked the bag with the book before going to the gate. "I'm glad that's done," she said. "Now all we have to worry about are the Eahta Frean fram Drycræft."

"How are we gonna get into their meeting?"

"It's important we get there before they do, so we can scope out the place."

"It's just a basement meeting room at the town hall. What's to scope out?"

"I don't know," she said. "I just want to get there before them."

DRAMATICANS ARE NORMALLY A PEACEFUL people, but the tax vote seemed to change even the mildest citizen's personality. Numerous arguments and more than a few fist fights broke out during the day among people with differing opinions. Furst witnessed several disputes for himself, and when word got back to him later in the day that infighting had escalated, he sent several of the troops protecting the library to Town Hall as public peacekeepers.

The reassigned Dramaticans brought their *original* Terrorian weapons with them, and the firearms had a chilling effect on their neighbors. The decibel-level immediately changed from *bar room brawl to worship hall*, and the voters' combativeness evaporated.

Voting on Dramatica was not sophisticated. It involved each voter taking three rocks inside a small room and dropping two in the barrel marked with the proposal they supported and one in the barrel they rejected. This insured that the guard at the door couldn't tell which position they supported. By mid-day, the barrel marked 'No Tax' overflowed with stones and a second barrel had to be set up.

Outside, Dramaticans milled about waiting for news about the vote. They broke out in cheers when they heard 'No Tax' was winning, and booed Dungen when he said voting would continue until the sun set, so *every* Dramatican would have a chance to vote.

"Something underhanded, he will try to do," some Dramaticans muttered.

"Send someone to follow him, we should. Keep an eye on him, we must," another stated.

But a friend of the new library board director criticized talk that Dungen might try to win by any means. "An upstanding citizen, he is. Talking crazy, you are."

One of the *ax-the-tax* voters looked for Furst in the library. "Trust them, I do not. Neither side. Something, can't you do?"

"With the voting, others would say I tampered. Best to see how it all plays out, it is. In our favor, the odds are. The barrels, watch. No one tampers with them, make sure."

"Right, you are."

"With you, I will go," Furst said. "A soldier to keep watch, I will assign."

"With the tax, won't the soldiers side? Trusted, can they be?"

"Worry, do not. Just whom to select, I know. Assign Lenc, I will. Trust him, I do."

NERO 51 STARED AT THE crowd gathered around him in the Terrorian library. He raised all his tentacles and addressed them. "My fellow countrymen, I have given what I am about to propose to you much thought, and

I know deep inside it is the right thing to do. The past few days have been dark and disheartening, but we must continue forward if we are to find the light. Tomorrow, we will commence phase two of our plan to take what should rightfully be ours—total mastery of all Libraries of Illumination within the Illumini system. While it may sound like a rehashing of our old plan, it is not. Our first step is to insure we invade Juvenilia first—a realm comprised entirely of children. Obviously, humanoid children do not have the intelligence or strength to rule themselves and should be easily overtaken. I wish to call our plan Operation Lethro 814 in memory of the general."

The sentiments of those surrounding Nero 51 began as a murmur, but soon built to a roar. Not a roar of dissension, but of complete accord. His kinsmen approved of his honoring General Lethro 814. Little did they know that Nero 51 visited the general just before his demise, promised him he would be exonerated, and then passed him a glass of poisoned merk.

JOHANNA AND JACKSON EMERGED FROM a taxi near Old Town Square in Prague. "Look at this place," Jackson said. "It's almost like we got here in a time machine. I mean it looks *old*. Really, really, old."

"No time for sightseeing," Johanna said. "We have to find a way into the basement of Town Hall."

"Is that the place with the clock?"

"From what I read, it's actually the entire row of buildings, but the clock tower is a good place to start."

"Look at all these people just standing here staring at the building. Kinda weird, huh?" A bell began tolling the hour. "Look. It's moving. That skeleton is ringing in the hour. That's hilarious!"

"It's the astronomical clock and it does this every hour." She pulled him away. "You can see it some other time. We've got work to do."

"You're no fun."

"This is important."

"I know. I'm just teasing you. You've got to learn to lighten up."

"I'm going to push on some of these doors. Just remember what I told you to do. If you see anyone coming, point out something to me in the guidebook."

"That's too obvious. I think I should do this instead." He spun her around and kissed her. A while later, he came up for air. "Pretty spontaneous, huh? And it gives us an excuse to ignore anyone who questions what we're doing. We could always say we're looking for a place that's a bit more private."

"Right." Johanna searched the outside of Town Hall looking for an entry to the lower level.

Jackson kept watch and intervened whenever necessary to make it look like they weren't looking for anything at all. He tugged her arm. "Why don't we just blend in with the tour that's going through that other door?"

"Good thinking." She grabbed his hand and they joined the group as they descended an old stone staircase. It led to a vaulted chamber.

"So this is where they're meeting?" he whispered.

"Not with all these people here. They're a *secret society,* remember? We'll have to look around, but I think we should take the tour first and see what there is to see."

They found the tunnels and rooms linked to other

451

tunnels and rooms, but many areas were off-limits to the public. When the tour started to wind down, they lingered, pretending to look at a point of interest. The sounds of the tour grew faint.

"Let's go down there," Johanna said, pointing to a lit chamber blocked off by a metal railing. She slipped under the railing while Jackson climbed over it, and they ducked inside a barrel-shaped room of stacked stone. Protruding from the wall, rusty manacles and chains dangled from primitive eyelets.

"It's kinda creepy down here," Jackson said. "I guess if you're a wizard with nefarious intent, it's perfect. But if you're just a regular person, it's spooky."

"You're scared?"

"No. I'm just making a point."

An ancient armoire stood in a corner of the room. "This is interesting," Johanna said. "It reminds me of something we might find in the library cellar."

"Yeah, like that Narnia book."

"*The Lion, the Witch and the Wardrobe.*"

"Right."

"By C. S. Lewis." She pulled the door open.

Jackson looked over her shoulder. "It's not very deep, unless it has a false back and it's hiding something."

"Like a portal to Terroria?"

"Yeah. But I guess you don't want to go there."

"You always expect things to be more interesting than they are. It's just the back wall of the cabinet. Look." She pushed against it to prove her point and inhaled sharply when it pivoted.

"You were saying?"

"We have a problem."

"That's what you call being wrong?"

She made a face at him. "We don't have flashlights."

"*You* don't have a flashlight." He dug around in his backpack and pulled one out. "I came prepared."

"I'm impressed."

"Yeah. I stuck one in here one night after I forgot my house key and had to search in the dark for the one my mother usually hides in the bushes."

"Did it take long to find?" she asked, following him into the tunnel behind the armoire.

"I didn't find it. So I threw stones at Chris's window to wake him up and get him to open the door, but the idiot opened the window and shouted, 'What do you want?' He woke my mother and Ava. Even Mrs. Caruthers light went on."

"I'll bet they loved that."

"I was grounded for three weeks—a week for breaking curfew, a week for waking them, and a week for disturbing Mrs. Caruthers."

They looked for signs that might help them find the meeting place of the Eahta Frean fram Drycræft. After what seemed liked hours, Jackson squatted down and leaned his back against the stone wall. "Can we go home now?"

Johanna sighed. She knew exactly how he felt. "Okay, but now we've got to find our way back." They navigated the maze and after a while, the silent void that surrounded them gave up a human voice. The two curators looked at each other and Johanna lifted her finger to her lips.

"Where do you think it's coming from?"

"Well it can't be coming from where we've been," she

whispered, "so I say we keep going in the same direction."

They crept along quietly, but stopped suddenly when they heard voices again.

"It sounds like it's behind us, but we just came from that direction. How could we have missed them?"

"Switch off the flashlight." She took his shoulders and twisted him around. "There's another tunnel that branches off this room, and it looks lit."

"The proverbial light at the end of the tunnel?" He laughed.

She jabbed him with her elbow. "Quiet."

As they inched closer to the spill of light, a voice became clearer. "… which is why we must determine who is responsible."

"I didn't think anyone knew about the existence of the book, except us," a stunning black woman stated.

"Neither did I," said Cathasach, but there was a recent breach in Skokholm. We found two teenagers wandering around our kitchen, a male and a female, who seemed to know all about us without our knowing anything about them.

"How did they get there?"

"I have no idea." He looked at another member of the group. "Beck?"

"I don't know either. They said they met me on one of my flights, but I have no recollection of them. I escorted them off the island and followed them to the inn they claimed they were staying at. When I saw them leave a short time later, I asked the proprietor about them. She said they tried to convince her they had reservations there, but she had no such record. They apparently hired a car to the airport from there. We have no idea what they may have discovered inside Myrddin's workshop before we found them."

"There's no need to worry," Cathasach added. "I sent the book away for safekeeping. It's at a secure site."

"What site?" asked one of the Eahta Frean fram Drycræft.

"One Myrddin designated it be sent to if the book were ever in peril."

"Don't you think you ought to share that information with us? What if something happens to you?" one of the eight asked.

Jackson nudged Johanna. "Who do you think said that?"

"I don't recognize the voice. Maybe you want to pop in there and ask them to state their names before speaking."

"Ha-ha."

"There were no Americans on the list. The man who just spoke has no discernible accent, so it's hard to tell which one he is, but it's safe to say he's not Veronika, Alianessa, Beck or Cathasach," Johanna said.

"I agree with Robert," a man with a South American accent said. "I think we all need to know where the book is."

Jackson's eyes lit up. "Robert Birk and Matteus Ferrari of Brazil. That solves that."

"I do not agree," a woman with a French accent stated.

Both teens whispered, "Alianessa Anjou," at the same time.

"Alianessa is right," a Russian-accented female agreed. "When the climate is uncertain, you don't take off your raincoat. The location of the book should only be disbursed when there is a need-to-know."

"Women," the Brazilian exclaimed. "It's a wonder your gender ever gets anywhere with all your caution. I find it hard to believe you were ever appointed to this council."

"But we were appointed to this council," Zendali Zendaga pointed out, "which means we're just as qualified to be here as you are—probably to make sure you don't run wild and do something rash."

"Rather than sniping, I suggest we get back to the task at hand," a man with a clipped British accent stated.

"Yes," Cathasach agreed. "The current location of the book doesn't matter as much as uncovering the person who's trying to steal it. That person must be stopped at all costs."

—LOI—

40

"So what would you have us do?" Beck asked Cathasach.

"Mine your usual contacts, even those a little further afield. Listen to the meanings behind anything that's said and note anything that sounds the slightest bit off kilter. Whoever is looking for the book has to have feelers out trying to discern its whereabouts. We need to listen for chatter along those lines."

"Has it occurred to you that one of us may be the culprit, after all we have full knowledge of the book and what it contains? What if one of us is behind the scheme?" Zendali asked.

"The thought has occurred to me," Cathasach said, "but I'm hoping the members of this group, whom I've grown to trust, would be above such betrayal."

The Eahta Frean fram Drycræft eyed each other suspiciously, contemplating which one among them might be responsible for wanting to steal Myrddin's memoir. But a sneeze from outside their chamber diverted their attention.

Beck and Mateus rushed out in pursuit of the sound, which came from an adjoining tunnel. They found Johanna staring at Jackson, who had closed his eyes as if to ward off attention. The wizards dragged the teens into the chamber where they had been meeting. "I believe we've found something that's *off kilter*."

THAT EVENING, AS THE LAST rays of the sun dimmed in the Dramatican sky, Dungen slipped into the voting room with one of his cohorts. They stopped when they saw Lenc standing on the far side of the room, holding a new decimator. Another unarmed militia volunteer stood nearby.

"In the voting room, no weapons are allowed," Dungen bellowed.

"Assigned by Furst, I am. Until the voting is finished, I'll stay. See him."

"Nothing to do with this, Furst has."

"Find Furst, I will," the unarmed volunteer shouted and ran from the room.

Dungen stomped up to the remaining soldier. "Follow your friend, you had better."

Before the new council leader could get too close, Lenc raised his weapon and trained it on Dungen. "For Furst we'll wait, or shoot first, I will."

Dungen's entire body clenched into a hard knot, but he took no action. He knew what the new weapons were capable of and didn't want to take any chances. But anyone could tell by looking at his tight curls he wasn't very happy. This young upstart had ruined his plan to redistribute the rocks and claim last minute voters had turned the tide.

BECK EYED JOHANNA AND JACKSON warily. "Those are the same two trespassers we discovered in Myrddin's workshop."

"I think we've found our thieves," Zendali Zendaga proclaimed. "And whoever designed this place conveniently left manacles chained to the wall, so we can detain them."

"But only enough for one person," Veronika Veselov noted.

"We don't need to cuff both their hands." Beck rattled one of the rusted manacles. "Just one hand and one foot each." He worked one of the manacles open and slipped Jackson's wrist inside. "Does anyone have a lock?"

Edmund Beasom walked over. "Secure the girl to the other manacle." While Beck chained Johanna, Edmund took a small bottle out of his pocket and put a few drops of what looked like metallic paint on the two ends of Jackson's manacle. He held them together. When he let go, the cuff around Jackson's wrist looked like a solid piece of forged metal that could not be opened. Edmund did the same to Johanna's manacle.

"What is that, Edmund?" Robert asked.

"It's a metal alloy I created, which has an alchemic base. It doesn't change lead into gold, but it does meld metal together as if it were melted and recast as a single piece. The only way they'll be able to get out of these is if they chew their hands off."

Johanna shuddered.

"What's with you people? That's plain evil," Jackson complained. "Myrddin never said anything about you being the bad guys…" He looked at Johanna. "Did he?"

"He suspects one of them may be responsible."

"Oh." He looked at the Eahta Fream fram Drycræft. "Strike my last sentence."

"You're either incredibly brave or incredibly stupid," Beck said to Jackson.

Johanna spoke with confidence she didn't feel. "Even if one of you is trying to steal Myrddin's memoir, I want to believe the other seven of you are fundamentally good. And I can't believe you would leave us here to rot, because that would be tantamount to murder. We're not here to steal the memoir."

"We already have it," Jackson said smugly.

Johanna would have kicked him, if she could have done it without anyone seeing her. "We're here at Myrddin's request—to identify the culprit and bring him to justice."

"You're bluffing," Robert said.

"Cathasach," Johanna opened her left hand so he could see her palm. "I'm from the Library of Illumination."

Cathasach's eyes widened. He approached the pair and studied Johanna's palm. Fantasia glistened in the Illumini system. "How do I know you're not being coerced by this young man?" He nodded towards Jackson.

"Because I'm a curator, too." Jackson opened his hand to expose his palm.

One of the men disagreed. "They're lying."

Jackson leaned toward Johanna and whispered, "Wouldn't this be a good time to show them the ring?"

Cathasach followed Jackson's gaze and twisted the

ring on Johanna's hand, revealing the sigil. He turned to Edmund. "Unlock their manacles."

"I can't do that. We'll have to send for a saw."

Cathasach stepped back. "You engineered a bit of alchemy you can't reverse?"

"I didn't intend to use it tonight. I only wanted to bring it up at the meeting and discuss its potential with the other members. I think it's a significant metallurgic breakthrough, and I wondered how we might best be able to use it."

Beck moved toward the door. "I'll find a saw somewhere."

Robert shook his head before turning back to Cathasach. "How do you know they're even who they say they are?"

Cathasach twisted the ring back to hide the sigil. "The mark on their palms," he replied. "I've only seen it once before, years ago, on a man who curated the Library of Illumination."

"You met Mal?" Jackson asked.

"Mal?"

"Malcolm Trees," Johanna clarified, "my predecessor."

"Yes, Trees, that was his name." He paused. "You called him your predecessor. Am I to believe he's passed on?"

Johanna smiled. "He passed on into retirement, or maybe now it's semi-retirement."

"He's alive and well," Jackson added.

"I'm really sorry about this," Edmund said, pointing to the manacles.

"Sorry?" Jackson questioned. "Just a minute ago

you seemed happy that we'd have to chew our hands off to get away."

"That was before I knew who you are. I do a lot of specialized work, and I'm actually an approved member of the Library of Illumination. I have nothing but the utmost respect for it and its curators."

"What so special about that library?" Veronika asked.

Johanna tensed. The last thing she wanted was a general announcement about the special properties of the library.

DRAMATICANS ERUPTED INTO CHEERS AND whistles when Furst and a reluctant Dungen proclaimed the tax vote had been defeated. Furst, knowing a new tax would soon be proposed, announced a series of meetings at the library to discuss ways to fairly cover the expenses of war. He invited his countrymen to submit ideas that would be read aloud at the meeting and debated by everyone in attendance. The citizens of Dramatica accepted this. They wanted a say in what would be done, and Furst's plan appeased them.

Still, they considered quashing Dungen's tax a victory. Before long, bonfires burned in the town square, and food and drink were brought in and shared with neighbors. There had been very few open celebrations on Dramatica before the Terrorian invasion. Life in the realm had always been predictable and low key. Now, the threat of war awakened a sense of nationalism and unity within the citizens, and small victories gave them a cause to celebrate. The devastating loss of life, liberty, and literature at the hands of the Terrorians inadvertently turned their library into a grail they needed to protect.

EDMUND DESCRIBED THE LIBRARY OF ILLUMINATION for those unfamiliar with it. "It's simply the best research library I've ever found." He smiled at Johanna and she relaxed.

"I find it almost insulting," Alianessa Anjou said with a sexy French accent, "that Myrddin suspects one of us of trying to steal his work. I say *almost* because I know someone is trying to steal it, and it could be anyone, including us."

"I don't agree," Mateus countered. "How do we know someone is trying to steal his work? We are taking the word of a complete stranger who claims she has spoken with Myrddin and was told he suspects one of us. Who started this inquiry in the first place?"

Cathasach's face reddened. "I did. I found the book slightly altered. I asked Myrddin's ghost about it and he confirmed that someone—possibly from another dimension—is trying to steal his notes, and he told me to send them to—"

"Stop! Not another word," Robert cried as he held out one hand. He appeared to be wearing thin, tan leather gloves that fit like a second skin.

"How come you're wearing gloves?" Jackson asked. "It's not like it's cold in here."

Robert glared at the teen. "What impertinence."

Edmund answered the question. "He has a skin condition. The gloves are like bandages, keeping the required medication from wearing off his hands."

Robert gave Edmund an equally withering look. "That is none of their business. Besides, I don't believe our young guests are who they claim they are."

"I'm Johanna Charette, curator of the Library of Illumination."

"I doubt that highly," Robert replied. "You're much too young to be a curator."

"But she is," Cathasach interrupted. "She already showed us the symbol embedded in her hand. From what I have learned, these cannot be duplicated."

"Anything can be duplicated," Robert said, studying her palm, "with the right know how."

"Yes," Cathasach continued, "but do you think this teenage girl has the know how to duplicate this on her own?"

Robert threw up his hands. "I guess not."

Veronika glared at Robert. "Are you saying that because she's a woman?"

"A woman?" he replied. "Really? She looks barely old enough to cross the street by herself."

"Then why did you accuse her to begin with?" Alianessa asked.

"I'm just saying she's not to be trusted—not with Myrddin's memoir—and perhaps, not with our wallets. They could be thieves of a more trifling variety."

"No," Cathasach said. "I believe they're who they say they are. Where is Beck with that saw?"

"That's another problem. I can't believe Edmund can't reverse-engineer his own drops. Here," Robert held out his hand toward Edmund, "let me see if I can do something."

Edmund slipped the bottle of drops in his pocket. "I prefer not to—not until I do more testing on it."

"Then why did you use the drops in the first place?"

Veronika asked.

"Because I saw those two as a threat. Now I don't. Since I do not fully understand how to reverse the drops," he continued, "I prefer not to use them again, until I do further testing."

Robert stepped forward and planted himself uncomfortably close to Edmund. "Afraid I might *best* you with your own elixir, Beasom?"

"No," Edmund responded. "I'm afraid you may cause harm with a potion attached to my name. I am willing to accept judgment for my own mistakes, but not for yours."

Beck entered with a small hack saw. He picked up Johanna's wrist and looked it over. "I hope I can do this without cutting flesh."

Johanna closed her eyes, but didn't say a word.

"Here," Jackson said. "Practice on me. I can take it."

Beck placed the blade against the metal. Jackson instinctively bent his wrist away from the manacle. "That's good," Beck said. "Don't move."

Beck sawed for several minutes. "Ouch," Jackson yelled.

"Sorry about that," Beck replied.

Cathasach took a handkerchief out of his pocket and blotted the blood on Jackson's hand. He then laid an amulet across the cut and recited a short spell, before he used his handkerchief to tie the amulet to Jackson's hand. It took several more minutes to cut the teen free.

Jackson massaged his wrist. "You've got to be more careful with Johanna," he said.

"I think I've got this," Beck answered, before placing the blade against Johanna's manacle.

The curator kept her eyes closed while Beck sawed away. It wasn't long before he freed her. She took Jackson's hand. "Let me see your cut."

He removed the amulet. His hand appeared unblemished. "It's gone." He held out the handkerchief. "I know I got cut because—A—I felt the pain, and—B—my blood is on the handkerchief. I guess it's like what Beck did to your ankle when you sprained it in Wales."

"What are you talking about?" Beck asked.

"Look, I know you don't remember because there's been a rift in the space-time continuum, but Johanna sprained her ankle running to catch the Skokholm ferry, and you put some blue gunk and twigs on her ankle and recited some mumbo jumbo and the injury went away by the next morning. You said the spell came from Myrddin. Johanna had a broken ankle, and you healed it."

"Did you say there's been a rift in the space-time continuum?" Cathasach whispered.

"Uh … yeah." Jackson mumbled.

Johanna grabbed Jackson's hand and squeezed it much harder than necessary. "It may have been an attempt to steal the book," Johanna said. "That's why we're so concerned."

"Right," Jackson added.

"I don't see how that could be possible," Robert said.

"Myrddin could be time traveling," Johanna said, turning to Cathasach. "Didn't you tell me he time traveled to the future thirty-five years ago and brought back a cell phone?"

"How could you know about that?" Cathasach sounded bewildered.

"You told us when we visited you in Myrddin's

workshop."

"Yeah." Jackson frowned. "That was before you forgot who we were and had Beck escort us off the island."

"We must get to the bottom of this, and quickly," Edmund said. "I do not like the direction this conversation is taking."

Jackson yawned, disrupting the ensuing silence. "Sorry, long day."

"That's true for all of us," Cathasach noted. "Maybe we should table the remainder of this meeting until tomorrow."

"Some of us have business to attend to," Zendali said.

"Yes, but I think we'll all benefit from a night's rest." Cathasach looked at the teens. "Where are you staying? The Old Town Square Hotel is right above us. I suggest you take rooms there. It would make meeting with us tomorrow convenient."

"I kind of hoped we'd stay at the Four Seasons," Jackson said. "Maybe it has burgers like the George V."

"I doubt it," Alianessa said. "Nothing here is anything like you'd get in Paris."

"Oh." Jackson's face fell.

The others began filing out, but Cathasach put his hand on Johanna's arm to detain her. He waited until the others' voices became faint. "I very much would like to speak to you before meeting with the others."

"We'll meet you in the center of Town Square tomorrow morning," Johanna responded.

"Why not in the hotel for breakfast?"

"Because Jackson wants to stay at the Four Seasons. I'm pretty sure he'd like eating breakfast there as well."

"Yes!" Jackson picked Johanna off the ground and twirled.

"What are you doing?" she asked.

"I'm doing this instead of a happy dance. I don't want to embarrass myself."

"I think it's too late for that," she murmured.

"Why don't I meet you for breakfast then, at *your* hotel," Cathasach said. "There would be more privacy there. The others are all staying at the place I mentioned earlier. It's actually better if we meet elsewhere."

"Works for me," Jackson said.

"We'll meet you in the lobby of our hotel around eight," Johanna added.

"Aw," Jackson moaned. "So early?"

"That's not early."

"It is when the beds are comfortable. The Four Seasons has *really* comfortable beds."

Cathasach tilted his head. "You're so young, I would never have taken you for a world traveller, and a luxury traveller, at that."

"You have no idea," Jackson answered and would have continued about all the places he'd traveled to recently, if Johanna hadn't squeeze his hand really hard. Again.

—LOI—

41

Recruitment on Terroria built steadily, if only because many of the citizens wanted to pay tribute to General Lethro 814.

Nero 51 looked on with a feeling of accomplishment. *If I had known this many people would enlist for battle, I would have killed the general long ago.*

He had promoted Barzic 922 to replace the late general. His *new* general now approached him. "Room 3 is overflowing with recruits. Would you like to look them over before we break them away for training?"

"I don't think that's necessary," Nero 51 replied. "Get them sorted and assigned. There are many things for them to learn. Make sure, however, they're drilled in parade formation first. I find the appearance of a well-deported military gives both the troops and the public a sense of pride and hope for the future. I will not abide sloppy formations. I want to see precision. They already know how to handle weapons. They learned that in school. And we don't need them to be tacticians. The upper echelon will handle that. I want them to be able to take orders and follow directions without question."

"As you command," the new general answered.

"You have twenty-four hours."

"Twenty-four hours? That's impossible."

"There's a lot at stake here, General. If you can't handle it, you can opt to be demoted back to private, and I'll appoint a new leader in your stead."

"I was a colonel, not a private."

"As I said, if you can't handle it, I'll have you demoted back to private. Do you understand?"

"Yes."

"Good. I'm glad we ironed out that annoying wrinkle."

The general turned to go. "It may go more quickly for you," Nero 51 continued, "if you withhold their meals. They'll learn precision quickly, if they understand that's the only way they'll be fed."

"That's brutish."

Nero 51 grabbed the general with all eight of his tentacles and spun him around. "That's *efficient*. And we need efficiency, right now. Twenty-four hours, General. Or should I say, Private?"

Barzic 922 answered through clenched teeth. "As. You. Command."

It took longer than expected for Pru Tellerence to gather the right mix of books for Dramatica. The class **R** library reorganized its inventory every day in order of importance, which made it take longer to determine which books needed to be replaced. That delayed her trip to the realm until the following morning.

The only original piece of furniture remaining on the upper levels of the Dramatican library had been the circulation desk, so the overseer arranged for shelves and new furniture to replace what had been lost. She believed this would be a welcomed surprise for everyone.

She completed her preparations, but first transported to Dramatica without books or furniture to make sure errant pieces of flying furniture would not bump off Furst or members of his militia.

Soldiers fired on her as soon as she appeared, and once again, she wordlessly thanked Ryden Simmdry for his protection charm.

The troops all spoke at once.

"The overseer, it is."

"Your fire, hold."

"Sorry, we are."

She held up her hands to silence them. ★*You are doing an excellent job of protecting the library. Carry on.* She walked past them and found Furst in the bindery, one of the few rooms that had not been disturbed during the invasion.

He meticulously pieced together an old book with a binding that had been charred by a flaming arrow. He looked up when the shadow of the overseer fell across his workspace. "Honored I am, Pru Tellerence, that to return, you have chosen."

★*If you will clear your soldiers out of the library— for only a moment—I have a surprise for you.*

"Of course, yes," he replied and asked the soldiers to move to the front of the lobby.

With the library cleared, Pru Tellerence recited a short spell as she moved her left hand with the Illumini constellation facing outward in a slow arc. The Dramatican soldiers gasped as the room filled with books and furniture. It only took a few seconds for the dean to refurbish the expanse. When she was done, some books flew about on their own, reorganizing in their order of importance for that particular day.

★*I believe that should take care of your literary needs for now,* she said with a smile.

"Grateful, we are," Furst replied, his eyes glassy with emotion. "To your posts, you can return," he told the soldiers.

★*Is there anything else I can help you with?*

"Make a decision, Dramaticans must. To collect taxes, we need, for war, to pay. Against it, the people are. But necessary, it is. Go into the square, would you, and to the people, speak?"

★*Of course.* Together they left the library to address the citizens in the town square.

CATHASACH MET UP WITH JOHANNA and Jackson at their hotel the following morning.

They talked in general about the city of Prague while they ate, and then settled down to business over a second cup of coffee. "So what do you want to discuss away from the others?" Johanna asked.

"I suspect someone. I didn't until last night, but after what transpired and what was said, I'm left with a question."

Johanna leaned toward Cathasach. "Whom do you suspect?"

"What's the question?" Jackson asked simultaneously.

Cathasach took another sip of coffee. "I refuse to name names—in case I'm wrong—but only one among us has ever claimed to have successfully performed Myrddin's most important spell."

"Traveling as sound and light," Johanna guessed, and Jackson nodded.

Cathasach's mouth opened in amazement. "How could you possibly know that?"

"Because you mentioned it on Skokholm," Johanna said.

"But you never said who it was. Does anyone want the last croissant?" Jackson asked politely before stabbing it with his fork.

"I hate to think the person I suspect is the culprit, because next to myself, he's been a member of the eight the longest."

"Is it the guy who wanted us to chew our hands off?" Jackson bit into the croissant, "because he's on the top of *my* list."

"No," Cathasach replied. "Although there's nothing to say he *isn't* the one."

"Tell us about the members," Johanna urged.

"Well, you know about me. I actually live at Myrddin's workshop, even though I'm originally from Scotland. We always select at least one member from Wales, and *that* person usually lives at the workshop as a protector. But the last couple of Welch wizards couldn't relocate to Skokholm because of familial or career concerns. The workshop needs to be constantly guarded. Since I'm on my own, I moved in. That was forty-two years ago. I've been there ever since."

"Who else is from Wales?" she asked.

"At this point, just Beck, and having to live on the island would cut into his active social life, not to mention his ability to easily get to the airport for work."

"Unless," Jackson said, "he's the one who can transmogrify into light and sound."

"No. It's not Beck, at least as far as I know." Cathasach sighed.

"So who is it?" Jackson asked. "We have six more people to go and not much time if you're having a morning meeting."

"There's Z, but she's always been such a staunch supporter, I doubt she's behind it."

"Z?" Johanna asked.

"He's probably talking about Zendali Zendaga of Zimbabwe." Jackson turned to Cathasach. "Am I right?"

"Yes. Then there's Mateus. He's a powerful wizard, but I've never had any reason to suspect him."

"Tell me about the Russian woman," Johanna said.

"Veronika can be argumentative, but I believe it's because she sees herself as a supporter of causes."

"What if one of her *causes* is to steal Myrddin's powers?" Johanna asked.

"She's already a force to be reckoned with. That would make her nearly impossible to deal with," Cathasach confessed.

"What's the deal with the French chick?" Jackson asked.

"Alianessa Anjou? She doesn't seem very aggressive, but I guess it's the quiet ones we have to worry about."

Johanna leaned back in her chair. "I noticed you

could hardly believe one of the men might be involved, while you're not as circumspect about the women."

"It may sound that way," Cathasach replied, "but I assure you, it's not what I'm thinking."

Jackson checked a scrap of paper he'd pulled out of his pocket. "That's everyone. Now what?"

"Now," Johanna said, "I think we should accompany Cathasach to the meeting, sit quietly by ourselves, and study the others as they conduct business."

"Whatever you need to do," Cathasach said, pushing away from the table, "you have my wholehearted support. But we have to hurry. We have just enough time to get there before everyone else."

NERO 51 DID NOT TURN on the light when he entered his private retreat. The portrait of his great-great-grandfather on the far wall glowed, illuminated by red-hot magma flowing behind the translucent rock that protected the curator's space.

He bowed his head for a moment before speaking aloud. "I will honor your memory soon, Garpa, with a Terrorian victory, just like we spoke about when I was a maturling." He walked over to the portrait and lovingly touched a corner of it. "I know to have done so yourself, would have meant a great deal to you. It wasn't meant to be during your lifetime, but I will forfeit everything I own to insure that it will come to pass during mine, and I will honor you by doing it in your name. Soon, now, Garpa." He bowed his head and saluted the portrait with each of his eight tentacles. Then he disappeared into his meditation room to mentally prepare for the Juvenile invasion.

* * *

MOST DRAMATICANS HAD SCANT KNOWLEDGE of the overseers, however, tales about the remarkable beings had begun circulating in earnest after Library Council members and soldiers encountered Ryden Simmdry and Pru Tellerence in the library. So when Furst accompanied Pru Tellerence to the town square, Dramaticans crowded around them, eager to see the overseer for themselves.

Pru Tellerence smiled at everyone she encountered and sent out powerful calming vibes. ★*We are doing everything in our power to crush any invasion attempts, but we cannot provide complete protection, only because the realms, even though connected, are separate and autonomous. We cannot barge in and accuse anyone without proof.*

A Dramatican citizen with a border of jewels on his caftan, but not much more embellishment, pushed his way to the front of the crowd. "Their weapons, we have. Proof enough, is that not?"

★*It could be, once it is determined who specifically is responsible for manufacturing them and arming their militia. Proof against the realm is not the same as proof against the guilty party in charge.*

"Bah!"

★*If Furst took it upon himself to invade another realm without your consent, would you want the overseers to retaliate against all of you? I don't think so. The College of Overseers knows about the devastation those weapons caused, but we must proceed carefully. And there are other considerations. Your invaders have stolen a device that makes them more dangerous than the sum of all their weapons. They have taken a machine from another realm that allows them to travel through time. It means they can transport back to a period when the portals were open and use them to invade any world. We are searching for a way to protect every realm, but we don't want to put whoever is responsible on the defensive, because we're afraid it would trigger even greater devastation.*

"An overseer, you are. Travel back in time, why can't *you*, and when to the portals you get, stop them?" Furst asked.

★*That is an excellent idea.* Pru Tellerence smiled. ★*Our primary goal has always been to trust each realm and its people and assume they would act fairly. In the past, we only stepped in to stop a problem once it had begun. I will talk with the others about your suggestion to prevent the problem before it starts or at least before it continues.*

The Dramaticans applauded politely.

★*I cannot promise the others will agree with me, so until that happens, you must prepare for war. That means building weapons and stockpiling food and supplies that would normally go toward you and your families. It is a sacrifice, but it is payment for future protection. Soldiers need to be fed and armed and may miss out on profit from their usual trade while they're working to protect you. They will need a stipend to keep their families clothed and fed. It is everyone's duty to make sure that's possible. You must pool your resources together in advance to help pay for it. It may be a hardship, but it's better to sacrifice a little now, than to sacrifice a much more significant amount—possibly your lives—if you're caught unprepared in the future.*

Only the soldiers applauded at this point.

★*Those with the most wealth should give the greatest amount. Those with nothing to spare should give the smallest denomination, but everyone should give.*

The applause increased, but the realm's most prosperous citizens did not join in.

★*I know you all to be open-minded and warm-hearted, and I trust you will do what is right. Furst tells me there will be a meeting, so you can all discuss the best way to join together to consolidate your resources. You all have a chance to be heard, but only if you go to the meeting. If you choose not to attend, don't be surprised when your future complaints fall on deaf ears. You are all members of this society and responsible for each other's well being.*

JOHANNA, JACKSON AND CATHASACH ARRIVED at the chamber under Old Town Hall and found Robert Birk already there.

"You're out early, Robert," Cathasach remarked.

"I have been giving this problem of an alleged thief a lot of thought, and I've come up with a plan to catch him or her. I wanted to speak with you before the others arrived. I didn't know you'd have the kiddie brigade with you."

Jackson clenched his fists. "Kiddie brigade? We're curators of the most prestigious library on earth. We weren't chosen because we belong to a kiddie brigade."

"I'll tell the U.S. Library of Congress and the Vatican and Bodleian Libraries they've been displaced by—where is it you work?"

Johanna squeezed Jackson's hand. He turned to look at her, and she almost imperceptibly shook her head.

Jackson pulled her out of the room. "You're going to let him get away with that?"

"There's trouble brewing and he's a suspect. Don't let his antics distract you from the main reason why we're here. It doesn't matter what anyone thinks of us, only that we prevent someone from stealing Myrddin's memoir. And the best way to do that is to identify the culprit."

"Yeah. Well," Jackson jerked his thumb toward the meeting chamber, "that guy gets my vote."

"Noted. Let's go observe the proceedings."

They walked back into the chamber to find several of the Eahta Frean fram Drycræft entering through a different entrance. "Where do you think that entrance leads?" whispered Jackson, nodding towards it.

"I don't know, but I wouldn't be surprised if it goes directly to their hotel."

"So," he reasoned, "they could enter and exit, and it would look like they never left the hotel."

"And that matters—why?"

"I don't know. I'm brainstorming here."

Johanna merely smiled and took up a position in the corner of the room. Jackson sank down next to her, and they watched as Cathasach called the meeting to order.

"I believe the best way to begin is to eliminate those of us who could not have possibly tried to take Myrddin's book," Cathasach said. "That means I'll need your verifiable whereabouts for the day in question."

"That's ridiculous," Veronika said. "We lead very busy lives. How are we supposed to prove where we were at any given moment?"

"Well, if you were in Saint Petersburg and someone there can vouch for your whereabouts for the day, that should be sufficient. You're profile doesn't mention the ability to transmogrify, so I would conclude that you are not the person responsible."

"But I wasn't in Saint Petersburg. I was in London that week, on holiday. I shopped, and museum hopped, and took in attractions like the London Eye. I'm sure the hotel will verify my stay."

"That wouldn't be enough. London to Marloes is only a four-hour trip. I'll need a detailed itinerary of where you were during the day, so I can rule out a side trip to Wales."

"Don't you think that's a bit much?" Robert said.

"No. I don't. I need to cross reference where everyone says they were at any given time for the day in question."

Alianessa shifted in her chair and crossed her arms. "And who questions you, dear Cathasach?"

"I'm the one who reported the tampering in the first place."

"Yes," said Mateus, "but who's to say you didn't take the book and concoct a ruse about sending it to that library you mentioned to cover your tracks?"

Robert tapped his pen against the tabletop. "Mateus poses an intriguing possibility, Cathasach. What do you have to say for yourself?"

"I was at the workshop, of course. I didn't leave the island. If I did, the ferry service would have a record of it."

"That doesn't prove you *didn't* send the manuscript to some obscure place for later pick-up," Robert continued.

"Or you could have helicoptered out," Veronika added.

Cathasach sighed. "This is not getting us anywhere."

"It's not so nice when the finger is pointed back at *you*, is it?" Edmund asked. "Now you know how we all feel."

"And it may not be one of us at all," Zendali said.

"Yeah," Beck said, "but as long as there's a chance it could be, we have to do this.

"I believe Cathasach," he continued. "And I believe those two." He nodded toward Johanna and Jackson. "But I'm not sure I believe it's one of us. Still, unless one of you has a better idea, you'd better start checking through your records and receipts and supply Cathasach with some details so he can check everyone's—dare I say the word—alibi."

"That is no easy task," Robert said. "May I suggest we adjourn for a couple of days before meeting again? It will give us enough time to fly home and put together what you're asking for."

"That's easy enough for you to say," Mateus uttered. "You don't have to fly to Brazil. I don't even know if I can get there, get the verification you need, and fly back here in a couple of days."

"You would if you were able to successfully perform Myrddin's transmogrification spell." The others turned to stare at the speaker—Edmund Beasom.

"We've all seen that spell," Alianessa said. "Who's to say one or more of us *can't* perform it successfully? Anyone capable of traveling as light and sound could steal the book and still provide the necessary documentation to prove they were elsewhere for *most* of the day in question. Even Brazil."

42

Nero 51 climbed to level two, the window level just below the library cupola. He rubbed the glass with his tentacle so he could see more clearly and looked down at the field to watch the military training. He winced as Terroria's newest soldiers attempted to maintain crisp military precision, and failed. *It's only been a few hours, but...*

He descended the stairs and headed out to the field. Maybe a few well-placed words to the soldiers and the general were in order. *It's time for them to learn why they need to pay attention to details.*

The soldiers were just about to take a break when he arrived. "My fellow Terrorians, this is no time to rest. That will be your reward when you learn to do this simple procedure properly.

"General," he said, "drill them again."

Nero 51 remained at the field for hours, refusing

to allow the soldiers to take a break until they marched in perfect formation. He made it known they would not be fed until they formed perfectly straight lines and maintained them throughout multiple parades around the field.

"You see, General, already they are much improved. Follow my lead and you will have no problem meeting my deadline. Slack off, and you'll find yourself marching beside them."

Furst and Dungen worked together to prepare for the upcoming tax meeting on Dramatica. Dungen crowed about the tax being his idea in the first place, however, Furst countered by saying—while a fundamentally good idea—it needed the input and acceptance of the populace. They continued to bicker for hours, until they formulated a basic tax proposal they both agreed on.

Furst created a large chart outlining the plan and displayed it in the main reading room. He surveyed the newly furnished space and decided they would need more chairs to accommodate everyone. "To bring up additional chairs, I'll need help."

Dungen squared his shoulders and lifted his hairy chin. "To help you, get a soldier."

"Here, now, you are."

"The president of the Library Council, I am. Do menial tasks, I do not."

Furst felt the roots on his neck start bristling, but chose not to pursue an argument with Dungen. "To the door, I will walk you," he said evenly and literally pushed Dungen out.

* * *

⌘*MALCOLM, I SEE YOU HAVE FOUND IT within your power to return to Lumi.*

"Selium Sorium came to Fantasia for a visit, and I traveled back with him. He told me about a tax they're trying to collect on Dramatica, and I thought it would be an excellent introduction for me in my new capacity as Chancellor of the Exchequer. It fits perfectly with what I'm *supposed* to be doing and will give me a chance to rehearse my new role and learn about the Dramaticans' military plans. Any realm I go to after that will be easier, because I could always refer back to *when I was on Dramatica* ... and it should give me instant credibility."

⌘*A superb plan.*

★*I'd like to add to it.*

⌘*Pru Tellerence. I didn't realize you had returned.*

★*The Dramaticans shot down the impromptu tax the new director of their library council tried to ram down their throats, but as Furst explained, the tax is necessary because they need the funds to keep their militia battle ready. I believe Mal should go to the meeting they plan to have tomorrow. I'll introduce him as the new Chancellor of the Exchequer. I think the Dramaticans will be happy about him being there because they're afraid the proceeds from a tax will be misused. If someone appointed by the College of Overseers is there to handle its collection and disbursement, the Dramaticans may feel a little better about parting with their hard earned goods.*

"Goods? Not money?" Mal asked.

★*Dramaticans have a barter society—labor for tailoring, food for tools, livestock for medicine. They have never had a need for other types of monetary units, although gemstones do hold a special place in their economy, with the most prosperous residents wearing the most luxurious jewel-studded caftans.* She smiled thinking of them. ★*Furst is now in charge of their army, as well as being curator of the Library of Illumination—the most important facility in the realm—but because very few Dramatican citizens require its services, his caftan is simple and unadorned. The College of Overseers gives him every-thing he needs, but in the eyes of his countrymen, he hasn't* earned *more prominent raiment. So I would also like to request military uniforms. The militia should have sturdy, serviceable attire that is more practical than their caftans, with more elaborate adornment for the officers. And for Furst, something exceptional that will immediately elevate him and alert everyone that he is a prestigious person in our eyes. It will give him sway over the soldiers and the townspeople—something I think he needs right now.*

⌘*Another excellent idea. I would like to be there when you present them with their uniforms.*

★*Of course. You may want to perform a protection spell for Malcolm. They have a tendency to shoot on sight.*

⌘*That gives me an excellent idea of my own.*

"So it's come to this, has it?" Alianessa griped. "The more proficient we are as wizards, the more likely it is that we're guilty."

"That is not what I originally meant," Cathasach answered, "but it is, in part, quite accurate. I will need to know who in this room has ever transmogrified."

"It is the most difficult of Myrddin's spells," Robert said.

"And yet," Cathasach replied, "I remember you telling me two years ago that you had successfully accomplished that spell."

"To some degree, I have. But not necessarily for the great distances or lengths of time that you're talking about."

Edmund and Mateus both sprang to their feet. "Why weren't we told this?" Mateus demanded.

"We have sworn, as members of the eight, to keep the others fully abreast of any and all successful recreations of Myrddin's work," Edward added. "Yet it seems that you, Cathasach, and Robert have been acting as gatekeepers."

"I have hardly kept my work a secret," Robert said. "I openly told Cathasach. It is *he* who chose not to inform all of you."

All eyes focused on their leader.

Cathasach reddened. "It's true I knew about Robert's advances. But as he said, he had only made minor inroads into the spell, and I felt he should have the privilege of informing you about his accomplishment when he felt ready."

"Disappearing for a moment or two is easy," Edmund said. "Traveling is much more complex."

Robert adjusted one of his gloves. "Spoken like a man who may have experienced some small measure of success, himself."

"Like you, I have only just begun to unravel the mystery of transmogrification."

"So both of you have been successful." Zendali's features hardened. "But neither of you made the rest of us aware of it."

"What does it matter?" Beck asked.

"If you've lied once or, in this case, withheld

information," Zendali continued, "who's to say you haven't done it a thousand times. This organization is built on trust and a mutual goal. If some members are using Myrddin's resources without disclosing the results to the rest of us, it's a betrayal."

"Betrayal is a little harsh," Alianessa said. "I did not feel like I betrayed anyone when I, too, managed to disappear. I never mentioned it because I reappeared almost immediately."

Veronika placed both palms against the table and half-stood. "Some of us haven't been so fortunate in our attempts, but pooling our information may have helped *all* of us make inroads."

Cathasach's shoulders slumped. "This is getting us nowhere."

"I don't agree," Mateus said. "The way I see it, we now know who among us is more focused on their own goals rather than those of the group. I believe we should take disciplinary action against those who have shielded their advances."

"That's ridiculous," Edmund said loudly. "We were all wizards before being asked to join the eight, and as such, were free to practice our skills. Calling for disciplinary action—when we have not broken laws of man or magic—is childish and inane."

Jackson leaned his head against the wall and closed his eyes as the meeting deteriorated into a shouting match. "Wake me when it's time to go."

"I know what you mean," Johanna replied. "It makes me wish *we* knew how to transmogrify."

* * *

NERO 51 APPROACHED THE TOP bio-engineer in his realm and explained he wanted a way to surveil troop placement and be able to track their "wellbeing."

The bio-engineer, Plala 6, had gained a measure of fame when he developed a bio-system to monitor mammoths grazing in the Terrorian countryside. The animals provided nearly sixty percent of the Terrorian diet and were closely watched. Plala 6 told the curator it would take only seconds to band each Terrorian soldier with a bio-band, and nanocytes would immediately permeate tissue and build an intramuscular network of molecular receptors and transmitters to report host telemetry. The nanocytes worked rapidly and telemetry would be completely operational within a few hours.

Nero 51 nodded his approval. "How quickly can you start?"

"I've just received a ten thousand unit shipment. I can begin whenever you want," the bio-engineer answered.

"Then pack up your supplies and report to Building 11 in the capital. We will begin immediately."

The bands caused excruciating pain for the first few hours, but soldiers received vouchers for free merk, which took their minds off the agony.

THAT AFTERNOON IN THE LUMINAN city of Fridi, clothiers busied themselves making patterns for Dramatican militia uniforms. The pants resemble jodhpurs, flared from the hip through the knee, with a snug fit for the lower calves and ankles. This allowed Dramaticans, who were not accustomed to wearing trousers, to flex and leap without hindrance. The jacket resembled a hip-length caftan. Short boots, and flexible knit caps that could hold back a Dramatican's abundant curls completed the outfit, save for a leather cross-body brace that contained a sheath for a knife, a detachable quiver for arrows, a shoulder strap for an optional crossbow, and a holster for the decimators that would be issued.

The uniforms were all created in two colors: fawn brown for day-to-day use and icy blue for dress uniforms.

The officers' uniforms were similar, however the caftan-like jackets were trimmed in braid and the dress uniforms came with sashes that could be adorned by jewels earned for deportment and bravery. The officers would also be given peaked hats instead of knit caps.

Then there was Furst's uniform. It was similar in line to the militias' uniforms, however, the fabric was a superior quality and the colors rich and jewel-like. Furst's day uniform was a brilliant bronze color, and instead of braid trim on his jacket, it was encrusted with Luminan diamonds. Gold epaulettes provided a distinguishing bit of adornment. Furst's dress uniform was cut out of a luxurious white fabric, and his sash was already adorned with colorful jewels surrounding a diamond depiction of the Illumini Constellation at its center.

Tailors worked through the night to complete as many different uniforms in varying sizes as possible. They worked in an assembly line, first the pattern makers, then the cutters, followed by the seamstresses and tailors. In another factory, shoemakers cut, hammered, and stitched away, making sure they would have a ready supply of boots and leather braces.

Further to the south on Zyco, work got under way for a special project for Ryden Simmdry.

And not far away from there, on the outcrop Munit, specialists in weaponry retrofitted machinery to churn out the parts necessary to duplicate Terrorian weaponry and began making decimators.

Back in the capital city of Lumi, Mal prepared notes for what he would say to the Dramaticans the following day when he was announced as Chancellor of the Exchequer.

"Malcolm Trees, you have a visitor."

He had become quite used to the disembodied voice that notified him of any pending action and reminded him to eat and sleep. "Open the door, please."

A courier handed him a sealed envelope. Mal ripped it open and found himself summoned to the College of Overseers. "I have a transport disk waiting to take you to the college," the man said.

Mal nodded and allowed himself to be whisked away to the chamber of the overseers.

JOHANNA AND JACKSON CAUGHT AN AFTERNOON flight back to Charles de Gaulle Airport and easily re-entered the Library of Illumination where everything was quiet. Almost too quiet.

"Do you think your family left?" Johanna asked.

"Not if they're getting free room service," he answered. And he was right. Inside the George V suite, Chris and Eva played with an Xbox.

"Where'd you get that?" Jackson asked.

Chris blasted Ava's soldier to pieces. "Room service."

"Cool. Where's Mom?"

"She's in her bedroom getting a massage."

"No way!"

"Yeah. I think the hotel manager likes her. He sent up the masseuse, and later on, someone's coming to give her a facial and style her hair. He wanted her to go downstairs to the spa, but she said she couldn't leave the room. But who needs to? Whenever we want something, they bring it to us."

"Well, I hate to rain on your parade, but we're back," Jackson replied grabbing Ava's game controller out of her hands. "And soon, this will all be just a memory."

"Can we at least get room service first?"

"You've still got a few days," Johanna said. "Jackson and I haven't yet completed our mission, and we need you to take care of the library."

"See," Chris joyfully blew up Ava's encampment. "We have to stay—for the good of the library."

Jackson shook his head as he addressed Johanna. "We've created a monster."

"Best monster ever!" Chris said. Ava reclaimed the controller and began attacking his troops.

—LOI—

43

ALL THE OVERSEERS WERE IN place around their chamber conference table, and Mal stood at the end of the table opposite Master Ryden Simmdry.

⌘*Ah, Malcolm, right on time.*

"What can I do for you?"

⌘*It's not what you can do for us, Malcolm. It's what we can do for you. I have proposed, and the deans have unanimously agreed, to confer upon you the majorious longevicus blessing. You will receive the complete complement of charms that, until now, have only been bestowed upon those who have risen to the rank of dean. You came very close to being an overseer yourself and only mitigating circumstances prevented that from happening. As our new Chancellor of the Exchequer, we feel you have earned the right to be blessed with the same benefits and abilities longevicus provides.*

⌘*We have chosen to dispense with the public*

challenge portion of the ceremony, considering you have already taken part in it and we know where your dedication lies. Please enter the circle of our table and stand on the Illumini Constellation.

Mal moved to the middle of the room and felt himself lowered into the ground. The surrounding crystal columns and brilliant light reminded him of when he received his blessing as a curator, except now the light was purple instead of blue, and the blessing he received would slow down his aging to one year for every thousand years that passed.

He had lived a long and fruitful life, perhaps not as long as some of the others who had received the blessing at a younger age, but still, he felt he had been blessed with a wonderful and illuminating existence. It seemed like only moments had passed when the platform rose, signifying the blessing had been conferred.

⌘*One last enchantment, Malcolm.* Ryden Simmdry recited the spell that would protect Mal should he enter a library cupola and find himself under attack. ⌘*One can't be too careful.*

"Thank you. Thank you all. I will do everything in my power to prove to you that you have not made a mistake in taking me into your confidences.

◍*We will need a sigil for Mal. Might I suggest ₵ considering he will be the receiver of taxes?*

⌘*A very appropriate symbol, indeed.*

JOHANNA JOINED JACKSON AND HIS family for dinner in the *suite* and was surprised when Naimh Roth entered the room. She looked completely transformed following her spa makeover.

"Mom," Jackson said with a touch of awe, "you look totally hot."

Mrs. Roth blushed.

"Stop it," Ava said. "She's our mother. You can't call her *hot*."

Chris kissed his mother's cheek. "Unlike Jackson, I think you look totally *cool*."

Mrs. Roth smiled. "It's just a little hair color and makeup."

"It becomes you," Johanna said. "Is that a new blouse?"

"It's on loan."

"On loan?" Ava asked, as she answered a knock at the door. "How'd you manage that?"

Two hotel employees wheeled in carts filled with food.

"If I like it, I can buy it. If not, I can return it." Mrs. Roth sat down at the dining table.

Jackson and Johanna had ordered burgers, but everyone else dined on steak and seafood. Chris tucked into his porterhouse while Jackson eyed his burger. He knew it would be good, but wondered if Chris's steak would be better. "So, Chris, are you paying for that with the earnings from your part time job?"

Chris chewed slowly, savoring the steak before swallowing. "If they ever send me a bill—in my name—I'd be happy to pay them. But as far as the hotel is concerned, we're the Oswald-Fitzpatricks of New York."

Jackson placed his burger back on the plate. "Where'd they get that idea?"

"Well," Chris said between bites, "Mom always told us not to give out personal information to strangers, so when room service didn't have our name on the bill the other night, I made one up for them. I thought using two names was a stroke of brilliance, and New York made us sound so ... so cosmopolitan."

"As opposed to just plain so-so?"

"Very funny. Want a bite of my steak?"

"Yeah."

"Well, forget it. I'm eating the whole thing myself."

"Who *is* going to pay for this?" Mrs. Roth asked. "I haven't really thought about that since that first night."

"Probably, no one." Jackson shoved a french fry in his mouth. "It's not real."

"I don't know about you," Ava said, scooping up the last of her Lyonnaise potatoes, "but this tastes 'real' to me."

"Yeah. Well. Enjoy it while you can." Jackson turned to Johanna. "Right? We won't get billed for this will we?"

"If we do, we'll just pay for it with a doubloon," she joked.

She felt Jackson nudge her under the table. "Don't go there," he said under his breath and looked covertly at his mother.

Johanna smiled.

"What doubloon," Chris said, pausing between bites. "Do you guys have a real doubloon?"

"No." Johanna shook her head. "It was just a joke."

"Too bad," Chris said. "Paying with a doubloon would have been awesome." He pushed his plate away. "Spending time with you guys is great and all, but it's Saturday night and Brittany awaits."

"What are the two of you doing?" Mrs. Roth asked.

"Nothing. Maybe we'll see a movie." Chris rose

from the table and headed toward the door.

His mother continued to pry. "Well, is it nothing, or is it a movie?"

"Does it matter?" Chris asked. "We're just spending time together."

"Movies, bowling, sporting events—all imply that the two of you will be in the company of others and fully occupied. 'Nothing' leaves too much room for temptation and getting into trouble."

"Okay. We're going to a movie. Is that all right with you, Mom?"

"It's fine, as long as that's what you're really doing."

"We're not planning on getting into trouble."

"I'm just making sure," Mrs. Roth reiterated.

"We're not!"

Ava leaned back in her chair. "Methinks thou doth protest too much."

"And what," Chris asked, color rising in his cheeks, "if we change our minds? Will we be liars then, as well as trouble-makers?"

"All anybody asked," Ava replied, "is where you're going, and you got all huffy."

"Next time I'll lie and act cool."

"Yeah, like Robert Birk," Jackson muttered.

"Who?" his brother asked.

"One of the guys we're investigating to see if he's after Myrddin's memoir."

"Who's Myrddin?" Ava asked.

"Only the greatest wizard who ever lived," Jackson answered. "And this guy, Robert Birk, may have recreated one of Myrddin's spells, without telling anyone."

"So what's so bad about that?" Christ asked.

"Nothing except he misled everyone about having done it."

"I have to ask Mal a question," Johanna said suddenly, rushing out of the room.

"What was that all about?" Ava asked.

"I don't know," Jackson replied, "but if I know Johanna, she probably just had a brainstorm."

IT MAY STILL HAVE BEEN Saturday night on Fantasia, but it was already the next morning on Terroria, and the military, resplendent in full dress uniform, marched in formation down the main street in front of the Library of Illumination. Each soldier carried a fully armed decimator and wore a glowing purple band surgically attached to his left fore-tentacle that transmitted telemetry to military headquarters.

Nero 51 summoned General Barzic 922 and Plala 6 to the library. "It is time to put your work to the test. I want two dozen troops here within the hour, outfitted for combat. I will accompany them to their destination in the time machine to insure we target the correct realm. Once all the troops are in place, we will crush Juvenilia like a lump of sand."

JOHANNA PULLED OUT MAL'S DIARY. "Who has been with the Eahta Frean fram Drycraeft the longest?"

The pages fluttered just as Jackson entered the room, however, the answer didn't appear until several moments had passed. *Cathasach Caird of Scotland has been with the group the longest continual time, but there's some indication Robert Birk of Sweden was with the group before Cathasach arrived on the scene and either quit or was forced out. According to one rumor, he was banned for practicing déofolcræft—the black art of devilcraft.*

"Did you read it," Johanna asked Jackson, who stood peering over her shoulder.

"Yeah. Are you surprised?"

"Not really. It would explain his slickness and self-assuredness. He has a smarmy edge beneath his bespoke suit."

"What's bespoke?"

"Custom made."

"I think I'm going to get me one of those bespoke suits."

"Just don't use the gentlemen weavers from Hans Christian Andersen's *The Emperor's New Clothes* or all your secrets will be out. Literally."

"Very nice talk from someone who acts like a proper lady." He sat close to her, and could feel the warmth of her body. "So what do we do about this Birk guy?"

"I think it's time for another visit with Myrddin."

He twisted around and encircled her waist with his hands. "Can it wait?"

"Unfortunately, no."

Nero 51 looked over the first troops who had assembled in the field where the time machine was hidden. He divided them into small groups and personally transported the first group to their target destination.

The portals scrambled and their first stop was definitely not Juvenilia. He was surprised to see a human woman with a horrified look on her face. He quickly exited that world and tried again.

He noted the soft colors and lyrical music at the

second stop. *Must be Romantica. They will get a turn as well, but not now.*

In the cupola of his third attempt, a telescope was trained on the heavens. *This must be Scientico.*

The next cupola was decorated in primary colors and he saw a child's game laid out on a table in the corner. "We have arrived."

Nero 51 instructed the troops to remain hidden in the cupola until all soldiers were accounted for and he personally gave them the signal to begin. It took time to travel to Juvenilia, because he could never be sure where the portals would take them, and even when they arrived, he could only transport a few troops at a time. Finally they were all in place—in the *correct* place.

INSIDE THE LIBRARY VAULT, IT took no time at all for Myrddin to appear.

"Have you found the person trying to steal my work?"

Johanna pointed her forefinger at him. "What do you know of a man named Robert Birk."

"I am not familiar with that particular name." His face stilled and his gaze lost focus for a moment. "However, it reminds me of a man who claimed to be a member of the northern Svear tribe, Rathbarth, son of Visbur, whom I befriended for a time until he tried to undermine my position at court. Over the years, his name may have evolved into Robert, son of Visburk, or Robert Birk. He was a wizard of notable skill and unbridled ambition. I doubt he would have survived into this century, but then, you are speaking with me, or at least my energy, so who am I to say he didn't find a way to persevere.

"You must promise me," Myrddin continued, "to be very careful and ensure you are alone when you enter this chamber. It would be better to not visit me here at all, until the situation is resolved."

"But what if we need to ask you a question," Jackson interrupted, "like we're doing now?"

"There is a book, *Historia Regum Brittanniae,* written by Geoffrey of Monmouth in the twelfth century that refers to me. If you were to open that book in this library, you should be able to speak with me. Wait." He disappeared for a few seconds and then reappeared. "I have made sure the version of me you will encounter within those pages is prepared to answer your questions."

Johanna quirked an eyebrow. "Version of you?"

"Yes. In that book, I'm known as Merlinus, a name that later degraded into Merlin the magician. "

"We knew that," Jackson quipped.

"Do not come here again. It is too dangerous." Myrddin disappeared into the pages of the book before Johanna closed the cover.

"He was sure in a hurry to get out of here," Jackson said.

"I don't blame him," she answered. "If the thief can transport as sound and light, what's to stop him from sneaking in here with us."

"Then let's lock the door and hide the key. After that, I think we should go see a movie."

"So you can spy on your brother?"

"I just want to make sure he's as good as his word."

PROUD WORKERS DELIVERED THE FIRST twelve decimators and time-correctors to the College of Overseers. Their foreman showed the deans how the weapons worked, then explained how the time-corrector necklaces simply protected the wearer from experiencing temporal rifts.

◍ *How ingenious.*

⌘*If our curators are affected by the temporal rifts, they will immediately forget about protecting themselves, as soon as the invaders travel back in time. The amulet will allow curators to maintain all memory, regardless of changes to the space-time continuum.*

Ryden Simmdry turned toward the workers. ⌘*Thank you all. We mustn't keep you. Your work is important and we need many more of these armaments and amulets to protect the realms.*

Ω*Twelve weapons is a very small start.*

⌘*It will be sufficient for now. We do not know where the Terrorians might strike next, but we do know it will be through a portal in the cupola. I would like you to transport immediately to your respective realms and present one of these weapons and an amulet to each of the curators for their protection.*

JOHANNA AND JACKSON RAN INTO Chris and Brittany at the movie theater and shared a pizza with them afterwards. Then the couples parted ways so Chris could walk Brittany home.

Johanna and Jackson entered the library and saw Ava run up the cupola stairs carrying a decimator.

"Where did she get that?" Jackson's shout brought his mother and Selium Sorium from the bindery.

◍ *There has been another change in the continuum. We have chosen to supply all realms with weapons identical to those used by the Terrorians.*

"But she's still a girl. You can't just give my little

sister a gun and expect her to know how to use it. One moment's hesitation on her part, and she'll be erased from the face of the earth."

◍ *Your sister has demonstrated a certain amount of prowess on what you call an Xbox. She has a good eye. She's certainly brave. And with both you and Johanna out of the library, we had to press her into action. She's guarding your portals. As a precaution, all overseers, as well as Malcolm, have received a protection charm that makes them impervious to the weapon. Since no one else should be using the portal system, she has been instructed to shoot on sight.*

"What if Furst comes through needing our help? What if Pru Tellerence finds Isabella and brings her back here using the portal system?"

◍ *Both Pru Tellerence and Furst have been apprised of the dangers the portals now pose. The only guests who will enter the cupola are uninvited ones.*

"Still, my sister …"

"What's up with Ava?" Chris asked as he walked through the front door.

Jackson did a double take. "It didn't take you long to walk Brittany home."

"Yeah. Her parents were up and must have heard us, because the porch light went on right away."

Jackson snickered.

"You didn't answer me," Chris said. "What's going on with Ava that's got you all riled up?"

"She's up in the cupola with a gun that will vaporize anyone she fires at."

"She's got the Xbox up there?"

"It's a *real* gun. Did you meet Selium Sorium? There's an invasion threat, and he armed Ava with a very powerful weapon. I wouldn't sneak up on her if I were you. But if you do and she blasts you, can I have your iPod Touch?"

"You told me I was a jerk for buying it second-hand."

"Well, if you're not around to enjoy it, I may as well."

"It's in my back pocket. If I go, it goes." Chris headed toward the cupola steps as he yelled, "Hey Ava, I'm coming up. Don't shoot."

Jackson spun around. "Mom, this is a really bad idea."

"You didn't see them, Jackson. Big, oily monstrosities with tentacles for arms."

Johanna finally spoke. "The Terrorians were here? You saw them?"

"I thought I might be able to see you and the boys walking back from the theater, so I went up to look out the windows. I didn't realize that staircase," she pointed toward the center of the library, "only went to the cupola. When I got to the top floor, I saw those things materialize for just a moment, almost ghost-like, then disappear. I almost died when Mr. Sorium appeared a moment later, carrying the weapon Ava now has."

The overseer smiled. ◍ *We do not use the honorific "mister" where I come from. Simply call me Selium Sorium. Everyone in Lumi has two names and is called by both together. I would never be Selium, or Mr. Sorium. I am only Selium Sorium—almost as if it were one name instead of two. Pru Tellerence, Ryden Simmdry—we all go by both our names spoken together. Never one or the other.*

"I don't want to sound disrespectful or anything," Jackson said urgently, "but what about the Terrorians?"

Suddenly, a high-pitched scream echoed down

from the cupola.

    Mrs. Roth broke into a run. "Ava!"

—LOI—

44

NERO 51 ISSUED FINAL INSTRUCTIONS to his first wave of Terrorian troops. "Begin by quietly destroying books. You should not encounter much resistance. If you do, capture the kiddlet in a force field and remove them from plain sight. Report back to me when you have destroyed the library. Do not venture outside this building without a direct command to do so."

"How do we report back, sir?" a trooper asked.

He pointed to a raised emblem on their bio-bands, "Press this button, and we will return for you."

The Terrorians decimated all the books on the top four levels of the Juvenile library and had destroyed half the books on the first level before being discovered by three pairs of twins. They managed to capture five Juveniles in force fields, but one Juvenile managed to escape. The Terrorians immediately barricaded the front door to prevent retaliation and continued their work.

* * *

GUFFLE, THE FOURTEEN-YEAR-OLD Juvenile who escaped the Terrorians, burst into the *wreck-wroom* of the Juvini city center—pale and sweaty.

"What is it, Guffle?" Duddu asked, putting down his pool cue. He was the official Juvenile leader—voted into power by collecting the most chocolate ingots. The only one considered a greater authority was Peer Meap, the curator.

Guffle gasped for breath between each phrase. "Big… ugly … monsters … captured Flugle and the others … in the library … destroying books … all the Mozo stories … my favorites …" He collapsed on the floor.

"Bring him some sweet water and do what you can to revive him." Duddu turned to Pollo, his right-hand guy. "Take some of the older boys and investigate the library. See what's going on there."

Pollo narrowed his eyes. "Sling shots and water cannons?"

"BB guns, stink bombs, and air-blaster horns. If what he's saying is true, water cannons won't be enough."

"Got it." Pollo snapped his fingers at one other boy and they left the room.

Guffle choked on the sweet water being poured down his throat and sprang back to life. "We've got to do something." He coughed. "Trouble in the library." He coughed again. "They've got Waxmo and Pokkie and Selly and Cici, too."

Guffle immediately tensed. Cici was the cutest girl in the capital city of Juvini, and Guffle adored her to the point of distraction. "I should go with them." He turned toward the door.

"No." Marbol held him back. "You can't afford to get hurt. I'll go."

Guffle clenched his fists. "Cici is mine."

"You can keep your precious Cici. They've got Selly, too. You're the leader now. You stay here and lead. I'm the old man. I turn sixteen soon, and we all know what happens when you turn sixteen. So it's no big deal if they capture me. I'm the oldest, so I have the most experience and maybe I can get everyone out safely." Marbol didn't wait for Guffle to agree.

Marbol rushed home to pick up his sonic-scrambler—an invention of his own design. He'd heard that high pitch frequencies and ultrafast vibrations could scramble peoples' sense of time and space and disorient them, while exceptionally low sine waves could make people cower in fear. For the past several months he had worked feverishly to create a secret weapon with high and low pitched settings. He planned to use it on a couple of bullies who liked to harass his little sister and make her cry. This would be a good test. If he turned out to be a hero and became more popular than Guffle, so be it. And if Selly and Cici both threw themselves at him—even better. He smiled as he ran to the library.

RYDEN SIMMDRY, PRU TELLERENCE, AND Mal arrived on Dramatica safely and accepted soldiers' apologies after being shot at. The overseers were dressed in their usual attire. However, Mal wore a robe of dark green velvet trimmed with gold braid, and instead of a miter, wore a dark green chaperon on his head. The trio was immediately taken to Furst, who fretted over the placement of a question box for the tax proposal.

"Come for the meeting, you have? Ryden Simmdry, I am honored."

⌘*I am here for more than the meeting, as you will presently learn.*

They heard banging on the front door. "Illumination," Furst called out.

The door slid open and Dungen practically fell into the library, shoved to the side by a hundred Dramaticans who all vied for a chair close to the center of the action.

"Not scheduled to begin yet, the meeting is," Furst announced diplomatically. "Outside, please wait." No one moved. The curator sighed.

⌘*Continue doing what you were doing, Furst. We will patiently wait here with your countrymen.*

"Offer you refreshment, can I?"

★*You need not worry about us, Furst. Do what you must to prepare for this meeting. We would like to speak to your kinsmen once you have called the meeting to order, to make some important announcements.*

Furst nervously eyed the front door as people continued to pour in. A scuffle in the back of the room diverted their attention. A heavily jeweled Dramatican demanded that a less-elite citizen give up his seat. The less bejeweled man would not comply.

"Not enough seats, there are," Furst mumbled.

Ryden Simmdry waved his hand and several rows of extra chairs appeared. ⌘*There will be room for everyone.*

Furst relaxed, but tensed again when a youngster ran up to him and tugged on his caftan. "To ring the bell, is it time yet?" Furst nodded and within moments, the bell tower pealed, signaling the beginning of the meeting.

Dungen walked to the podium. "Fellow citizens and honored visitors ..." He looked directly at Ryden Simmdry and faltered when the master deliberately shook his head.

Pru Tellerence walked over to the podium. ★*I am glad to see that so many of you have come out for this very important meeting. It is a credit to your curator, Furst, who put this together on such short notice.*

Dungen huffed.

★*We know how important it is for you to establish a militia to repel outside invasion forces, and we know you have been asked to sacrifice goods and services to make that possible. Of course, you have concerns about the oversight of your taxes and how they will be used, which is why we are here. For those of you who do not know Ryden Simmdry and myself ...* She tilted her head toward to master ★ *... we are overseers of the Library of Illumination system. We supply the library with its books and equipment and make sure your curator is compensated for his services. While many libraries continue the age-old tradition of appointing a library council ...* She nodded at Dungen ★*... it is a ceremonial position only. Please look to your curator, Furst, to make any and all decisions regarding library business.*

The color of Dungen's face matched the rubies on his caftan.

★*Now, I would like to introduce Ryden Simmdry, the master of all the deans at the College of Overseers. He has an important announcement for you.*

Polite applause followed and Ryden Simmdry took his place behind the podium.

⌘ *The College of Overseers recently created a new position that reports directly to us. The Chancellor of the Exchequer will be responsible for making sure taxes collected in each of the realms are handled honestly and used efficiently. He will be responsible for your militia tax, but is not allowed to take any of it in payment for his services, nor remove it from your coffers. I would like to introduce Malcolm Trees, who will make sure you get, in the parlance of his home world, more bang for your buck.*

No one laughed, and more than one Dramatican scratched his head. They knew a bang meant noise, but had no idea what a buck could be.

Mal took the stand and looked out at a sea of curious faces. "The overseers have selected me for a very important position, and I am honored to be able to serve you. I hope to meet many of you individually during the day's proceedings and would like to hear all your concerns so we can address them. I am not here to intrude on your daily affairs or put undue pressure on anyone. My only duty is to make sure your contributions are used wisely. I look forward to speaking to you at the end of this meeting." He nodded at Pru Tellerence and Ryden Simmdry who both returned to the podium. Ryden Simmdry waved his hand and two mannequins appeared.

⌘ *Over the centuries, in realms like your own, soldiers have worn clothing designed to establish uniformity and rank. While uniforms distinguish members of the militia from the general public, they mask societal position, which allows the best to rise to the top regardless of wealth or prominence.*

★ *As our gift to you, each of your soldiers will be*

given two uniforms. The brown ones are for every day. The pale blue ones are for more formal meetings.

The master waved his hand again and the officers' uniforms appeared.

★ *These uniforms are for military officers. You'll notice they have sashes on which to attach jewels bestowed upon them by the Library of Illumination for deportment and bravery.*

Ryden Simmdry waved his hand one last time and Furst's uniforms appeared.

A collective "Ahh," rose from the crowd when they saw the rich material and gemstones. Many of them pointed to the jeweled sash containing the Illumini constellation. Pru Tellerence smiled. She had been waiting for this moment. ★*And these last two uniforms are for your curator, Furst, a most important person. Look to him to lead you during these trying times, and listen with care to everything he tells you. It is an honor of the highest order to be chosen as a curator of the Library of Illumination—the repository of all knowledge—and the position is not assigned lightly. Furst is knowledgeable, patient, and wise. The adornment of his new uniform is in direct relation to the power and skills he holds. Support him and respect him, for he is your leader and the best man for the job.*

The crowd applauded, nodding and smiling at Furst. They knew Furst to be pleasant and easy to get along with, and he had already led them to victory against the Terrorians. If the overseers wanted to give him their endorsement, the Dramaticans would as well. Except Dungen, who stood to one side, silently seething.

* * *

FOLLOWING THE MEETING ON TERRORIA, Mal returned to Fantasia where the blast from a decimator gave him a moment's pause. "Oh dear, I was warned this might happen," he remarked, "and I am protected, but it's still unsettling when someone shoots at you."

"You're okay?" Ava's question erupted between sobs.

"Yes, I'm quite fine. And I can see they chose the right person for the task of protecting the library. No one is going to get by you."

Chris couldn't believe Mal's praise of Ava. "I would be just as good if I had a decimator."

Mal smiled. "I'm not saying you wouldn't."

"What happened?" Jackson asked as he ran up the last few steps of the cupola stairs, ahead of his mother and Johanna.

"Jackson." Mal smiled and extended his hand. "Your sister has a lot in common with Phoebe Ann Mosey."

"Who?"

"A woman better known as Annie Oakley," Mal answered.

"Uhhh. She shot at you?"

"And I wouldn't be here to tell you about it, if the overseers hadn't taken a few precautions. Ava's a crack shot."

"As opposed to being a crackpot?" Jackson joked.

"It was luck," Chris said.

"And I'm sure you're brother would have been just as good if the weapon had been in his hands," Mal added diplomatically. "It may come to that, soon. I'm told additional weapons are being created and will be distributed."

◍ *Malcolm, I see you came to test Fantasian defenses.*

"I give it my wholehearted endorsement and none too soon. The Terrorians have apparently stepped back in time again and have attacked Juvenilia. Zenith Fullova says they have taken several Juveniles hostage and they fear Terrorians will extended their reach outside the Juvenile Library of Illumination."

◍ *Oh dear. They're just children.*

"Surely, there are adults there who will figure out some way to keep the Terrorians at bay," Mrs. Roth said.

"There are no adults, per se, on Juvenilia," Mal answered. "All the inhabitants are between the ages of three and fifteen. They literally die of old age before their sixteenth birthdays. But then their energy is reborn into a duplicate of their three-year-old selves, and they live once again. That's not to say they don't mature. They age very slowly. A fifteen-year-old Juvenile is the equivalent of a seventy-five-year-old Fantasian. However, while some of them grow to be quite wise, they rarely lose their childish ways."

"So they look old," Jackson reasoned, "but act like children? Or do they look young and act like adults?"

◍ *Neither. They look young and they act young. It takes more than 1,800 Fantasian days for Juvenilia to orbit its sun, so its residents age very slowly.*

"How will they protect themselves?" Mrs. Roth asked.

"The same way your daughter just protected you when I suddenly appeared in the cupola. The young have agility and quickness, and they don't fear mortality quite the same way someone older does. They can be excellent soldiers. Unfortunately, war and invasion are foreign to the Juveniles, and they have no experience protecting themselves against an alien attack."

"I'll bet we could protect them," Ava said, holding her decimator at the ready.

◍ *I've no doubt that you could.* And at that moment Selium Sorium felt the consensus of all the overseers.

BUOYED BY REPORTS THAT TERRORIAN troopers had taken several Junveniles hostage and had wiped out a large portion of their library, Nero 51 told General Barzic 922 and Plala 6 to ready another contingent of soldiers for a secondary invasion. "The females of Romantica with their foolish notions, whimsy, and frivolity will be just as easy to conquer as the children of Juvenilia."

He prepared the troops' orders, and once they were assembled, personally transported them to Romantica. It took several attempts to find the correct cupola, but before long, Terrorian troops stood ready to destroy another library.

CHRIS NUDGED JACKSON WITH HIS ELBOW. "It's a good thing you two are back from your, uh, mission. It looks like things are about to heat up around here."

Mal turned his attention toward Johanna and Jackson. "Did you learn what you need to know?"

Jackson sighed and looked down at his feet. "Not really."

"But we're close," Johanna said. "I think we need to go back to Scotland to talk with Cathasach."

◍ *There is someone you suspect of trying to steal Myrddin's Memoir?*

"Yes," Johanna answered, "but it's still only a

suspicion. I think we need to tell Cathasach about it and see what he thinks."

Chris's face lit up. "Is this about that birch tree guy you mentioned?"

Jackson mocked his brother, "Birch tree?"

"Yeah." Chris stepped in close to his older brother's face. "You mumbled something about him at dinner, and then Johanna said you needed to talk with Myrddin."

⌘ *Who is the culprit?*

Everyone jumped. No one had heard Ryden Simmdry enter the library. A Luminian man stood behind him with a crate filled with weapons.

Chris practically salivated. "Can I get one of those?"

⌘ *Once you've been instructed in the proper safety and handling of the weapon.*

"Hey, you gave one to my little sister," he exclaimed. "Was she instructed in the proper safety and handling of the weapon?"

◍ *I instructed her myself, and I will do the same for you. But you are almost too eager, and that could be disastrous. This is not a toy or an instrument for one-upmanship.*

Chris turned bright red. "I know that."

◍ *Then we shall begin.* Selium Sorium took a weapon from the Luminan and led Chris away from the others.

Ryden Simmdry reclaimed Johanna and Jackson's attention. ⌘ *Please tell me who covets Myrddin's memoir.*

"It's not written in stone," Johanna answered, "and I hate to name someone without more to go on."

⌘ *Then why suspect that person at all.*

"It's just a general impression we got when Cathasach questioned the Eahta Frean fram Drycræft. One man seemed to always have an answer or excuse and was adept at re-directing suspicion away from himself whenever anyone questioned him. His name is Robert Birk. Myrddin said there was once a man named Rathbarth, son of Visbur, who was a powerful wizard back in the day. He says the names are similar enough to indicate a possible connection."

Ryden Simmdry's eyes widened for a millisecond before his calm countenance resurfaced. Most people might not have noticed, but Johanna had been staring at him so intently, she witnessed the small, nearly imperceptible, moment.

"You know him," she said quietly.

⌘*I was acquainted with Rathbarth, son of Visbur at one time—around the same time Myrddin was believed to be the most powerful man in existence. Rathbarth wanted that title and publicly swore to take it away from Myrddin. That was just before Viviane turned Myrddin's magic against him and trapped him inside a rock. I always wondered if Rathbarth had a hand in that.*

Johanna pulled out her cell phone and navigated to a picture of Robert Birk. "This is the man we suspect."

Ryden Simmdry froze as he gazed at the picture on the tiny screen, and once again Johanna picked up on it. She looked at Jackson and then turned back to the master.

⌘*He must be stopped.*

—LOI—

45

Jackson stared intently at Ryden Simmdry. "So you know Robert Birk?"

⌘*The man in that picture is familiar to me. He is a former Mysterian curator who hasn't been heard from in many millennia and is believed to have perished in the Two Millennia War. He was known as Odyon, a high priest and shapeshifter. Perhaps I should say "is." His appearance has changed, but the gold starburst radiating from his pupils, along with this oddly shaped scar,* he pointed to the side of Robert Birk's nose, ⌘*tells me he is the same person. Were you able to see his hands?*

"No," Jackson answered. "He wore gloves—indoors—which I thought was kind of weird."

Ryden Simmdry nodded. ⌘*He is hiding his Illumini constellation and the white disfiguring scars left on his hands after he tried to maim me with acid. I deflected the container's trajectory and it burned Odyon's hands when*

517

he put them up to protect himself.

"What are we supposed to do, now that we know it's him?" Johanna asked.

⌘*Nothing, at the moment. I will devise a plan that will eliminate the danger he poses.*

Jackson rubbed his head. "Let me get this straight. You're saying this guy has been around since the Two Millennia War. How is that even possible?"

⌘*Mysterian high priests have many special powers, and he was the most powerful one among them. Odyon personally created the majorious longevicus blessing that protects overseers and curators. It is not at all surprising that he is still alive, considering he probably used the blessing on himself. And as a shapeshifter, he can change into an inanimate object when injured or pursued, so that he may rest and heal undetected.*

"It sounds like his skills are on par with Myrddin," Johanna said.

⌘*They were close in power. Odyon was dangerous because he practiced déofolcræft. However, Myrddin was more powerful because he had the strength of goodness—engelcræft—behind him.*

Jackson tilted his head as he thought about the problem. "Do you think this guy Robert Birk, or Rathbarth, or Odyon can travel as light and sound?"

⌘*Undoubtedly.*

Johanna and Jackson groaned in unison.

⌘*I see you share my sentiments.*

MARBOL JOINED UP WITH THE other Juveniles, who had gathered outside the library. "Did you try to go inside?"

Pollo nudged a stone with the toe of his shoe.

"Not yet. We're working up to it."

One of the others stared at the weapon in Marbol's hand. "What's that?"

"It's my sonic scrambler."

"Will it get rid of them?" he asked.

"I don't think so. It's just supposed to confuse them and scare them."

"Maybe they have one just like it," Pollo joked, "and that's why Guffle was so scared."

Marbol pressed his lips together into a tight line. "Nobody has a weapon like this."

One of the local bullies who had been picking on Marbol's sister, approached. "Hey you stupid gripps, this is my turf, and if you want to meet here, you're going to have to pay the price." He smacked his right fist into the palm of his left hand.

Marbol shot him with his sonic-scrambler. Then he flipped the switch and shot again. At first the bully just seemed confused, but then, he eyes widened in fear and he turned and ran.

The others stared at his retreating figure and then at Marbol. "Where'd you get that?" Pollo asked Marbol, nodding at the weapon.

"I made it."

"Can you make me one?"

"Depends."

"On what?"

"Just depends. Ask again when this is all over." He lifted the weapon and nodded at the library door. "Let's go inside."

"It's not going to be easy," Pollo said. "It's never easy to get inside the library. It's like the door is stuck shut, except when Peer Meap doesn't want it to be."

"I know how to get in," one of the boys said. "Follow me."

NATALIA DALURA, HAD CLIMBED HALFWAY UP the spiral staircase with an armload of books, when she heard footsteps and whispers in the cupola of the Romantican library. She had been alone in the library, and the door was locked, even to Dame Erato, the former curator.

Natalia felt her heart skip a beat. She quietly edged her way back down the stairs hoping to get help before being discovered.

THE NEXT MORNING, RYDEN SIMMDRY returned to Fantasia with a plan and a package. He found Johanna and Jackson sitting in the main reading room, studying books on Terrorian military tactics. ⌘*I have given this a lot of thought, and it appears to be our best course of action.* He unwrapped the parcel and withdrew a perfect black cube about the size of a ring box. The color, or lack thereof, was so intense that the box looked like a black hole in the middle of the overseer's hand. ⌘*This box has special properties. It absorbs transmuted or "imperfect" light and sound that subsequently cannot escape it. I have spent the night creating and perfecting it. It will safely hold Odyon's essence inside.*

Jackson looked up as he cupped the back of his head in his hands. "So all we're suppose to do is say, 'Hey Odyon, get in the box'?"

Johanna poked him in the side before standing. "What do you want us to do?"

⌘*You will need to conceal the box within your robes.*

Ryden Simmdry paused to study Johanna's clothing.

She wore form-fitting, black jeans with a slinky wrap top. She tensed under his scrutiny.

⌘*I can see how that might be a problem.*

"Wait." She ran up to her residence and exchanged her blouse for a bulky, hip-length sweater with pockets, before returning. "How's this?" She stuck her hands into pockets that were hidden within the seams.

⌘*That will do nicely.* He handed her the box. ⌘*Hold it in both hands.* He recited a spell. ⌘*Now, only you can open and close it.*

Jackson jumped to his feet. "Hey, what about me?"

"Jackson has a point," Johanna said. "If something happens to me, we don't want to lose our chance to capture Odyon."

⌘*All right, Jackson. Hold the box in both hands like Johanna did.* The master recited the spell again before continuing.

⌘*You must invite the Eahta Frean fram Drycræft here for a meeting.*

"Here?" Johanna shook her head. "Myrddin strictly advised us against that."

⌘*Regardless, you must invite them here. Tell them you cannot see how any of them could possibly be the culprit. Explain if they all come here they can speak directly to the spirit of Myrddin that's trapped inside his memoir, and together you may be able to determine what outside source is posing the threat. Having access to the book is too much of a temptation for Odyon to pass up. Have them meet in the conference room. I will ensure that access to the lower levels is sealed off to prevent anything from happening to the memoir, which I presume is in your vault and must remain there.*

Johanna shut her eyes for a few seconds, while she thought over the plan Ryden Simmdry had just laid out. "You don't think they'll see right through that?"

⌘ *I will provide an acceptable facsimile of the memoir with an interactive hologram of Myrddin. They will not question its authenticity.*

"You still haven't explained what to do with that box." Jackson nodded at the small black cube.

⌘ *Using the box will require a bit of finesse. After convincing everyone that you don't suspect them, you will have to deftly steer the conversation toward building evidence against Odyon, without saying he is one of them. Then you must suddenly turn on Birk and accuse him. I believe he will try to escape by turning into a beam of light or sound. All you need do at that point is open the box to absorb his energy. The box will do all the work. But don't let him see it first, or he'll recognize its dark properties and find a way to flee before you get a chance to use it.*

Jackson scratched his head. "How do we open it?"

⌘ *Telepathically. If you think you want it to open, it will.*

"How quickly can a whisper of sound or beam of light exit the room?" Johanna asked.

⌘ *Very quickly indeed, so as soon as you see his image waver, open the box.*

Jackson sat on the arm of one of the reading room sofas. "What if he's not Odyon?" he asked quietly.

⌘ *Then the search renews.*

"So the box is harmless to everyone else," Johanna reasoned.

⌘ *Not entirely.*

Jackson sprang back up. "What do you mean?"

⌘*As I said, the box will absorb imperfect energy, and that may include any protective charms cast upon you and the others. Odyon's energy should provide the strongest vibration. In its absence, the cube may interpret the longevicus charm that protects the two of you, and suck you inside before you have a chance to react.*

Jackson's voice boomed. "That's not good."

⌘*If that happens, I will do everything in my power to retrieve the box and set you free.*

ONE OF THE BOYS LED the other Juveniles around the block to the alley leading to the back of the library. They passed a pile of crates and he instructed the others to grab one. When they got behind the library, he piled them up and climbed on top and looked in the back window.

"What do you see?" Pollo asked.

The boy spit on his hand and rubbed the dusty glass pane. He gasped as he jumped off the crates. "I'm not going in there."

Pollo climb up and peeked in. "Farzz!"

"What do you see?" Marbol asked.

"The ugliest creatures you can imagine holding heavy tubes that make stuff disappear," he whispered, crouching down.

"What stuff?" one of the boys asked.

"Books."

"Can they make people disappear?"

"I don't know," Pollo said, "and I don't want to find out."

The boy looked at Marbol. "Will that thing work through the window?"

"There's only one way to find out."

Pollo jumped down and Marbol took his place. The blood drained from his face as he stared at the Terrorians. He felt his knees weaken, but he knew if he chickened out, he would never hear the end of it. *Might as well go out in a blaze of glory. Or stupidity.* He aimed his scrambler at the Terrorian doing the most damage and pulled the trigger.

JOHANNA EMERGED FROM HER OFFICE WITHIN minutes. "I just spoke with Cathasach. He's calling the others and instructing them to meet us here by midday tomorrow."

⌘ *The plan is in motion. By sunset tomorrow, the threat to Myrddin's memoir should be eliminated. I will take my leave of you until then. The Terrorian invasions of Juvenilia and Romantica command my attention.*

"Romantica!" Jackson exclaimed. "Is Natalia Dalura okay?"

⌘ *That—I cannot answer. I was only advised of this latest attack while Johanna spoke with Cathasach. I must return to Lumi and review what has happened with the other deans.*

IN LUMI, THE USUALLY UNFLAPPABLE overseers injected a lot of nervous energy into their discussion with Ryden Simmdry about the Romantican attack.

⌘ *It was sudden. I was taking a cache of weapons to the realm to use against the Terrorians if needed, and I seemed to be suspended in time for several long moments before appearing in the cupola. I immediately noticed shelves and books missing, and in communing with the others learned from Pru Tellerence that it had happened that exact same way on Dramatica. I returned here hastily with the weapons. I didn't want to leave them for the Terrorians to claim.*

⌘*Has Dramatica been attacked again?*

★*Not that I have heard, but the Dramaticans have proven themselves to be formidable opponents, so I can understand why the Terrorians might focus their attention elsewhere.*

Ryden Simmdry nodded. ⌘*And what of the battle on Juvenilia?*

§*The library interior has all but been destroyed, save the vault, which remains impenetrable to all but the curator.*

⌘*Have we heard from Peer Meap?*

§*No. I do not know if he is hiding or has been captured, but the vibrations from the vault seal tell me it has neither been tampered with nor recently accessed.*

⌘*Do any Terrorians linger within?*

§*I do not know.*

⌘*Zenith Fullova, you must return to the Juvenile library and seal the entrances and windows. Then immediately return here, sealing the portals behind you. We must strand the Terrorians on that world until we come up with a greater plan. We do not want them to be able to report back to their leaders. Horatio Blastoe, you must do the same on Romantica. It's too late to stop them from invading, but if we can prevent them from returning to their home worlds, we may be able to undermine the Terrorians' invasion strategy.*

★*Hopefully, we are not subjecting the beings in the invaded territories to further threat.*

⌘*They have already been threatened Pru Tellerence.*

Our mission is to mitigate the danger by undermining the continuance of war. If we don't, who's to say Lumi won't be next.

◍ *They would not come here, unless they successfully conquered* all *the other realms. That would take a great deal of funding, effort, and time. I don't believe we would have to consider the possibility of an attack on Lumi for at least another millennia. Possibly two.*

⌘ *You are correct, of course. For now, we must focus on the twelve realms that make up the Illumini system.*

FOR SEVERAL SECONDS AFTER MARBOL pulled the trigger of his sonic scrambler, nothing happened. Then, the soaring glass window he aimed the scrambler through—shattered.

A unified roar erupted from the Terrorians who all turned to face the window.

Marbol jumped off the box. "Stink bombs, NOW!" The boys threw a combination of stink bombs and firecrackers inside the window and then ran as fast as they could. The only one to stay behind was Marbol, who shinnied up a tree and repeatedly fired the sonic scrambler through the window.

—LOI—

46

ONE BY ONE, THE EAHTA FREAN FRAM DRYCRÆFT arrived at the Library of Illumination, and Jackson showed each of them into the conference room.

At noon, Johanna entered the room, carrying a facsimile of *Myrddin's Memoir*. "Thank you all for coming. As I said on the phone, Jackson and I have gone over what little information we have, and we've concluded that no one from the Eahta Frean fram Drycræft could possibly be posing the threat to this book. However, your help is needed to determine who is. We've taken it upon ourselves to invite you here, so we can discuss the problem directly with Myrddin through his memoir. Please, make yourselves comfortable." As the wizards took their seats, Johanna looked at each member of the group and saw their eyes were all riveted to the book she held.

Jackson nodded at her. "Let's get this show on the road."

Johanna opened the book. "Myrddin, the Eahta Frean fram Drycræft are here to help us find whoever is trying to steal your life's work."

A 3-D image of Myrddin appeared to hover over the pages. "What further information do you seek? I have told you all I know."

"Myrddin," Edmund Beasom began, "how do you know someone is trying to steal from you?"

"I don't," the image answered. "I only became aware of the problem after Cathasach came to me saying the book had been moved. He asked me if I had perceived any astral changes from within."

"And did you?" Robert Birk asked.

"No," Myrddin replied. "If someone had disturbed my work, it was done quite deftly."

Robert exhaled, almost imperceptibly. The tiniest hint of a smiled played at the corners of his lips.

"Who do you know who would want to steal this book? Veronika Veselov asked.

"I don't know of anyone, anymore. Many years have gone by, and my colleagues have all passed on. I am blind to who would want to steal my work at this current point in time. Surely, what is contained within my collection is now archaic, and my spells and elixirs have been far surpassed by more effective charms and potions."

"No, my friend," Mateus Ferrari commented, "your work remains without equal."

"Then you must prevent it from falling into the wrong hands, especially if the threat is coming from another dimension."

Zendali Zendaga leaned forward in her seat.

"What do you mean by another dimension?"

"Outside of our *known* world. I have traveled the astral plane, and there are realms, foreign to our own, where threats may lie."

Beck shook his head. "As far as I know, speaking with your *spirit* is the only other dimension I've ever encountered. How would we even get to another *realm?*"

"As long as you hold onto your notion of earthly bodies, it may not be possible. You must be willing to give them up—to become one with the elements."

"Hah!" Edmund Beasom exclaimed. "I've been trying to do that for years, but can't get past the second step."

"You cherish your own flesh and blood too much. There is much to behold beyond it."

"So what are we supposed to do?" Beck asked. "Kill ourselves to free us from our mortal chains?"

"It is your mental chains that must be cast aside," Myrddin replied.

"Give me an example," Robert said. "Tell me what I can do to cast away my mental chains."

"You must possess the ability to travel as sound and light by clearing your mind and becoming one of those essentialities. Once you control that ability, you can go *anywhere.*"

A moment of silence ensued as everyone pondered Myrddin's answer. They had all tried to master the transmogrification spell—purportedly with limited success.

Johanna stared at Robert. "Robert, I believe you have had the most success with that spell."

He looked up at her, his eyes filled with fire, and

then ice. "No more than anyone else," he said quietly.

"I think you're lying," she replied.

THE ROMANTICAN LIBRARY DOORS SWISHED open more loudly than Natalia Dalura expected. She prayed whoever had invaded her cupola, was too preoccupied to hear it. She slipped out to search for Dame Erato.

The former curator was on her knees, pruning the fragrant blossoms that bordered her garden. She heard frantic footsteps and looked up just as Natalia rounded the corner of her cottage.

"Dame Erato. I think we are being attacked."

"What do you mean?" the older woman asked, brushing dirt from her gloved hands.

"I was locked in the library, about to shelve the last shipment of returned books, and as I climbed to the cupola, I heard footsteps and whispering above."

"Perhaps it was the overseers."

"No," the curator replied. "There was a funny odor. The overseers smell like the flowers you grow in your garden. Whatever stood above smelled more like a chemical factory built in a field of rotting flesh."

"Terrorians?"

"I think so. I would contact the overseers, but the Terrorians are *in* the cupola. What would you do in this situation?"

"I would use my diary, of course. Horatio Blastoe gave it to me when I succeeded him as curator of this library. Come inside. We'll contact him and he will ask the other overseers what we should do."

Natalia breathed a sigh of relief. Having an ally who was once an experienced curator helped lessen her burden.

Several minutes passed before an answer appeared.

We are aware of the breach. The libraries will soon be sealed, as will the portals. The invaders will be stranded.

THE OVERSEERS WHO TRAVELED TO the Romantican and Juvenilian libraries completed their assigned tasks from the cupolas, without having to engage the invaders. As they retreated, they sealed the portals causing a slight temporal rift, since the portals had not previously been sealed at that precise moment.

NO SOONER HAD JOHANNA CALLED Robert Birk a *liar*, than the whole room seemed to waver. Everyone's gaze zigzagged from her to him and then back to her, until Jackson broke the tension by saying, "Ten will get you twenty Nero 51 just used the time machine to invade another realm." All eyes suddenly diverted to him.

"Time machine?" Matteus asked. "What is this, some kind of hoax?"

"No, it's…" Jackson turned to Johanna and caught her glaring at him. "Just a joke."

"Actually, it's quite feasible. Haven't we discussed this before?" Cathasach asked.

"We talked about time travel," Beck answered. "But not about a specific piece of apparatus or time machine that would make that type of travel easy."

"Who's Nero 51?" Veronika asked.

"He, uh, stole the time machine we borrowed and is using it to storm the portals of the Libraries of Illumination so he can invade them?" Jackson's voice trailed off. He looked to Johanna for help, but she only glared at him.

"This is ridiculous," Robert Birk said. "We're not accomplishing anything here. I'm leaving."

"Running away ... Odyon?" Johanna asked. "You can't, you know. The door's locked."

His eyes narrowed for a moment, and then his face froze. His image wavered and Johanna pulled out the black cube, but her movement was awkward. *Open,* she commanded telepathically and suddenly Robert disappeared, but that didn't startle her as much as what happened next. At nearly the same moment, Alianessa Anjou faded into wisps of gray smoke that were immediately sucked into the cube before the top slammed shut.

"What just happened here?" Mateus demanded.

"What happened here," Johanna said quietly, "is that Odyon, the person responsible for trying to steal Myrddin's memoir, got away."

Veronika pounded on the table. "What happened to Alianessa?"

Johanna looked at the black cube in her hand before closing her fingers around it. "She's in here."

Odyon. His secret was out, but what did it matter. He'd escaped the room in time, traveling as sound through the air vent. Inside the cupola, he used his shapeshifting abilities to change into a book on a shelf near the portals. He was familiar with the portal system. Back at the onset of the Two Millennia War, he had been the curator of the Library of Illumination on Mysteriose and had sided with Terroria and Adventura against the other libraries. When the tide turned against them, he had transmogrified into a book at the Fantasian Library of Illumination knowing they would never knowingly destroy a book. In time, he escaped the library and set out to make his fortune on Fantasia. The portals had been sealed all these years, trapping him far away from Mysteriose, but now, all he had to do was wait for someone with a time machine to storm the portal system, and he would find a way home at last.

THE PLOT THICKENS ... WITH MORE TO COME

Turn the page for a preview of the next
Library of Illumination adventure …

THIRD CHRONICLES OF ILLUMINATION
Escape to Mysteriose

Coming soon from Artiqua Press

THIRD CHRONICLES OF ILLUMINATION

Escape to Mysteriose

JOHANNA CHARETTE AND JACKSON ROTH stared at the little black box overseer Ryden Simmdry had given them. He'd created it so they could capture Robert Birk, otherwise known as Odyon—a powerful wizard who wished to steal the workbook containing spells and potions created by Myrddin Emrys—otherwise known as Merlin the magician. But Odyon, a shapeshifter, had transmogrified into light and sound too quickly to be captured. Instead, the tiny black box had sucked up the essence of Alianessa Anjou, the French member of the Eahta Frean fram Drycraeft—the group entrusted with protecting Myrddin's legacy.

Johanna chewed her lower lip. The 18-year-old curator of the Fantasian Library of Illumination had failed. "I wish Ryden Simmdry was here."

"No you don't," Jackson countered. "Then we'd have to tell him we bungled capturing Odyon and admit the threat against the Library of Illumination is still hanging over us. He's going to give us one of those disappointed looks, like my mother gives me when I've let her down. Let him stay where he is—thinking we're saving the world.

The remaining members of the Eahta Frean fram Drycræft glared at her.

Veronika Veselov walked up to her and tried to snatch the box from her hand.

"No." Johanna twisted away from the Russian woman. "There's only one person who can open this now, and he's not here. I have to keep it safe until we find him."

Veronika turned to the other members of the secret group of eight wizards who had sworn to protect Myrddin's legacy. "I'm leaving. Anyone who wants to further discuss this debacle, follow me." She grabbed Cathasach's arm and dragged the startled man from the room. The others followed, with Beck bringing up the rear.

Johanna grabbed Beck, missing his hand, and wrapping her fingers around his wrist instead. He twisted and the Illumini constellation on her left palm rubbed against his sigil. Suddenly, she felt lightheaded. Her knees weakened and she thought she might faint. Her lids fluttered as her eyes rolled back.

Beck's brow furrowed. "Jackson, there's something wrong with your girlfriend."

Jackson rushed to Johanna's side and lifted her into his arms. He tried to walk away but couldn't. "Let go of her."

"I'm not holding her." Beck wriggled his fingers. "She's holding me.

"Johanna," Jackson kissed her forehead. "Let go of Beck."

But she couldn't respond. Waves of energy and power she had never experienced before surged inside of her and her mind became both clearer yet more confused than it had ever been before.

"What did you do to her?" Jackson asked.

"Nothing. I was walking out the door. She grabbed me."

Johanna didn't know how much more of the energy surge she could take. Even as the strange new power entered her being, it sapped her own resources, and she felt herself shutting down—losing consciousness.

Her grip on Beck's wrist released when she blacked out.

He pulled his hand away. "I'm going. I don't know what you two are up to? If it's no good, we'll be back. Otherwise, think of this as our final goodbye."

"We're on the up and up," Jackson said. "This is Odyon's doing, or didn't you notice how he magically disappeared when we accused him?"

"For all I know, he's stuck in there with Alianessa. You've taken on the wrong group if you think you can pull one over on us. We weren't selected for the Eahta Frean fram Drycræft because we're weak. On the contrary, we're the most powerful wizards in the world. Pray we don't have to return, because if we do it won't be pretty."

Jackson's voice increased in volume but lowered in pitch. "We didn't do anything."

"Two wizards are missing. If one or both of them are responsible for trying to steal Myrddin's memoir, we would have dealt with it. Internally. You did do something, and you'll have to pay for it." He stormed out of the room.

Jackson carried Johanna toward the hotel suite, hoping his mother still had some spirits of ammonia left. The wizards were arguing loudly as they crowded the front door.

"How the hell do we get out of here?" Beck shouted.

"Illumination," Jackson said quietly, and the door slid open, allowing the wizards to escape.

Johanna felt her blood surging through her veins. Her eyes flew open. "Where am I?

Jackson knelt at her side with an ampoule in his hand. "The hotel suite in the library."

She admired the interior of the George V hotel suite. "I've never been in one of the bedrooms before. … Nice."

"Are you okay? What happened? I thought Beck did something to you and you were going to die. That's one of Myrddin's spells, isn't it?"

"I'm fine, I think," she said sitting up.

"So …?"

"Something weird happened when I grabbed Beck. Like all his knowledge and power seeped into my body. He's studied Myrddin's spells quite closely, and now I feel like I know them by heart." Her focus dulled as she searched her memory. "I do." She grabbed Jackson's shoulders. "I know them all by heart."

"How could you know that?"

"I just do."

"I think you and I should go downstairs and have a little chat with Myrddin."

"He told me not to visit him in the vault anymore.

He gave me the name of a book to use instead." She searched her pockets. "Wait a minute, I wrote it down." She finally pulled out a scrap of paper.

"It's a wonder you can fit anything in your pants pocket."

"What do you mean? Do you think they're too tight?"

He threw both hands in the air, palms facing out. "Don't change a thing. They fit you like a glove." He smiled.

She made a face. "You can stop staring now."

"Just admiring your form."

Johanna set the box down on the floor. "I hope Alianessa was telling the truth about not being able to transmogrify for any length of time."

"Why?"

"Because I'm going to set her free."

"I thought only Ryden Simmdry could do that?"

"Maybe that was true, until now."

"Really. You think you're that powerful—that you can undo the protective charm Ryden Simmdry placed on that box?"

"Yes."

"Even if you can, I don't think you should."

"Why not?"

"Because she's going to be mad as hell, and may try to take it out on us, and frankly, I'm tired of being defensive."

"We have to do something. We can't just leave her in there."

"Maybe you could just tell Mal. You know? Write something in your diary and then say, *don't you agree,*

Mal? He'll try to figure out what you mean and might even pay us a visit. Then we can sort this out."

"I don't know," she answered. "It doesn't sound very pro-active. It makes us seem like children waiting for a parent's approval."

"Mal has never steered us wrong."

"No, he hasn't," she agreed, "and I don't want to tarnish his reputation now, by dragging him into this."

"Well, that's all I'm going to say. If you want to open the box, open the box."

⌘*You will find it is not possible.*

Johanna cleared her mind, envisioned a pinpoint of light, and forced it to grow larger before opening her eyes. A swirl of gray motes took form and within seconds, Alianessa Anjou appeared. The dazed wizard stood apart from them—staring.

Ryden Simmdry inhaled sharply. ⌘*Something has changed since last we met.*

"She held hands with Beck from the Eahta Frean fram Drycræft one moment," Jackson nodded toward Johanna, "and said she knew all of Myrddin's spells in the next one."

Ryden Simmdry used his mind to plumb the depths of Johanna's consciousness, and found he couldn't. ⌘*Explain to me what happened with Beck.*

Johanna told him about grabbing Beck's hand and suddenly feeling both lightheaded and energized at the same time. "It's like I absorbed all his knowledge."

⌘*Did this sudden influx of knowledge feel like it entered through the Illumini constellation on your left hand?*

Johanna thought back. "Yes."

⌘*And you were merely holding his hand … his palm?*

"No. Not his palm. His wrist." Here eyes widened with recollection. "His sigil."

A commotion coming from the main reading room interrupted their conversation. They found Alianessa pounding on the front door. "Let me out of this place."

⌘*In good time. First, I must determine why the cube chose to induct your essence. I designed this box to absorb unnatural energy that is imbued with protective powers or special charms. It chose you as the most likely source after Odyon managed to disappear.*

The Frenchwoman pouted. "I do not know of any Odyon. It's something you're making up."

Johanna held her gaze. "You were right there when I accused Robert Birk of being Odyon. You know precisely whom we're talking about."

"I've never known him by that name," Alianessa said.

⌘*But you do know him. The question is, how well?*

"He's just one of the eight. I don't know him any better than the others."

⌘*That's too bad because it would have explained why the cube worked on you. I will have to investigate your relationship more directly.* He placed his left palm against her temple.

Alianessa backed away. "Don't touch me."

⌘*I hate you involve you Jackson, but would you please hold her?*

Jackson grabbed Alianessa from behind and wrapped his arms around hers, so she couldn't move.

⌘*Once again.* Ryden Simmdry placed his palm against her temple.

Alianessa stomped on Jackson's instep with the five-inch stiletto heel of her shoe.

"Ow," he shouted loosening his grip on her. She squirmed away and ran for the door.

Jackson started to run after her.

⌘*It is all right, Jackson. I have what I need.* Ryden Simmdry picked up the box. Once again, Alianessa dissolved into a smoky haze before being reabsorbed by the cube.

"Why not let her go?" Johanna asked.

⌘*Because she is more than she claims to be.*

—LOI—

If you enjoyed this book, kindly review it on Amazon, Goodreads, and/or LibraryThing. Your reviews are what make books like this possible

ABOUT THE AUTHOR

C. A. PACK, author of *Chronicles: The Library of Illumination* (a *Kirkus Reviews'* Best Book of 2014), is an award-winning journalist and former television news anchor/ assignment manager at *LI News Tonight*, who has also worked as a news writer at WNBC-TV and Cablevision News 12. She served as president of the Press Club of Long Island for several years and is a proud member of International Thriller Writers, Sisters in Crime, and Mystery Writers of America. She lives on Long Island with her husband and a couple of picky parrots.

Manufactured by Amazon.ca
Bolton, ON

23893514R00326